YOURS TRULY, FROM HELL

Books by Terrence Lore Smith

Novels
The Thief Who Came to Dinner
Grownups and Lovers
The Devil and Webster Daniels

Written with research associate David Alan Doman
The Money War

Leo Roi mysteries written as Phillips Lore
Who Killed the Pieman?
Murder Behind Closed Doors
The Looking Glass Murders

Nonfiction
Different Drums
(Written with Charles Merrill Smith)

YOURS TRULY, FROM HELL

A NOVEL BY
Terrence Lore Smith

WRITTEN WITH RESEARCH ASSOCIATE
David Alan Doman

St. Martin's Press
New York

YOURS TRULY, FROM HELL. Copyright © 1987 by Terrence Lore Smith. All rights reserved. Printed in the United States of America. No part of this book may be used or reproduced in any manner whatsoever without written permission except in the case of brief quotations embodied in critical articles or reviews. For information, address St. Martin's Press, 175 Fifth Avenue, New York, N.Y. 10010

Design by Claire Counihan

Library of Congress Cataloging-in-Publication Data

Smith, Terrence Lore.
  Yours truly, from hell.

  I. Title.
PS3569.M538Y68 1987   813'.54   86-13690
ISBN 0-312-89828-2

First Edition
10 9 8 7 6 5 4 3 2 1

*For the Williamsons—Doug, Dianne, Mary
and Tami; family, friends, good companions:
In hope that this scary story will amuse.*

The evil that men do lives after them . . .
—*William Shakespeare*

PROLOGUE

The London Daily   August 1, 1988

RIPPER ANNIVERSARY

Special to the London Daily
by Carl Collins

He remains history's most famous murderer. His bloody crimes have been legend for a century.

Sometimes he called himself ''Saucy Jack,'' and his trade name passed into the language, but no one knows who he was.

As the hundredth anniversary of the Ripper crimes approaches, theories abound as to his identity. Some say a prince of the realm or his Cambridge tutor; others, an anonymous butcher or common midwife; still more suggest several convicted killers of the time or a particular failed lawyer or a noted physician. All the evidence is circumstantial. None of the theories would pass muster in even an informal hearing, let alone secure an indictment or conviction.

What we know is what he did.

Over a period of nine weeks in the autumn of 1888, he murdered and mutilated five women in the mean streets of Whitechapel, the predominantly Jewish slum of London's East End. The victims were all derelict alcoholic prostitutes. Around 4:00 A.M., August 31, 1888, he slashed the throat of Mary Ann ''Polly'' Nichols and made extensive mutilations of the abdomen and internal organs. A week later, at 5:30 A.M. on September 8, he killed Annie ''Dark Annie'' Chapman in the same manner, but with greater mutilation. Some of the internal organs were lifted out of her body and draped across her left shoulder. On September 30, between 12:30 A.M. and 1:45 A.M., he struck again. Twice! Elizabeth ''Long Liz'' Stride, found in the middle of Berner Street, was less mutilated than Annie Chapman. Experts theorize that the murderer was disturbed by the approach of those who found the body and fled before he could satisfy his bloody appetites. In any case, he killed again less than an hour later and less than a quarter mile away. Catherine Eddowes' body was discovered in Mitre Square. Her slashed throat looked like a canyon, her eyes, ears and face were slit and her lower body had been ripped entirely open. Her entrails were lifted out and flung in a heap about her neck. Her uterus and a kidney were missing. On November 9, at around 3:30 A.M. in a small room on Millers Court, Mary Kelly, twenty-four and pregnant, had her throat slashed so viciously that her head clung to her body only by a strand of skin. For more than two hours, in the privacy of her shabby room and by the light of a glowing fireplace, the killer ripped her to pieces in one of the most savage butcheries of a human body in recorded history.

The killer disappeared. He did not strike again, and remains unknown, anonymous, mysterious but not forgotten, even after the passing of a hundred years.

Why?

Other mass murderers have run up bloody scores substantially larger. Leaving aside individual entrepreneurs, the twentieth-century totalitarian triumvirate of Mao, Stalin and Hitler murdered more than fifty million.

Perhaps it is the unparalleled bestiality of his crimes that still resonates in our minds after a century. Or is it the audacious manner in which he continued his gross murders? All were in the open (save only the last), all were in a confined area (less than a half mile separated the two most distant sites) and the last four in the midst of one of the most active manhunts in history. Do we remember him because he killed as freely as if invisible?

This reporter wonders if it might be because of the era he lived in. Is there some echo of evil set up by the proper Victorians and their mythic murderer?

Do we remember the stolid muttonchopped burghers, the large-boned heavy-jawed women of the world's most far-flung empire? Or their namesake queen's popularized penchants for black clothing, humorless public propriety and private excess? Do we remember the brutal sex crimes of that fall, one hundred years ago, because of the prudish Victorians' prurient and vicarious obsessions with them? Is the resonance from the revelation of the dark, secret side of that most rigidly self-restraining society?

More simply, perhaps, we remember *Yours Truly, Jack-the-Ripper* (the ''trade name,'' as he called it, with which he signed some of the letters taunting police and press) because he was never caught, never identified. Leaving us, a hundred years later, with a still-unsigned open-ended cruelty:

Yours Truly
?

I
Mary Ann "Polly" Nichols and Annie "Dark Annie" Chapman

> I would far rather be ignorant than wise in the foreboding of evil.
> —*Aeschylus*
> Maxim 453

Lees rode in a black Austin taxi through a discarded section of London. The night world had turned a grainy black and white with a faint sepia undertone, like an old motion picture.

The streets were narrow and took quirky turns. They were pebbled with flotsam men, jetsom women, momentarily pinned by pale headlight beams. Tired faces, eyes glazed by generations of malnourishment, caught the light, lost it again. They were a listless table-scrap population.

The fat tires of the taxi whispered slowly across the cobblestones.

Something about the people, the place, seemed off, but he couldn't think what.

The driver did not speak; the windows were closed, the motor muffled out of hearing. The silence tightened the knot of fear in Lees' stomach. His head hurt. He sweated despite the air-conditioned cool.

At a tight channel between a board fence and a brick wall, the driver downshifted to nose through a clump of people. They shuffled to either side reluctantly, their faces floated in the windows. Unshaven men in dirty derbies and sad suits; blowsy women in rag-barrel dresses. The very blankness of their eyes accused him of something. What? He wanted to protest his innocence as guilt flooded him, but he was distracted.

A woman, with scattered hair struggling beneath wilted flowers in the crown of her mashed hat, pressed her face close to the glass. She held to the arm of a lean, bowlered man with muttonchop sideburns. He was uninterested, puffed a black cheroot.

Lees turned in the seat, stared as they receded through the rear window. They looked so . . . Victorian.

The large black auto turned into a broad street that was straight as far as his eye could see, and the driver downshifted again, bringing the taxi to a gentle stop beneath a gas-jet streetlight.

The cabbie spoke to the windscreen. " 'Ere's where you get out, guv'ner. Whitechapel Road."

Lees shrank into the corner. "Nonsense. Drive on."

"Sorry, guv. It's yer destination."

"No."

†

3

The cabbie asked the windscreen, "Did yer change yer nyme?"

"No," he admitted.

"That's ryght, guv'ner. There's no escypin' some things."

Still, Lees stalled. "How much do I owe you?"

"Not a brass farthin'. T'other gentleman pyed, guv."

Lees' voice cracked. "The—other?"

"The one who *sent* fer you. 'E pyed, guv," answered the driver, as his head swiveled slowly. "The ride's free, guv. On 'im." The cabbie laughed as his face came round.

Only there was no face.

Between the whipcord cap and coat collar was a dark space broken only by eyes suspended in the black; eyes perfectly round, flat silver and opaque, like ball bearings—blind eyes reflecting only dead light from the yellow gas-jet.

Lees wondered, Where does the laugh come from?

The dark space spoke again. "Free ride, guv'ner. On 'im," and laughed again.

Lees fumbled out the door, hampered by his cloak and walking stick. He stopped, stared at the heavy ebony stick. Cane? Cloak? he wondered.

His head pounded hard, slowly. His heart hurt.

He looked around carefully.

The grimed, gray-black sky was a canopy of coal smoke reflecting chimerical shards of gaslight, casting everything in ugly tones, like the madness of a doomed, despairing painter. Across the wide thoroughfare loomed a vast brick building with the legend THE GREAT GENERAL HOSPITAL FOR EAST LONDON.

This was the main artery; the side streets had been minor tributaries. Here, there were shops and pubs, and the eddies, creeks, and streams of leftover people swelled to a busy river—deeper, faster, more energetic, as if drawing some strength from mere numbers. The sound of horses' hooves and the iron of hansom cab wheels on cobblestone shattered the humid night air, made it impossible for Lees to think.

"Go on, guv. 'E's wyhtin'."

Lees looked.

The ball-bearing eyes were suspended in the dark space between the top hat and the black cloak collar. The horse stamped a forefoot nervously and the hackie leaned out from his narrow seat atop the small commercial carriage.

"Go on, guv'ner," he repeated. " 'E's wyhtin'." The chill, humorless laugh welled up again, and he cracked the whip and pulled away, gathering speed in a deafening roar of metal-on-stone that nearly drowned out the insane laughter.

God help me, thought Lees, involuntarily. He turned and walked.

He had no conscious thought. He was pulled, led, and he was afraid, but he could not resist; his will was suspended; he was powerless and alone, and that made him more afraid.

He walked briskly, easily, almost floating, even though his limbs trembled.

A woman leaning against a doorjamb called to him, "Handsome gentleman care for a party? Old Joan'll show you a right treat, Mr. Lees."

Startled by his name, he glanced at her.

She ran her tongue lewdly over her lower lip and four dirty upper teeth defined dark gaps, like caves of decay.

Lees shivered, walked on.

A small, plump workman tugged his forelock in passing, but his eyes were blank without respect, the gesture a remembered ritual without meaning.

A newspaper lay curled around the base of a lamppost, and, in the hissing light, Lees could read only the date—August 31, 1988.

He turned, without thinking, off Whitechapel Road into a side street. Entered the maze of back alleys, closed courts, the twisting warren of board-and-brick-sided lanes where the street lamps were few and ineffective, where the crowds of people thinned and stretches of deserted walk loomed, where the dark and the quiet grew terrifying, where the thick fear of the hideous lurked—where "t'other gentleman" beckoned him, led him, waited for him.

He turned a corner and there was no one. He walked fifty paces and the street bent out of sight. His steps rang loud, hollow in the still.

He glanced down and his legs had disappeared; he was wad-

†
5

ing through thigh-high fog that hung and curled and clung like odorless smoke. He sweated in his broadcloth suit and slowed as he approached a widening in the lane, a small closed court.

He stopped at its edge.

A peninsula of brick bounded by a shore of board fence with shadowed tenement breakers beyond. The last streetlight was twenty yards behind; the next gas-jet was at the far side of the court, perhaps thirty paces away, and flickered low, unevenly; the light was amber yellow and insufficient.

He stood still, powerless to go further.

There was a woman halfway across the court, standing by the far fence. There was something wrong with her, but Lees was distracted.

There was another presence.

He turned his head slowly to the right. Blank brick facing of a semi-retired warehouse, windowless and senile. He swiveled his head left and stopped. Fear choked him and he nearly fainted.

There was a deep doorway a few paces off, and in it stood the vague bulk of a man's image. The blood in Lees' veins slithered and itched like hot pus. The man was medium-sized. Dressed, as Lees was, in broadcloth suit, cloak, top hat. Something in his hand, not a walking stick, something bulkier, yet more . . . compact.

"Glad you came." The voice was peculiarly husky and the words were not a question.

"Glad you came?" The voice was a rich, musical interrogative.

"Glad you came." The sound was a growl and not a question.

"No," Lees whispered.

"Watch," answered the figure.

"No," pleaded Lees.

"It is the path you have chosen—to watch."

The man emerged from the doorway and turned into the courtyard. Lees looked back to the waiting woman and, now, saw what was wrong with her. She was cleaved neatly down the center. Half of her was old, sagged, lumpy in the cos-

†
6

tume of a Victorian streetwalker—an abandoned soul who would hump you on the pavement for a tot of gin; the other half of her was young and candy firm, dressed in a contemporary silk blouse and skirt, with soft, creamy skin, swelled breasts and taut thighs—a trendy tart at twenty-five pounds a throw.

She smiled at the oncoming man and her grin was repugnant—half, even white teeth; half, yellowed stumps and black holes. Only her eyes matched.

Dulled yellow; opaque; jaded with the tedium of a garbage life, bored by the endless banality of evil—her soul was in her eyes and they were a void.

"Care for a party, dearie?"

The man bounced a cloth pouch in his right hand and it jangled with metallic heavy harshness. Lees saw the something in his left hand.

It was a small black bag.

I must stop him, Lees thought. But he could not move. I must stop him. But he was frozen as if encased in a solid shell, a paperweight of a man in a Lucite cube, suitable for desktop decoration, non-functional. I must stop him, Lees thought. Please, please, I must stop him—God help me, he thought again. But he did not believe in God; he was powerless, impotent, reduced to a spectator of dread.

"Twenty guineas?"

"Gold?" asked the woman, and the man nodded. She agreed. "That's a bit of alright, then, dearie. I've done for less in films. With dogs. Bloody, great German shepherds, mind."

"Yes." He nodded, handed her the pouch and turned her around.

"Fancy dog style yourself, do you?"

The woman bent obligingly, her forehead resting on the fence, and flipped her skirts up, revealing naked, unmatched buttocks. The man set his bag down and opened it, then withdrew something, something that gleamed.

I've got to stop him. But Lees was frozen.

The man nestled into her buttocks, pinned her against the fence, asked, "What's your name, girl?"

"Polly Nichols." She giggled and reached back for his

†
7

crotch. "Say, you're not undone, dearie." She squeezed and turned her head, puzzled. "You're not . . ."
She stopped; she saw the something in his hand; her eyes widened.
The knife flashed, winked once in motion, bit deeply into her throat, sawed swiftly.
She opened her mouth wide to scream, but no sound came. Great gouts of bright blood sprayed from her throat as her head banged the fence and she convulsed.
Lees opened his mouth wide to scream and no sound came. The woman fell and the man rolled her over. He slashed her clothing open and plunged the knife in while her dying body still thrashed and kicked her feet on the bricks in a parody of ecstasy.
He ripped her.
From chest to uterus, with obscene, cracking, tearing sounds and blood boiling out.
Lees screamed soundlessly.
He ripped her.
And picked hot organs from the carcass and flung them across her shoulder.
He ripped her.
And Lees could see her open dead eyes, finally bright yellow, life returned in the instant of dying, vitality returned at the price of terror, the price of knowledge of evil beyond banality—and something more, something almost like . . . hope.
He ripped her again.
And again.
And again.

Lees screamed aloud.
And woke thrashing.
He blinked and looked around slowly.
He was kneeling on the king-size bed. The strangled pillow in his hands was covered by a cranberry slip that matched the sheets. He stared dully at cream walls. Built-in bookshelves of dark hardwoods. Did he recognize the grain of his own handiwork? Hardbound volumes of poetry and essays and military history swam before his glazed eyes. And silver-framed photographs of his family.

†

A tall and pretty middle-aged woman stood by the door, hand on the light switch. Her oval face was tired, her blond hair askew, her blue eyes filled with hurt and fear and compassion. Ann Lees asked, "The dream?"

He sank to a sitting position on the bed. "Yes. The same."

"More progression?" she whispered.

He shut his eyes and nodded.

She came to him and put her arms around him, just held him tight in one of the oldest healings—mate comforting mate.

"This time the taxi didn't change to a carriage until I got out. And the woman was half . . . like today, like . . . a modern woman. And the newspaper had a date. I saw it clearly."

"Wha"—she struggled to control her voice—"what was it?"

"August 31, 1988," he said flatly, and she despaired at the resignation in his tone even more than the dread fact.

"One hundred years exactly."

"Yes," was all he said.

Some desire for motion in him communicated to her and they rose, went to the sliding doors of their bedroom's balcony. He snared cigarettes, a lighter, and an ashtray while she slid the screen back. They stepped onto the balcony and the unusually humid August air greeted them like a wall. Below and away stretched the bowl of downtown Colorado Springs; the lights were bright and still, did not twinkle in their ordinary manner.

"Storm," they muttered as one and turned their eyes toward Pikes Peak. The Rampart Range ridges were melted together, dark bulks grayed over by a moving mass. They sat in chaises to wait for the storm.

He lit cigarettes and passed her one. They smoked and said nothing.

Eight or nine tall buildings dominated the carpet of lights below them. The city skyline was mushrooming upward, but the Holly Sugar Building of the Chase Stone Center was still tallest. Its companion, the Antlers Hotel, completed the set, drew the eye, maintained pride of place.

In minutes, the air freshened, cooled as the storm descended from the mountains.

She stared at him in the dim light drifting out from the bedroom. He was an exceptionally handsome man in his fifties—perhaps handsomer than when young—lean, ruddy-faced and silver-haired, with luminous blue eyes. But he was shaken now. Again. By the dreams—the visions.

For three years, the recurring nightmare had come to her man, over and over and over. Finally, she asked the question. "What now?"

He shook his head.

The rain was heavy, but the wind was easterly and sent it skittering by their north-facing balcony in flimsy sheets. Their bodies drank the cooled air, and the sight, the sound, the gray drape of night rain closed off the world and eased their wounds.

He sighed and it was a defeated sound.

She asked again, "What now?"

He shrugged. "It's August thirty-first now. What time is it?"

"About four."

He smiled wanly. "Should have known. Just about when it happened. How many time zones is it to London—five or six?"

"Six, I think."

"So in six hours, something will happen. Or it won't."

Ann pressed her palms against her thighs hard. "If nothing happens, will you . . . will you see someone?"

He laughed acidly. "A shrink or a priest?"

"Someone to help you."

"What if something *does* happen?"

Ann was silent.

They returned to bed and there were no more dreams that night, but she lay awake wondering just what *was* happening to her husband?

Polly Nichols was a disposable person, and her life was a no-deposit, no-return existence. Her one-room cold-water basement flat on a run-down street near Soho was an undecorated wreck of broken furniture, cracked crockery and abundant flies, roaches and the occasional rat.

†

10

She was thirty-two years old and not really sexy. Her face was hard and ordinary of feature, her blond hair as lifeless as her button-blue eyes and her scrawny, malnourished body had large breasts as its only alluring characteristic. She had been a street prostitute for seventeen years, an alcoholic for nearly as long. The only change or "improvement" in her dreary life had been her relatively recent introduction to the lower fringes of "show business."

Polly had become a "star" of private-rental pornographic films specializing in bestiality and sadomasochism as well as a popular "featured player" in theater-release porn epics. She had recently received third billing in *The Nun Habit*, a grotesquely antireligious porno "comedy" by a demented director who thought of himself as the young Bunuel of the erotic genre. Polly's perverse popularity was due to a combination of massive mammaries, simulated zeal and a frantic, hyperactive tongue that sometimes appeared, on screen, to be of gargantuan dimension.

All this seemed an improvement in condition to her. Humping, licking, sucking, whipping or being whipped for a camera were larks compared to fucking some pimply kid standing up in a drafty hall or blowing some fat bank clerk while kneeling in a rain-drenched alley for a quid or two.

Her comparison had nothing to do with the acts themselves (she had no emotional investment and scant attention during them), but were based on animal considerations. "Movie" work was inside and warm; fees were larger—she'd been paid sixty quid for *The Nun Habit*; there were fringes such as occasional parties with free food, liquor and dope. And the odd, well-paid, private "date."

Like the one tonight. The cabbie had promised a hundred pounds!

Polly took another deep swallow of Jameson's. She was sprawled on her narrow bed and only mildly high. Plenty of time for that. The date wasn't until almost three. Funny time for it, but the cabbie had said the gent was a swell, had to be careful not to be seen. The cabbie said the gent had seen her pictures, fancied her a lot—"starstruck" was what the cabbie said.

†

It didn't matter to Polly. His money was good. The hundred pounds would be the largest lump sum she'd ever have seen in her life.

She drank again and lit a cigarette. She'd finish the tumbler and take a bath, do herself up real pretty. Then give the gent a right treat. Maybe he'd fancy his pretty Polly for another time or two. Or regular like.

Polly smoked and drank and drifted in her fantasy.

No relationships of value to people, places or things existed for her. Her knowledge of life was of a non-reusable world, and she thought of herself that way. So she became a throwaway, a one-time trick.

She finished her drink and fumbled in the pocket of her robe for the shilling she'd need for hot water in the upstairs bath. Plenty of time; maybe she'd have another little nip. It wasn't two A.M. yet and the cabbie wouldn't come for another hour. Rather swell having a cabbie pick her up for the date. Almost like having a chauffeur. Almost like being somebody. She liked that.

If it wasn't for his creepy silver eyes.

Polly sat in the corner of the taxi's back seat, enjoying the quiet luxury of the ride, the plush appointments, the cool of air conditioning, the smooth handling of the large auto.

She ignored the silvery eyes in the mirror.

The steamy rain was tapering off and patches of ground mist were already rising. A streetlight made her window a mirror and she saw her reflection—lank blond hair combed straight; rubied lips and heavily azured eyes; red flowered dress.

They turned a corner and whispered down a narrow street. A gas lamp made her window a *yellowed* mirror.

A gas lamp? she wondered as she stared at her reflection in awe and horror. Her face was blunt and heavy, with brown and gray hair straggling beneath an outdated bonnet. Her mouth gaped open, revealing a lack of five front teeth. She wanted to scream her shock, but her head was pulled, swiveled around to face forward, drawn against her will and her eyes directed ahead to the shadowed figure of a man waiting at the corner. An ordinary-size man in Victorian clothing—

black broadcloth three-piece suit, half-boots, white linen shirt and gray silk cravat, dark cloak and top hat. He had a small black bag in his left hand.

The taxi slowed, stopped.

The man got in next to her.

"Ev'nin', guv—'Yde Park?"

The man nodded as Polly stared in fascination at his outlandish costume. She was excited, filled with dread and anticipation. He had creamy, pale skin, theatrically curly dark hair that bushed his muttonchop whiskers and thick mustache, thin lips beneath an aquiline nose and dark, glowing, hot brown eyes. Her whiskey-addled brain groped for lost and unfamiliar feelings.

Release me, she thought. He will release me. And she wondered where the words came from.

The man did not speak.

She did not speak.

They turned a corner and, momentarily, all was ordinary again. The streetlamp was electric; her face was her own; a cheap tart, late 1980s style; her feelings were of boredom about the job ahead, disinterest in what particular brand of kinkiness this john fancied. Probably has his favorite fetish device in the little black bag.

The ground mist was thick now and obscured the features of the park to either side of the Ring. The taxi was the only auto on the road, and the cabbie shut off the headlights as it glided to a stop.

The Ripper spoke in a husky voice. "Let's take a walk, Polly. Down by the Serpentine."

She did not want to go, but she was without will, defenseless, compelled to obey. She caught a glimpse of herself in the window as she opened the door. She was the old drab with missing teeth, and she felt the weight of the black velvet bonnet on her head.

Why?

But she received no new answer.

The ground was damp and springy underfoot. The Ripper took her arm to steady her. His touch was electric, and shot through her with heavy warmth, pleasure-pain and fear comingled, like the first time a penis had penetrated her.

†

13

She heard a horse neigh softly and stamp his hooves.
She glanced back.
The hackie sat calmly atop the hansom cab, clucking softly to quiet the horse.
A carriage? she wondered. But the ground mist floated, rose, obscured the image.
They walked and the silence was awesome, the landscape felt underfoot, but mostly unseen in the dark and fog.
The Ripper glanced upward, ahead, seemed to slow a fraction at some vague intimation of light from Park Lane beyond and muttered something.
"Lees," was what it sounded like, but she was not sure and it made no sense and did not matter, for the touch had full control of her now and she would follow it to the destiny she feared and she welcomed.
The mist broke and they were dimly reflected in the waters of the Serpentine.
In the short seconds she had left to think, to feel, she was filled with wonder that the knife came as no surprise.
A patch of yellow moon broke through the clouds and the fog wandered away from them a space. The blade gleamed everywhere—in her eyes, in the waters of the Serpentine, in the Ripper's eyes. And everything gleamed in the blade—eyes, moon, water.
"You know?"
She nodded.
A bible verse, from Chapel school twenty-five years earlier and unremembered all the intervening time, flickered in her mind:

> *Without the shedding of blood,*
> *there is no remission of sin.*

She stretched her hand and touched the blade, bent forward and kissed it—her bonnet dropping at her feet as she did. She straightened and stared into the hot brown eyes.
She smiled.
Screamed!
He leaped, and the blade flash-slash-sawed her throat, cutting sound like the slamming of a noise-proof door, and she

dropped dying with the Ripper on her instantly, slashing away her tawdry clothing, baring her body from pelvis to throat.
He plunged the knife.
He ripped her!

Constable Johnathon Kneilly, a lanky young man, walked up Park Lane, welcoming the sight of the Dorchester ahead. The doorman was friendly, and Kneilly always stopped for a minute or two to break up the monotony of his customarily uneventful beat.

The scream—high-pitched and rising, a siren sound of dissolution into terror and ecstasy—stopped him in mid-stride before it was chopped off with final abruptness.

He trembled, then ran.

Into the mist.

He ran blindly in the dark and fog, stumbling over paths and slipping on the rain-slick grass; he ran a long stretch quickly toward the Serpentine as if the scream were a homing beacon planted in him.

The fog lifted lightly.

He saw the mutilated body, blood dark in yellow moonlight. He saw the Ripper, finished, turning away, saw only in the brief instant of turning—three-quarter-face, profile, back retreating.

He chased him into the fog and lost him and caught one last glimpse as the Ripper leaped onto the running-step and into the carriage, slamming the door behind him. Saw the cabbie and the silver ball-bearing eyes in the dark; heard the laugh and the crack of the whip and the horses' cries; stood stunned by the sight of the carriage and the sounds of iron hooves and iron wheels on concrete as the hansom cab lurched forward, gained speed and rolled away into the dissipating fog.

Taking the blunt fact of anachronism from flat sight, leaving the innuendo of mirage insinuated on his brain, Kneilly stood, breathing raggedly, gasping for air and reason. "Daft," was all he could croak to himself.

He knew what he had to do. With reluctance like the weight of the world, he turned to retrace his run. To go back to the body.

†

*   *   *

As dawn was breaking with the promise of daylight, Sir Malcolm Stuart, deputy commissioner for CID of New Scotland Yard, was embroiled in a scene from Bedlam, an experience from hell. In the thin, weedy light all the faces looked pale, drawn, shocked. Officers and technicians moved about the park inspecting, photographing, cordoning off the press and public, keeping early traffic in the Ring and on surrounding thoroughfares going; but their motions had a quiet stylized quality. They were like characters in some absurdist drama where an overwhelming shift in perspective causes ordinary behavior to appear grotesque.

Kneilly had uttered, in dead-flat and lucid manner, an account of a scream and fog, a Victorian murderer and an escape in a nineteenth-century carriage driven by a Victorian hackie who had blind-looking silver eyes.

The body was dressed in the remains of a cheap red flowered dress, but a black velvet Victorian bonnet lay at her feet. She was blond and ravaged-looking even without the mutilations, which made the corpse grisly beyond anything in Stuart's experience.

Roused from a comfortable sleep in the arms of his mistress, Stuart was not yet awake, which added to his disorientation and general grumpiness.

Christ, he thought, this is all we need: some murderous fool who's decided to dress up and play Jack-the-Ripper just because a hundred years've gone by.

While Stuart took charge of pulling the pieces of the investigation together, a flippant headline writer for one of the less respectable tabloids was composing a two-word summary of the whole horrid situation:

Special Edition   Special Edition   Special Edition
The London Daily   August 31, 1988

JACK'S BACK!

†

16

SEPTEMBER 1–7, 1988

The Commons Club drew its name from a famous remark of Churchill to the Queen. It was made as he declined elevation to a Dukedom. He said he would not accept because to do so would deprive him of membership in the world's finest club—the House of Commons.

Founded in 1959, it was a toddler among gentlemen's clubs, yet had already achieved prestige and desirability. The Commons Club was top-heavy with important Tory MPs, knighted business tycoons, influential military men and professionals as well as a generous sprinkling of nobility with long lineages.

The criteria for membership were simple enough. A candidate was required to possess at least comfortable wealth and a great respect for the person and politics of the late Sir Winston Churchill. Additionally, the candidate's personality could not be too eccentric or abrasive (an often repeated maxim was "One doesn't mind a member holding peculiar views, one merely does not wish to be bored by them"). Useful, if not requisite, was a career that was perceived as dynamic. And, while it was not a closely studied phenomenon, there were more Harrow graduates than Etonians, and Sandhurst was nearly as well represented as Oxford and Cambridge.

If a single member had to be selected as almost perfectly representative of the entire body (this was just the sort of queer notion that, if voiced, could cause a candidate's exclusion), Sir Malcolm Stuart would have been as accurate a choice as possible.

Stuart was handsome, beautifully groomed and permissibly dashing in a way that bespoke breeding and character rather than acquired manners; had an inherited trust income of two hundred thousand pounds, tax-paid, per annum (he donated his professional salary, after-tax, to charity); he was an honors graduate of Harrow, Sandhurst and Cambridge; he held political views slightly more conservative than Mrs. Thatcher's. His career had initially been with military intelligence, but had been diverted to executive police work at the urging of Edward Heath, a family friend, and he was now being groomed for a decisive spot in the civilian intelligence community.

Stuart was also one of the original one hundred members. His single venture into public print was a slim volume recounting Churchill's adherence to principle during the ebb of his career (the 1930s) entitled *The Candle of the Prophet*.

Sir Malcolm embodied everything that the Commons Club held dear and fell short in no respect of their standards.

The club was situated on Berkley Square and ran to leaded windows, old leather and wood, pungent tobacco smoke, dim lighting, quiet conversation, largish drinks and goodish dinners. The most prominent feature of the decor was an enormous collection of portraits and photographs of prime ministers, past and present—with Sir Winston represented at least once in every room.

As Stuart crossed the dining room, freshly shaved, bathed and clothed, he noted (as usual) how blessedly relaxed and comforting the atmosphere was. He gave a quick, silent thanks for refuge.

A dapper man with slicked dark hair, pencil mustache and tedious eyes rose and extended a pale hand.

"My dear Malcolm, how kind of you to invite me."

"Dezzi, you know my theory. Business *must* be combined with pleasure if one is to retain sanity."

They were settled at a rear corner table with no other luncheon guests near. Stuart ordered a Scotch and the salmon grill; his guest, Lord Desmonde, chose pink gin and kidney pie. Desmonde, the home secretary, Stuart's superior and mentor, was close to sixty, wealthy, politically astute with hope of one day becoming PM, and had an earned reputation for briskness that just skirted rudeness.

"I hadn't meant to cadge a lunch, Malcolm, but I was insistent that we get together because I want to know how much trouble this murder is going to cause the government."

Stuart sipped Scotch and eyed Lord Desmonde carefully. "There isn't a great deal I can tell you. We've only had this thing for eight hours."

"Tell me what you can."

"At approximately four A.M., a constable, walking a beat along Park Lane, heard a scream from Hyde Park. He ran into the park and came upon the body near the Serpentine. He saw the murderer fleeing and gave chase, but the murderer entered a hansom cab and was driven away."

The home secretary almost choked up a swallow of gin, coughed briefly, then asked, "You did say a hansom cab?"

"Yes. Both the murderer and his driver-accomplice were dressed in Victorian clothing."

"Dear me."

Stuart nodded. "Apparently, two lunatics dressing up as Victorians and acting out the initial Ripper murder on its hundredth anniversary. One has to consider the possibility that they intend to reenact them all. The second Ripper killing was in the early morning of September 8, 1888."

"Thursday week."

"Yes, a week from tomorrow."

Both men finished their drinks as the steward served their meals. They tried the food in silence. Lord Desmonde smiled appreciatively.

"The kidney pie is marvelous. How is your salmon?"

"Excellent, as always."

The HS nodded. "Your Anatole is the envy of every other gentlemen's club in London."

Stuart smiled.

"I tell you what I'm thinking, Malcolm. I want you to downplay the whole thing as much as possible. Don't release any of the costume-drama details without clearing it with me."

"And the commissioner?"

"Ah, yes."

Lord Desmonde reflected upon the character of Sir Edwards William, commissioner for New Scotland Yard, and the reflection brought no pleasure. Sir Edwards was a holdover appointee from the previous home secretary; he was incompetent, ambitious and disloyal, and had been a thorn in Lord Desmonde's side for several years. Why the prime minister would not acquiesce in his dismissal remained a mystery. The HS frowned.

"Have you briefed him?"

"No. I expect a preliminary report this afternoon, which, in the normal course of events, I should be obliged to pass along to him."

"Quite."

They ate in silence for several minutes.

"Malcolm, the last thing we need, presently, is a domestic crisis for this government. Especially one which presents Sir Edwards with an opportunity to make political capital. I shall ring him up directly and tell him that the prime minister is taking a particular interest. I shall say that she has asked that you report straight to me so that I may keep her informed. You will have to give him some reports, of course, but keep them in precis and omit the gaudier details."

Stuart sighed. "He'll be scratchy."

"Quite. If he becomes *overly* tiresome, refer him to me, but do be your usual charming and diplomatic self."

"I shall tread lightly, Dezzie."

"Wonderful. Then, do you suppose we might finish with some of that superb cognac?"

Sir Malcolm smiled. "Ah, Dezzie, if only the club cellars could solve all my problems so easily," and turned to beckon the steward.

When Stuart returned to the Yard, he seated himself behind his desk, punched a button on his intercom and said, "Send me Inspector Hughes and Sergeant Clive."

Chief Inspector Richard Hughes was a tall, blond, clean-featured and handsome man who looked more like an advertisement for Savile Row tailoring than for the police academy. Sergeant Clive, in contrast, was dark-haired and chunky, with reddish coloring, blunt features, steady eyes and the plain-and-hearty countenance of a comfortable domestic stew.

Hughes laid a manila folder on Stuart's desk. Sir Malcolm waved his subordinates to chairs and said, "Tell me about it, Richard. I'll read this later."

†

"We found a doorman at the Cumberland Hotel who saw the carriage come out through the Cumberland Gate, near the Marble Arch, and proceed up Edgeware Road. Working along that route, we discovered a citizen who saw the carriage on Marylebone Road turning into Regent's Park. After that, they seem to have vanished." Hughes crossed his long legs. "Forensics are not much help yet, but it's early for them and they're hard at it. No identification found on the body, but a few minutes ago one of our men came forward with a tentative ID."

Stuart frowned and his tone was irritable. "A few minutes ago? What took him so long?"

Clive smiled apologetically. "Well, sir, he was embarrassed."

"Embarrassed?"

"Yes, sir. He's a married man and the woman . . . well, he says he *thinks* she might have been a performer in pornographic films."

"Oh. I see." Stuart fingered his mustache. "Tell him—and quite firmly—in future not to withhold information, even for a few hours. And, then, reassure him that the Yard respects that sort of confidence."

Clive nodded.

Hughes cleared his throat. "The fact is—he says he thinks the woman's name is Polly Nichols."

"Polly Nichols? Wasn't that—"

Hughes nodded. "The name of the original Ripper's first victim."

Stuart gazed out the window wall at blue sky and a few fat white clouds in the distance. Too bizarre, he thought, too grotesque. He turned back to his men.

"What else?"

Hughes sighed. "Presently, the only other thing is the bonnet that was found next to the body. Black velvet and obviously new, but a very good replica of a Victorian style. Clearly not appropriate to the victim's other clothing. We've started with the maker's label, Hanby and Sons, but so far we can find no listing in the commercial directories."

"Still," said Clive, "the picture already tells us a good deal."

Stuart smiled at Clive. He was fond of the sergeant and his sensible earthy powers of reasoning, hoped, before his tenure as head of CID was over, to secure Clive's promotion to deputy inspector.

"Describe it, Sergeant."

"We know they've got money, and they've put a lot of time into this. Money because the replica bonnet, their clothes, a genuine hansom cab and horse can all be had, but not cheaply. Time for the same reasons. As I say, those things can all be had, but you can't saunter into Harrod's this morning and order them up for tea time."

"Go on."

"Yes, sir. And time to research the Ripper crimes to get at least some of these details right. And, well, the woman. If her name *is* Polly Nichols, we'd have to assume it was no coincidence."

"Mmmm."

"We'd have to assume she wasn't just out for a stroll in the park and they happened on her. They had to seek her out—find a woman named Polly Nichols—and set it up. Tell her it was a lark or hire her for something and take her there. I won't pretend it's a complete picture, sir, but it's a start."

Stuart nodded. "I agree. Richard?"

Hughes uncrossed his legs, sat upright. "I agree with Sergeant Clive. The best leads seem to be tracing the carriage, the bonnet and the woman. And one other idea occurs. We might begin to go through the metropolitan directories for women named Annie Chapman."

Stuart asked, "The second victim?"

"Yes."

Stuart dismissed his aides and picked up the written report. He frowned as he opened it. The deputy commissioner, CID, did not regularly involve himself in individual investigations, but Sir Malcolm had a premonition that he would be tied to this murder case until its course was run.

On Thursday morning at ten-thirty, Chief Inspector Richard Hughes gazed about the shabby basement flat of the late Polly Nichols and sighed sadly. It was a depressing place, and everything in it and about it—the white cracked enamel teapot, gray paint peeling from the door and frame, split and pockmarked plaster walls and chipped linoleum floor, the faded poster of Sean Connery as James Bond, the seedy bits and pieces of furniture—all of it spoke to an uncommitted and fragmentary life.

Hughes rocked on his heels with his hands shoved into his trouser pockets and watched the technicians examine, collect, poke and pry, dust and photograph. He absentmindedly recapped an open bottle of Irish whiskey on the night stand. Glanced down at the sagging lumpy bed, and saw a peep of blue vinyl at the pillow's edge. He bent over and extracted a cheap blue diary, then flipped through the pages, reading at random. It was as sad and scattered as the rest of Polly Nichols' life, part childish journal recording exhilarations and depressions based wholly upon momentary gratifications or the lack, part haphazard commercial ledger confirming what Hughes had already suspected—Polly Nichols was a prostitute.

One more parallel with the original, he thought.

He flipped to the last entry:

Date for a.m., 8/31
Arranged by L.N.
100 POUNDS!

Clive was right; whoever they are, they have money.

A young constable stuck his head in the door. "I've interviewed the landlady, Inspector. Elderly type with the gout. *Says* it woke her about two A.M., that morning. She heard Polly go out around three, went to the window and saw her ushered into a taxi."

"Did she happen to get the number?"

"She says not; didn't occur to her."

"Anything else?"

The constable smiled. "If you can credit it. She says the driver was wearing a top hat and cloak. She couldn't see much more because her eyes aren't good and the light from the streetlamp was yellowish that night. I told her you might want to interview her as well."

†
23

A taxi *and* a carriage, he thought. Quite a bit of money. He nodded at the constable. "All right. I'll be up directly."

Sergeant Clive was enchanted. Magic!

He stood grinning broadly, his brown eyes twinkling, his face radiant and aglow with the sheer delight of the little boy that lived inside of him.

The castle hall was high and broad and light, airy. Glorious tapestries in browns and greens and silvers muted cool marble walls. Velvet pennants of scarlet and blue and purple, blazoned with gold and silver heraldry, hung overhead from wooden lances set in brackets. Thirteen large, handsome men in chain mail and embroidered jerkins encircled a huge round wooden table. King Arthur drew golden jewel-encrusted Excalibur and laid the broad blade upon the table.

"From this day forth, I—King Arthur—and my court of Camelot shall be known as the Knights of the Round Table. By this sword, I pledge my life and honor and ask all who would follow me to do the same."

The dozen men covered their hearts with their right fists and forearms and chorused, "My Lord—we so swear!"

"Hold it . . . hold and *cut!*"

The director clapped his hands happily and the camera dollied back while the actors broke their poses and relaxed. The director turned to a script girl who held a bound script and pointed to a page while technicians climbed metal scaffolding and began to inspect, adjust and tinker with dozens of high-intensity lights.

Sergeant Clive turned to the dark, pretty young woman next to him. "Thank you, Miss Pringle." His broad grin was still boyish. "I've never seen a filming before. It was wonderful."

Marcy Pringle searched Clive's face, smiling quietly. "Most people say it's disappointing."

Clive's features registered surprise as obvious as his delight had been. "Do they, now? I can't imagine why. I like seeing how special things're done."

She smiled again, said, "Now, if you'll follow me, we'll see if we can't get your questions answered."

†

She led him, at a brisk pace, out of the huge soundstage and along a line of barbed-wire-decorated World War I trenches that were being soaked with garden hoses for just the proper texture of mud and slop. They passed through a sleepy eighteenth-century Transylvanian village where pitchfork-and torch-bearing peasants were being instructed to cultivate frenzy for the storming of Count Dracula's castle. Then they cut across another large soundstage where, upon a set of the Old Bailey, a murder trial was being filmed.

Behind the soundstage was a four-story high, four-block square concrete warehouse. They stepped inside out of the early morning light.

Shadows and dark fought widely spaced squares of light for dominance.

Things were everywhere.

A pale-blue 1925 Rolls-Royce Silver Cloud phaeton nestled under the wing of a khaki-colored Grumman Albatross seaplane; three puny, archaic World War I tanks fronted a trailer-mounted nineteenth-century single-masted sailing schooner; chests of pirate treasure and mounds of cutlasses and swords filled one corner beneath racks of bayoneted muskets; one whole wall was lined with wardrobes filled with uniforms and dresses and suits and capes and furs and hats and shoes and boots and sandals and togas from every period of history in the record of man; a circus wagon and a calliope flanked a bottle-green Lotus Formula I racing car; high overhead, red, brown, black, white, yellow and royal-blue Spad, Sopwith Camel and Fokker biplanes were suspended by wires in tiers; deep in the shadowed recesses were rows upon rows of carriages—hansom cabs and fringed surreys and large, open four-seaters and gilded glassed vehicles of nobility and royalty.

Clive rocked back on his heels, his bright grin returned. He laughed with joy. "Do you suppose they'd let me come and play here when it's time for my second childhood?"

"I'll speak to the management."

A pale-skinned middle-aged man in soft tan slacks and blue pullover sweater stepped from a cubicle office, crossed to them.

"Mr. Sudlow, this is Sergeant Clive of Scotland Yard. He needs to ask you some questions."

†

Sudlow nodded. "Certainly, Miss Pringle," turned his narrow hawklike face to Clive.

Clive smiled at her. "Thank you again, Miss Pringle. You've been most kind."

She cocked her head to one side and her brown eyes sparkled. "Thank *you*, Sergeant. I don't feel half so *blasé* as when I came into work this morning." She walked away quickly.

"Fancy a morning cuppa, Sergeant?"

"Wouldn't mind, Mr. Sudlow."

They crossed to the six-by-eight glassed cubicle, which was as paper-stacked and littered as the warehouse was object-crammed. Sudlow served tea in plain white mugs and seated himself behind a small desk. Clive sat in the only other chair, in front of the desk, and they peered at one another across irregular hills and ridges of forms and magazines like playful children engaged in peekaboo.

"How can I help you, Sergeant?"

"We're trying to trace a hansom cab that was used in conjunction with a felony. If I wanted to secure a hansom cab, how would I go about it?"

"Tottenham Court Studios'll rent you one—if you've a thousand quid to put on deposit, can afford sixty-guineas-a-day rental, possess proper identification and references so you're bondable for purposes of our insurance."

They both sipped at their tea, and steam dampened their faces.

"Have you rented any . . . lately?"

Sudlow smiled. "Last rental of Victorian hacks and carriages was second week of August to BBC. Nothing since."

"Are all your carriages here?"

"Yes. We've eleven hansoms at present. They're all out there in storage."

"Could anyone get one out of here, surreptitiously, and return it?"

"Could if they were magicians, I suppose. Storage is guarded clock-round and inventory on larger items—boats, cars, planes, carriages, the like—is run weekly."

"When was your last inventory?"

"Wednesday afternoon." Sudlow leaned over to peer at a

†

26

desk calendar, then returned his black eyes to Clive. "The thirty-first."

"Where else could I secure a hansom?"

Sudlow sipped tea, thought. "Not too many places. Tottenham's the largest studio rental operation in England. Ealing, I suppose. Pinewood. Perhaps six or seven others."

"Can you supply a list?"

Sudlow nodded, set his mug aside, began jotting on a notepad.

"Anyplace other than a studio that I could find one?"

Sudlow frowned and chewed on the end of his pencil. "Mmmm . . . museums, maybe—but how'd you get it out? Private collections? There might be a few about. Duke of Blandford is supposed to have the largest down at Singleton Castle, but I don't know if he has a hansom. Not an ordinary item to lay your hands on."

"If I wanted to have one built?"

Sudlow whistled. "Be expensive. I'll give you a list of the few people I know who can do it, but they won't run one up for you for less than seventy-five hundred pounds or so. Be a very costly whim."

"The other studios have rental terms as stringent as yours?"

Sudlow nodded again as he finished writing, tore off the page of note paper and passed it to Clive. "Have to do. We rent it to you and you damage it—you pay. We want to be certain you can and will pay, or our insurance rates would be higher than this roof. We don't want to be making insurance claims and neither do the other studios."

"One last thing, Mr. Sudlow. Could we just see your inventory of hansoms. You've been most helpful and I'm not doubting you, but just for the record?"

Sudlow's narrow face showed a sly grin. "Besides, it gives a good reason to poke about amongst the toys for a little longer."

Clive laughed. "That it does and I won't have such an opportunity often."

Sudlow stood, still smiling. "Come along, then. We've a vintage steam locomotive I'd be glad to show you as well."

Clive grinned.

†

27

* * *

Lees delayed for another day.

He alternated between television and radio all his waking hours, listening to each fragmentary report of the Hyde Park murder, and read the still sketchy summary in the afternoon edition of the *Gazette-Telegraph*. It didn't sound like his dreams; it hadn't happened in Whitechapel or in the manner he had "seen."

Ann aided and abetted the delay. She said it wasn't his vision at all, might be coincidence, and asked, "How could what you dreamed have helped prevent what happened or help solve it?"

Which was a perfectly logical question.

But logic didn't stop the churning of his stomach, the clinging feeling that he was holding back when that was unacceptable.

But he delayed.

That night, he dreamed again. The same dream.

But the date on the newspaper curled about the lamppost base had changed—to September 8, 1988.

When he told Ann the next morning that he had to go to London, she asked, "Why? What good will it do? Do you really believe all this?"

He shrugged. "I don't know. But I have to go."

They sat at the oak breakfast table in the kitchen. Through a tall, narrow window he saw the sun create an aura of intensified light around the raw red point of snowless Pikes Peak. They looked at one another.

We're becoming neurotic, he thought. She can't stop worrying about me; I can't let go.

She asked softly, "What about your health? Dr. Friedmann says stress could push your blood pressure to cause a stroke or an aneurysm in an instant."

He grinned lamely. "I'm a soldier. Soldiers don't worry about health when it's time to do our duty."

"*Were* a soldier."

He shrugged again. "Once, always . . ."

"Jim, have I ever asked you not to do your duty? Even when you went back to Korea voluntarily, the second time? Or Vietnam, voluntarily, the second and *third* times?"

†

"No."

"You survived that. We survived that. You're retired, and this is *supposed* to be an extra-special time. No money worries, the kids on their own—our time to enjoy one another." She shook her head, and tears of frustration were in her eyes. "But ever since the dreams started, you're tense, distracted, irritable. Your health is a worry, and you won't listen to Dr. Friedmann or me. You won't talk to me, or tell me what this is really about. I have less of you now than I did when you were away on duty months at a time!"

He said sadly, "I know."

"It's not fair!"

"I know."

"I don't see this as your duty. And you won't tell me why it is your duty, or even what you expect to accomplish!"

"I can't tell you because I don't know those answers myself."

She stared down into her coffee cup as if afraid of the answer she would see in his eyes. "And if I asked you not to go?"

"Please, don't."

The face she raised to him was angry. "I *am* asking! *Don't go!*"

He shook his head. "Everything inside me wants not to go. But something at the center of me says I *have* to."

"And you expect me to go with you?"

"I want you to come."

She shut her eyes. "Will you at least see Dr. Friedmann?"

"Yes."

He couldn't get reservations for a flight before Thursday evening. Ann packed and he went to the doctor—who disapproved—and, later, to see his friend Pat Cochran, who was puzzled.

For James Robert "J.R." Lees, brigadier general, U.S. Army, Ret.—a man who had been drafted in 1950 and worked his way up from private to one-star general in thirty-five years, a man who strode up Pork Chop Hill amidst the screaming and the dying, angered by the rain of gunfire, a man who had slogged resolutely through the iron triangle of Vietnam, a man who had married young and remained faithful, a man who

†

had raised sons and daughters with discipline, grace and compassion, a man who had angrily denied God and his family heritage of precognition for more than half a century, a man who had led a fine, courageous, useful, loving life—for him it would be the longest journey.

A seamless terror trip through the living hell of essential confrontation with essential evil—an invitation to evil.

Jim Lees was as good a man as a wholly secular world view could produce. An excellent man. And he shortly would discover that that was not good enough.

Not nearly good enough.

He booked their plane connections at Denver and Chicago unnecessarily close, almost as if he hoped they might be stranded. However, luck was with them, and they made both connections with at least a minute to spare.

Lees was apprehensive, afraid to sleep. He did not want the dream to come and, especially, he did not want to awaken screaming.

So he fought sleep. He refused alcohol with dinner, accepted coffee as often as it was offered, popped No-Doze, and smoked constantly.

The flight would bring them into Heathrow at 9:00 A.M., London time; now it was full dark over the unseen Atlantic. Ann slept and Lees tried to keep his restless mind from rattling the bars of its cage.

He thought of his children and grandchildren—not an altogether soothing subject. Bill, thirty-nine, had been a young army captain because of Vietnam, but now was an aging major, wondering if he ought to jump to the private sector while he still had the opportunity. Lees did not know what to tell his son and felt inadequate because he did not. Tommy, thirty-six, was a whiz-bang success as a computer-program designer for TRW, but had a shambles for a marriage. Lees had not inquired closely, but there were plenty of indications that Tommy and Joan had both had affairs—anyone could see that they were driven by the Broadmoor success/prestige/money business. And did Tommy drink too much? Was Joan running on Valium? He and Ann had tried to impart sensible ethical values, and Ann had seen to the children's religious training (Lees

†

would have none of that), but what could he say about extramarital sex, materialism, alcohol and drugs—bad, don't do them?—in a world preoccupied with just those things?

The twins, Karen and Ann, thirty-two, *appeared* happy enough; Karen seemed to be able to juggle marriage and motherhood with her clinical psychology practice; Ann was art director for a Denver ad agency and talking about the leap to New York, but men came and went in her life in no pattern discernible to her father.

And what effect did the jumpy lives of his children have on the minds of his five grandchildren? There was an entire new generation knocking on the door of his worry closet, ranging from Billy, sixteen, to Patty, five.

He sighed and turned to glance at Ann, who was sleeping peacefully.

That was when the shot came.

It jabbed his skull as if a blood clot had lodged in his brain, and the pain was sharp and excruciating. He felt instantly nauseous and clammy.

The cabbie's voice played in his head. —*'Aven't got it right, guv'ner. 'Tisn't pretty Polly's innards. That's Dark Annie's guts you see.*

Images of blood and flesh and organs steaming in the dark alley flashed through his brain. The agony in his head had forced him to bend at the waist and he thought he would vomit. He closed his eyes against the pain and the image changed to a dusky-skinned woman, screaming.

That's right, guv. You've got it now. Be seein' you. Soon!

Lees heard the cabbie's laugh. His brain and bowels felt aflame. The other voices played in his ears.

Glad you're coming. Husky declarative.

Glad you're coming? Musical question.

Glad you're coming. Growl of finality.

Then it was over.

Did it last forty-five seconds? A minute? No matter. The pain, the shot, the incident vanished, leaving him shaken and drained. All the previous Ripper visions had come in dreams, at night, asleep. He had not had a waking vision in twenty years, not since . . . not since he saw the ambush in his head two minutes before the choppers were to land his men in the meadow of elephant-grass. They thought he was crazy ordering the choppers to turn away, crazy calling in the air strikes—until the rockets and napalm flushed an NVR company and a VC mortar platoon. Afterward, the word had gone out—the "Old Man" has a nose for Charlie. Was the "gift" returning in full flower? Was it all true? Was someone planning to "do" the Ripper murders all over again?

He thought of his father and squirmed in his seat. Large red letters appeared in his head like a bleeding wound: LEES SEES! His father's dark greasy hair, thin pale face, intense yellow eyes.

NO! he thought, *no!* I can't think about that now. With an almost physical tearing, he channeled his thoughts back to the children. The effort of not thinking about that which he did not wish to think about kept him awake and sweating the entire flight.

He was exhausted and dazed when they arrived at Heathrow Airport. They drifted through customs, and Ann secured a taxi to take them to the Dorchester.

Most sights along the dual carriage way made little impression on him. The houses and factories were uniformly drab, mainly of dingy red brick. There were more billboards than he remembered. Every other one seemed to be advertising Scent of Love Perfume. A tawny-haired model, ten times life-size, stared out with hungry dark eyes; her face was so classic, its essential beauty could not be hidden by its sensual pout. A long, slinky body in a long, slinky, glittery gown beckoned and invited. She held a needle-shaped bottle-stopper to her throat with her left hand and a squat glass bottle of Scent of Love Perfume in her right hand. The image was the soul of naked allure, of impersonal desire, of universal tease. There were three bold lines of copy:

   HER NAME IS VANESSA
   ALL MEN KNOW HER
   SHE IS THE SCENT OF LOVE

The campaign was pervasive. They passed a dozen identical billboards on the drive into London's center. Lees soon tired of the repetitive, slightly obscene image, fully obscene implications; his conscious mind refused to grip them.

Hyde Park was summer green and Park Lane elegant as memory.

Only after the bags had been collected by a porter did Lees turn back to the taxi and look at the cabbie. He nearly swooned in the heavy August heat. His tired eyes blurred the man's features. He saw only the eyes—eyes so gray they were as silver as a fox coat and, seemed in sunlight, nearly opaque, nearly blind. His laugh was low but horrible, humorless, as he took the ten-pound note from Lees' outstretched, frozen hand.

"Thanks, guv."

It was the voice of the nightmare driver.

"Welcome to London, Mr. Lees."

The taxi pulled out into a convenient hole in traffic, turned the corner onto Curzon Street before Lees could think to take the license-plate number.

Ann touched his arm. "J.R., is everything all right?"

"Did you notice the taxi driver?"

"I didn't pay much attention. And his cap was pulled so low. Why?" She looked frightened now.

"His eyes were silver-gray and he . . . he called me by name."

"He could have seen it on the luggage tags."

"Yes," he said. "Perhaps that's it."

Their suite was Wedgwood-blue and cream-white and overlooked the park. The decor was stylish, crisp, reminded one of Noel Coward between world wars or Bertie Wooster at handsome loose ends between snacks, but luxury seemed thin comfort, did not cheer Lees.

He showered and shaved and, for the first time in three years of retirement, donned his uniform with the breastful of ribbons and the brigadier's single shoulder star. The familiar dour green suit, tan shirt and brown tie were reassuring. He adjusted the hat with its gold braid on the hard bill to just the angle he preferred. He drew strength from his image in the mirror. That was the Jim Lees he could accept.

†

It was eleven when he emerged from the Dorchester, and he looked quite carefully at the driver's brown Pakistani face and eyes before he entered the cab.

The twin towers of New Scotland Yard's office block on Victoria Street had been renovated the previous year. A floor had been added to each tower. The one in the rear building housed three deputy commissioners (formerly called assistant commissioners) and their immediate staff in—by police standards—rather palatial offices. Atop the leading tower it housed the commissioner and the deputy commissioner for Criminal Investigations Division and their immediate staff in offices that were grand by anyone's standards.

It was to Sir Malcolm Stuart's office atop the forward building that Lees was shown after presenting his calling card and dropping a name that Stuart knew well.

It was a reassuring room. Properly spacious, book-lined on two walls, appointed with deep wine carpet, teak desk, discreet lighting. A trio of comfortable leather armchairs around a slate table sat near a wall window overlooking Wellington Barracks, St. James Park and Buckingham Palace.

Sir Malcolm was a reassuring man as well. He was big—six-three and sixteen stone. He had the relaxed, peaceful air some large men have when they are unconcerned with the intimidation potential of their own physiques. He was about Lees' age, perhaps a few years younger; dark with receding hair, intelligent brown eyes and a marvelous mustache; handsome in the manner of a matinee idol who has aged well, acquired subtleties of character.

They sat by the windows, and Stuart read Lees' letter of introduction.

<blockquote>
FROM THE DESK OF

Patrick J. Cochran
Major-General,
U. S. Army, Ret.
9911 N. Meade
Colorado Springs,
Colorado 80907
</blockquote>

Sir Malcolm Stuart, KB
Deputy Commissioner, CID,
New Scotland Yard

Dear Malcolm:

It has been far too long since we last corresponded, and whatever happened to your long pledged visit to Colorado? We can't get properly pissed and swap lies with you there and me here. I still have some bottles of Glenlivet set aside.

The bearer of this letter is another treasured comrade in arms. Jim Lees is as brave and loyal a soldier and friend as any man could imagine. He wasn't explicit about his need for this letter, but I gather he has some information for you.

Whatever Jim says you may rely on completely.

If you don't come see me soon, I may just drink the Glenlivet myself.

                                       Best,
                                       Pat

    Sir Malcolm dropped the letter and Lees' card on the slate table and looked at the middle-aged soldier. He was clean and trim and splendidly uniformed, but the eyes were red, pouchy; his hands were clasped tight and his jaw rigid. If Pat says so, he thought, but this lad looks tighter than a Hammersmith bus schedule.
    What he said was, "Welcome to England, General Lees. A high regard from Pat Cochran is a complete recommendation for me. When we worked together at NATO, I always thought Pat would be running that show someday."
    Lees shrugged. "He should have been, but the Carter Administration decided he was 'unduly pessimistic' about Russian motives and intentions. Pat retired rather than face the frustration of force-feeding reality to Foggy Bottom."
    "Sorry to hear that. Will you take tea, General? Or is it not too early for something with a little more bite?"

Lees' smile came and went like a swift illusion. "Not too early for me."

"Whiskey?"

"Yes, thank you. Neat, please."

Stuart grinned and it spread across his entire face. "You're a friend of Pat's, truly." He fetched tumblers of Johnnie Walker from the bookshelf bar, and they touched glasses. "Cheers, General."

"Cheers."

They took swift swallows.

"Now, General, Pat said you might have some information for me, but"—he eyed Lees' uniform—"the letter didn't give the impression that this was an official call."

Lees smiled and turned the Galway crystal tumbler. "That's diplomatically put, Sir Malcolm. No, this isn't an official visit. I suppose I wore the uniform because I needed reassurance."

They both sipped.

Stuart said, softly, "You'll forgive me for saying so, General, but that's a passing strange remark."

Lees nodded. "It's a strange situation. One that I find extremely uncomfortable . . . very hard. Does my name, James Robert Lees, mean anything to you?"

"It seems as if it should."

"Perhaps, if the first names are reversed—Robert James Lees?"

Stuart shifted uncomfortably in his chair. "Mmm . . . a Victorian psychic?"

Lees smiled coldly. "Yes. Except the term, then, was spiritualist. Robert James Lees was a noted medium who conducted seances for Queen Victoria at the palace. He was also involved in the investigation of the Jack-the-Ripper murders in Whitechapel. He had visions, precognition of several of the crimes, and his vision detail was particularly accurate in the last murder. That of Mary Kelly."

Stuart frowned and took a swallow of Scotch.

"Robert James Lees was a distant cousin to my grandfather. Many members of my family have had the gift to greater or lesser degree." Lees paused and made an unpleasant face, then repeated, without affection, "Gift!"

He closed his eyes.

Continued, "I have always despised that aspect of my heritage. My father was . . ." His jaw locked, as if he was physically unable to go on. Stuart waited. "My father was a half-assed medium. We lived on what he could grub from private séances, readings, performances in carnivals and fifth-rate nightclubs. It was a squalid, gypsy existence. Loathing is not too strong a word for my feeling about"—he made an irritable shooing gesture with his hand—"about all that." He sat silent, run down.

Stuart prompted, "But you have the, er, ability?"

Lees pressed his lips tight, as if to forbid the word.

"You have this faculty?"

"Yes," said Lees, angrily. "Yes, I'm cursed with this nonsense. I had my first 'vision' when I was five or six, had them regularly in my teens. My father wanted me to exploit it. At eighteen, I welcomed the draft. To go to Korea, to fight, was not too high a price for escape. I stayed in the army after the war for its buttoned-down way of life. Routine, chain-of-command, no ambivalence, no room for the bizarre."

"Did the visions continue?"

"They came less frequently. I became adept at blocking them, at cultivating states of mind that were unreceptive. When they came anyway, I ignored them. Denied them."

"And now?"

Lees lit a cigarette and offered one to Stuart, who accepted.

"Three years ago I retired. Without the routine, I dropped my guard. Visions began again, regularly. A long series of the same vision with variations. They begin as a dream of the Victorian crimes in Whitechapel, the Ripper murders. But parts of the dreams became contemporary in detail. They began to make me afraid the crimes would be recreated on their hundredth anniversaries. I told myself they were just nightmares, meaningless, but after the news of the Hyde Park murder came . . ."

"Yes. You had better tell me about the visions, General."

Lees nodded acquiescence without enthusiasm.

He related the visions and variations in outline form. Stuart listened politely, asked only a few questions. Lees was tighter at the end than when he'd entered the office; relating the visions had no cathartic effect, provided no release.

Ready to explode, thought Stuart. Compassion moved Stuart to the window, where he stood with his back to Lees. He glanced away and down to Wellington Barracks, where a single soldier walked his jet-black mount, his plumed silver shako gleaming, winking in the sun. An anachronism, a polished relic of another time, thought Stuart, but was it simpler? Nostalgia welled in him momentarily. Then he remembered that another soldier in an identical scarlet tunic had trod the same ground a hundred years before; that simpler time had, after all, produced the Ripper.

Stuart turned and saw Lees straightening his tie, pulling himself together.

"General Lees, I'm grateful to you for making the long journey. I realize the enormous discomfort this has caused you and, just as Pat Cochran says, you are a brave man. However, I'm not really sure how your, er, dreams are helpful. We know there has been a 'recreation' of the first murder, may be others to follow—but you don't, as yet, seem to have any information that helps." He shrugged.

Lees shifted uncomfortably in his chair. Stuart was an imposing bulk against the window, framed by the sun-hazed sky. Quietly, he said, "There's a bit more."

He narrated his premonition on the plane flight and the encounter with the cabbie.

Stuart sat again. "And what do you make of that?"

Lees sighed. "The 'flash' *might* mean I'm . . . my visions might intensify. As for the cabbie—I was tired, under stress, the sun was bright and in my eyes and the whole thing probably lasted less than thirty seconds. His eyes *looked* silver, like in the dreams, and his voice *sounded* like the one in the dream. He did call me by name, but he could have gotten that from the luggage tags."

"Yes. Of course. And you didn't get his cab number, so . . ."

Lees nodded. "Not much help. Again."

Stuart hesitated, but honor bade him speak as well as decency. "I will tell you one thing, General Lees. It is a detail we are reserving for the present and I shall have to require you to treat it as classified."

†

"Certainly."

"The Hyde Park murderer had an accomplice. A hackie." Stuart hesitated again, decided not to mention the hansom cab just yet. "We have only a partial description, but the principal feature is silver eyes, much as you describe. We are checking the taxi firms, but, so far, without success."

"I see." Lees stared at his highly polished wing tips. *So there is some link with my dreams.* He laughed inwardly. *However small.*

"General, I have no more idea what to make of this than you do, but it seems . . . you might be needed. Will it be too inconvenient for you to stay on in London?"

Lees shook his head. "No. I will honor my duty. I have always tried to do that." He rose. "My wife and I are staying at the Dorchester."

Stuart led him to the door. "Good. Thank you again for coming, General Lees. I shall ring you up soon and, if you— well, *receive* any more information, don't hesitate to call me. Anytime."

They shook hands tentatively, unsure of one another.

Stuart left his office shortly after Lees. He had a telephone call to make and he wanted to be sure that he had a fully secure line—one that didn't go through the Yard switchboard.

The ride from Victoria Street to his Duke Street townhouse on Grosvenor Square was pleasant in the warm afternoon, but he did not enjoy it as much as he customarily did. He hated to impose on old friends, especially in ways that might have serious repercussions for them. And Pat Cochran was a great friend and an extraordinary man. Still . . .

He let himself in quietly, went straight up to his second-floor study, sat at his desk. It only took six-minutes to get a transatlantic line.

"Malcolm, you dog—when are you coming over to see us?"

The booming, cheery voice at the other end of the line sent an unexpected shiver up Stuart's spine.

He remembered.

It was a rain-gray, bone-cold night in Berlin—had it been October of '69 . . . or '70? A British agent had been blown,

†

39

was on the run. An American agent was going to bring him home. They were both Stralsunders, Baltic eyes for the West, and for two interminable days Stuart and Pat Cochran had stood watch at Checkpoint Charlie, wondering if their men were still making their torturous way down from the icy north or had already been taken by the Abteilung, lost. Cochran recognized his agent's battered rust-colored Volvo when it was only third in line across the way. He practically threw Stuart into the sleek, waiting Cadillac (chosen to impress and infuriate the GDR border guards) and roared across the neutral zone to their checkpoint. Inside the hut, he gave a twelve-minute performance of the Ugly American that was positively Oscar caliber. He demanded service. Instantly. He raved about nonexistent rights. He pounded on the counter and jabbed his finger against the chest of the guards or into the pages of passports they were examining. He shouted insults at the East German government, the Russians, bureaucrats and border guards. Stuart played a supporting role as best he could, but Cochran carried the hour. As it was designed to, his act drew all attention to them. Two guards carefully inspected the luxury sedan, dazzled by its opulence. One tried to placate Stuart; one tried to placate Cochran. Most importantly, the man behind the counter, in order to show the American ruffian that the GDR could be swift, efficient and courteous to those who behaved themselves, insisted on making Stuart and Cochran wait while all outgoing traffic was passed through. Cochran finally stomped off to a window and watched as the rust-colored Volvo passed safely into West Berlin, then turned and marched back to the desk, snatched up his and Stuart's phony passports, snarled, "Well, if this is the way you run your pissant little country, we damn well don't want to visit this dung heap!" He led Stuart to the Cadillac and drove back to the West. They had gotten thoroughly and properly pissed with their agents and laughed through the long night. It remained in Stuart's memory a harrowing and brilliant experience.

He spoke into the telephone with affection and genuine regret. "Sorry, I haven't made it recently, Pat. I shall do so soon. Just now, we're a bit of a balls-up over here, and I have to ask you about your friend, Lees."

"Jim—good man. The best. What about him?"

"Well . . . your letter was quite complete, of course, but I may need to rely on him in an extremely important matter. You've known him long?"

"Fought with him in Korea for more than a year, briefed and debriefed him in Vietnam. I've been drunk with him and sober with him; he was best man at my wedding. I'd trust him with my life—hell, I'd trust him with the lives of my family. Good enough?"

"Almost."

Cochran whistled. "My God, Malcolm—what do you want?"

Stuart swallowed hard and hesitated before he answered. "His service jacket. His dossier."

"Jesus H. Christ, Stuart!"

"I know it's rather much to ask, but I'd prefer not to go through channels."

Silence.

"Pat, you still there?"

"Just thinking, old buddy, just thinking. If I get caught they'd hang my ass higher than a full moon on Halloween, but . . . I *could* get it."

"Will you?"

"I don't suppose you want to tell me what it's all about?"

"I'd rather not. At the moment. Later, perhaps."

"Okay, my friend. I'll get it for you. It may take a few days. Once you're done with it, you destroy it—PDQ!"

Stuart gazed out the casement windows at the Roosevelt Memorial in Grosvenor Square. Relief and gratitude moved him. He said simply, "Thank you, Pat. I shan't forget."

Cochran snorted. "Don't thank me—it isn't nearly enough. Come see us some time. Bring that lady friend you wrote me about."

As if conjured by the American's words, Vanessa Cilone came quietly into the study with a high-collared blue silk robe flowing loosely about her long young body. She sat on the apricot carpet near Stuart's feet and stared up at him through the heavy frame of tawny-blond hair. Her flawless fair skin and high strong features were a perfect setting for the velvet-amber eyes that gazed at her lover in contented possession.

†

He smiled at her and spoke into the phone. "I will, Pat. Soon. There are just one or two questions I'd like to ask you about Lees."

"Go ahead, it's your nickel."

"In the time you've known him, has he ever spoken of or shown any special intuitive ability or a gift for . . . oh, precognition?"

The silence lasted so long Stuart wondered if the connection had been broken.

"Pat—you there?"

"Thinking, old buddy. Thinking. It's curious you should ask. I was remembering the other day a thing that happened in 'Nam. Hadn't thought about it in years."

"Would you share it with me?"

"Sure. Once, early on, in 'Nam, Jim was taking his troops out on an S-and-D operation. Riding helicopters into the boonies. Two minutes before they're supposed to land, for no apparent reason, Jim pulls back and calls in air strikes around the landing zone. Place was crawling with Charlie and NVR. Jim never could—or never would—explain how he knew. All his time in 'Nam, he seemed to have a nose for Charlie. Nothing as spectacular as that first time, but a sense for traps and feints."

"You said you fought together in Korea. Did he display this talent then?"

Cochran said, "Uh?" as if startled. "Now who's a mind reader?"

Stuart frowned. "I don't follow."

"You hit exactly the thing I was thinking about. Nothing like that ever happened in Korea, but that was a more conventional war. Most of the time, we knew where the unfriendlies were, they knew where we were. In 'Nam it was all that hit-and-run guerrilla shit. A guessing game. It was like Jim had a sixth sense he never needed till 'Nam. When he needed it—it came to him."

Stuart felt uncomfortable, didn't like what he was hearing, but didn't know why. His eyes wandered as he listened, as if searching for some sedative, some soothing sight to ease a mild ache. Gunmetal leading of the casement windows; broad ebony desktop with inlaid ivory trim; lustrous cherry-wood

†

42

paneling and built-in bookshelves crammed with the unprogrammed selections of wide and varied taste; ornate gold chandelier; Vanessa's soft face.

"What about his . . . mmmm, I don't want to be offensive, Pat, but—did he ever show signs of instability?"

"You know, Malcolm, this conversation is getting a little weird."

"I know, Pat. I'm sorry, but I hope you can believe me—it really is necessary."

"Is Jim in some kind of trouble?"

"No, I don't think so. But we do have something of a situation here. His 'information' may or may not have a bearing on it, so I have to consider the reliability of the source."

Cochran sighed. "That's not real forthcoming, old buddy. Okay. Instability? Who doesn't show some from time-to-time? If you mean, Is Jim flaky? the answer is an unqualified no. Bottom line for a soldier is combat. Jim was the best, and I mean *the best*! Always looked tight as a drum going in, but he was a tiger in the close spots. Never got anybody killed from being either timid *or* gung-ho foolish. Like I said, I'd trust him with my family's lives."

Stuart turned the conversation to reminiscence, and Vanessa laid her head against the side of his leg. He stroked her long hair. When he rang off, she smiled up at him.

"I see you're still up."

Stuart deadpanned, "You can see no such thing. This suit is fully concealing."

She mock-bit his knee and wrinkled her nose at him. "I'm willing to play that sort of game if you are."

"I have to get back to the office."

"It's late enough in the afternoon to justify calling it a day. And, I remind you—momentous investigation or no—you will be home Saturday week. The dinner party has been on for two months and no beastly killer shall be allowed to interfere."

He nodded. "I haven't forgotten. You must tell Hathorn that there may be two more guests than planned for. General and Mrs. Lees. If I need him, we'd best make them welcome."

She smiled wickedly. "Only if you scrap your return to the Yard. I've just made plans for the next hour or so."

†

He laughed as he pulled her up into his arms. "As long as all that? Mightn't you be overestimating this elderly sort's capacities?"

As their lips neared, all she said was, "No."

Saturday morning, Jim Lees pushed away his half-eaten breakfast, lit a cigarette and stared at the milky-brown residue in his teacup. He leaned his elbows on the crisp linen of the room-service table and dug the heels of his hands into his eyes. Ann stood by the window and stared out at the drizzle falling on the park.

"What do you want?"

"Honesty," she said without looking around.

"That's a little vague."

She snapped, "Don't play games, Jim! You *know* what I'm asking about. For forty years all you've told me about your family was that all your immediate relatives were dead, that your father was a 'pretend psychic,' a charlatan, that your family were all lunatics who 'thought' they had ESP talents and that you had a relative that once held séances for Queen Victoria. Now it's obvious there's more to this. If you're not going to tell me, just say so; but *don't* pretend that there's nothing to share."

"What I told you was all true."

"But what was left unsaid?"

Lees sighed, felt the teapot, splashed a little lukewarm liquid into his cup and then ignored it. "My father was a fake, but he did have a little of the ability. Not much, but a little."

"What's a little?"

Lees shrugged. "He was pretty good at reading cards. You know—I pick a card, the ace of clubs say, and stare at it, and he tells me what the card is. He could get that right six or seven times out of ten. And some of his astrology stuff was fairly accurate. The rest—mind reading, prophecy—he faked all that."

"And?"

Red letters floated in his tea—LEES SEES. He closed his eyes and bit his lip. Images in his head—the sallow face covered with a week's stubble; the yellow eyes; the violence of his thrashing and the crossed arms tugging, pulling, straining un-

†

44

til the neck muscles bulged and the forehead vein popped up throbbing.

"And?" she repeated.

His father's scream echoed in his mind—"*I've got to warn the president!*" Lees stubbed out his cigarette and forced himself to concentrate.

"Some of my relatives *were* psychic. Eccentric, anti-social, unprosperous and just plain goofy, but . . . oh, I don't know—attuned to something *outside* themselves. And my grandfather's cousin, Robert James Lees, was involved in the investigation of the original Ripper crimes. Gave the police some details ahead of time, especially about the last murder."

Her voice was a velvet whisper. "What about you?"

Her question remained in the room. Alive.

He put his face in his hands.

"Oh, Jesus."

Silence.

"Yes," he finally whispered.

"Yes—what?"

"Yes. I have it. Remember the time I told you we were going to Europe, and a month later I was posted to NATO Command?"

She nodded. "Yes."

"I'd had a dream . . . a dream of NATO Headquarters and an office with my name on it. Things—the dreams, the *special* dreams—aren't always that simple or clear. Sometimes they don't seem to mean anything."

"Is that all?"

"No. Sometimes things . . . have come to me while I'm *awake.*" He told her of the flash on the airplane. "Things like that. That was the first one in twenty years."

She was silent.

Watched a red double-decker bus pull slowly away from a stop on Park Lane below. The red metal and the black street gleamed from the rain. A small fair-haired boy with an umbrella held above his head ran after the bus. She could see his mouth wide, shouting, but she could not hear him. He ran in the street, leaped at the back platform and secured a precarious hold. Ann held her breath. His feet slipped and he started to fall down and away from the bus. She stiffened. An

†

arm shot out the back door. The conductor grabbed the child's collar, hauled him upright and in the door.

She sighed and looked at her husband.

"Jim, this is going to take some getting used to for me."

"I know."

"I love you, and this . . . doesn't mean you're a *completely* different man than I've known, but it's obvious you've kept a whole dimension of yourself hidden."

He nodded. "I'm sorry. It wasn't fair or right—it's just that I always hated it so much."

"You're going to have to talk to me about it. Not everything all at once, maybe, but I—I have a right to know."

"Yes."

"One thing—I don't understand your anger. You make it sound like a disease."

The breakfast plates and cutlery jumped as he crashed his fist down on the table. *"It is a disease!"*

She crossed, stood behind and put her arms around him. He was trembling and she held him tight.

"I always understood why you didn't like the sham, the fake things. But why make a secret of what's real? Why be angry at what's true? That's different."

Her husband whispered, "Not to me."

Stuart didn't like working Saturdays, but he was three full days behind on his mail because of the Hyde Park murder.

The letter was near the bottom of the stack.

The envelope was pale-yellow, of a superlative paper and hand-inked in an arresting shade of deep blue. It gave him a strange sensation, almost electric to touch, and he slit one end gingerly.

He removed two sheets of matching notepaper also hand-inked in the riveting shade of blue. Something about the ink and paper seemed to make the letter alive, produced a glow in the cool light of his office. The words, the message, seemed to rise from the paper, seemed almost to hang suspended in air, free of the medium of paper, solid and electric like an advertising sign, a trick of depth perception, as if lettered on the invisible molecules of oxygen.

†

<u>FROM HELL</u>
August 31, 1988

Sir Malcolm Stuart
Deputy Commissioner, CID,
New Scotland Yard

New Boss:

Hello again. I'm Jack; I'm back. You're not finished with me yet.

> The time is nigh and I am high
> To work with knife and pen again,
> To coax a final frightened sigh
> And shrieks of pleasure-pain.
>
> I've slept a century and kept
> Fears still, but now I'm back
> With blade and rhyme adept
> At fun for Saucy Jack.
>
> I did my bit
> O' work last night;
> Took fast flight;
> Gave you all a fit.
> Now do you believe?
>
> I can't wait 'til Thursday next!
> I'll cut her guts and proper
> And leave you—copper,
> Hexed by my bloody text!
> Then, will you believe?
>
> I come to show, for you to know
> My name's not Clarence. Never was
> Gull or Stanly—oh no!
> A man's name is as he does.
>
> I laugh at Druitt, Chapman and Cream,
> While Pedachenko's simply a scream.
> I'm not Leather Apron or a midwife,
> Just Jack—come back to life.
>
> I wasn't on Thuggee weaned,
> I'm me—not a foreign skipper.
> Accept it. I'm your own true fiend,
> Yours Truly, Jack-the-Ripper!

P. S. New Boss, you know the nights—catch me if you can!

†

Stuart dropped the letter on his desk and rubbed his eyes as if to eradicate the thing from his brain. Contradictorily, he then looked back at it. He got up from his desk and walked across to his window wall, stared out at the grandeur of Buckingham Palace misted by a soft summer shower and the muted light of a wet gray sky.

Bloody crank letter, he thought. But it didn't make him feel like a crank letter did; it felt like reading something much worse. Spooked me, he thought. Maybe it's this business with Lees that's got me edgy.

He crossed back to his desk and lifted the letter.

Something spooky about touching this thing, he thought. He reread the text, set it aside and pondered.

The poem—Stuart shuddered—still that's what it was—had several noteworthy aspects. It was more or less literate. It showed considerable knowledge of Ripperology, as it denied most major suspect theories from the Duke of Clarence to the anonymous midwife, and it borrowed heavily from some of the poems and letters received by police and press during the period of the original Whitechapel murders. That it was addressed to him personally was also unusual (as head of CID, he was not a faceless public servant, but he was far from being a household name).

Stuart picked up the envelope. Really fine paper. Might give Clive and the lab something to work with, he thought. The cancellation mark was not uniform, had a series of knicks around the lower edge, but Stuart didn't know how that could be of any use.

The rain intensified momentarily, drummed on his window wall beckoning his attention. Rain was another simply solved problem. Just wait. It always went away of its own accord, sooner or later stopped.

This case wasn't going to be like that. And the secondary problems were multiplying.

Lees.

Genuine or kook or fake, whatever, an American general, even retired, was a delicate element. The Foreign Office would fry the home secretary if there was a flap, and Dezzie would fry Stuart. The press would love to know about him, too. On the whole, they had given large but balanced coverage

†

to the murder—so far. Of course, they don't know about the costume-drama stuff or her name, he thought. Yet.

Sir Edwards William, he thought. He was already irritable about the sketchy information he was providing and that would get worse.

Stuart sighed, made a mental note to have lunch or dinner with Dezzie on Monday (he should have Lees' dossier by then, could fill the HS in) and punched his intercom button to summon Sergeant Clive.

The raven shook its head against the drizzle. It was dampened to lustrous black, large, fat and ugly. Its glistening beak had a razor look, menacing, and its bright empty eyes were vacant and vicious.

The raven looked at Lees.

Lees met the bird's eyes.

Animosity passed between them.

The raven cawed, startling in its volume, and half-flapped its wings and flexed its taloned feet. It ran at Lees with an overpowering urge to tear and rip and savage flesh.

In a flash of scarlet, a Beefeater stepped onto the grass and stamped his foot. The raven cawed angrily and wobbled away. The Yeoman smiled at Jim and Ann.

"They're overfed and spoiled. Their soft life at the Tower makes them a bit saucy. Hope he didn't upset you folks."

Ann smiled. "Just startled me."

Lees shrugged.

The Tower of London, a medieval castle, seemed even a touch gloomier in the gray and light rain than it had a moment before.

Ann was delighted with the exhibit of the Crown Jewels, but Jim was distracted. He was not sorry when the tour ended and they left.

He was glad the day's sightseeing and shopping spree had lightened Ann's mood. Maybe it'll help mine in awhile, he thought. Westminster Abbey was next and after that—Harrod's for gifts for friends and family. Lees smiled to himself. Hope I brought enough money. Ann had become a legendary shopper since he had retired.

†

The taxi passed Waterloo Bridge and bent fully into the curve of the Victoria Embankment. The driver was a cheerful, loquacious Irishman who seemed to regard concentration on traffic patterns as an impediment to the flow of conversation. At least he had clear blue eyes. Lees found himself now in the habit of scanning the driver's face and eyes before entering any cab.

Cleopatra's Needle loomed ahead.

Lees looked out across the Thames. On the far bank he saw the Royal Festival Hall and the pier below. Sun was breaking through the clouds and rain.

Suddenly his head hurt—stabbing pains, like those on the airplane.

A column of mist rose and hovered over the river. Beneath it, the water, in a widening pool, was changing color from its muddy amber and dull blue-green and brown.

It was red—blood red.

He rubbed his eyes and his head stopped hurting. He looked back and the mist was gone, the Thames was ordinary and the sun had disappeared again.

He glanced at Ann. She was looking away, to the right, at the looming facade of the Savoy Hotel.

Trick of light, he said to himself.

Fished out a cigarette and lit it, blew smoke.

Detective-Sergeant Clive stared irritably at the smirking young lab technician. He was a lithe, dark-haired, good-looking young man who probably spent too much time peering at himself in the mirror. Clive bent forward to see the plastic badge attached to the breast of the white lab coat.

He straightened. "No bloody cheek, Johnson. Just take the envelope and make your tests and give us a report."

Johnson shrugged indifferently. "All I was suggesting, Sergeant, was that we don't do our best work in the dark. Helps if we know what we're looking for."

Clive's voice was acid. "Take the envelope. Do whatever hugger-mugger you like. Tell us anything you can discover that will help us locate the manufacturer. It is obviously an expensive paper. Can't be too many like it around. What you can tell us may lead us to source and sale. *That* is all you *need* to know and that is bloody well all you will be told."

Johnson smirked. "Right. CID. Cops-and-robbers, hush-hush, Alfred bloody Hitchcock, mystery and all that."

Clive walked away before he lost control and slapped the young, insufferably smug face. Glad it's nothing more important than a crank letter. He did not consider the letter a priority lead. Can't remember a case where a fool letter amounted to anything.

Detective-Sergeant Peters dropped the three typewritten sheets onto Chief Inspector Hughes' desk and said, "Preliminary report on the bonnet found by the victim's body, sir."

Hughes looked up at the slim, balding young man. "And?"

"Well, sir, as you'll see, we've been unable to locate any manufacturer of ladies hats, *currently operating*, by the name of Hanby and Sons."

Hughes caught the emphasis. "Currently operating, Sergeant?"

"Yes, sir. Constable White deserves full credit, Chief Inspector. When we'd exhausted the contemporary directories, he got the idea of checking some of the older commercial guides. Reishards' volume for 1888 lists a Hanby and Sons, milliners, on Court Street. It is also listed in the volumes for 1883–87, inclusive, but not in the '89 edition or any thereafter."

"Went out of business," said Hughes.

"Most likely, sir." Peters hesitated.

Hughes again caught the nuance from his subordinate. "There's more."

"Yes, sir. White went to the trouble to look up Court Street. It's only a few paces from Buck's Row in Whitechapel."

Hughes stared at him.

Peters shifted uncomfortably.

"Buck's Row was where the body of Polly Nichols was discovered in 1888."

Peters nodded. "Yes, and the one thing known about Polly Nichols' movements during the day before she was murdered was that she bought herself a new hat. A black velvet bonnet."

†

51

Grotesque charade, thought Hughes. "Well, Sergeant, it seems as if our killers have gone to elaborate lengths to echo the Ripper murder."

"Very elaborate. Shall I put some men on checking specialty manufacturers of women's clothing? The bonnet would have to be a custom order, and specifying the replica maker's label would surely make it an unusual one."

Hughes nodded. "Yes, do that, Sergeant Peters. And give my congratulations to Constable White."

"Yes, sir."

The Boeing 757 streaked thirty-two thousand feet above the Atlantic Ocean, winging toward night and London. In the first-class cabin, a bulky, balding, bearded Irishman stretched the collar of his turtleneck jersey with a forefinger and rotated his head from side-to-side.

Damn things look good, thought Pat Cochran, but they don't help a headache.

He took a generous swig of his Wild Turkey on the rocks and fingered the fat unlabeled manila envelope in his lap. He had touched it every minute or so since takeoff to reassure himself of its presence. A friend's service jacket isn't something you dare mislay, he told himself again.

Stuart's energy dried up in early evening. It began to fade further shortly after he settled into the back seat of his chauffeured car. He had not had regular sleep for many days and he was completely exhausted.

He *ought* to stay at the Yard. He *ought* to oversee and pull together the myriad details that the investigation called for. He *ought* to deal with the howling press and try to make sense and use of General Lees. He *ought* to.

Still, Stuart was sensible enough man to know that *ought* was theory; reality was that he was too tired to be of further use until he had rested. He chose reality and gave his driver orders to take him home.

He leaned his head back and closed his eyes as the car accelerated smoothly into traffic. In the instant his lids were descending, his eyes flicked across one of the ubiquitous

Scent of Love Perfume billboards; his retinas captured the spotlit image and froze it.

Mild irritation rose in him for the thousandth time, and for the thousandth time he tracked the irritation through his mind, trying to resolve it. There was the likeness of the beautiful woman in an attitude of sexual suggestion with a perfume bottle in her hand. There were the three outrageous lines of copy:

**NAME IS VANESSA
ALL MEN KNOW HER
SHE IS THE SCENT OF LOVE**

The advertisement was, quite successfully, selling perfume by means of two lies. The first and obvious lie was the most familiar in advertising: linkage. Here is a desirable thing; this desirable thing has our product; if you want to have or be this desirable thing, buy our product. If you want to be this woman, buy our perfume; if you want to have this woman, buy our perfume for your lover.

The second lie was the better lie, for it contained a truth. It was the lie about love. This woman's physical beauty is erotic; eroticism is love; this woman's physical beauty is love. (If you want love, buy our perfume.)

The truth and the falsity of the syllogism was in its reduction. Physical beauty is a component of eroticism; eroticism is a component of love; physical beauty is a component of love. The correct syllogism implies elements outside itself and the necessity of searching for them. The billboard syllogism allowed no larger implications. Its reduction was a false perfection, making a tight, hard circle, self-contained and tiny, while infinite, yet completely untrue and utterly mad. The billboard seemed to Stuart both the dominant and symbolic syllogism of modernity. Many pursued the superficial exclusively, accepted the incomplete and despaired of love.

All this might have been solely an exercise in abstract moral contemplation, in which case, Stuart would never have pursued it through his excellent brain a thousand times. What removed it from abstraction for Stuart were the facts that the Scent of Love girl was Vanessa Cilone, and Vanessa Cilone was Sir Malcolm's lover.

The exact refutation of the billboard syllogism was that, as the car pulled up to his three-story townhouse on Duke Street, he was far too tired for sex, but he desperately hoped his lover was home. He wanted to see her, talk to her, share with her. He adored her physical beauty and enjoyed their sex acutely, but he loved her for far more, and in a multitude of manners. He was as fully entranced by her habit of blushing when complimented or her total disdain for blank verse as by the suppleness of her limbs.

In anticipation, he left the car hurriedly and rushed up the steps without so much as a passing glance at darkening Grosvenor Square across the street.

Lees dreamed.
    He dreamed a pillar of mist above a widening pool of blood.
    He dreamed jazz played by uninspired, inept musicians.
    He dreamed a tall dark woman with large bare breasts dancing an erotic dance that was not erotic.
    He dreamed the wounded white trailer with the large legend emblazoned in red letters—LEES SEES—behind the dusty pickup on the road.
    He dreamed the road—American highways from Bangor to Big Sur, from Seattle to Key West.
    He dreamed his father's anguish-distorted face screaming, "I must warn the president!"
    He dreamed the Ripper.
    He dreamed the knife, long and narrow, thumb-notched, with the gleaming, winking razor-keen blade mirroring a pillar of mist above the widening pool of blood.
    He dreamed the cabbie with silver eyes.

He woke in the middle of the night lying in sweat-soaked sheets, his pupils dilated in the dark, his heart hurting from pounding, his limbs trembling in terror of forces at work in the world with malignant design, of forces in his mind

†

beyond his conscious control, of forces within him waging a war, with his soul as their battleground.

Lees opened the door. Pat Cochran stood there grinning at him in a trenchcoat and trilby hat. Lees couldn't help smiling and shook his head. "Imagine my surprise when you phoned up from the lobby."

Cochran shifted a fat unlabeled manila envelope to his left hand, extended his right. Lees laughed and pumped it and led him into the suite's sitting room.

"Still in pajamas at noon? Retirement has made you a slugabed, Jim."

"Didn't sleep well."

"Yeah." Cochran nodded as he peeled coat and hat, dropped them and the envelope on the sofa. "You look like hell."

"Thanks, old buddy." Lees sat in a blue chair; Cochran dropped onto the sofa next to his things. "Like I said, didn't sleep well. You look good, even with that fur on your face."

Pat scratched his beard. "Itches sometimes, but I kinda like it. Where's Ann?"

"Mass," replied Lees as he fumbled a cigarette from his pack, lit it and tossed pack and lighter to Cochran. "Pardon my French, Patrick, but what the fuck are you doing over here?"

Cochran lit a cigarette, tapped the envelope. "Malcolm Stuart called me and asked me to get this for him."

Lees face was guarded. "What is it?"

"Your service jacket or, rather, a highly illegal Xeroxed copy of same."

"That's pretty far out of line, but I suppose I can't blame him."

Cochran shook his head. "Pardon *my* French, but what the fuck's going on, Jim?"

"Stuart didn't tell you?"

Cochran shook his head in the negative. "Nope. Malcolm was not forthcoming."

Lees stared at his bare toes. When is this going to end? Does the whole world get to pry into my private life? But Cochran was his best friend; he trusted no other man half so

†

much. The pressure of carrying things alone was grinding him down.

He sighed. "Want some breakfast?"

"I could eat."

Lees picked up the phone and ordered from room service. He explained the basic situation while they waited, as they ate, and after they were finished.

Cochran sipped the dregs of his coffee and shrugged. "Sounds to me like you're fighting Godzilla with a kid's peashooter."

"Huh?"

"All this running around wishing this and that, hating this and that, wanting things not to be the way they are is kid stuff. What is, is, and what ain't, ain't. It's tough enough fighting the unreal; fighting the for-reals is always a losing proposition."

"Thanks a bunch, buddy."

"You got this whatever-it-is ability—so use it."

"It's not that simple, Pat."

Cochran shrugged again. "Okey-dokey. Your choice, pal." He tapped the envelope with his hand. "What do you want to do about this?"

Lees stubbed out his cigarette. "Won't tell him much. Shrink report says I have a deep-seated resentment against my father, but if he was my friend, he'd already know that." He yawned. "Fuck it. Give it to him."

The hansom cab was restored and cleaned and polished to a high gloss. It stood on a rectangle of brown-and-tan parquet flooring framed by a thigh-level purple rope strung between four brass posts. The black horse in the traces was a wooden refugee from a carnival merry-go-round. The bowlered driver atop and the Victorian couple inside were special-order wax dummies.

The large, well-lit room was filled with similar displays of other varieties of horse carriages and summoned a handsome smile to the seventy-year-old face of the fifth Duke of Blandford. "Rather an eccentric indulgence, but I love the buggies, Sergeant. Family thinks I'm a bit potty, but I don't mind."

Detective-Sergeant Clive gave a return grin. "I admire your taste, My Lord."

"Good of you to say so, Sergeant. I suppose this isn't much help."

"I'm afraid not, My Lord. We're looking for a hansom that's missing—not those that are where they're supposed to be."

"Done the movie studios and museums, did you say?"

"Yes, My Lord. And the few specialty firms that can manufacture to order."

"Which leaves only collectors."

Clive nodded.

"Not many of us. We all know each other and, as far as I can tell you, there are only five hansoms restored to operational quality in private collections. In the islands, of course. Don't know about Europe. Let's see—Dickie, er, Sir Richard Puling has two at Wepton Hall. Tried to buy one of them a few years back. Fancied a set, but so did he."

Clive said, "I've spoken to Sir Richard by telephone, My Lord. His are accounted for."

"Mmm, Teddy Tavistock in Birmingham and Sir Horace Blatt at Wimbledon own the others."

Clive sighed. "I also phoned Mr. Tavistock and I've been down to see Sir Horace's."

"Bit of a blunt end, then, Sergeant."

"I'm afraid so, My Lord."

As Clive drove down the graveled drive of Singleton Castle with the stone turrets and bricked battlements filling his rearview mirror, his frustration level rose rapidly.

Where in blazes did those idiots get a hansom cab?

They sat in the study in Stuart's Duke Street townhouse.

Stuart took in Cochran's pale-blue turtleneck, navy double-breasted blazer and gray flannel slacks. "You're looking well, Pat. Even the beard—though I can't quite get used to it."

Cochran smiled and held his glass of neat Scotch up to the light, swirled the oily liquid. "After I retired, I woke up one morning thinking, I've shaved every day for the last thirty-seven years and decided to take a break. Didn't shave for nine weeks. By then, I decided I liked the beard." He sipped his

†

drink. "Curious thing is that with a beard, shaving is more of a high-tech task than without."

Stuart smiled. "It looks fine." He lifted his glass. "Berlin."

Cochran raised his. "Berlin."

They drank.

Stuart put a large hand flat on the envelope atop his desk. "I know thanks aren't adequate for this, Pat."

Cochran grinned. "No, they aren't." The grin disappeared like quicksilver in a change of light. "Jim Lees is my best friend, Malcolm. He gave me a rough draft of what's going on here. All that file will tell you is what I've already told you—in spades. He's a good man. I don't know what you're thinking or wondering about Jim, but you can trust him with your life. I stopped by the Dorchester before I came here. Jim okayed my giving you the file."

"I see."

"I hope you do, buddy. Jim's struggling with this psychic stuff, got some grudge against it. I don't understand all that, but that's his choice." Cochran's face was unsmiling. "But I would become very angry—even at a friend like you, Malcolm—if I thought he was getting a raw deal."

Stuart nodded. "Understood, but recognize my position, Pat. I've a bizarre, nasty murder and Jim has involved himself. Considering his ... professed attitude, I have to ask myself why."

"Jesus Christ—his conscience! His sense of duty and honor."

The two friends eyed one another.

"Yes," said Stuart, "I am making that assumption, but ... *my* clear duty and honor force me to document Jim's motives as best I can."

Cochran agreed. "Fair enough."

"I wonder, Pat, if you could be convinced to remain in London for a week or so. Jim and I are still acquainting ourselves like your American porcupines—*very carefully*. You might be able to facilitate the relationship."

Cochran tossed back the remainder of his whisky, stood and grinned again. "I'd already decided on that, Malcolm. You couldn't blow me out of London with a cannon."

* * *

†

Sunday night Lees dreamed again.

A column of mist above a spreading pool of blood next to a police station.

His father leather-bound and twisting in torment.

The scream, *"I must warn the president!"*

Rhythmic chugging noises and the grinding sound of wood scraping and tearing at wood.

Ann's face turning away. Her back. Walking away. Walking toward a figure in shadow.

The Ripper's smile. The cabbie's smile.

"Glad you came?"

The bright blade of the long knife.

He awoke in fear again, in the middle of the night again and, again, in sheets soaked by his own sweat.

I smell like a goat, he thought. Maids must think I'm a malaria case when they change the sheets.

He slipped out of bed without disturbing Ann and stole into the sitting room to smoke a cigarette in the dark.

Constable Colin Colson was a handsome, ambitious young man of twenty-six, blond and fair, compact, but muscular and athletic. His ambition was timetabled and precise—to make detective-sergeant in two more years, deputy inspector by thirty-three, inspector before his fortieth birthday, chief inspector by his late forties and, after that . . . deputy commissioner?

Constable Colson was excited to be on the neo-Ripper killing. It was the sort of case that had attention-getting possibilities. Since he was young and confident, he didn't consider that "being noticed" was a double-edged sword with negative as well as positive potential.

Of course, he was only just on the case, being one of the team checking taxi companies with the very sketchy description of the murder acomplice. In fact, "an ordinary-size-man with bright silver eyes," was so sketchy as to be slightly embarrassing. It was also not bringing success. Almost all the taxi firms had been covered, with no results. The firm he was heading for first thing Monday morning was not even on the list. It was new and small and he had stumbled across the

†

closed garage by accident while off-duty Sunday afternoon. It was a measure of the constable's youthful eagerness that he did not bother to report in before calling on the South Kensington & Chelsea Hire, Ltd., off Fulham Road not far from St. Stephen's Hospital.

It was a smallish stone building with a cramped two-desk office in front and a modest garage behind. The receptionist directed him to the rear for the driving superintendent, Mr. Falcon.

The garage was dimly lit, with space for a dozen or so vehicles. Only three taxis were in sight; two on lifts being repaired and one dusty cab in the corner with a cracked windscreen, dented fender and a flat tire.

Falcon was a short burly man, not ten years older than Colson, in blue overalls with oil and grease stains like an absurd abstract canvas. His voice was chest deep and his manner brisk. "What can I do for you, Constable?"

"The Yard is making inquiries for a taxi driver of rather ordinary size and features, but with quite striking silver eyes."

"What'ch'er want him for?"

"In connection with a felony."

"That so." Falcon hesitated, took a closer look at Colson's handsome, hungry face. "What sort of felony?"

He knows him! He knows him! pounded through Colson's brain while he strived to keep his expression bland.

"That's the Yard's concern, Mr. Falcon."

"So it is."

Falcon seemed to hesitate while he produced a cigar stub and a kitchen match from a coverall pocket. He clamped his teeth on the stub while striking the match with a greasy fingernail, brought flame to the cigar tip and sucked it into life. He blew the flame out with a massive stream of blue smoke and dropped the stick on the floor, where it sizzled a second in a puddle of not-quite-dry oil.

Falcon shrugged. "No skin off my ass; Luke's an arrogant bugger anyhow. Now listen, Constable, if Luke's in Dutch, that's not any part of SK and C. We don't employ drivers, we just lease taxis to them on a monthly basis."

"No difficulty, Mr. Falcon."

†

"Right then. We've one driver might fit your description. Luke Nicholas."

Colson left the garage moments later with a pocket photo of a full-bearded blunt-faced man with silver eyes that shone even in the poor black-and-white copy of his driver identification picture. The card it was laminated to had his full name and address.:

LUCIAN T. NICHOLAS
#11 CLAYMOOR ROAD
BRIXTON

He also had the adrenaline high that comes with the idea of a high-risk, high-reward opportunity.

He ought to go straight back to the Yard with his lucky find.

He ought to . . .

Hughes, Clive and Stuart were seated in the conversation area of Sir Malcolm's office. Nine A.M. sunlight was just beginning to haze the window-wall glass and steam rose from their teacups.

Clive continued, "So, at the moment, we're stymied. I don't know where they got their hansom cab. Constable White has had the bright idea of going at it from the aspect of the horse."

Stuart frowned. "I beg your pardon?"

"They had to get the horse somewhere and they have to keep it somewhere. White suggested we begin a check of horse sales in the London area, livery stables, riding schools and so forth. It's thin, but possible. Tentatively, I've put White in charge of a four-man team to tackle it."

Stuart crossed his legs. "Enlarge that to a dozen."

Clive and Hughes exchanged expressions of surprise.

Stuart stretched his long, large body against the couch cushions. "This *is* CID's top priority and we've only until Thursday early morning to open something up—if these lunatics are bent upon recreating the entire Ripper sequence."

Hughes set his teacup and saucer on the table. "I think we have to assume that from the elaborate detail they've gone to reconstructing. The identical matching of the victim's names—"

"—Not quite," interrupted Clive.

Stuart and Hughes looked at him.

Clive scratched a reddish area of his throat where he had irritated the skin shaving. "It may be a meaningless quibble, but our woman's name is Polly Nichols. The original Ripper victim's name was Mary Ann Nichols. Polly was her nickname. It's a thin hair to split, but it has a bearing on the Annie Chapman search, which I'll get to in turn."

Hughes nodded. "Quibble accepted, Sergeant," and he smiled. "In any case, the *similarity* of names, the Victorian costumes, the hansom cab, commission of the murder on the hundredth anniversary evening at precisely the same time as the original and the bonnet planted by the body—you've seen the report on that piece of detailed reconstruction—all these items speak to careful long-term planning. It would be hard to imagine such effort just to recreate only one of the five Ripper killings."

"Quite," agreed Stuart, and Clive nodded.

"There's more." Hughes opened a folder, extracted three stapled sets of reports and handed one each to Clive and Stuart. "This is the final autopsy report. It came down Saturday. I'll read a bit, and if you will, follow me. Let's pick up in paragraph three on page two. 'The victim's abdomen was sliced open from a central point beneath the right ribs and beneath the pelvic area to the left of the stomach, where the wound became jagged; the omentum was cut in four places and there were two stabbing or thrusting wounds upon the vagina.'"

Stuart frowned again. "Are you making a point, Richard? I don't see the particular relevance of the section you are reading."

"The relevance," said Hughes quietly, "is that while you are following my words precisely from the autopsy summary of the woman murdered in Hyde Park last week, I am not reading to you from that file."

Clive and Stuart stared at Hughes hard.

"I am reading to you from the report of the autopsy done

†

on Mary Ann Nichols in 1888. It is virtually identical to the current report."

The trio sat in uncomfortable silence.

Finally, Clive said, "Well, let's not make too much of this. The language of autopsy reports is fairly limited. It's not *so* surprising that the reports would be similar."

"Yes," Stuart replied, "but virtually identical is . . ."

Hughes shifted uncomfortably. "The precise wording of the two reports gives pause for thought, certainly, but that is not the larger point."

Clive slapped his knee. "Of course!"

Stuart nodded. "I see. In order for the reports to be virtually identical the mutilations of the separate victims would need to be the same."

"Yes," said Hughes. "How did the new Ripper know—with precision—the location, length, depth and number of cuts, slashes, stabs and incisions to make in order to replicate the attack perfectly? And we know that he had only a few feverish minutes to do his cutting, so—even assuming knowledge—how did he do it so accurately, so quickly, under so much pressure?"

"Have you any answers?" asked Stuart.

"Not yet. That will require some collaborative thinking. It does cement the idea of painfully detailed planning. These men are lunatics, but methodical and skillful madmen. They will be difficult to catch and there's no doubt in *my* mind that they will attempt all five murders."

Stuart nodded. "Which brings us back to my point. Use all the men you need for any task, however chancy it may look. If the Chancellor of the Exchequer gets shirty about overtime hours and unbudgeted costs—let that be my worry. I am giving both of you carte blanche where manpower and expenses are concerned. Now, Clive, what about the Annie Chapman search?"

Clive smiled. "I'm glad of that generous attitude, Sir Malcolm. I've been using two dozen men on this because I judge it our best hope. And since there was a hair-splitting difference in the names of the first two victims, I broadened the search to women with names similar to Annie Chapman.

†

Ann, with or without an *e*, Anna, Annie, Anny with a *y*, Anya and Chapman, or *mun* or *mon* with all the potential variations in spelling."

"Excellent." Stuart smiled.

"Thank you, Sir Malcolm. We've limited it to the London metropolitan area and so far have come up with two hundred and eleven possibles. We are interviewing them and eliminating by age—twenty to fifty, since the original Ripper victims were within that range—and are looking, at least initially, for women who are or have been prostitutes."

"Sound," said Stuart. "And since we are to release the name Polly Nichols at this morning's press conference, we can publicize the search for Annie Chapman."

"Yes, sir."

"Anything more?"

Clive and Hughes exchanged glances, shook their heads.

"Then, keep me apprised at all times."

Claymoor Road in Brixton was little more than a collapsing alley of overhanging and aggressively seedy rowhouses that were too close and leaning toward each other across the narrow brick path like lovers straining for that initial kiss, sordid red-and-brown buildings peeled, corroded, settled and sagging in companionly, communal decay.

Constable Colin Colson stood a few paces off from the lacquer-black door to Number 11. He stared down at the license plate on a black Austin taxi—RDX-11988.

He's home, thought Colson.

There was something compelling about the automobile that held his eyes. It was too large for the narrow street, like a clot in an artery. And it glowed strangely. Colson frowned at it.

Glowed wasn't exactly the right word. It was polished to a perfection of newness, but where a plank of sunlight had wedged its way between the looming rowhouses and made a stripe across the car the vehicle was dulled, had somehow lost its luster. Still, it . . . perhaps radiated was the word? Radiated something . . .

Constable Colson pulled his eyes away and turned to the door. He ought to call in at least, ought to . . .

He walked briskly up the three small steps and rapped on

†

the door with his bare knuckles. The door was out of place also. Newish-looking. Or at least the lacquer-black paint was and it, like the car, radiated . . . something.

Strange faint smell, too, some mild aroma that he couldn't place.

The door opened.

He was ordinary size. About five-ten and eleven-stone, with blunt fiftyish features and a full red beard beneath a thick thatch of sandy hair. He wore a tan corduroy suit, lemon shirt and chocolate tie.

His eyes were silver.

Blind-looking.

Unreadable.

Queer eyes, thought Colson, and suppressed a shiver.

"What can I do for yer, Constable?"

"Mr. Lucian T. Nicholas?"

"I'm 'im."

"I need to ask you some questions about several fares you may have had in your taxi."

"Yer may as well step in, then."

Colson entered and Nicholas closed the door behind them.

It was empty.

A parlor opened off to the left and a kitchenette-dining room to the right, while directly ahead was a bedroom. All the doors were open and, even in the dim light, Colson could see the flat was barren. There was not a stick of furniture anywhere. No carpet over the dark-brown hardwood floors. No pictures or paintings or prints adorning the deep-brown walls. The only visible light was the naked overhead bulb.

There's nothing here, thought Colson. It's as if no one lives here.

Those were his last formulated logical thoughts. All that was left were sensations. Feeling and reaction and fear.

The iron grip of the hand cupping his chin.

The sharp pain of the knee in his back.

The wonder at Nicholas' strength.

The tearing pain of ripped muscles as his head was savaged backward.

The awful sound of his spine snapping in three places.

The pain.

†

Death.
Release.

The journalist liked to think of himself as a foreign correspondent. It had a nice toney ring to it and conjured up romantic and glamorous images—images of handsome men and beautiful women in Burberry or London Fog trenchcoats holding microphones on camera and speaking earnestly of world issues or crises, with the Champs-Élysées or Lake Geneva or the medieval walls of Luxembourg as background while a spellbound viewing audience of millions watched. Deadline pressure that meant something because a major story might affect world politics and mean praise and prizes and large sums of money; personal audiences with prime ministers and generals or dukes and sheiks; investigative digging with discreet sources met at rainy-night back-street amusing little bistros.

If one was a foreign correspondent, those images might or might not contain some fragment of reality. But the reporter was not a foreign correspondent in any ordinary sense of the phrase, and the romantic, glamorous images had nothing whatsoever to do with the reality of him.

Which was that he was an alcoholic expatriate Canadian who eked out a subsistence living as a devalued stringer for a number of sleazy English, Canadian and American tabloids and scandal sheets. His specialty was sensationalizing sex-and-gore stories beyond their inherently lurid details.

The reporter had never held a permanent position in his life because he was a mediocre journalist and writer, he was too often drunk to be reliable and because he was an unnattractive man—short, pudgy, bad-skinned and none too scrupulous about his bathing and grooming habits. He was ignored by the respectable press as less than contemptible, but was "known" around the Yard and lesser constabularies, in hospital emergency rooms, by ambulance drivers and doctors, solicitors and barristers. He had become something of a talisman of misfortune and cruelty.

Whenever there was a particularly bloody motoring accident or a leak about the sexual indiscretions of a member of the House of Lords or an especially nasty murder—those whose jobs entailed sorting out the mess began to glance over their shoulders expecting the acne-scarred visage and slightly glazed eyes. And there he would come, slewing around the corner in his quarter-century-old Triumph Spitfire that only ran from habit, lurching into the bloody emergency room, bringing the reek of alcohol and stale sweat to mix with the acrid odors of pain, death and adrenal-hyped fear.

For more than a decade he had been a ubiquitous totem of disaster, a walking Ghoul's Housekeeping Seal of Approval, certifying a tragedy's dimension. His role had earned him a nickname—the Vampire.

"How was it last night, Reggie?"

"Awful smash-up out on A-Eighteen, Tom."

"Vampire there?"

"Didn't see him."

"Ah, well, couldn't have been the worst then, eh Reggie?"

Today, the Vampire was humming to himself as he coaxed his junkyard Spitfire through traffic along the Embankment. He was drunk and happy and expectant. There was something special about this neo-Ripper killing. Instinct told him it was going to be a hot story and it was just his sort of thing, his specialty. Maybe this would be his big break, propel him to journalistic fame and riches—and a better grade of booze than the cheap gin his present pocketbook could only barely manage in sufficient quantity.

The Vampire was disappointed and puzzled.

The turnout for the Yard press conference was so small that the press lounge looked more like a tea-time get-together than a hot story breaking. And the conference itself was low-key and insubstantial despite the presence of Deputy Commissioner Stuart. Constable Kneilly, while walking a beat in Mayfair, had responded to a scream about four A.M., Wednesday morning, August 31, 1988. He had crossed into Hyde Park on foot and, near the Serpentine, discovered the murdered and mutilated body of a woman. Constable Kneilly chased the suspect, who was leaving the scene of the crime, but in the dark and fog was unable to apprehend him. Owing

†

to the conditions, the suspect's description was limited to that of a dark-haired white male, about thirty years of age and of ordinary height and build, blah, blah, blah, blah.

The Vampire yawned and wondered if anyone would notice if he took a quick one from the pint in his pocket.

A somber young beat-reporter from the *Mirror* asked, "Sir Malcolm, has the woman been identified?"

"Yes. She was a thirty-one-year-old 'performer' in pornographic films with several arrests for prostitution on her record. Her name was Polly Nichols."

For the first time there was a hint of electricity in the air.

A middle-aged man from the *London Times* asked, "Sir Malcolm, did you say Polly Nichols?"

"Yes. The Yard is, of course, aware that a hundred years ago, the initial victim in the Whitechapel killings was a forty-two-year-old prostitute named Mary Ann Nichols, nickname Polly. We are, presently, working on the assumption that some deranged person or persons unknown has attempted to recreate that murder with some attention to detail."

Stuart paused to sip from a glass of water and clear his throat.

"We are also not unmindful of the *possibility* that the murderer *might* intend to recreate other Ripper killings on their anniversary dates. While that is not certain, we are making intensive inquiries of women named Annie Chapman or variations thereof. In fact, one of the main reasons for this conference is to request the aid of the press in publicizing this search for any woman who *might*—I cannot emphasize the *might* too strongly—might be an intended next victim."

The Vampire sat up straight. This was better; this was more like it, the sort of twist you could get your teeth into.

The Vampire had an intuition. There's more of this, he thought. A bloody lot more of this duplication business. That's why Stuart came himself. There's a lot more of this voodoo and he's here to sit on the lid.

Stuart and Lord Desmonde sat in corner easy chairs in the reading room of the Commons Club. Above and behind them hung a bright, rather impressionistic and excellent oil painting of a field near Checkers, the country retreat of English

†

Prime Ministers. Observable in the lower right-hand corner of the canvas were a few gold daubs of paint that formed the signature *Winston S. Churchill*.

The home secretary steepled his fingers beneath his chin and asked, "Well, Malcolm, what do *you* make of him?"

"He seems sincere enough. Pat Cochran, for whom I have the utmost respect, gives him an unreserved recommendation. None of the, er, 'product' of his visions is particularly revelatory or helpful. Yet."

"What about his dossier?"

"Very much as Pat suggested. Excellent record—especially distinguished in combat. Family man, dependable, innovative officer, but comfortable within the system, the chain of command. Psychiatrists' reports show a long-held resentment against his father, but consistently labeled him as extremely well-adjusted and psychologically stable."

A steward shimmered across the room bearing a silver tray that held afternoon brandies in outsized snifters. He set them on the small table between chairs.

"Thank you, Goodson." Stuart smiled.

The steward nodded. "My pleasure, Sir Malcolm," and he shimmered away.

They sampled the cognac. The HS smiled. "This nectar is treasure, Malcolm. How many cases did you say your club cellars hold?"

"One hundred and seventy-nine at the last audit. Our sommelier made a fortunate find two years ago. Got three hundred and fifty cases from a small firm in Normandy at a bargain price."

"Amazing. As for Lees—even a *retired* American general could be a delicate policy problem. Go very gently and let us just keep him our secret for the time being."

Stuart set his brandy on the table. "I'll have to let Chief Inspector Hughes and Detective-Sergeant Clive in on it soon. But they are totally reliable; we can certainly keep the commissioner in the dark for now."

"Good. The Foreign Office are still not recovered from that flap last May with the Canadian tourists. I do not fancy another series of cabinet meetings with the foreign secretary administering the cane to my spiritual backside."

†

Stuart smiled. "Dezzi, I've never known you to accept a caning without retaliation. It may come to nothing. As I say, nothing he has said, so far, has been much of a guide. I know psychics—Peter Hurkos, for example—have been useful to the Yard in the past, but . . . well, I don't dismiss them out of hand. Still, I prefer things more straightforward."

The HS finished his brandy. "Don't we all, Malcolm, don't we all."

Monday morning—as it had for four weeks—the sign case outside the bar featured a flattering air-brushed glossy photograph, twelve-by-twenty-four in size and lewd in mood. The act being advertised was billed with only two words, in French above the photograph and repeated below in English:

> DARK ANNIE

Inside the bar, sweat oozed over Annie Mackey's writhing dusky flesh as if with a life of its own, slithering from under her meaty arms, gushed across her heavy breasts, made a sheen on her thick thighs. Her full head of long black hair was damp as it whirled and tossed in the amber and blue light of the smoky room. She flung her brown arms outward, rolled her ample stomach and popped her wide hips, thrusting her crotch upward and outward in the ancient gesture of suggestion, of invitation. Her bare breasts vibrated to the twisting of her torso and her gray nipples were a blur.

The inept music, from a local Le Jazz quartet, was nearly inaudible over the hoarse shouts, whistles, cheers, foot-stomping and hand-battering applause of the two score sailors, pimps, drug dealers and toughs that were the mid-morning audience of Le Club Hot. She was the lead attraction of the waterfront saloon, which was one of the roughest in the port of Marseille—not an easily earned, if dubious, honor.

The almost unheard music did not carry her through her frantic, lewd dance, nor did the noise of the sexually aroused crowd. Perhaps it was the lines of cocaine she did before each of her nine daily performances. Or the vodka she sipped steadily all her waking hours. Or had she done the dance so often for so long, and was the routine so ancient in form, that she could rely on muscle and racial instinct?

No matter.

She was able to put herself into a trance while working, so that in some literal sense she was not present. She spun and leaped and bucked and gyrated and moved her Amazon body as if possessed, feeding the frail fevered fantasies of drunken observers, giving them back exactly the sexual illusions they brought to her performance while she ignored them with a rapt indifference that could not have been shattered had some handsomely gifted stud bared a grandiose rigid member and banged it on the stage for attention. This, in fact, occasionally happened. All it ever provoked in Annie was an instinctive winking of one dead, dark eye, a moue of her acne-scarred cheeks and plump mouth and no thought or emotion. She danced on mechanically and thought of other things.

Annie Mackey was, that morning, twenty-nine years old. She had been a prostitute since age seventeen; a stripper for nearly a decade; an alcoholic since age twenty-two; a cocaine addict for more than a year. She was a British citizen, of a Cockney father and West Indian mother. She had "liberated" herself from the cozy hell of Brixton with her quite remarkable body, but her poxy face kept her from the top of her profession.

As it was, her month's booking at Le Club Hot guaranteed her fifteen hundred pounds, less agent's commission, a spectacular sum in the balance of her "career."

Still, she earned her money.

Nine dances daily, six days per week, was not an unusual contract. And, in addition to the physical toll of performance, her tall body carried numerous scars from the knives of importunate customers who took rejection rather too seriously. The relatively recent addition of cocaine to her list of necessities had caused her to supplement her stripper income with a return to turning an occasional high-priced trick.

Presently, she was contemplating the end of her booking, tomorrow night, and her Wednesday trip back to England for the heavy date that night. Three hundred pounds, nearly a week's wages, for one night's fornication or whatever prefer-

†

ence the customer had. She'd gotten a hundred pounds in cash advance from the creepy cabbie (even *her* dead eyes disliked his). Much as she despised all sexual acts, they seemed a small price to pay for her powdered heaven.

Lees dreamed.
　He dreamed the pillar of cloud and the pool of blood.
　He dreamed his father.
　He dreamed the Ripper in shadow and the cabbie's mad laugh and the silver blade.
　He dreamed a dark-skinned stripper's scarred, pitted, furrowed face and her progressively naked body writhing in dance, in pain, in torment.
　He dreamed her fear and sweat and musky odor and woke thrashing in the bed again—his own fear and sweat and smell matching the whore's.
　Insane, he thought in the dark. I am going insane, just as . . .

The Ebury Wine Bar in a brick Belgravia townhouse with a bay-windowed front was pleasingly cool. Muted light was also a happy contrast to the heavy heat and unwavering brightness of midday.
　Cochran, Lees and Stuart sat in a row on the last three bentwood stools at the bar in the rear. Luncheon was a cucumber-tomato-cauliflower-and-pepper salad accompanied by large chunks of crusty bread and a crisp Côtes de Provence dry white. The high hum of the noontime crowd was a conversational cover that assured their privacy.
　Lees shrugged. "I'm not sure what use it'll be, but Pat persuaded me I ought to share what I've 'seen' with you. Saturday, in a taxi on the Embankment, I glanced out over the Thames. I saw a pillar of mist above a spreading stain in the water that was the color of blood. It vanished quickly, but I've dreamed that image every night since. A column of cloud above a spreading pool of blood."
　Stuart asked, "In the dreams was it located in the Thames?"
　Lees shook his head. "No. In the dreams it has been . . .

†

isolated from geographical locale. Self-contained, as dreams often are."

"Of course."

"I've also dreamed the Ripper and the knife and the silver-eyed driver, as in the past. And strange sounds. One was a rhythmic engine or machine noise, the other was a grinding, tearing noise with cracking and splintering sounds, like wood battering wood."

"No images to go with the noises?"

Lees swallowed a bite of bread. "The sounds were background for the images I've described."

"Anything else?"

"Yes." Lees swallowed wine. "Last night I dreamed most of the images I told you about, but at the end I also saw a woman doing some sort of physical gyrations, a dance to jazz music."

"Can you describe her?"

"I had an impression she was tall. Very long, very black hair and deep brown skin—more racial than a tan. A powerful and voluptuous body, mostly naked. She had strong, clean features and dark eyes, would have been stunning, but she had"—Lees put his hands to his cheeks—"prominent scars, pitting here on her face. Like pox scars or, maybe, the remains of hideous acne."

"Anything further?"

"No"—he lifted his wineglass—"and I don't know—"

The pain in his head snapped his eyes shut, tightened his face in a grimace.

Cochran asked, "Jim? Jim, you all right?"

The cabbie's voice was in his brain—"*Can't get it, can yer, guv? Try 'er 'at fer size!*"

A black bonnet in his brain. Velvet and new.

His hand shook and he dropped the wineglass and seized his skull.

"General Lees?"

"Jim?"

"In my head . . ." he whispered. "The cabbie's voice and a hat . . . black hat . . ."

His skin was white, clammy; the pain nauseating. The hat

†

in his head aged and shriveled and died in his mind's eye—
"*Go figure that, guv!*"

The image and sound left; the pain released him.

He opened his eyes. Cochran and Stuart hovered, worried. Customers from the next room were looking, whispering. A hearty middle-aged woman approached behind the bar.

"Any difficulty, Sir Malcolm?"

"Air," whispered Lees, "need to get some air."

Stuart said, "Pat, help him out; I'll settle here," and turned to the matronly woman. "Our friend needs some air, Yvonne. If I might have the bill."

Lees sat on the sofa in Stuart's office.

Fresh air, a short walk, time and a glass of whisky had brought color back to his face, ease to his movements. He had described the vision in detail. Now, Stuart sat at his desk across the room and Pat Cochran paced while they waited for the bonnet to be brought from the laboratory, where tests upon it had been completed.

A uniformed officer entered with a large square box and crossed to Stuart's desk, laid the box upon it. "The evidence you requested, Sir Malcolm."

"Thank you, Reed. And the report?"

"Lab says it'll be up in the morning."

"Mmmph—if that's the best they can . . . That will be all, Reed."

"Yes, sir." He left.

Cochran and Lees crossed to the desk as Stuart removed the lid, revealing the black bonnet nestled in packing paper.

"What the hell?" muttered Stuart.

"That's it," said Lees. "That's the hat I *saw*."

This can't be right, thought Stuart. The hat was faded and worn, with all the bristly texture gone from the velvet and the color metamorphized from deep black to a dusty dark shade that implied gray. The black linen band was wrinkled and dirty and sagged from the crown. Threads were unraveling everywhere and it was nearly shapeless, all crispness gone.

He lifted it gently and inverted it. The maker's label was

shriveled and sweat-stained, greasily discolored, and the firm's name had blurred to HA BY & S N.

"This hat was brand new," said Stuart, "when we found it by the body a week ago."

Cochran leaned closer, peered. "It's not new, now." He poked a finger at a hanging thread and the light brush of his fingertip dislodged it. It curled and dropped to the desktop. "It's disintegrating, by the look of it."

Hugh and Meg Brandon had had a lovely evening.

It was their second wedding anniversary, and Hugh brought roses and champagne home from his day at the brokerage offices. They made delicious love and took in an early showing of a new film at the Times on Baker Street. Afterward, they taxied to the Churchill Hotel on Portman Square for a late dinner. Over Bordeaux and Chateaubriand for two, they talked of children. Money was no difficulty (she had an independent income and his commissions ran to six figures), but time was relevant (he was thirty-three, she twenty-nine). After dinner, they decided to walk home the less than a mile to their townhouse off Norfolk Square.

The evening was pleasantly cool after a stifling day and the air intimated fall. They held hands as they strolled along Porchester Place. Ahead, in the aura of a streetlamp, they saw a tiny figure.

A small boy stood with one foot in the street and one on the walk. His feet were bare and the cuffs of his too large black broadcloth pants were rolled up, exposing bony ankles. He wore a shirt and soft railway cap of matching cloth. As they neared, they saw he had a large wooden box, supported by a string around the back of his thin neck and opened so that his small chest was obscured by the high broad lid. It displayed a bright blue and yellow and purple advertisement:

BRYANT & MAYS
ALPINE VESUVIANS
LONDON 1888

†

The body of the box served as a tray for smaller wooden boxes, one of which he held at shoulder level in his right hand. His high, piping voice was slightly dissonant, like a tone not quite centered.

"*Matches!* Ha' penny the box! Matches! Ha' penny the box!"

They neared.

His black hair, flopping from beneath the cap, was thick and grainy rather than sleek. Everything about him was thin, and his skin was so pale it implied translucence; their eyes almost anticipated seeing visible veins and subcutaneous tissue, musculature and bones.

They stopped a few feet away.

His teal-blue eyes were shiny as marbles, but his expression was curiously blank, fixed. He cocked his head at an odd angle. "Matches! Ha' penny the box!"

Hugh asked, "What are you doing out so late, son?"

Meg added, "You'll catch your death, going barefoot, and no sweater either."

His head moved, angling an ear at them as if he were hard of hearing. His voice was hesitant. "Matches. . . ?"

Meg wrinkled her nose; he *looked* clean enough, but he emanated a strange aroma she couldn't place.

Hugh asked, "What's your name, son?"

The boy's brow furrowed; his face became sullen as ignorance asked unexpected, unanswerable questions; his head moved back and forth. Listening?

Hugh decided to joke with him. Smiling, he said, "You're awfully young—I ought to ask to see your vendor's license."

The boy's face showed irritation; he moved a step toward them, shrieked, "*Matches! Ha' penny the box! Matches! Ha' penny the box! Matches! Ha' penny the box!*"

They jumped back a pace and the boy's face glowered at them.

Meg held Hugh's arm tight, whispered, "Buy a box and let's go."

Hugh dropped a coin in the tray, snatched a box of matches, mumbled, "Keep the change."

The boy grappled the air in front of him as if searching for something. Hugh stepped aside and they hurried off.

†

All the short two blocks to their home, they heard behind them, fading on the night air, the high, piping, dissonant cry: *"Matches!* Ha' penny the box! *Matches!"*

Warm in bed with windows closed and after making love again drifting toward sleep, Hugh thought about the boy—something about him. Something . . . oddly Victorian.

Meg shivered to herself, wondered. Do I really want to have children? Maybe I'm not ready yet.

Wednesday, September 7, 1988, was an entirely unsatisfactory day for Sir Malcolm Stuart.

Over breakfast, he read an editorial in the *Times* that tasked CID, himself, Commissioner William, Lord Desmonde and the government for "failing to report any significant progress in the Hyde Park murder as the hundredth anniversary of the second Ripper murder is upon us."

Lord Desmonde called to complain about the editorial almost before Stuart's bottom had touched the seat of his desk chair at the Yard. Stuart could only reply, "Dezzi, I didn't write it! And we're doing everything we can!"

The lab report on the bonnet stated baldly that in material, style, and construction "this hat appears to be an artifact of nineteenth-century manufacture." It also stated, equally baldly, that no "fiber content or chemical composition that would explain the article's accelerated dissolution can be discerned."

Clive brought a further thorn with the news that a young officer assigned to the cabbie search had disappeared. Constable Colin Colson had not reported for duty in three days. His room had been checked, his father and his fiancée questioned. No one knew where he was.

When he filled Hughes and Clive in on the "Lees aspect," Hughes was reserved and Clive openly skeptical. "Sounds a bit too much like a retired officer with not enough to occupy him. They often go a bit eccentric."

The only effort that brought any reward was the cut-and-dried numbers and plans for the evening. So many extra men on duty, patrols here, patrols there, timetables for sweeps of parks and public places, codeword ANNIE to be used for all radio communications of Ripper developments (if any) and to be

†

77

given instant priority, any codeword ANNIE communications to be relayed immediately to Stuart's office, which would be used as a case-action command post, etcetera.

And even that left him with the lingering feeling that they were overlooking something simple and obvious and important. But the simple obvious something remained elusive.

Annie Mackey returned to London aboard the Calais–Dover cross-channel ferry train in late afternoon. She went straight to her shabby Whitechapel flat to rest before her "heavy date."

Lees, Ann and Pat Cochran took in an Alan Bates–Diana Rigg revival of *Blythe Spirit* at the Haymarket and had dinner and drinks at Hostaria Romano in Soho. As it always did, Pat's wit and sense of fun cheered them.

Stuart had an early dinner, made love with Vanessa and took a nap, setting his alarm for two A.M.

†

SEPTEMBER 8, 1988

4:32 A.M.

The Ripper dressed slowly.

The clothes were heavy and unfamiliar, alien, anachronistic. Gleaming black half-boots, polished to a reflective shine and thick dark wool socks. Heavy black broadcloth trousers and white linen shirt and braces. A gray silk cravat and stiff wing collar. Black broadcloth waistcoat. Black broadcloth suitcoat.

On the bed was a small black leather bag with hard leather handles. It was open. The twin knives lay on the velvet lining. The blades shone silver, hypnotically drawing the eye.

The Ripper lifted the knives, tested the blades. They were whisper sharp. One drew a dot of blood. He dropped them back into the bag and closed the case, while he sucked salt red fluid from his thumb.

Resumed dressing. Black silk top hat lined with silver satin. Broad black silk cape lined in scarlet, like blood.

Minor adjustments to buttons, tuggings and smoothings of cloth.

The Ripper turned to survey the effect.

The image in the mirror—an image of a late-Victorian gentleman—glowed with dim deflected light. Medium height and slender, theatrically dark, curly hair with huge muttonchop whiskers and a thick mustache that did not conceal the sensual lips; hot brown eyes glowing out from a pale, ascetic face, penetrating the gloom with a look of dreamy madness.

The change came with an electric shock to the base of the Ripper's skull.

The modern Scandinavian furnishings of the bedroom vanished.

The frame of the mirror, the dresser and wardrobe, the bed's headboard and the tables were now ancient oak and cherry. They were heavy, dark and hand-carved in the ornate style of the late nineteenth century. Gas lamps hissed and sputtered yellow light high along the walls, wafting sulfurous residue into the room. The paintings, the small Chagall and the Klee, were absent, and the wallpaper was no longer a textured apricot burlap but had become a rose-and-gray rococo floral pattern.

The Ripper's face glowed, ecstatic and fulfilled. Yes!

Aloud: "Yes! Come now!" What powers!

The Ripper knelt at bedside, bowed his head, prayed silently.

I will bend my will to thy purpose, Master, as I have promised. I will do thy bidding. Only grant me thy powers, thy swiftness, cunning, savagery that I might take *my* revenge on her, on the one who has stolen all from me.

Annie Mackey did two more lines of cocaine, rubbed her nose and dabbed tissue to her watering eyes. Good shit! she thought.

It was 4:44 A.M. and her untidy room above a sordid Whitechapel grocer was stuffy with the stink of cat, human sweat and menstrual flow. The latter caused Annie some concern. She hoped her heavy date would prefer fellatio, SM, bondage or some other perversion (most did). If he demanded intercourse (few did), she hoped he would not be put off by her period (some were, some weren't). She needed the remainder of her fee because she was broke, as usual, and her cocaine stash was dwindling, as usual, and she could not stand the idea of even a day deprived of her remedy.

She shuddered down a stiff, straight vodka and looked herself over in the cracked mirror above her washbasin. Her springy body was still taut, large, lush in a tight black leather jumpsuit all adangle with silver zippers and chains and highlighted with silver studs. The irregular Y of the mirror's fault split her pocked face into uneven, webbed sections, returning her a torn, disorienting reflection. Fragmented woman.

She poured herself another straight vodka and sipped it, letting the coke rush overpower her. She began to feel

†

taller, larger, stronger. She sipped vodka and laughed.
"Fuck the rag." I know how to handle johns, she thought. Fuck the rag, I'll get my money.
She drank.
All I've got to do is remember who's in charge.
She drank.
When she knew she was ten feet tall, she left her room abruptly, shoulder bag briskly thumping her hip, and descended a runnerless flight of stairs to the street.
The taxi was waiting at the curb.

The taxi cruised along Westminster Bridge Road.
It was 5:11 A.M.
Annie Mackey was mesmerized by the image in her cab window. Light came and went, played tricks. Her face was smooth, unscarred, without blemish. Perfect—just as she had always imagined it might be—if it were perfect.
She touched her face.
It was smooth.
No scars, she thought. And then: He is waiting!

A constable on foot patrol glanced at the taxi as it passed. The cabbie returned his gaze. The constable felt a light tingle in his hair, like mild electric static, and walked on—now clothed in the high hard helmet and buttoned-up uniform of an 1888 bobby.
He caught sight of himself in a window and stopped to stare. His reflection was clearly Victorian, down to whiskers and mustache.
The hair tingle came again.
He blinked.
He was as before—clean-shaven, in modern uniform—himself again.
He stood for minutes wondering what the trick was, if it would happen again.

5:18 A.M.
Detective-Sergeant Clive hung up the telephone, made a notation on the graph in front of him and laid his pen on the clipboard. He looked across the desk at Stuart.

†
81

"Five-fifteen check-in complete, Sir Malcolm. No extraordinary action reports and no codeword ANNIE calls."

Stuart and Clive locked eyes.

"I don't like it," said Stuart.

"No, sir."

"Sitting. Waiting. Having to give them the first move."

"No, sir," said Clive. "The next hour we'll be acting. Major sweeps through all public parks and meeting places, open areas, train stations."

Stuart shrugged. "We don't have enough men. A patrol sweeps Leicester Square and moves on; five minutes later, *they* come."

Clive sighed. "Yes, sir. Or they could commit this murder indoors, out of sight. *Anywhere.*"

Hughes turned from the wall of glass where he had been gazing at the city lights. "You really think so, Clive? I think, if anything happens, it will come in plain sight again."

Stuart cocked his head. "Why do you say that, Richard?"

"Ego."

Clive frowned. "Ego?"

"We are operating on the assumption that Polly Nichols was not murdered for personal reasons, but was sought out merely because her name closely resembled that of the victim of a hundred-year-old crime. We assume that the Hyde Park murder was done entirely as an exercise in replicating that century-old murder. An abstract, because-it's-there sort of thing. If that's true, it requires a monstrous ego, and part of the purpose would be to rub our noses in it. The letter addressed to Malcolm had that tag line—'catch me if you can.'"

"We don't know," Clive objected, "that it was genuine, that it was from the murderers."

"We don't know that it wasn't. In any case, the whole sense, the style of the Hyde Park crime was theatrical, insolent, a kind of detached arrogance. If they strike again, it'll be public."

"If?" said Clive.

"If," echoed Stuart, glancing at his watch.

5:22 A.M.

* * *

They stood on Lambeth Pier.

The castle, home for Archbishops of Canterbury for seven centuries, loomed above and behind them, its pale accent bricks outlining dark towers, turrets, battlements and columns, suggestive even in the last hour of full dark. Lambeth Bridge arched high away to their left, like an observatory platform for gods. The Thames was calm, lapping gently at the pilings.

As if in a dream, Annie Mackey said, "Queer place for a date."

The cabbie's silver eyes held hers. "Yer bein' paid enough t' fuck the gentleman onstage at Royal Albert Hall, if that's what 'e fancies."

They turned at the rhythmic chugging sound.

A boat approached.

The man at the tiller was dressed in the same Victorian costume as the hackie and the boat was old. It was black wood and perhaps twenty feet long, shaped like an enormous canoe, bowed broadly in the center and high-sided, with a blunt stern.

It traveled under a pillar of steam.

It was 5:32 A.M.

Lees dreamed.

He dreamed the cabbie and the woman and the boat.

He dreamed the river and the Ripper.

He woke shaking and sat up, fumbled on the light and swung his feet from under the sheet, off the bed and onto the floor.

Ann raised her sleepy face from her pillow. "Jim. . . ?"

The images were still in his head. It's real, it's happening, he thought.

"Jim. . . ?"

"I see it, Ann. I see it happening in my head. They're on a boat on the river. The cabbie and the woman and the Ripper!"

He glanced at his watch as he fumbled for the telephone receiver: 5:36 A.M. He asked the switchboard operator to get him New Scotland Yard.

Images were in his head—broad water, the river gently

†

rocking the boat and, elevated and angled, high and away—familiar buildings . . . what?

"Is there anything wrong, sir?"

"Operator—would you just *please* get me New Scotland Yard, *immediately*! It's an emergency!"

Parliament, he thought. Those are the Houses of Parliament.

"Is it something the assistant manager could help you with?"

"*Operator!*" he roared, "*put me through to New Scotland Yard!*"

The boat. The pillar of mist. It's steam, thought Lees. Steam!

"Yes, sir. There's no need to shout. I shall put you through."

A bridge high overhead. Westminster Bridge, he thought. He glanced again at his watch.

5:39 A.M.

The steam boiler was a black cast-iron tube dominating the center of the launch. The single vent stack was a pale white tube rising phallically in the dark. Steam billowed upward.

Annie Mackey sat in the bow and watched the man with the black bag coming forward past the boiler.

No more scars, she thought, and touched her face, felt the smooth unblemished cheeks.

She noticed her arm was no longer leather-clad. Gray muslin. She stared down at herself. A dress.

Where is my jumpsuit? she wondered.

Horror gripped her heart.

No more scars, she thought soothingly. No more scars. She touched her cheeks again.

The man was beside her. He set the bag on the plank seat and opened it.

She saw the knife blades glowing dully in the dark.

"The lines are all busy, sir."

"*At five-forty in the morning?!*"

"There's no need to be rude, sir. They are busy. I can't change that."

†

84

Lees shut his eyes.

Images in his head: the R.A.F. Memorial. A bag, knives, the woman, the Ripper. Another bridge looming ahead.

"I'm sorry, operator. This is an emergency. I can't take time to explain, but it has to do with the Hyde Park murder. It's a matter of life-and-death. You must keep trying. Please."

"Yes, sir. Of course, sir."

He shut his eyes tight.

Please!

The Ripper drew a knife from the bag.

No more scars, was the last thought left to her, the last small comfort.

The Ripper plunged the blade deep into her throat, sawing across it with animal savageness, driving her head back to the edge of the bow, nearly tearing it from her neck and shoulders.

Blood spurted out in streams and sprays, soaked everything, jetted and splashed over the side of the launch, darkened the dark river water.

The Ripper slashed her garments open with furious hacking strokes and plunged the blade up to the hilt into her abdomen.

He ripped her!

Cut open her stomach in swift abandon, stabbing and sawing, severing organs from connective tissue, dropping bloody heaps by her shoulder.

He ripped her!

By 5:44, when the Yard switchboard operator finally put him through to Stuart, the images had left Lees' mind.

"Why the hell are your phones tied up at this hour?" he gasped rudely in his anger and frustration.

"Phone as well as radio reporting of our major patrols—"

"Never mind," Lees cut him off. "No time! They're on the river, in a boat—the cabbie and the woman and the Ripper! I had a dream and woke, and the vision stayed with me until about a minute ago. It's never happened that way before. I feel certain, Malcolm! They're on the river!"

"It's a big river, Jim."

†

"Sorry, too excited—the last image I had was the R.A.F. Memorial, and whatever bridge is just beyond it. Going toward the broad bend and . . . *Jesus!*"

"What?"

"Going toward the broad bend in the Thames—in sight of Cleopatra's Needle. Where I had the vision Saturday."

Stuart snapped, "I'm going to ring off now, General. Talk to you later."

"Right," said Lees, but the connection was already cut.

Stuart snapped at Clive. "Lees says they're on the river near Cleopatra's Needle! Call the river police and have them send patrols to the area! Richard and I will head for the station under Waterloo Bridge. Meet us there!"

Stuart and Hughes were already up and moving as Clive reached for the telephone.

The boat stood alongside the pier fronting the Royal Festival Hall. The plume of steam rose steadily, and the small steam engine throbbed as if eager to move on. The Ripper was already on the pier waiting for the hackie.

He secured the tiller, shoved the engine into gear and leapt free of the launch, which plowed back out into the Thames on a northerly course, a water hearse for the blood-drained corpse wedged into the inner V of the prow.

One limp arm of the thing that had been Dark Annie Mackey trailed over the side, rapping the wooden hull to the rhythm of the river's rise and fall, beating a low funeral dirge unheard by the sleeping city.

It was 5:50 A.M.

At 6:11 A.M., Stuart and Hughes stood on a pier of the River Police Station beneath Waterloo Bridge where the launch's course, by design or chance, had delivered the body.

They stared down into the harsh police floodlight. The boat had battered straight into a wooden piling and gouged against it until an officer had jumped aboard and shut off the engine. Now it was lashed to the piling awaiting inspection by the forensics experts.

The body was unavoidably gruesome in the harsh light,

†

with corpse-pale flesh and savage wounds and dark, clotted stains glaring as if in silent outrage.

Stuart passed a hand across his brow, wondering momentarily what he might have done, what anyone might have done to prevent this. . . . Dead is dead, he thought to right himself. The real question is—now what. . . ?

Reflections From the Ripper's Journal

We must picture Hell as a state where everyone is perpetually concerned about his own dignity and advancement, where everyone has a grievance, and where everyone lives the deadly serious passions of envy, self-importance, and resentment.
—*C. S. Lewis*

JULY 1986

At last!
  The sham is ended—at least in my mind.
  It is not love I feel for her, for them, despite all the pronouncements and protestations of custom, morals, society and the world—yes, even the weight of the cold and dread cosmos—despite everything—it is not true. I do not love her or any of them. That is fact; truth. I do not love her, and all the rights and justs and musts hold not a candle to my reality.
  Which is: I hate her!
  There, it's said and I feel ever so much better. Do they not say, "Know the Truth and the Truth shall set you free"? Very well—that is what I shall do. Explore my Truth and let it free me.
  I feel already a cleansing, a purifying. It is a fire I have banked long years, a fire that would not die, and the choked smoke from that trapped flame has fogged my mind for a seeming eternity.
  I will not damp this fire again!
  I free thee, flame.
  I hate her!
  Oh, lovely! I feel the dead smoke fleeing my mouth and ears and eyes and every orifice, from even my pores, fleeing, freeing, cleansing. I am aflame and it is beautiful. Adrenaline flows and my heart sings and my mind soars and I am alive. What are the highs of narcotics or alcohol compared to this grand elation I feel? As nothing.
  Burn, flame—I free thee to burn blinding bright.
  I hate her!
  Burn!

SEPTEMBER 1986

It is not enough to hate her blindly, dumbly, with the passion of a hairy, plodding beast. That is too clumsy, that is the club of the caveman. My fury requires the focus of the laser. To fully free my hatred, I must understand it so it may grow and multiply.

I've just had a droll thought.

Why and how do I hate thee—let me count the ways!

I hate you because you have what I want—what belongs to me!

I hate you because you have stolen all the meaning from my life. Your very existence is a blot upon my birthright and your name is a blasphemy. If only you did not exist—then I could live! Be free!

I hate you and I will not be mocked—I will be avenged.

I hate you!

†

DECEMBER 1986

A curious comfort has come to me. Your name, bitch! Not the one you use, but the name you ought to wear for all the world to see. The comfort came casually as I was watching a not very well done film about the Ripper murders. His last victim, hilariously, bore your name.

What a delicious thought!

I warm myself in bed, drifting off with the happy vision of what he did to one of your name—slaughter!

Mutilation!

Disembowelment!

He ripped her body to bloody pieces. Precisely what I should love to do to you, bitch!

I shall visit the library; I must read about this delight!

FEBRUARY 1987

Lovely, lovely!

Not only is your name the same as the Ripper's last victim—in one year you will be the same age as the Ripper's final victim was when he killed her.

More!

Next year will be the hundredth anniversary of those bloody, beautiful, immortal murders!

Can the confluence of facts and events be mere coincidence?

No! I reject coincidence.

And, if not coincidence, why should I suddenly become aware of these facts and events?

Is someone, somewhere trying to tell me something? And who might it be?

Do I see destiny on the near horizon?

II
Elizabeth "Long Liz" Stride & Catherine Eddowes

> Thinking means connecting things, and stops if they cannot be connected.
> —*G. K. Chesterton*

SEPTEMBER 8–19, 1988

Stuart and Lees sat in easy chairs in the center of the sitting room. Ann sat on the sofa a few feet distant. Stuart had left Hughes and Clive in charge at the scene and come straight to the Dorchester. Early morning now made clear comfortable light in the suite.

"And you 'saw' nothing after that?"

Lees shook his head. "No. The Ripper near, and a knife in his hand. It was as if I were plugged into the victim's head, could see with her eyes. When she was killed, I was . . . disconnected."

Stuart leaned forward. "Describe the boat again."

Lees sighed. "This is—" He stopped, staring at Stuart. Words were in his head.

There was contact . . . there will be contact. . . .

A pale-yellow envelope floated in his mind's eye and then was gone.

"What is it?" asked Stuart.

"Words suddenly in my head," said Lees softly, "and an image. The words—'there was contact, there will be contact.' And an image of a long pale-yellow envelope. Now it's gone."

Stuart sat back in his chair and stared hard at Lees. What have we got here? Psychic—or accomplice?

"What do you make of it?" he asked.

"Have you received a letter from the Ripper in a long pale-yellow envelope? If not, maybe you will. Or maybe it doesn't mean anything."

"Yes, of course. Perhaps, you'd be willing to come down to my office in an hour or so. Let us take a formal statement."

Lees nodded.

* * *

†

After he showed Stuart out, he came back into the sitting room and stood staring at Ann.

"Let's go home."

Her eyes widened. "What?"

"I'll go make the statement for them, you pack and we get out of here. Let's go the hell home."

"You don't mean that."

"Yes, I do. It was a mistake to come. I can't help them and this is torture. I want out!"

"No."

She rose and crossed to him and took his hands and locked eyes with him. "No. You can't run, Jim. I don't like this either. I'm more confused than you are, but *something* is happening. Something that requires *our* response. We can't run and you can't hide." She held him in her arms. "Let me help you, Jim."

"I wish I knew how."

The Ripper walked in sunlight.

Laughing inside.

Laughing at the dolts passing on the street, rubbing shoulders with the fools in crowds, smirking at the passing cars.

If only you knew! I kill, I have power, I work my will and you don't even recognize me on the street in broad daylight. Fools!

The Ripper laughed aloud and didn't mind a strange stare from an elderly man passing on the pavement.

Walking down Broadway, he neared New Scotland Yard. The two glass-and-steel office towers gleamed in the sunlight.

How perfect! All those busy men inside and wondering who I am. I wonder if I should stop in, say hello, introduce myself properly. Hello, my name is Jack!

The Ripper laughed aloud.

Father Eric Mueller walked easily across the familiar courtyard, absorbed in thought. He was an ordinary-sized man with delicate, handsome features and quick blue eyes, blond hair showing a few streaks of silver. His temperament and intellect were far more effervescent than the stolid tradition of his

†

national heritage; he was a gentle German Jesuit, a scholar-priest, a man of clarity and wit.

He was considering an article he had just read about Peter Hurkos, the Dutch housepainter turned psychic, and attempting to fit it into the thesis of the book he was engaged in writing, *Limited Prophecies: Parapsychology and Spirituality.*

His consciousness was so concentrated that the midday sun did not bother him, despite the weight of his traditional soutane. He took no note of the rust-colored bricks of the path or the bits of clay soil that adhered to his black shoes. Acid-green lawn and bushes of English tea roses did not draw his eye. He was not even aware of the wall, through which he must pass to reach the street, looming a few paces off.

He stopped suddenly, froze quietly.

His thought was dissolved, but no new thought came in its place. His consciousness was blank. No sound had alarmed him; nothing overt had occured.

He gazed around and he was alone and nothing moved.

The high stone wall stood still; the arched gate remained in shadow. Towering off to his left, the Gothic church was stable; to his right, the slight stone chapel was immobile.

He glanced over his shoulder. The rectory had not fled. "Lord. . . ?" he asked softly.

At his feet, the path forked, leading ahead to the gate in the wall or right to the side door of the chapel. Grass trembled.

He stared at the arch of the chapel entrance. Sunlight broke its shadow, diagonally, into roughly equal portions of scarred wood and black imagination.

He had no business in the chapel this moment . . . had he?

The ancient pewter door handle bounced light away from its dull gray surface.

He was on his way to a luncheon with his editor to discuss publication schedules. He would, likely, be late even if he hurried now.

Again: "Lord. . . ?"

A tea rose nodded to a whisper of air.

He submitted to what he believed; crossed to the chapel door, opened it and entered.

†

The dark was vast after the sun.

A shadowed woman lit a candle from, and added it to, a small pyramid of candles. She crossed herself, knelt and prayed.

Father Mueller stood and watched her, waiting comfortably with the calm of surety. He felt something from—no, *toward*—her; this was his purpose. He was content as she prayed for long minutes.

She crossed herself again, rose and turned to leave. She started in her tracks at sight of him, stopped, stared.

He stood in an arch of brilliant light fanned from door to floor; his skin glowed as if scrubbed with a special soap.

Warm air; flame-cleansed odor; light and dark softened by searching eyes.

She was an attractive, middle-aged blonde with startled blue eyes. Mueller read bewilderment in her face, and longing.

"I'm Father Eric Mueller. Can I be of service to you?"

Her shoulders sagged. "Ann Lees, Father. I . . . I need to talk to someone."

He took her back to the rectory, made tea, phoned his editor to cancel the luncheon, and sat with her an hour. She poured out the story of her husband, his dreams, his confusion and hers, the link to the Ripper re-creations.

Finished narrating, she sat exhausted. He stared away, muttered, "Lack of power, that was our dilemma."

Ann looked at him. "What?"

He smiled and his eyes were soothing. "Nothing, just an old, familiar thought."

"Can you help me, Father?"

"What would you have me do?"

"Save Jim!" The words exploded from her with such passion that he felt a savage pain in his heart, as if he had absorbed a share of her suffering. It rocked him, and he let it burn, dim and subside before he spoke again.

"From what?"

"From *all that!*" Again the words were passionate and again they burned him and he let them go.

"From all what? I assure you, I'm not being obtuse for no purpose. You *must* say what you mean. Clearly."

She pulled her thoughts to a center, spoke slowly. "From the hell he is enduring. From his confusion . . ."

"Ah," he said and nodded. "And what about yours?"

She stared at him, thinking, and then nodded in turn.

"That's what it is, isn't it, Father? I don't understand why it's become so real, now. In the past he always made light of . . . that part of his past. I mean—I know this is very different for you, the precognition and all that—this is a little out of your field."

Images came to him. The brick path; the arched door; the pewter handle; the nodding rose. He smiled to himself. "No. As it happens, it isn't. I am something of a scholar in the field of extrasensory perception and am, just now, working on my third book dealing with that subject."

She stared at him, dumbfounded.

"Yes, it is true. A *coincidence*?" He shrugged. "Let us leave that to the skeptics to rationalize. But you have touched, obliquely, the central issue. His denial."

She frowned. "Denial?"

"So long as he, in his heart, denies gift and Giver, he will be blocked from full use of the power, however great or limited it may be. And it mocks his posture of helping to save lives. Thus, his internal strife. And yours. This is what you want me to save him from."

"Perhaps . . . perhaps that's it."

"I can talk to him, if he will listen, but only he can make a decision to accept or deny. We cannot help someone who will not, at least, cooperate in his own salvation."

"Will you come with me to our hotel?"

"Certainly."

Lees was angry and frustrated and upset with Ann for not being with him. She had gone to church. That was fine for her—what about him? He was left alone and lost. Helpless. Powerless.

His face brightened momentarily as he called, "Ann?" but froze when he saw Father Mueller following her into the suite's sitting room.

Ann introduced them.

Stiff handshake and mumbled amenities.

†

Offered drinks. Father Mueller accepted mineral water; Lees took a neat Scotch and poured vodka-and-tonic for Ann.

They sorted themselves out into a rough triangle. Its base was parallel to the window overlooking the park, with Ann and Lees in easy chairs separated by ten feet, defining its limits. Father Mueller was its point on a sofa some eight or nine feet distant and seated approximately at a mid-spot between them.

The priest sat upright, hands flat on his thighs, and began without preamble. "Ann has told me of your predicament. She asked me to talk to you. She thought I might be of help."

Lees shot an uncharitable glance at his wife.

"This angers you?"

"Yes."

"Why?"

As Lees considered, then answered, an arrangement of afternoon cloud slowly drove a shaft of light through the window; broad to begin with, it expanded until it nearly flooded, the full center of their triangle.

"We have always . . . accorded each other respect in matters of faith and philosophy. I have never, for a moment, questioned Ann's religion or interfered with the children's education and choices. In return, she has—until now—let me follow my own path."

Lees shot Ann another unhappy glance, and Mueller noted that he squinted at the massed light blocking his view of his wife.

The priest stared, dreamily, into the light as it sifted motes of dust, particles of the air's impurity. "She loves you and fears for you, and has turned to the solution she knows. She has intervened on your behalf. This should anger you?"

"What you call intervention, I call interference." Lees finished his whisky in a gulp. "In any case, Father, how will you help me? Tell me to go and sin no more?" The sneer in his voice was so evident that Ann sucked in her breath and flushed with shame.

Mueller merely smiled and shook his head. "No, that is not my approach to any problem. As it happens, I am a scholar in the field of parapsychology, ESP and the supernatural. I thought we might talk about your case."

†

Lees stared at him, openly surprised. "How did she find you?"

"You ask a philosophical question, General. But I believe you desire a mechanical answer. She went to a chapel to pray, and I was drawn to it by a feeling that I had business there without knowing what it was."

Lees' face was sour. "A miracle, I suppose?"

Mueller shrugged. "Or a coincidence. One or the other, but not both. Would you like to talk about your difficulty?"

Pain stabbed Lees' skull. His mind swam with the leering image of the cabbie's silver eyes, his black facelessness. His ears rang with mad laughter.

Lees turned pale and cried out, pressing his hands to his head. The cabbie's voice was in his brain. *Can't cut it, guv? Need a bit o' help? The letter's coming for Stuart! The letter tells the secret, guv!"*

Laughter.

The vision ended. Lees sat with eyes closed, very pale and breathing rapidly, shallowly.

Mueller stared intently into the heart of the light and spoke softly. "You have just had an episode?"

Lees nodded.

Ann's hand was at her throat. "Jim?"

"It's all right. Gone now."

"Can you tell us about it?" the priest questioned gently.

Lees opened his eyes, nodded. "Ann told you the basic details of my visions?"

"Yes."

"This time it was pain, then the silver-eyed, faceless cabbie. His image. His laughter. His voice. His laughter."

"What did he say?"

"'Can't cut it guv? Need a bit o' help?' He talked about a letter for Sir Malcolm Stuart, head of CID."

The priest stared into the light, allowed himself a small smile, a barely perceptible nod, whispered, "Yes, of course."

Lees frowned. "Of course what?"

"He does not want you talking to me. He fears my presence."

"Who—the cabbie?"

†

103

The priest shrugged and his silk soutane whispered with movement.

Lees pressed his lips tight, then asked against his will: "Who?"

"He has many names."

The words, spoken matter-of-factly, filled the room with weight. The triangle quivered; the light steadied, grew.

Lees shook his head without scorn, almost sadly. "I just can't, Father Mueller. I know I've been rude, and I apologize. I'm sorry."

"I took no offense."

"That is kind of you. But I simply can't talk to you about this."

Mueller smiled. "I know you can't—if you could, you would. I will go now, General, but I would like to leave you with a thought. I will quote you a famous atheist and ask you to consider his words. Will you do that?"

"An atheist?"

"Yes."

"All right."

"Herbert Spencer said, 'There is a principle which is a bar against all information, which is proof against all arguments and which cannot fail to keep a man in everlasting ignorance—that principle is contempt prior to investigation.'"

All three sat in silence for several minutes, staring into the unwavering light.

"I see," Lees muttered at last.

No, you don't, thought the priest, but I shall pray that you do so. And soon.

At the door, Father Mueller took Ann's arm lightly and whispered, "Do not fight him. Love him and pray for him as I shall. And I may not be the one to reach him, but when the pupil is ready, the teacher will appear."

When she returned to the sitting room, Jim had gone into the bedroom to lie down. The afternoon clouds had been rearranged once again, withdrawing the shaft of light, making a gray, pensive sky. The room was cheerless and gloomy.

†

<u>FROM HELL</u>
September 8, 1988

Sir Malcolm Stuart, KG
Deputy Commissioner, CID
New Scotland Yard

New Boss:

Hello again! Now—do you believe I'm back?

> Two little whores
> Looking for Hell,
> Found what they wanted
> As they fell.
>
> Two little whores
> And more alive;
> Do you really think
> I'll stop at five?
>
> I'll do you a favor
> And give you a hint;
> Let Lees catch my flavor,
> He'll cut short my stint.
>
> Chase me up the hill,
> See me in the well;
> I'll give you a glance
> Into Hell.

P. S. New Boss—double event next time and something special—won't that be fun? Catch me if you can!

Stuart passed the letter to Hughes and turned to Clive. "What can you tell me about the first letter I received?"

Clive reddened. "Not a great deal, sir. I'm afraid I gave it a rather low priority. Lab report is due on Monday."

Stuart pursed his lips. "Sergeant, I *want* to know where these letters are coming from. Now, what can you tell me about the boat?"

Hughes said, "I can answer that," and passed the letter across to Clive. "An expert from naval museum says that it is a steam launch of the kind commonly used in trade on the Thames during the period 1865–1890."

"Where did it come from?"

Hughes shook his head. "*That* he doesn't know. He says that his only knowledge of the type is from extant photographs and drawings—not models."

Stuart controlled his temper and spoke evenly, but with ice in his tone. "I want to know where the *boat* came from. Where the *letters* came from. Where that *bonnet* came from. Where these idiots got a hansom cab. They didn't materialize out of thin air. I want to have some answers. *Soon.*"

His subordinates exchanged glances, swallowed and nodded.

"The woman?" he asked.

Clive chewed his lip.

Hughes said tentatively, "No identity as yet. There were no papers in the pockets of her jumpsuit. We've been thinking of giving a head shot to the press. Suitably cleaned up, of course."

"Do it," said Stuart. "They're busy enough calling us incompetent—let them solve a problem for once. And, gentlemen, speaking of the press raises the issue of political implications in this case. Sir Edwards William is badgering me and irritating the prime minister in the bargain. *She* is giving the home secretary fits, and Lord Desmonde is asking me questions for which I have no answers. So far, I have been able to absorb this discontent. Without some answers soon my ability to do so will cease."

"Yes, sir," said Clive.

"Understood, Sir Malcolm," said Hughes.

"Now, the one aspect of the case we haven't discussed today is the psychic."

"Lees," said Hughes.

Clive made a face, but remained silent.

"I have been giving the brigadier much thought," Stuart continued. "If he *is* a genuine psychic and able to help, we'd better find out and foster his, er, gift."

Hughes crossed his legs. "Tests, sir?"

Stuart nodded. "Exactly. What I propose—if General Lees

will agree to it—is to assemble a team. A physician, a psychologist, some experts in the field of ESP. I would set them up down at Hedgemore and let them have at him."

"If he agrees."

"Yes." Stuart drummed his fingers on the desktop. "What do you think, Richard?" He smiled. "We already know what Sergeant Clive thinks."

They laughed.

"First rate." Hughes chuckled. "Get him into a scientifically controlled situation and, at the very least, we can find out if he's of any use."

"Or something else altogether," replied Clive, tapping the letter. "Don't forget this mentions him. You know I've not much use for extraordinary things like psychic explanations. Suppose I'm right. Where does he get the knowledge he has if he's not implicated?"

Stuart nodded. "That possibility hadn't slipped by me, Sergeant. I think the Hedgemore project would be ideally suited to discovering that truth as well." He smiled broadly at Clive. "Despite your objections, Sergeant, do you think you could arrange for the security detail, in case the General agrees? I won't ask you to assemble the team of experts."

Clive laughed. "Security's right up my alley, sir."

Hughes said, "I take it you want me to arrange for the team."

"Yes," answered Stuart. "There's also one other thing about that letter which we don't want to overlook. The author says not to expect him to stop at the original five murders. He's recreating them, but he seems to hint there will be more."

Clive closed his notebook and laid it on his lap. "And if he doesn't play by the original in one aspect, how can we assume he'll follow the old pattern in other details?"

Stuart frowned. "You're saying he might strike at any time, at any place, in any manner?"

Clive nodded. "It seems as if—assuming we believe the letter is authentic—these jokers'll recreate the original murders. But the letter opens the question—what *else* will they do?"

†

* * *

Clive hadn't bothered to tell Stuart or Hughes that it was just as well they had a second letter and envelope to trot around with. It would come to them in the lab reports soon enough.

The original letter paper was beginning to age as poorly as the bonnet. Not quite so quickly, but, when he had looked at it the previous day, the paper was not as shiny, not as new. It was acquiring a soiled look in small patches, and one corner of one sheet had started to curl.

Bloody nonsense, thought Clive. He shrugged and went back to his work.

At the back of Sir Malcolm's townhouse on Duke Street was an enclosed garden, nearly square and some forty feet to a side. It was Vanessa Cilone's most recently completed project in her two-year renovation of Stuart's home, the final area to submit to her touch. Indeed, the dinner party was a celebration and showcasing of the home's transformation.

The garden's old masonry and stone walls had been painted a subdued coral and lined with evenly spaced slabs of latticework teak rising to a height of seven feet, where they supported a conical roof of the same material. The effect was more of an outsized gazebo with an interior garden rather than the other way around. The latticework was interwoven with mature grape vines supplemented by hanging plants in reproductions of Ming pots. A fieldstone floor was bordered narrowly by pebble-covered earth, Japanese stone lanterns and tiny shrubs. A trio of small reflecting pools completed the tranquil, summery effect.

Vanessa wandered about her creation, sipping a glass of Taittinger, scrutinizing the garden and decorations and refreshments for even minute deviations from her expressed design. Everything seemed in perfect order, from the vases of cut flowers to the English "country pâté," yet something nettled the beautiful young woman, gnawed at her in a way she couldn't identify.

What bothered her about the garden was a vision of it she had in her subconscious—in vivid dreams she didn't remember upon waking—a vision she could not allow herself to see. The vision was of herself in a traditional white wedding gown being married to Sir Malcolm Stuart in the garden's gazebo.

Vanessa knew she could not allow herself to "see" this, because to visualize it would authenticate the very real longing she had for just that event. She loved Stuart passionately and comfortably in the balanced paradox that strong relationships contain. She cared not a fig for the vast differences in their chronological ages; she was his wife in all save name, and she dearly wanted that final closure.

They had never really discussed the subject, but she assumed he feared the differences in their ages, and had no desire to change his widower status (his wife had been killed in a motoring accident a decade earlier).

The finishing of the garden, however, completed her two-year renovation of the townhouse, making it theirs rather than his. This produced a sense of imminent decision; of a turning point. What was all this activity about? Was their relationship real and substantial—as it seemed to be—or merely more post-sexual-revolution artifice?

She checked the garden again, making sure that every detail was just right, yet certain that she was overlooking something.

Stuart, in semi-formal black-tie, stood with his hands in his pockets and watched the love of his life pace her renovated garden. The tall, blond girl, all long lines and elongated curves, caused, with her youthful distraction, easy movement and physical grace, an ache in him he hated to acknowledge.

He also had a vision of their marriage, but he believed it would never happen. His fears, however, operated on a clear and conscious level. He only mouthed contemporary clichés about "open relationships" because they seemed to be the attitudes of her contemporaries—and he assumed they were hers as well. He also assumed that Vanessa did—or eventually would—care about the differences in their ages, and that her career was paramount to her, assumed she believed that marriage would hamper or crush her career. To Stuart, a deeply conservative and traditional man, these casual relationships were profoundly repugnant. It was a measure of his love that he was more concerned for her happiness than for the justice of his own principles. It was also a mistake.

She saw him suddenly and they paused, observing each other self-consciously. Simultaneously, love overcame their preoccupations. They crossed the gazebo, met, embraced.

He poured himself a glass of Taittinger and gazed around. "It really is lovely, Van."

"You truly like it?"

He touched his glass to hers. "You've made the whole house come alive. You've changed it from a fusty, male domain to a home."

She curtseyed. "Your pleasure in it is my own, Milord."

Stuart mock-grimaced. "Don't press it—there's a good girl."

General Sir Arthur Kelly, Vanessa's uncle, and Jillian Kelly, Vanessa's cousin and booking agent, arrived for the dinner party just as Jim and Ann Lees were mounting the steps of Stuart's townhouse. Neither of them paid much attention to the driver of their taxi (although, as he paid him, Sir Arthur noticed that the man had most peculiar silver eyes), but, as they were turning away from the taxi, they had to step aside quickly to avoid Lees' rush down the steps and across the walk toward the cab. The driver had put it in gear and was slowly pulling out from the curb as Lees arrived. Loudly and distinctly, he said, "Ev'nin', General Lees. 'Ave a nice dinner," as the taxi gathered speed and scooted up Duke Street.

Lees stood, white and shaken, at the curb, staring after the taxi, reading and repeating the license number aloud, trying to memorize it: "RDX-11988, RDX-11988, RDX-11988." He turned to find Sir Arthur and his daughter staring at him as if he were a two-headed man. Lees flushed with embarrassment.

Sir Arthur smiled and asked dryly, "Long-lost friend?"

Lees flushed again. He recognized the tall, lean, distinguished-looking man before him; Sir Arthur had been the hero of the previous year's short, successful and popular war in the Caribbean Basin. Lees, struggling with his discomfort, spoke bluntly. "That, er, man, the taxi driver, is involved in the Ripper business."

The Kellys stared at him as if he were mad; Sir Arthur recovered his manners first. "You come to this knowledge through divination, no doubt." He smiled smugly.

"Unfortunately, Sir Arthur, that is correct."

Again the Kellys were pulled up short and Lees cursed his honesty and lack of wit.

Ann had descended the steps and, for several seconds, the quartet maintained the awkward tableau. Jillian, the bony, brunette daughter, broke the silence.

"How do you know my father's name?"

Lees regained enough composure to laugh. "Not by divination. Your father is a hero and I am more than ordinarily interested in military affairs." He extended his hand. "Retired Brigadier Jim Lees, United States Army."

Kelly shook his hand, limply, disdainfully. "How very droll—a psychic general. The mind reels at the possibilities." He half-turned and indicated with a nod of his head. "My daughter, Jillian."

Her handshake was firm enough to be a relief after her father's and she tried to smooth the discomfort. "Never mind father—he has only two postures; the sarcastic arrogance of Wilde or the heroic arrogance of Wellington."

Lees half-bowed. "Mr. Wilde, I presume." Lees introduced his wife as they moved up the steps and were ushered inside by Stuart's man, Hathorn.

Jillian gushed something to Vanessa about a movie offer being firm now and the terms nearly set as they hugged, and Lees drew Stuart aside to ask for a few minutes in private.

They stepped into a small elevator, paneled in creamy raw silk, and Stuart pushed the button for the third floor. "We'll be more comfortable in my study and I wanted a private word also. But guest first."

Lees said, "Sir Arthur and his daughter arrived by taxi. The driver was the same one who brought Ann and I from Heathrow. The silver-eyed man from my dreams. He spoke to me by name again."

The elevator stopped smoothly; the door whispered open.

Stuart and Lees eyed one another.

Stuart gestured with his arm. "Please."

They stepped out and walked to the end of the hallway, entered the study and sat in chairs near the desk.

†

111

"I got the license-plate number."

"Excellent," said Stuart. He rose, crossed to his desk, sat and took up pen and notepaper.

"RDX-11988."

Stuart scribbled down the number, picked up the phone and dialed, waited.

"Yes. Malcolm Stuart, Constable Brown. Who's on dispatch desk tonight?" He nodded to himself. "Put me through to him, please." Waited again. "Sergeant Sanders, Malcolm Stuart. Take down a license-plate number, please. RDX-11988 . . . yes, that's right. Put out an all-officer alert—that cab is to be stopped as soon as spotted and the driver detained. He is wanted for questioning in the Hyde Park murder. Please advise me as soon as he is located and don't be bothered if the hour is late. I want to know immediately. Thank you, Sergeant."

He hung up and swiveled his chair to face Lees, who was sitting with his back to the windows overlooking Grosvenor Square. "Curious how this man keeps popping up casually," he said.

Lees shrugged. "This is all more than curious, Sir Malcolm. It is grotesque."

Stuart nodded. "Quite." He opened the top drawer of his desk and pulled a photocopy of the Ripper letter out, rose and carried it to Lees. He sat in a neighboring chair. "That arrived in the late-mail delivery Wednesday afternoon. I didn't get to it until yesterday."

Lees read it twice, then stared angrily at Stuart. "How in hell. . . ?"

Stuart nodded. "Yes, indeed. That is the question."

There was a long, nasty silence.

Finally, Lees mastered himself. "But this is no good, Sir Malcolm. The question raised in your mind impugns my honor; the question raised in mine impugns yours or your staff's."

"Yes. If honor left me another course, I should gladly take it, but duty forbids me. I must ask—have you an explanation of your name in that document?"

Lees shook his head. "No. None whatsoever."

Stuart sighed. "And I have none either."

†

They were two strong, tough-minded men and when their eyes met it was like a test. Neither wanted to look away.

"Paranoia," Lees said at last, "is an insidious insanity. Reason and order rest upon trust. Once ordinary faith is abandoned, where shall we stand? So where does that leave us now, Sir Malcolm?"

Stuart smiled. "At a place where it becomes increasingly uncomfortable to have you address me so formally. Malcolm will do nicely."

Lees smiled in return. "Good enough. My friends call me Jim."

"Good, Jim. I have a proposal I want to put to you."

Stuart explained the idea of the Hedgemore project, but couched the reasons in rather more diplomatic terms than had been discussed at the Yard.

Lees closed his eyes. Oh God, he thought. Then he remembered that he had closed that door himself.

Stuart said, "Hedgemore, my country estate, is quite comfortable."

Lees smiled, eyes still closed. "A lab rat is a lab rat even if you dress the laboratory up like the Taj Mahal."

He opened his eyes and met Stuart's frank gaze. "Just two days ago, I wanted to go home. Ann talked me out of it. I still want to go home, but— You spoke of duty. I have mine also. Yes, if I'm to try at all, I suppose I must go the distance."

"Good." Stuart rose. "Let us join the others, Jim. After I ask Sir Arthur where the taxi picked him up, I should like to forget this business for a few hours and merely relax."

"You're on, Malcolm."

The unseasonably mild night led the party to linger in the garden beneath the suffused light of gay paper lanterns. The Taittinger flowed, making the surface spirit lively and upbeat.

Vanessa moved unobtrusively from one pocket of guests to another, trying to feed the positive mood with a laugh here, a smile there, a compliment or a joke or some brief chatter for everyone. She appeared relaxed and completely at ease, but she was alert for the slightest drag in conversation or any undercurrent of unrest or clashing egos. The occasion was important to her. This was her evening to prove, to herself and

†

to Stuart, that, despite her youth, she was a competent hostess for a man of Malcolm's stature.

She glanced at Lord and Lady Desmonde in close conversation with General Cochran and Mary, her widowed mother, still beautiful in her mid-forties. Her mother said something and the others laughed; that was a given; she could rely on her mother's charm to carry that quartet.

She joined Arthur, Jillian, the Lees and Malcolm in a small circle directly beneath a hanging lantern that dropped a textured glow on them.

"Your frontal assault by land and amphibious assault on the flank was brilliantly done, Sir Arthur. The Tobongo campaign will be a textbook classic for generations."

Kelly's slender features were bemused, "But General Lees, aren't you going to point out the clear parallel with MacArthur's strike at Inchon? *All* my American friends are ever so anxious to remind me of it."

Kelly's sarcastic tone of voice and cutting remark was such a rude rejoinder to a handsome compliment that the rest of the group stiffened slightly.

Malcolm's eyes met Vanessa's, who wondered what to say to ease the tension.

Lees saved it.

Shrugging, he said, "Superficially, of course, but your use of helicopter wings for the third assault in the midst of enemy concentration gave the plan an entirely new dimension. Very daring, very risky, but success proved your plan."

Kelly smiled again, but, for once, wholeheartedly. "How terribly charming of you to raise that point. Exactly the issue I should use to defend my originality if I were inclined to that sort of thing."

Lees sipped his champagne and said mildly, "I don't know that comparison to the innovative abilities of Doug MacArthur really warrants a defense. It's not an insult. But the parallel also falls apart when results are reviewed. What did the Tobongo campaign require—six, seven weeks? Korea dragged on for years. I know. I was there the whole time."

"Of course, the Chinese made your equation rather different. Still, it is kind of you to credit me so generously. We must lunch next week, General Lees."

†

Vanessa relaxed as Malcolm smiled.

Jillian touched her arm, winked and whispered, "His ego is monstrous, but what can you do? That's father."

Vanessa drifted off toward the last quartet of guests.

Aubrey Mayhew, youngish Tory MP for Bretonshire, and his perky wife, Pamela, were plainly puzzled by Ronnie Graham and Barbara Jensen, mid-twentyish up-and-coming stage actors. Ronnie was tall and blond with sulky pretty-boy looks and Barbara had an attractive face made dazzling by almond-shaped amber eyes, silky black hair that hung to the middle of her back and a firm, voluptuous body.

Ronnie shook his head. "But whyever should one have to give up either? Why choose? Both are perfectly delightful—I enjoy a firm boy or a soft woman. Or various combinations." He grinned wickedly at Vanessa. "Of course, if Vanessa would only say the word—she is the one woman in the entire world I would give up boys completely for."

Barbara put her amber eyes on Vanessa, licked her large pouty lips and said huskily, "I'd give up boys for her, too."

Vanessa smiled at the Mayhews, feeling her face so tight it might break from brittle strain. "You mustn't mind these two. They are so sex-obsessed their brains are softened. The only other passion they have in life is acting. Fortunately, they are quite good at *that*, so one forgives them their adolescent kinkiness." Lord, help me out of this, she pleaded silently.

Hathorn appeared in the open French doors, caught Stuart's eye and announced, "Dinner is served, Sir Malcolm."

Heneage Street was almost deserted at 2:05 A.M.

Kevin Boyle was an indigent twenty-three-year-old painter who suffered from insomnia fueled by his longings: a longing to dazzle the art world with a creative flame so fierce that all sensibility of beauty would be drawn to it irresistibly, an artistic torch too hot not to burn out (a romantic, lingering death from ennui and tuberculosis—at say, thirty-nine—was one of his semi-conscious formulations); a longing for fame and praise and riches, a Mediterranean villa with silk sheets and servants and a cellar chock-full of legendary vintages; a longing for Dora Watson, an upper-class fellow art student with no talent, but a pretty and kind face on a sensational

†

body. Prosaically, he could not sleep because he was unknown and untested, broke and horny, and wished not to be any of those things.

Between the hours of ten P.M. and five A.M., he often walked far and wide from his shabby furnished room in Spitalfields. Often his nocturnal wandering led him to the night-quiet commercial no-man's-land where Spitalfields and Whitechapel joined.

He was alone on Heneage Street. It looked . . . disoriented slightly. Some of the buildings weren't quite as he vaguely remembered. They looked slightly older, yet— Is that possible? he wondered. The ambiance was almost of another time.

There was a faint glow ahead. And, coming from it, something like a sound that wasn't quite audible. Perhaps more like vibration. He walked toward it.

It was the brick wall of an old building, phosphorescent and luminous in the dark.

His artist's eyes widened, delighted and enriched. He stopped ten paces off and drank it in.

It was a commercial collage of dated advertising posters. A white-wigged man in a planter's hat puffed a fat cigarette that blazed and smoked like a forest fire:

SMOKE ALLEN & GINTER'S RICHMOND GEM CIGARETTES

He tasted tobacco and coughed.

A top-hatted Victorian gentleman and bonneted matron sat behind a broad board with their newly booted feet poking through:

LILLEY & SKINNER'S	**Boots**
Finest Stocks	**and**
in London	**Shoes**

His ankles ached. Why does it glow? he wondered.

DISINFECT WITH SANITAS FLUID SOAP POWDER
WORLD'S FINEST SAUCE   YORKSHIRE RELISH

†

> **STOWERS LIME JUICE**
> **NESTLÉS SWISS MILK**
> **FELTOE'S LEMON SQUASH**
> **HENKEL'S BLEACHING SODA**

Smells of bleach, ammonia, lime and lemon clogged his nostrils and steak sauce and milk coated his tongue. He felt dizzy, nauseous, and wavered on his feet.

A pink-gowned woman stood next to a black horse with a blue-silked jockey mounted and he smelled sweat and horse manure and heard animal breathing:

> **The**
>   **SPORTSMAN**
> **For**
>   **FULLEST**
> **BEST**
>   **RACING**   **NEWS**

A sidewheel steamship plowed through whitecapped waves and salt tang was in his mouth and the ground rocked and slipped beneath his feet and a stiff sea breeze flattened the hair on the sides of his head, whipped top-curls as if trying to straighten his kinky mane:

> **MARGATE & RAMSGATE**
>   **DEAL**   **YARMOUTH**
> **DOVER**
> **SOUTHEND**
> **GENERAL STEAM NAVIGATION CO**

Boyle fell to his hands and knees and vomited into the street—a strange bile with steak he hadn't eaten in sauce-coated gristly chunks and residues of soft drinks he hadn't drunk. He heard music—tinkly-piano bawdy-hall booze-and-smoke-and-sweat music. An outsize stiffly corseted Latrecian-lithograph woman danced and kicked her legs and swirled her skirts:

> **A GAIETY GIRL**
> **DALY'S THEATRE**

†

My God! Boyle recognized the poster from a textbook. Dudley Hardy drew that . . . in . . . in—1880 or 1890? He heard the shouts of an angry mob and saw flashes of silver—swordblades and scythes. A man in a long white coat stood on a raised wooden platform with a guillotine in the background and Boyle recognized another textbook example of Victorian poster art. John Hassal, he thought, as the screams of the mob filled his ears:

THE ONLY WAY
A Tale of Two Cities

MR. MARTIN HARVEY
as Sydney Carlton

He covered his ears and shouted, *"Stop!"* as words and pictures and line ran together. The building bulged and throbbed and the light glowed blindingly as colors ran together in a nightmare abstraction of oozing white and black and pink and lemon and purple and red and orange and green.

Boyle pushed himself to his feet, turned and ran.

Lees dreamed but did not wake or remember.

He dreamed the pillar of steam and pool of blood and giant spiky spider legs overhead and iron wheels on cobblestone and unconcerned crowds and the smell of flowers and fruit.

The Ripper dreamed.

Dreamed blade slash and scream song and blood spray.

Woke alert and tight, focused.

What have I done? What am I doing?

"No!" the Ripper shrieked, *"I will not submit!"*

Conscience must die!

"I will it so!"

She must die, so they must die.

The Ripper whispered, "I will . . . it so . . ." and fell back asleep.

Dreamed knife tearing, siren scream, red rivers.

Came in sleep-dream, drenched a circle on the sheets.

†

* * *

Sir Arthur had told Stuart that he had called South Kensington & Chelsea Hire, Ltd., for his taxi. Now, Clive stood in the small garage off Fulham Road and Sunday morning light and shadow play of the interior swam before his eyes. He tried to absorb what the man, Falcon, had just said to him.

"I already gave Luke's name, address and photo to one of your constables. Last Monday. Luke told me it didn't come to anything."

Colson! thought Clive.

The air seemed suddenly chill and his heart beat slowly and insistently in his chest.

Father Eric Mueller stood in the sunny, salty air bathing the steps of St. Martin's Church near the Chelsea Embankment. He greeted the parishoners exiting the mass he had just celebrated.

Ann Lees approached.

He took her hands.

They smiled, eyes searching.

"How are you, Ann?"

"Bearing up, Father Eric."

"And Jim?"

She shook her head. "In pain. We're to go down to Kent, be secluded. He's to be tested . . . about this."

"I don't mean to be facile, Ann, but we're all . . . to be tested."

She smiled and nodded.

She looked unusually attractive in a tan wool wrap-dress, her golden blond hair and deep-blue eyes accented by discreet gold-and-sapphire earrings and pale makeup. He was extraordinarily handsome, his silver-streaked blond hair, fair complexion and trim body complemented by the black silk soutane.

They looked at one another.

The church towered above them, a gray-stone semi-Gothic bulk representing solidity and safety, tradition beyond time.

The moment became awkward.

They dropped hands, turned toward the Thames and began to descend the steps.

†

"I would offer you luncheon this week, but . . . when do you depart?"

"Tuesday, I believe."

"Tomorrow, then?"

"Yes, Father Eric. It helps to talk."

Claymoor Street in Brixton was choked with uniformed policemen. Fragments of faces and curious eyes floated in the grimy windows of the overhanging gossipy rowhouses. Detective-Sergeant Clive knocked on the glistening black door of Number 11.

It was his third try.

He waited.

No response.

He jerked his head toward the black door. "Open it."

A uniformed constable with a set of peculiar-looking and quite illegal tools stepped forward and bent to the lock. He selected a thin metal shaft, fitted it and fiddled. After a few moments, the bolt popped with an audible click.

Clive opened it.

"Christ!"

The stench was overwhelming. Colson lay face down in the hallway, a putrifying mass swollen to bursting in his rancid uniform.

Clive put a handkerchief over his nose and breathed through his mouth as he entered. He glanced at the parlor to the left, the kitchenette-dining room to the right and the bedroom dead on: pale-yellow walls and mocha carpet; common contemporary furniture of the hundred-pounds-for-the-complete-set variety; some unremarkable abstract paintings. Nothing extraordinary for that sort of flat in a place like Brixton.

Damn fool! thought Clive angrily as he stared down at the disgusting corpse. You always were too eager by half!

The photograph of Lucian Nicholas, recovered from Colson's pocket, made the evening television news accompanied by the terse tagline, "Sought for questioning in the death of an unidentified police constable."

Luke Nicholas turned his silver eyes from the television screen, looked at the Ripper and laughed.

†

"This begins to become truly amusing."

He laughed again.

The Monday newspapers would splatter the front pages with the photograph, silver eyes dominant even in crude newsprint reproduction, but with no mention of any connection to the Ripper murders.

Stuart stood in the hallway of the flat while Lees wandered through the rooms. They had come alone at Lees' insistence. The forensics people had finished in the early morning hours and since then only a single officer had remained outside the door to guard the murder scene.

Probably won't come to anything, thought Stuart. But at least worth a try.

Lees walked slowly around the parlor.

Royal blue walls and muted gold carpet; pale blue-and-rose-striped period furniture, heavy and ornately detailed; mediocre reproductions of Delacroix and Manet.

Lees walked stiffly, like a man injured. Silver-Eyes was in his head, laughing at him. *Can't get it, guv. Helter-skelter! First yer go up, then yer go down! Helter-skelter and yer can't get it, guv!*

Then it stopped, vanished.

Lees sat in a chair, his rear barely perched on the edge. His breathing was shallow, his skin pale and his hands shook slightly.

"Jim?"

"I'm all right, Malcolm. Just had a—flash. The cabbie in my head, taunting me, laughing. Just need to rest a minute."

He's genuine. The thought startled Stuart. He's not acting. Stuart fought the intuition. Have to reserve judgment. Facts, he thought, have to build a foundation of facts first.

Lees raised his head and brought his tired eyes to bear on Stuart.

"Build your foundation of facts, if you must, Malcolm. But I am genuine—whatever I am—and I'm not positive of what that is at the moment. I am genuine and"—he smiled wanly—"I never have had a gift for acting."

"How . . . ?" Stuart started a question and, then, let it drift away.

†

Lees sighed. "It's growing. I'm not just 'getting' things about the Ripper business, now. I'm beginning to 'read' the people about me." He stared at his now steady hands. "And I don't like it. Don't like it at all."

Clive frowned as he read the lab report:

> The paper subjected to laboratory examination is a highly unusual blend of rice pulp, high-quality linen pulp and silk, which makes it one of the finest papers this lab has ever studied. The content removes it completely from the mass-market arena, which may help in locating the source.
>
> However, it is such a costly blend that none of the experts contacted (see attached sub-file GA222) could suggest where to start. One consultant ventured that, if available, this paper might well retail for 150–200 pounds per ream (500 sheets).

Don't be condescending, you snots, thought Clive irritably. I know what a bloody ream is and so will anyone else reading this report. He went back to it:

> Additionally, the chemicals used in manufacture also constitute a problem area (see attached sub-file GA223). The chemicals, as well as their combination or mixture, are suggestive of 19th-century production methods and processes rather than contemporary techniques. Some of the particular constituents, ferrous-malidium for example, are wholly unknown in 20th-century industry and might prove virtually impossible to secure. Nitrous-galvanorite, for another example, has not been produced or utilized in the Western world since the approximate period 1885–1890.

The principal report continued in that vein for an additional two pages. He finished it and skimmed the attached sub-files which only documented the experiments conducted, research undertaken and consultations sought to produce the report.

Clive closed the folder.

Bloody cheek, bloody cheek and nonsense! *Somebody* made the damn paper and envelope. And this old son will damn well find out whom.

†

* * *

Ann Lees twirled the wineglass in her hand, staring through the pale, transparent fluid as if searching for a flaw in the crystal or the odd piece of cork in her dry white. "I suppose all this has revealed a whole area of Jim that is so unknown, it . . ."

Eric Mueller swallowed a bite of fettucine alfredo and finished her sentence for her. "Frightens you? Alienates you?"

She nodded.

The late luncheon crowd at the Palm Court of the Ritz Hotel was thinning, but the conversation was still lively enough to provide a background hum.

"I never faced it before, but my faith, my Catholicism, gives us such radically different world views. . . ."

Mueller sipped mineral water and waited for her to finish.

She held his eyes with her own. She forced her next words, "I feel so separate!" and then drank off some wine to hide her embarrasment.

"I see the difficulty, but what would you do?"

"I don't know. I just know that I feel helpless trying to talk to him about his pain."

Mueller nodded as he cut another forkful of pasta. "Because you have a remedy and he doesn't, and you can't give him yours."

"Yes. That's what I feel." She looked down at her barely touched Sole Veronique, smiled faintly and shook her head. "You see—I can talk to you and you understand right away."

"Shared perspective."

"Yes."

He finished the last bit of fettucine and pushed the plate aside, drank some Perrier and dabbed his mouth with the spotless linen napkin.

"You've barely touched your fish."

"Not hungry."

He smiled. "I so seldom eat at such wonderful tables, I can't resist. I'm going to have dessert as well and I insist you try some of their excellent strawberries and cream with a cup of espresso."

She smiled back. "Do I sound very foolish?"

He laughed and shook his head. "As you say—you haven't

†

faced this before. You're in shock. And under enormous stress. The instinct is to withdraw, and it's fully human and natural." He patted her hand and then signaled to their waiter. "But, as you also say, you have a solution. You have your faith, and the spiritual tools to see you through. And I will help in any way I can."

She felt little-girl foolish and said, "Yes, Father," in the tone of the contrite child.

He laughed, but it was gentle and understanding, not distant.

Lees called Pat Cochran for help Monday evening. His plea was simple.

"Pat, I'm going nuts. I gotta get out for a while. Just a few hours away from this."

"Sure, buddy. Whatta you want to do?"

"Let's get drunk. Real drunk."

"You got it, J.R."

They got drunk on Irish whiskey and imperial pints of draft Guinness, got drunk at half a dozen pubs, got falling-down-leaning-on-everything-singing-soldiers'-songs-laughing-madly-red-faced drunk and wound up at Pat's room at Browns, passing a bottle of Paddy back and forth and trying to focus their eyes and to top each other with outrageous soldier's stories that were more than half true.

When Lees got back to the Dorchester, he lay down on the sitting room floor and promptly fell asleep. He snored, but he did not dream. He had succeeded in anesthetizing his central nervous system; all the lights were out and nobody was home.

Tuesday morning was barely illuminated by a weedy gray sky that bled a thin drizzle, a climatic cliché for early autumn in southern England, a cold, wet and gloomy day that could only be described as bleak.

Bleak was also the best adjective for the mood in Stuart's Jaguar sedan on the seventy-five-mile trip down to the Kent coast. Lees had a massive five-Excedrin hangover. And Ann was feeling disgust at his binge.

Stuart had tried. He had made brisk, cheery talk at the Dorchester until he recognized Lees' symptoms and Ann's disaffection. Once he sensed the mood, he gave them the space of silence and concentrated on driving carefully through the nasty weather, keeping an eye on the mirror to see that he wasn't losing the quintet of unmarked police cars following with the eighteen constables who would serve as security at the estate.

Even in the rain, Hedgemore was a beautiful sight.

Set in Romney Marsh on the Kent coast between Hythe and Rye, it occupied more than a hundred and fifty acres just north of the Dungeness headland. At a point where the blacktop country road curved gracefully away from the coast, a gravel drive exited toward the shore, running straight as a taut piano wire for a mile-and-a-quarter between inner walls of closely trimmed hedges and outer walls of tall, evenly spaced hardwood trees.

The drive split Hedgemore into nearly equal halves. The heavily forested fields to the north were called The Shoots and were used for the small-game and bird hunting of Sir Malcolm and his guests; the rolling, lightly forested fields to the south were called The Rides and were used for fox hunting and horseback excercise. At the end of the drive, a large clearing opened on a coastal depression and a shallow cliff above a stretch of white-sand beach protected by two tentative outthrusts of coast too minor to be named headlands.

Two buildings dominated the clearing. To the right immediate edge and angled southeast was a low shingle-covered structure with fourteen narrow wooden doors that proved to be a fourteen-car garage. Dead on was a three-story Georgian mansion with two-story wings angled coastward at either end. The south wing was for the servants; the north wing for spillover guests who did not rate a room in the main house.

Even in their current unhappy state and despite the gray damp gloom of the day, the Lees could not but be overwhelmed. Cheerful servants saw to their bags, served tea in the library of the main house, and settled the policemen into rooms in the servant's wing. Later, the butler, Granby, a warm, polite, lean, silver-haired man, showed the Lees to adjoining bedrooms on the third floor, with a common bath and

†

a broad connecting balcony overlooking a pool house at the north side of the clearing, the lush, grassy sweep to the cliffs and the beach and channel beyond.

Lees stood at the French doors to the balcony and stared out. The rain had stopped and the wind had freshened and riffled the grass playfully. The light was pale, brighter, as if the overcast was breaking up, moving on. The sea was green-gray, white-flecked, swift.

Lees felt better, though he wasn't sure why. Maybe just getting out of London, or the clearing weather. Perhaps it was the beauty and serenity of Hedgemore or the sight of the sea. Or renewed hope. He believed a team of competent experts might enable him to "break through," use his power to thwart further killings. Whatever it was, his burden had lightened, his spirit had lifted.

He heard her moving about in the next room, called out, "Ann."

She stopped, then came to the open door, waited.

He turned, "I'm . . . sorry, Ann. I lost it last night. I have no excuse."

She nodded ruefully. "I'm sorry too. I just . . . hate to see you thrashing about in . . . so much pain."

"I know. We'll see."

Ann smiled. "This has come to a pretty pass. After forty years we get separate bedrooms."

Lees smiled in return. "That is just for appearances. Mustn't offend the servants' sensibilities."

She laughed. "No, I don't suppose that would be good form."

He called down to the staff area, got Granby and inquired if the pool was in use; it was; asked if swimming trunks were available; they were.

"Medium, sir? About a thirty-four-waist?"

"Exactly, Granby."

"I shall send them up directly, General."

Lees swam in chlorine-blue light and the cloying air of a heated, closed pool. He did not mind the eye strain or stuffy air; he swam hard.

†

Quick laps—one, two, three, four. He rested, holding onto the pool edge; breathed deeply, exhaled explosively.

Swam slow, stretching laps—one, two, three, four, five. Rested; breathed.

Swam sprint-furious laps—one two, three. Rested; breathed.

He repeated the series ten times. Swam for more than an hour. Swam nearly a mile in the forty-foot pool. Swam methodically with determination to dump his tension and the hangover poison from his system, tire his muscles, rest his mind.

Then he napped.

Dreamlessly.

At dinner, Stuart explained that he would be driving back to London for a press conference. "Try to get the bloody wolves to stop their yapping for a space." The team would begin arriving tomorrow.

Dr. Henry Percy, Stuart's personal physician, would come for the day to give Lees a thorough physical, and would leave a registered nurse for the duration. On Thursday, Dr. Samuel Hobart, a London psychologist, and Dr. George Frounle, a Cambridge don in history and a parapsychologist by avocation, would arrive with Billy Topp, a former Liverpool dock worker and noted "sensitive." The tests would begin immediately.

After dinner, Stuart left for London.

The Lees retired. And, restored, made tender, gentle love. Slept.

Lees sat in a bedroom on the first floor of the guest wing at Hedgemore. In a chair across from him sat Dr. Henry Percy. The bedroom had been converted to a temporary infirmary and Percy was taking a medical history from Lees.

Born in December 1898, Percy was only weeks short of his ninetieth birthday. Officially, he was head of the prestigious Harley Street practice of The Doctors Percy, Ltd. (himself, his son, grandson, and great-grandson—Henry Percy V), but, in fact, he had in the last twenty years reduced his client list to a handful of favorite patients and friends, of which Sir Malcolm Stuart was by far the youngest. An ordinary-sized man, with modest, sloped shoulders and a trim torso, Percy was the sort of man who enjoyed watching to see if he would outlive his remaining clients. His pink, egg-shaped head had exactly two gray hairs on either side, which gave it a lightly pinstriped look, like a sports coupe. Nonetheless, he had lucid blue eyes, was spry of limb and mind and looked and behaved as a man twenty-five years his junior might. He continued to digest the latest developments in medicine, had always been an intuitive, sensitive physician and had more than sixty years of general practice experience.

He was also the only man directly involved in the current crisis who was born while Victoria still occupied the throne of the English Empire, who remembered Edward VII vividly and personally and who had experienced the speculation about the identity of Jack-the-Ripper as something other than ancient history.

Lees and Percy liked each other immediately, recognizing in each other competent, decent, no-nonsense men.

"Any known problems with heart, lungs, liver, kidney, any of the major organs? Hereditary diseases?"

Lees' recital was a sustained parade of negatives; for most of his fifty-eight years, his health had been unswervingly excellent and he knew of no major problems that ran in either side of his family.

"Hypertension, high blood pressure?"

Lees sighed. "Not until recently, and not anything way out of line."

Percy smiled. "Diagnosing yourself? I've noticed an increasing tendency of my patients to dabble in medicine over the last fifteen years. It would make me angry if there weren't so many incompetent fools posing as doctors. When did the problem arise and what have you done about it?"

Lees shifted uncomfortably in the leather easy chair. "About three years ago, when—I began having these dream-visions—I showed a slight increase at my annual physicals."

"How much is slight?"

"Most of my life I've run in the one-thirty over seventy to

†

seventy-five range. Three years ago, I began running one-forty over eighty-five; it stayed that way for two years." Lees smiled at Percy. "My *doctor* said it was still in a comfortable range, so we would monitor it but not worry."

Percy chuckled. "Quite right. And recently?"

"A year ago, it moved up to one-fifty over ninety; four—no four and-a-half months ago, it escalated to one-fifty-five to one-sixty over ninety-five to a hundred."

Percy nodded. "Top line's uncomfortable, bottom's pushing toward dicey. Treatment? Medication?"

Lees shrugged. "I refused medication. My doctor told me to relax, which I would very much like to do, but I haven't been able to with . . . with all this." He made a contemptuous gesture of dismissal with his hand.

Percy locked eyes with him. "Why did you refuse medication?"

"Don't like it. Don't like drugs. I use alcohol and tobacco moderately most of the time, and I stay away from everything else, including prescriptions."

"I don't care for drugs either, but sometimes we have to use them. Are you going to cooperate with me or shall I have Sir Malcolm find another, more pliant physician?"

The two men eyed each other for a silent minute. Finally, Lees sighed again and nodded.

"I'll accept your direction, Dr. Percy. Within reason."

Percy grunted, "Within reason. Alright, we'll see how it works. I don't know what I'll prescribe until we complete the physical." He rose and set the chart on an end table. "Might as well take your clothes off and hop up on the end of the bed there. I'm going to poke and prod you for a bit."

Lees stripped, and Percy poked and prodded for two hours with hands and instruments and machines. Throughout he said little and registered less to what he saw, heard and found. The only thing Lees could discern from Percy was displeasure with the blood pressure and EKG results; he took both those tests three times. On the last EKG, he monitored Lees' chest with a stethoscope.

Lees dressed and sat in the easy chair again. Percy sat near him, making notes on the chart. He finished after fifteen minutes.

†

The two men eyed each other.

Lees asked, "Problem?"

Percy's blue eyes were gentle. "Yes. Your blood pressure averaged one-sixty-two over one-oh-eight. In addition, the EKGs gave me an echo."

"An echo?"

Percy nodded. "A minor, faint irregularity. So faint and so infrequent that I wasn't sure it was really there until the third reading."

"But it is?"

"Yes."

"So what are you telling me?"

"General, my suspicion—and that's all it is at this point—my suspicion is that three years of high stress, hypertension and high blood pressure are beginning to exact a toll on your heart. We can probably medicate the blood pressure, but that's a symptom. What we really need to do is get your stress level reduced."

Lees shrugged. "Considering what's immediately in front of me, how would you suggest we manage that?"

"Going to be a bit difficult, isn't it? Malcolm has told me what you're involved in, what's going to go on and what you're trying to do. He also gave me what small background on you he had. If I understood him correctly, this ability of yours is rather repugnant to you."

Lees was cold. "You understood correctly."

"You have resisted it most of your life?"

"Yes."

"Yet now you are trying to use it for positive effect, are even going to submit to tests and stimuli designed to encourage the faculty?"

"Yes."

"How do you feel about *that*?"

"I hate it," hissed Lees with reptilian intensity.

Percy sat back in his chair and closed his eyes.

TRAFALGAR SQUARE, SEPTEMBER 14, 1918

Major Percy, still in uniform, walks toward the Golden Cross Hotel in brilliant sunlight. He stops by Nelson's column. A corporal of the 10th Fusiliers sits beneath a supine stone lion. He has a young, dark, handsome face, clean-featured and honest and pleasing to the eye—a ladies' man, no doubt. His shoulders are broad, torso large, arms muscular beneath the tight dress blouse. His hands are strong-looking, but still delicate, finely shaped.
 He is twenty or so.
 His legs stop at mid-thigh and he is blind.
 He sings.
 His voice is baritone, clear, sweet-toned. The song is some bouncy music-hall hit of the season. The corporal sings with feeling, élan; he smiles and gestures with his hands, arms, body. His upturned helmet rests on the concrete beside him and he salutes, without interrupting his song, the few sounds of coins rattling into it.
 Most traffic passes by with no more than a glance. Some faces assume expressions of disgust or revulsion.
 The song ends.
 Percy fishes in his pocket for a small wad of notes, crosses to the corporal, squats on his heels and drops them in the helmet.
 The soldier smiles in his direction. "Thank you—sir? Madam?"
 "How could you tell, son?"
 "You're blocking the sun, sir. I felt the cool."
 "Sorry, all I have to give you is money and not much of that."

†

"Bless you, sir, I don't need much. Soldier, sir?"
"Yes."
"It's mostly soldiers that trouble to stop."
"No trouble, son. You've made my day."
"Bless you, sir."
"Bless you, too."

The hotel lobby is gay, colorful, active.

A ravishing raven-haired girl in swirls of coral silk and a fantastic hat greets him with a sly hug, coy kiss. She complains he is late, complains about the service in the restaurant, complains that they must have tea rather than lunch because he gave most of his money to a cripple, complains about the food.

She complains.

In contradiction to the desires and expectations of both their families, he does not ask her to marry him.

Lees and Percy opened their eyes simultaneously.

Lees rubbed his temples. Quietly, he said, "You were a soldier. You met a crippled soldier in Trafalgar Square. It looked much different than now. Some buildings I didn't recognize, older vehicles, must have been near the end of World War I. He sang; you gave him some money, talked. You met a girl in a hotel I can't place—"

"The Golden Cross Hotel was torn down in the thirties."

Lees shrugged. "You had tea; she was irritating."

Silence.

Percy nodded.

"You do have the gift."

"Yes."

Finally, the old man sighed. "That happened seventy years ago, today. I lied to Corporal Tewes that morning, though I didn't know it at the time—he didn't make my day, he made my life."

"How so?"

"I was in a period of despair and bitterness. The trenches were a degrading, brutalizing experience. I had, in my twenty-year-old wisdom, decided life was a meaningless charade, stupid and rotten. I was preparing to walk through a tedious, predictable, foolish existence for the rest of my days—a place in a prestigious law office, an 'appropriate' marriage, a vapid, upper-class life of endless ennui.

"Then, for a mere moment, I saw things from Tewes' point of view. If he could be happy, if he could feel not loss of limb but love of life, if he could see, in his blindness, the sun—what right had I to despair?"

"I see."

"I hope you do, General. I remembered that experience, as I always do on this date, because you brought it to mind."

Lees' mouth tightened and he stiffened.

"In more than sixty years of medical practice, I would guess that most of the physical diseases of my patients have been brought on by discontent, unhappiness, bitterness, anger and despair. I can treat the body and I'm very good at it. But that is merely a holding action; my patients have to treat their spirits. Some do; some don't. Those that do live comfortably. Those that don't die miserably—day-by-day."

"How do you know the soldier wasn't just acting, putting up a facade?"

"My but you're stubborn, General. And, perhaps, a touch cynical?"

"Perhaps."

"I know because I went back and found him. Allen Tewes became my best friend and I thank God every day for putting him in my life. Allen had wanted to be an actor. The war ended that, but we found him work at a variety of odd jobs. Eventually, he married and had children; I've never known a happier man. Then he met some people who got him a position as a studio singer, a fill-in voice as recording began to get big. Later, he did dubbing for musical films and made a handsome living."

"And?"

"And what? Isn't that enough? Allen is still alive, eighty-nine, retired and happy with his wife, children, grandchildren and great-grandchildren. We lunch every week and he hasn't been sick ten times in the seventy years I've known him."

"You're telling me to be happy."

"Yes, I am, General. If you continue to impose stress on yourself you will be committing suicide. And the stress *does* come from you—not the situation. You are the cause of your illness."

"And it may kill me."

"And it will kill you."

The recently renovated press room at the Home Office was high-ceilinged, ornately paneled and carpeted in Wilton Scarlet (the latter choice, some wags said, was so that the blood let at Lord Desmonde's press briefings wouldn't be too obvious). The room was appointed with sixty plush, high-backed Edwardian chairs for the media minions, facing a raised dias dominated by a long, glowingly polished, intricately carved oak table (legend had it that the top had been hewed from the mainmast of one of Drake's ships; in any case, it was a handsome and ancient table).

Seated behind the table, the short, slender figure of the home secretary was overshadowed by the flanking bulk of Stuart. Lord Desmonde let the technicians set and adjust their lights and position and check their television cameras, allowed the photographers their incessant flashbulb popping and, when he judged they had had a fair run, rapped his knuckles lightly on the rich grain of the table.

"Gentlemen and ladies, if I may have your attention." He waited for quiet. "Thank you. It is not customary for a press briefing concerning a current Scotland Yard case to be held at the Home Office. Nor is it ordinary for the home secretary to attend such affairs. This departure from routine is at my request. I feel compelled to reply to the savage attacks upon the competency of the Yard that have been made by some members of the media. Accordingly, I shall read a brief statement, and Sir Malcolm and I shall take questions after."

The HS pulled horn-rimmed reading half-glasses from his pocket, put them on and read from a sheet of paper on the table before him.

"The neo-Ripper affair has been discussed in private conversation with the prime minister as well as in full Cabinet session. The government is fully satisfied with the ongoing efforts of New Scotland Yard and, in particular, with the leadership of Sir Malcolm Stuart, deputy commissioner for Criminal Investigations Division."

†

He repocketed the glasses. "Sir Malcolm?"

Stuart had no notes and spoke freely from memory and feeling. "Despite the efforts of the more lurid elements of the gutter press, New Scotland Yard has not lost its head." There was a ripple of appreciative laughter and Stuart paused to let it run its course.

"Nor, I daresay, shall the vast majority of the sensible British public. It seems apparent that some incredibly demented maniac has seized upon the centennial anniversary of the Whitechapel murders to act out his own unfathomable fantasies. While no arrest seems imminent, I have no doubt that the Yard will acquit itself honorably, as has long been its history."

The HS nodded and asked, "Questions?"

"Was the murder of the Yard constable connected to the Hyde Park and Thames murders?"

Stuart answered, "It is not a certainty, but seems *probable.* He was engaged in the investigation and was murdered in the course of his duty."

"Are you ready to release his identity?"

"Yes. The officer in question was Constable Colin Colson. His name was withheld until his family could be notified. A photograph and a summary of Colson's life and career will be made available at the end of this conference."

"Is the taxi driver being sought for questioning a suspect in the neo-Ripper killings?"

"He is suspected of being an accomplice."

There was a momentary hush.

"Are you saying that there may be more than one murderer?"

Stuart shook his head. "Not in the hands-on sense. We, presently, believe there is one murderer and one accomplice. And we suspect Lucian Nicholas of being that accomplice."

The Vampire snuck a surreptitious sip of gin and returned the pint to his coat pocket, started a yawn that developed into a belch.

Bleedin' buncha bullshit, he thought. *"Carl Collins, the London Daily—What about the barmy boat the woman was found on?!"* he shouted.

The room turned to face him.

†

Stuart made a face of distaste. The Vampire, he thought. Wouldn't you know he'd *have* to turn up on a case like this.

"The boat is a steam launch of nineteenth-century manufacture and we have, to date, had no success in locating its contemporary source."

The Vampire wobbled to his feet. "Don't you find it bizarre that a re-creation of a nineteenth-century murder should occur on a nineteenth-century boat that nobody can figure out where it came from?"

Stuart nodded. "I certainly do." Laughter. "I find this entire case grotesque beyond the madness of routine murder, but crime comes *as is*, not in a tidy, acceptable package."

"Does Lucian Nicholas have a prior criminal history?" was asked from another corner of the conference room.

The Vampire sat down heavily.

"Not that we can locate through Yard or British Commonwealth records, or those of Interpol."

They don't get it, thought the Vampire. This isn't just weird, there's something *really* kinky going on here. And Stuart knows it. You're too cute by half, Sir Malcolm, but you're not fooling this old hand.

The Vampire dosed himself with another swallow of gin. Eructed.

Too clever, you are, he thought. But you're not going to get away with it forever, my fine Scotch friend. I'm going to find you out.

Soon.

The office was another converted bedroom in the guest wing. The bed had been moved out; two desks with chairs had been moved in along with a filing cabinet and a bookshelf, books, office supplies, the cliché couch and a grouping of easy chairs. The room itself was at the end of a wing with windows on the corner of the clearing and views of The Shoots. The same creamy plaster walls with oak trim, blue carpet and two ordinary landscapes.

Lees sat stiffly in a chair by a desk.

Dr. Samuel Hobart sat behind the desk.

He was a chipmunk of a man with a round head and stubby

†

body, tufty brown hair and round hooded green eyes. He was, that morning, forty-one years old, dressed in a tweed sport coat with leather elbow patches, fawn slacks and loafers. He was smoking a largish briar that looked like a facial deformity. He was also a man of many nervous mannerisms: ear tugging, nose pinching, temple rubbing, tooth tapping, cuff shooting, watch checking and the like.

"I have, uh"—tooth tap—"some idea of the tests you will be, er"—ear tug—"undergoing. My function"—leg cross, cuff shoot—"will be to ascertain your present"—nose pinch—"psychological state, background and, hmm, to counsel you on the"—clenched teeth grin—"accompanying stress."

*Wo*nderful, thought Lees. For a shrink, I get a nervous squirrel.

"Now, hah, fortunately, we don't have to begin from"—watch check—"scratch. I have, heh-heh, rather illegally I believe, your army service jacket or, hmm, rather, a facsimile. Most interesting. High intelligence scores averaging around a hundred and fifty-five. Mine, heh-heh"—clenched teeth, smile, wink—"consistently run in the one-seventies. Anyway, no outsized psychological signals on your tests. Graphs running in the—well, hmmm"—neck stretch—"we don't like the term 'normal' much anymore—let's say ordinary range, shall we?" (Nod.)

Lees unclenched his teeth. "Let's."

"One obvious blip—I don't think you liked your father."

"He wasn't a very likeable man."

"Why, hah, don't you tell me about that."

Lees crossed his legs. "Why the fuck should I?"

"Ah," said Hobart, and rose from behind the desk, circled around it and sat in a chair a meter away from Lees. "Why shouldn't you tell me about your father?"

"Cute," said Lees.

Hobart's nervous mannerisms ceased. He concentrated on Lees with an unwavering gaze. "The rule is," he said evenly, "whatever you don't want to talk about is, regularly, the precise thing you most need to discuss."

They stared at one another in silence.

Memories flooded Lees' mind.

†

* * *

He is a small boy in a sordid Maine trailer camp and he holds his father's large, moist hand and sees the tree falling on them and says, "Daddy, we go in. The tree is falling," and they look at the pine tree standing next to them as its branches waver in the wind of freshening storm, and he says, again, "Daddy, we go in," and they do as thunder and lightning begin and rain comes and, three minutes later, lightning splits the pine trunk neatly and the tree topples, shaking the trailer with the fury of its sudden fall, precisely where they had stood, unprotected.

His father's eyes are lemon-yellow and ravenous in his clammy albino-white face framed by dark hair, a pseudo-ascetic look cultivated for its "stagey mystery." His father's lemon-yellow eyes are always on him, at him, after him, wanting and digging and prying, "Do you see anything?" and, when he says no, the eyes are shadowed with . . . what? Fear? Disbelief? Distrust? Something . . . He is a little boy and he tells things he doesn't see—"The truck is crashing"—and they don't happen—the truck drives on safely—and, gradually, the eyes are less. Less on him, at him, after him and . . . bored? The word *fluke* comes into his life and he likes the word; it is safe, reassuring.

The sick white trailer with—LEES SEES—a red-letter wound on either side rolls over the long highways of America from Portland, Maine, to Galveston, Texas, to Hattiesburg, Mississippi, to Dayton, Ohio, to Charlotte, North Carolina—"Daddy, can't we stay? I like the school and the kids"—to Rapid City, South Dakota, to Billings, Montana, to Muskegon Michigan—"Can't we stay, Daddy? I like the lake"—to Laguna Beach, California, to Joplin, Missouri, rolls on and on through bad weather and flat tires and broken axles and overheated pickup engine and limps a little more each stretch of the endless trip like a blind animal running to death in pain, too sick to live, too tortured to die, too numb to shed its skin, too weak to be reborn.

He is seven and off-guard and the words come out of him without warning: *"Daddy, stop!"* he shrieks. *"Daddy, stop! The cars are crashing!"* and his father edges the rig off the road just before the intersection of Route 14 and Route 75 near Lake Benton in green, western Minnesota as two coupes

†

ram each other head-on like willful stags, bringing sudden combustion and pyramids of flame less than thirty feet away. The brief screams might have been theirs, and the lemon-yellow eyes turn back toward him, come around slowly, pushing the child's dread in front of them; the eyes are on him again, at him again, after him again and never give up again—"Don't badger the boy, Jack"—the lemon-yellow eyes never leave him alone again.

The manager of the stationery department of Harrod's was very polite. "I am sorry, Sergeant Clive. I've never seen a paper of quite this quality before and, other than checking all the quality stationers, I can make no suggestion as to locating its source."

"I see," sighed Clive.

The manager smiled brightly and handed Clive his business card. "But please do take my card, Sergeant. If you should discover the supplier, I would appreciate knowing their name. That is the sort of magnificent merchandise that Harrod's is always seeking to add to our inventory."

The request left Clive speechless and he exited the department store shaking his head in wonder at the man's effrontery.

Friday, Lees took tests.

In the morning, the Shipley Intelligence Test and the Minnesota Multiphasic Personality Index. In the afternoon, the Rorschach Test and the Thematic Apperception Test.

When it was all over, Hobart summarized the results. "I find you"—wink—"to be an intelligent"—tooth tap—"man with"—neck stretch—"basic social adjustment"—ear tug—"and excellent perceptive faculties." (Nod.)

"Pretty much what the dossier told you."

Pipe puff. "Yes. I would like to continue to talk with you a bit about your father. That's a strong enough distress to be worth pursuing."

Lees shrugged.

Clive stood outside Smythson's, 54 New Bond Street, and wondered whether to keep going or stop for lunch. He had

†

only four stationery shops left on his list that catered to clientele wealthy enough that they might carry such an expensive paper.

He sighed. What had the manager said?

"You might try to locate Cecil Gravender. He managed More's for many years before they went out of business. They were sold to Trafalgar Shares, the conglomerate, and the parent company closed More's two years ago, but they might have an address for Gravender."

Daft, thought Clive. I'll soon be chasing men without any names and names without any men.

He decided that the last four stationers on his list could wait until he'd had a grilled chop and a pint of lager to soothe his irritability.

Bloody letters, he thought.

Hughes stared at the glass case in the laboratory.

They'd put the bonnet in a vacuum case to protect it from elements that could foster further deterioration.

The lab technician shook his head. "We put it in the case nine days ago as you instructed, Inspector."

"Yes."

"It should be preserved perfectly since."

"Yes."

"But as you can see . . ."

Hughes' brain felt dull, slow.

The bonnet no longer resembled a bonnet. It was now no more than a small mass of black velvet with a trace of soiled white linen. No shape or form, merely a lump, dirty and decaying.

"Keeps up at this pace," continued the technician relentlessly, "in a month there'll be nothing there but dust."

"Yes," was all Hughes' dazed mind could conjure for comment.

Billy Topp, forty-two, was a muscular bantam in blue work shirt, work pants, hiking boots, red knit tie and suede aviator jacket. He had brown eyes, olive skin with a boozer's flush, a hawk nose and a handshake like an automobile crusher.

"Nice to meet you, General . . ."

†

140

Electric touch held too long.

Lees saw a cargo net break, cases falling, Topp hit on the head, driven down, limp. They released hands slowly, eyeing one another.

"That's right, General. Happened about six years ago. It's when I became 'sensitive.'" He turned to the man next to him. "He's got it, all right."

Dr. George Frounle, a pudgy sixty-one, with heavy black horn-rimmed glasses that gave him a rather froggy look above his natty blue blazer and gray flannel trousers, extended his hand. "George Frounle, General Lees. If Billy says you've got it, you do."

They took their places for breakfast in the small dining room—Stuart, Lees, Ann, Percy, Hobart, Frounle, Topp and Percy's nurse, Cynthia Logan, a well-groomed forty-three-year-old brunette with a straightforward, quiet manner and efficient eyes. The team leaders, Percy, Hobart and Frounle, talked about the problem, about the tests, about their expectations and, mainly, about Lees. They talked about his history; his health, physical, spiritual and mental; talked about his gift, his visions—dissected him like a laboratory animal as if he weren't present listening.

Lees sat rigidly, barely eating, mortally offended. He rejected them all, could not stand their sight, made almost no eye contact, offered no comments unless elicited and, then, the barest adequate response, could barely restrain himself from rising and marching from the room. He hated it all; he hated them.

What am I doing? Why am I here? I don't want to be here. Can't they all go away and leave me alone?

Please!

The bedroom had been cleared for tables and books and files and equipment. Topp sat on one side of a table with a chest-high barrier down the middle; Lees on the other. Frounle sat in a chair nearby.

"We'll begin with some simple tests trying to define General Lees' sensitivity level and areas. The first test is quite standard and ordinary. We have a deck of cards that consist, as you see, of four black shapes against a white background—

stars, circles, squares and crescents. One of you takes the deck, shuffles and begins looking at the cards, one at a time. The other will attempt to read the cardholder's mind and see the shape. We will start with General Lees as the 'sender' and Mr. Topp as the 'receiver.'"

Lees shuffled the deck, placed it in front of him, turned a card over and laid it flat—a circle.

Topp said, "Square."

Lees turned over a square.

"Square."

Circle.

"Crescent."

Star.

"Circle."

Crescent.

Topp shook his head. "I'm not getting it . . . I'm guessing."

Frounle looked up from charting cards and responses. "Please continue."

They went through the deck twice. One-in-four were the odds for pure guesswork. Topp had "received" a little less, twenty-two percent correct.

"Now, Mr. Topp, if you'll take the cards, we'll try the general as a receiver."

Frounle moved his chair so that he could record the sequence of cards turned by Topp. The first was a star.

Lees saw it clearly in his mind, said, "Star."

Topp turned a crescent.

It was easy. "Crescent."

Square.

"Square."

Star.

"Star."

Circle.

"Crescent, I think."

Crescent.

"Crescent."

Circle.

"Circle."

They went through the deck twice. Lees' accuracy rate was seventy-nine percent.

†

142

Topp and Frounle exchanged glances and Frounle said softly, "A remarkable score, General."

Lees shrugged. "I can do this all day. It doesn't mean anything."

Frounle cleared his throat. "Yes, well, perhaps. In any case, let us take a long luncheon break. This kind of mental work is . . . tiring. Meet back here at, mmmm, two o'clock. We'll repeat the same tests as a control measure."

Detective-Sergeant Clive's desk butted up against that of Detective-Sergeant Peters' in a small office next to Hughes' and down the hall from Stuart's. The two sergeants were sitting at their respective desks muttering about their respective headaches. Clive kept alternating his gaze from a map to a slip of paper with a name and address:

> Mr. Cecil Gravender
> Twombley Cottage
> Felpham

"Where in bloody blazes is Felpham?"

Peters glanced up. "South coast, near Bognor Regis."

Clive found it on the map. "Oh, grand—a drive down to the coast's just what I'd in mind for Sunday afternoon. And me with tickets to the football match."

Peters grunted. "You've the easy part, mate. You should have the finding of this Nicholas sod. Picture of the bastard in the hands of every copper from here to Edinborough and not a peep. And where'd he come from? Landlord at Brixton says he showed up a month ago and paid cash for a year's lease, so of course the bleedin' landlord didn't ask for references. At the taxi firm he showed papers, but registry says they must've been forgeries. And Birth Records don't seem to think there's ever been a Lucian Nicholas born in the UK. For all we can find, the bugger doesn't exist."

In the afternoon, Frounle and Topp repeated the tests with nearly identical results.

Frounle had a Sunday tutorial in Cambridge, so it was agreed to take a break and resume testing Monday.

†

* * *

Hughes sat on one of the plank seats of the steam launch tied to the pier of the River Police Station.

Clayton, his expert from the naval museum, stood in the launch examining its surfaces and fittings and angles and details. He was a lean man like Hughes, but shorter, sixtyish and balding with soft precise hands and skeptical brown eyes flanking a bent-bridge nose.

The late afternoon sun was fading and a chill crept across the Thames. The water's surface was translucent reds and golds and orange layered above the weedy greens and browns of the opaque depths.

Clayton sat facing Hughes. "You're quite right, Richard. This boat has aged remarkably since I examined it last week. It appeared dockyard new then. Now the boiler's rusting badly, the caulking's brittle and cracking, seams are opening and the wood—look at the wood." He squeezed an edge of his plank seat with thumb and forefinger. Chips and splinters came away and he held fragments up for Hughes to see.

Hughes nodded.

"Richard, the wood of this boat is rotting at a pace beyond the ordinary that I am helpless to explain."

Hughes looked away across the river toward Southwark. "It's almost as if . . . we have a century-or-so-old boat that was made new . . . and now . . . is returning to its appropriate state."

Clayton frowned. "Dear me, Richard—that's a very fanciful notion."

Hughes smiled. "I know. Think of it as an analogy or a metaphor rather than an explanation."

Clayton nodded. "All right. As an analogy, it fits. Still, we need an explanation, and—"

Hughes smiled again. "Yes. As an explanation it's not fanciful, it's quite mad."

Both men were silent.

The breeze blowing upriver had become chill.

Clive was irritable—as was beginning to seem almost his natural state—when he arrived at Felpham. Not only was this supposed to be his Sunday off, not only had he given up his tickets to the Arsenal–Tottenham football match, but early fall rain had blanketed the country south of London and his drive down had been tiring and cheerless.

He had received directions to Twombley Cottage over a pint of bitter at a local pub. It was outside Felpham, on the shore, a stucco bungalow painted a cheery blue and perched on a cliff overlooking the sea. Clive pulled into a tiny gravel drive and scampered up the steps to a cozy overhang that sheltered him from the rain. He dropped the polished brass knocker three times.

The man who answered the door looked old enough to have been the original Tiny Tim.

"Mr. Cecil Gravender?"

The old man's hair was thin and white, his face and hands wrinkled and his eyes a spectacled misty blue. He nodded slowly. "Yes."

"Sergeant Clive, Scotland Yard. You have been recommended as an authority on stationery and we need your help in identifying some note paper."

He opened the door wide. "Come in out of the rain, Sergeant. I'll be happy to help if I can."

He led Clive through a small neat kitchen where a pot of tea was steeping and into a slightly larger lounge with a bay window view of the Channel that, on a clear day, might have stretched to France. The room was amiably cluttered with elderly hardwood furniture, including a rolltop desk and stool that would have made Bob Cratchitt at home.

Gravender seated Clive in a straight-backed chair and brought strong tea in Royal Doulton cups and a plate of chocolate-iced cakes with raspberry jam layering. He sat at the desk, took a bite of cake and washed it down with a swallow of scalding tea. "How can I help you, Sergeant?"

Clive produced the second envelope. "This came with a letter on matching note paper"—he handed it across—"and we'd appreciate anything you can tell us about it."

Gravender's eyes had become alert and steady at first sight of the paper. He switched on a high-intensity gooseneck lamp clamped to the desktop and brought the light to bear.

Clive ate a cake, drank tea and watched the steady rain swell the strident sea below and hammer the window glass

†

with monotonous insistence. He stole occasional glances at the old man absorbed by the envelope. At last, Gravender set aside a magnifying glass and turned the envelope in his liver-spotted hands.

"Impossible," he muttered.

Clive frowned. "You can't identify it?"

Gravender spoke as if to a retarded pupil. "Certainly I can identify it, but the paper is impossible. Where did you get it?"

Perhaps it was the man's age or his quiet air of authority, for Clive lost his official manner, answered boyishly, "I asked first."

Gravender chuckled. "So you did." Then he laughed, shook his head in amusement and repeated, "So you did, Sergeant."

Clive set aside his teacup. "You said you can identify it."

"Yes, it is a More's paper."

"How do you know? There's no watermark."

"Sergeant, I was with More's from 1926 until a few months before they were sold to Trafalgar Shares, Ltd. The firm has been my whole life and I have recently completed a history of More's for private circulation. I doubt if there are as many as half a dozen papers ever produced, handled or sold by the firm that I can't recognize on sight. Of course, I can identify it."

He closed his eyes and recited as if reading.

"Yellow-Moon Notepaper, house patent 111, 59.1 percent best bond-grade linen, 6.2 percent industrial grade silk, 34.7 percent A-grade pulp-and-rice, uncoated brush-finish texture, colored with a special yellow dye that featured some extract of lemon peel. First manufactured in 1853 for Benjamin Disraeli."

He opened his eyes.

Clive regained his business manner. "I will require a current location list for stocks of that paper."

The old man chuckled again. "That will be a very short list, Sergeant, very short indeed."

"Why?"

"Mr. Disraeli had exclusive use of the paper until his death in 1881. As was custom, the firm then made it a reserve stock available to all registered clients, but, after seven years, the proprietors decided that the private paper of a great statesman

†

such as Mr. Disraeli should be retired altogether. That's why I said this paper is impossible."

The two men stared at each other.

"Sergeant, there has been no Yellow-Moon Notepaper manufactured since August of 1888."

The statement hung in the air between the men as palpable as stone, as fragile as thought.

Gravender broke the silence gently. "The final sales were on Christmas Eve day, 1888, and the remaining stock was destroyed. A small quantity, to be sure, but, owing to its extreme cost, a handsome gesture to the earl's memory nonetheless."

Clive felt angry and couldn't place the cause, snapped, "Nonsense! Look at the paper! It's fresh, crisp, new!" He controlled himself, said reasonably, "That envelope is not so much as six months old."

Gravender, nodded sagely as if acknowledging a well-scored point, rejoined, "That is why I said it is impossible."

"Forged manufacture?" Clive queried hopefully.

Gravender shook his head as if with great regret. "Chemical tests can determine its age and exact composition, but because of the complexity of the manufacturing process there isn't a firm in the world equipped to produce it. Replication would entail starting costs of . . . let me see now . . ." Gravender stared over Clive's shoulder squinting as if seeing at a distance, muttered to himself. "There would be the presses that would have to be special ordered to specifications . . . replication of the dye . . . a new source for that mix of pulp-and-rice . . . hmmmm." His eyes came back to Clive. "I should say start-up costs in the neighborhood of a hundred thousand pounds. And one would need the formulas and processing details, which only More's possesses. In point of fact, since old Mr. More is dead—only I possess."

Clive blinked, murmered, "Ridiculous."

"Yes, isn't it. May I tell you something else?"

Clive wished he wouldn't but said, "Please."

"I would need an ultraviolet light to be sure, but I believe this ink is also a More's private patent. Phoenician Blue—so-called because of a tiny content of royal purple dye extracted, in the ancient Phoenician manner, from the humble snail. Phoenician Blue, house patent 232, was only manufactured and sold by the firm in the years 1885–1888 and was abandoned due to its cost pricing it beyond any reasonable market."

Clive realized he was sweating like a pig, and not from the room's closeness or the heaviness of the rainy day. "But what you are saying is that this envelope does not exist."

Gravender saw Clive's discomfort, smiled and spoke in a soothing voice. "Not at all, Sergeant. Here it is. I am holding it. Obviously it does exist. I merely say it is *impossible* for it to exist."

Rubbish, thought Clive.

"Yes." The old man smiled as if reading his thoughts. Gravender rubbed the bridge of his nose gently. "There is a method to confirm this. You noted the paper has no watermark, but More's, like any sensible firm, had a means of identifying its own product against forgery. I don't have the chemicals here, but they're readily available at any laboratory. I'll jot down the formula for you. You take the solution and brush a very small amount on the lower left corner of the envelope back or one of the note sheets. If it is genuine, letters and numerals so pale as to be nearly white will appear. If the paper is genuine, it should read—More's, Yellow-Moon Note, followed by the month, date and year of manufacture, which—again should the paper prove genuine—would have to be in the years 1853–1888, exclusively."

"And if it should so prove . . ."

Gravender nodded. "Yes. Of course."

He took a scratch sheet, wrote some chemical symbols and figures on it, handed it and the envelope to Clive. He switched off the gooseneck lamp, stood and stretched, crossed to the bay window and stared out at the rain.

"Should it prove genuine, you would be brought back to the aspect of its fresh crisp quality, its obvious newness."

He turned and smiled gently at Clive.

"That is the cause of my original comment. Impossible."

Ann had gone up to London for mass and more spiritual counseling from Father Mueller. Lees was lonely all day, and when

†

she returned she was calm but reserved. The thought crossed Lees' mind that he was glad Mueller was a priest. He was under no illusions about the emotional rift growing between them or the attractiveness of his wife of forty years.

Still a damn fine-looking woman, he thought. I have to talk to her. Tell her. I can't.

He had bad dreams that he didn't remember.

Monday morning, Clive took the envelope back to the lab and had it tested, along with the first envelope and all the sheets of paper, with the formula Gravender had supplied.

The results were uniform.

The lower left corners of the stock each raised pale white letters and numerals in response to the lightly brushed chemical solution. The manufacturing signatures were identical:

MORE'S YELLOW-MOON NOTE AUGUST 31, 1888

Bloody hell! thought Clive.
He felt like crying and didn't know why.

He walked the headland before dinner.

The marsh grass was green and gold in the late afternoon light, a calf-high sea of vegetation that bent to the will of the breeze off the Channel. A quarter-mile off stood a small lighthouse, abandoned by its look, and from it strode the small figure of Billy Topp, moving easily through the wild weeds and coarse grass. He bore down on Lees, waved and smiled.

Lees forced a smile and a vague hand gesture.

Topp stared up at Lees with mildly mocking brown eyes. "Nice country for a stretch of the leg, General."

"Yes."

Topp squinted out at the churning sea. A gull skimmed the surface. "What I can't figure is why you fight this so much. Take me—I don't know why I got 'it' from the accident, but it's been a right boon. I get fifty pounds a day and found for these larks and that beats dockwork for certain."

Lees laughed. "I'm sure it does."

"I know you wouldn't do it for the money, but why go so hard against the grain? What's the point?"

†

Lees stared at the breakers foaming upon the shore.

Momentarily, a wave peaked offshore, looked like the lips of a man drooling.

Lees shuddered. Remembered.

The hospital is a low-slung, sprawling complex that hugs the cracked earth of sun-baked sagebrush country north of El Paso, Texas. Lees stands at the walk leading to the door of the administration building. The door is screened and its frame painted a cool blue. Lees does not want to go in, stands hesitant and sweating. His hair is cropped so close it looks like stubble and announces, along with the lonely yellow PFC stripe on his sleeve, that he is fresh from basic training. He appears too young to wear a soldier's uniform. His blue eyes are vulnerable, unsure. He shifts his weight from foot to foot, a mild dance of indecision. Sweats. Sighs. Begins to walk slowly toward the cool blue door.

Lees pushed memory aside, looked at Topp and smiled sadly. "I wish it were that simple for me, Billy. But my . . . 'gift' has a history. A family history." A morbid history, he thought. "A history that I'm not fond of or comfortable with."

Topp shrugged again, then hesitated. "I'd say something, but I don't like to talk out of turn."

"Go ahead."

"I've noticed blokes like you have a habit of takin' simple things and makin' them complicated, takin' schoolboy sums and turnin' them into riddles. Sometimes I think it's done for fun—like playin' at a puzzle. But you don't seem to be gettin' any laughs from your jigsaw."

Lees had a wild impulse to unburden himself, to dump the load, to confide in the straightforward soul of Billy Topp.

He fought it.

Said instead, "Right. No laughs at all."

Hughes and Clive were reflected in separate sections of the cracked mirror in Annie Mackey's bathroom. Horace Phipps, a quite short, very round and red-faced man, stood beyond the door frame and apologized for the tenth time.

"I would have come forward before, but I never connected

Annie with the murdered woman. I've many clients and can't keep in constant contact with the lot. I'd no idea she was missing until Saturday when a booking opportunity came up and I tried to locate her. Yesterday, the landlord finally told me that she hadn't been home since the seventh, and I went straight to the morgue."

The fat man shivered and his jowls quivered.

"Horrible sight that was . . ."

Clive wished the booking agent would shut up, but fear or horror or the thrill of being next to a sensational murder had loosed a torrent of loquacity, so Clive tuned him out and concentrated on a brown plastic vial half full of white powder. A tiny taste on his tongue tip triggered an immediate tingling.

"Cocaine," he said as he recapped the vial. "High quality."

Hughes nodded as he stared at the oily clear liquid in a half-empty vodka bottle resting on the sink's shelf. "Booze and drugs," he muttered without surprise.

Phipps nodded. "A drunk and a coke-head she was, but she was a stripper of rare fine talent. Great body, but a poxy face. If it hadn't been for the scars, Dark Annie'd have been a superstar."

Hughes' and Clive's heads turned as one and they asked in unison, "What was that?"

Phipps was startled. "Eh. . . ?"

"The name, man!" snapped Hughes. "The name!"

"Why, er, Dark Annie. She was mulatto, dusky she was. That was her professional name. Billed herself as Dark Annie."

Tuesday was the color test.

Morning and afternoon.

Lees put his hands through a slot in the barrier, touched a series of pieces of colored paper and pictures. He received nothing significant.

When Topp stared at the series, Lees got colors accurate at a rate of eighty-eight percent. He also was able to supply some details for more than half the pictures.

As a "sender" he was as flat as he had been with the cards.

"He's gettin' stronger, George."

Frounle nodded. "Yes, Billy. He's right, General. As the

tests become more complicated, your results become correspondingly amazing."

Lees ran a finger across the bridge of his nose. "I know, but my dreams, my . . . well, spontaneous activity seems in decline. How do you explain that?"

Frounle shrugged. "Perhaps psychic energy is similar to other kinds of energy. You have a supply that can be drained, must be recharged."

"Then all these tests might well be taking me farther away from the point: seeing something that might help stop the murders."

Frounle smiled. "Or it might not. Because the tests seem to be developing your gift."

Billy Topp grinned. "Damned if you do and damned if you don't, General."

Lees chuckled. "I'm glad my dilemma is amusing to someone. Somebody ought to get the missing laughs you mentioned yesterday, Billy."

Ann Lees rode a calm six-year-old gelding through The Rides.

It was pleasantly cool in the fading sun. The rolling, uncultivated fields were green with the brilliance of intense life just before death. The distant trees were tinged with the promised crescendo of color. The motion of the horse was soothing, flowed in her, eased her pain.

She was angry at Jim in a way she'd never allowed herself to be before. She'd never given herself permission to fully dislike that core of him that refused to submit or accept or surrender. His coldness, his increasing hostility to the tests, the testers, to everything, had peeled a layer from her vision. She now saw that all the genuine goodness in him, the courage, the love and concern, the decency he'd always displayed, could be discarded, in some sense negated, lost by his completely conscious choice of rebellion against reality.

And presently, that was the direction he was moving.

And, it made her furious. She felt tricked, deceived in the man she'd loved and lived with for forty years.

And anger has consequences.

She was realizing some of them.

She knew why she hadn't called Father Eric today. She had

†

reached for the phone . . . and stopped her hand. What was the sensation of anticipation?

There was something more in her than just feelings of friendship, some desire beyond that for spiritual advice and comfort; a need to be held and comforted and loved like a child . . . and like a woman.

There. She'd said it to herself, acknowledged the great, terrible, human fact; with her man turned inward and away, she had unmet needs; her unmet needs were pulling her, turning her toward a sensitive, attractive man.

Who happened to be a priest.

The horse cantered and she let the motion be in her and she felt flow and the the image of Eric's silvering, blond hair, his sinew-sculpted hands, their subtle strength and grace. The horse sensed her and carried her and she felt warmth. . . .

She pulled the horse up sharply, abruptly, and tumbled from the saddle in a near leap. She stood and breathed deeply and felt her face flush. Talk about clichés, she thought. Anger, tension, frustration with my man and riding a horse, thinking of another man, going limp and warm inside to fantasy and desire and the rhythmic motion of a mass between my legs.

She was ashamed.

Knelt in the grass with the horse pacing near.

Prayed.

She was especially warm and considerate at dinner and virtually seduced her husband at bedtime with perfume and a peignoir and supple touch. In his arms, she used her willpower and prayer and concentration to be with him and let no other shadow enter their bedroom as they made love for what, she later realized, must have been some number beyond the five thousandth time.

Lees dreamed.

A pillar of steam and spider legs overhead and crunching sounds and harsh clattering sounds and the smell of soot mingled with the smells of country—flowers and fruit and fresh air. He dreamed harsh clattering sounds and abrasive deafening sounds and shrieks of agony at periodic intervals

†

and mad derisive laughter and the looming blackness of the cabbie's no-face with the blind silver eyes.

He dreamed and only remembered scattered fragments when he woke.

Hughes and Clive sat silent in Sir Malcolm Stuart's office.

They had reviewed the case to date: "Dark Annie" Mackey as another name, not a perfect echo but a clear resonance of the Whitechapel crimes; the elusive Lucian Nicholas; the disintegrating bonnet and boat; the lab report on the stationery and the observations of Cecil Gravender and the More's marks just as he had predicted.

Now Stuart eyed them. And they looked away. Morning rain dripped on the wall of glass, obscuring the view of the near familiar world.

"What are you two suggesting?" asked Stuart.

Clive shook his head firmly. "I'm not suggesting anything, sir. Just reporting."

"Richard?"

Hughes lightly touched his perfectly knotted blue silk tie and smoothed nonexistent folds in the waistcoat of his impeccable gray suit. "Not so much a suggestion, Malcolm, as an expression of feelings. Feelings stimulated by the increasingly bizarre findings of our investigation."

"Which are...?" asked Stuart impatiently.

"That everything is clicking into place in a pattern we are being almost *led* to believe. As if a chain of evidence were being forged and fed to us, but evidence for a conclusion of no earthly use."

Stuart allowed himself a thin smile. "Come, come, Richard. Don't be so elusive. We aren't in court yet."

"Yes." Hughes smiled. "And that is the point. If the conclusion we are moved toward is correct, we never will get to court. You can't put the ... supernatural before a Queen's Bench."

"Are you saying that this case is supernatural?"

"Not quite. Only that the evidence so far certainly points to something ... extraordinary."

Clive's face was red and furious. "Rubbish! Pardon me, Inspector, but there's got to be a natural explanation for all this. We just need to find it, is all."

Hughes said softly, "Ah yes, but the finding seems increasingly distant. If we are to work away from the extraordinary explanation—we are, presently, going in the wrong direction. Rapidly."

Stuart frowned. "Let's cut across, Richard. Do you believe this is a case of the supernatural?"

The question hung suspended in the air, like an aura of anticipation and fear mingled with startling desire. The rain ceased as if shocked by the bald voicing of such an outrageous question.

"I'm . . . I'm not convinced," said Hughes.

Stuart and Clive breathed relief.

Not convinced yet, thought Hughes. But it mightn't take a good deal more.

The night was a warm, perfect evening for a party.

South of the Thames lay Kennington (known locally as The Oval after the Surrey County Cricket Club's stadium), an undistinguished area of small factories and working-class flats. Its back streets held a recently rediscovered treasure of Victorian homes. Middle and upper-middle income families had begun to renovate and restore them for the good property value near the heart of the city via auto over Vauxhall Bridge or underground on the Northern Line.

Adam and Jocylen Allen, an upwardly mobile late-thirtyish couple (he a barrister junior partner in a small prestigious law firm; she chief copywriter for a largish advertising agency), had invited the dozen most socially useful friends of their twin children (quaintly named Adam and Eve) for an eight-year-old's delight—an overnight housewrecking party.

By 9:48 p.m., the fourteen "little darlings" had eaten their way through eleven pounds of Yorkshire pudding, thirteen pounds of chips, two gallons of ice tea and one of milk, as well as tidying up with two bakery-special triple-tiered chocolate layer cakes. After gluttony, the children retired to the side yard for after-dark hide-and-shriek and other mild forms of sado-masochism, while Adam and Jocylen spelled one another for the horrors of yard-police duty alternated by the relative relief of sucking on gin-and-limes while shoveling away at the wreckage of the kitchen debacle.

At 10:01 P.M., the Hokey-Pokey came down the street.

It was a small wooden pushcart with a pointed-peak square canvas awning in chartreuse and raspberry stripes. Its wooden wheels rumbled on the stone street as it moved slowly, pushed by a short man in a straw skimmer calling his wares in a cracked baritone: "Ice cream! Cool ice cream!" The cart rocked with a shaking sideways motion as it rolled from pool of streetlamp light to tree-canopied shadows to pool of light again.

A small girl of not more than four skipped and hopped beside the cart, chanting in a musical singsong: "Hokey-Pokey, Penny a lump; That's the stuff To make you jump!"

Around the corner popped another pushcart.

And a third.

Both were unawninged, the second and larger cart pushed by a bull of a man in black suit and derby, while the third cart, a wheeled traylike contraption with a tall barrel in the center, was propelled by a dark-haired teenage boy. The wheel-and-axle grumbling of their carts blended with the Hokey-Pokey's to form a chorus like low contained thunder on the move. The vendors joined the skipping girl's singsong: "Knives sharpened! Sharp knives!" "Fish! Cheap fish! Fresh fish!" "Cool ice cream!"

"Hokey-Pokey, Penny a lump; That's the stuff To make you jump!"

Seven more people came around the corner, flocking about a fourth pushcart, loosing their vocal advertisements to the warm still air: "Flowers, fresh flowers!" "Get the *Gazette*! Latest news! New Ripper murder!" "Muffins! Hot muffins!" "Sam Hall—chimney sweep! Sam Hall—chimney sweep!" "Cat's meat here! Cat's meat man!" "Rabbit! Rabbit for sale!"

They were a ragged parade moving between pools of light and lakes of dark, like illusions in a shadowbox.

Silence fell on the side yard in fragments as a puzzle being fitted until each of the dozen children, attention drawn, ceased their noise altogether. They crept to the brick retaining wall that ran the twenty meters between homes and clus-

†

tered in a tight row, small curious faces, their noses hooked on top the wall, twenty-eight wide eyes peering across the street.

Trees to either side made a high proscenium with dark limbs drooping and a light rustle of leaves under small nervous feet.

Jocylen stood a few feet back in full dark, frowning with arms folded across her breasts, absently swirling the last ounce of her fifth gin-and-lime with her left hand.

The Hokey-Pokey stopped in front of the wall. The strawhatted man loosed the large wooden handles and wiped his hands on his long black apron. His white shirt-sleeves were clean, but his vest was spotted with dried ice cream of various flavor colors. He was old and soft-faced, with wrinkled skin like bleached leather and shiny button-brown eyes.

The small girl skipped in a circle beside the cart. Her toolarge boots were cracked and worn, and wobbled on her dancing feet. She was covered neck-to-boots by a blousy brown coat, and her dirty blond hair hung lank and long, eyes like black marbles peeped from beneath a knitted cloche hat of the same chartreuse and raspberry stripes as the cart awning. Her voice was piercing: "Hokey-Pokey, Penny a lump; That's the stuff To make you jump!"

"Adam, go get your father."

Her son did not turn his head. "I want to watch."

Jocylen's heart pounded as the parade came closer and she seized his small shoulder.

"Sharp knives!" "Fish!"

"Adam, go get your father! Instantly!"

"Ow! That hurts!"

The burly, derbied man put his foot to a pedal suspended beneath his cart. A grindstone mounted near the handles spun. He took a gleaming long-bladed knife and began to sharpen it against the spinning stone, sending small sparks shooting into still air.

The scrawny teenage boy, barefoot below his trouser cuffs, shirt-sleeves rolled, stopped his cart and tipped the barrel, spilling a short swift stream of water and silver fish onto the tray.

Jocylen put her long tanned face close to her son's pale,

freckled oval. "Run and get your father," she hissed. "Run!" He fled.

The two flower girls were shawled and bonneted, wearing black dresses and carrying wicker baskets of lilies and roses and gardenias. "Fresh flowers!" The fourth pushcart was the smallest of the quartet, hardly more than a deep box on wheels, bearing a mound of various chopped tissues in front of a wiry, cross-eyed, floppy felt-hatted man who cried in a thin tenor, "Cat's meat! Cat's meat man!"

Lights began to flick on in lower rooms of neighboring homes and, here and there, a window was raised or a door opened a crack.

Jocylen shivered despite the warm. She took a step closer to the silent, fascinated children.

The rabbit-seller was tall and cadaverous, with a small blue soldier's hat above a flowing auburn mustache and sharply pointed goatee. "Rabbits here!" He was supporting a pole on either shoulder from which, rear feet tied and heads dangling, bounced the bloody carcasses of fifteen brown rabbits. "Fresh rabbit!"

The muffin man was plump and balanced a wooden tray of muffins and rolls and ginger cakes on his head while ringing a small bell in his left hand, his white linen apron fluttering about his legs. "Muffins! Ginger cakes! Hot rolls!"

She heard the back door bang and her husband's voice. "Jocylen?!" The children were whispering and pointing.

The news-vendor wore a frock coat and a high gray hat, some bastard cross between a topper and a bowler, and had a bushy white beard that puffed out from his chin and face like a spiky aura. "Gazette here! Another murder in Whitechapel! Ripper strikes again!" From his hand dangled a broadsheet, reaching from above his waist to past his knees:

GAZETTE
September 9, 1888
ANNIE CHAPMAN MUTILATED
RIPPLER SLASHES ANOTHER POOR WOMAN
WHITECHAPEL REIGN OF TERROR

†

"What the hell. . . ?" her husband muttered.

She grimaced. "It's not the little theater guild doing an historical pageant."

"Fresh flowers!"

"Cat's meat man!"

"Sam Hall—chimney sweep!"

"Hot muffins!"

"Ripper murders another in Whitechapel!"

"Knives sharpened!"

"Fish!"

They hovered near their row of carts making small movements back and forth in a contained space. They were pale-skinned to near translucence and shiny-eyed, but oddly oblivious, blank, fixed, their voices an unwholesome a capella mixture of bass, baritone, tenor, contralto and soprano, with the girl's piping falsetto leading the choral dissonance: "Hokey-Pokey, Penny a lump: That's the stuff To make you jump!"

There was a conglomeration of smells now that they were close, a stew of fish, flowers, chopped meat, dead rabbit, coal dust, sweat, bread and some other, overriding aroma—sickly sweet and choking, like a dead forest creature rotting in a heap of withered flowers.

"SamHallRabbitFishFlowersCat'smeatRipperKnivesHokey-PokeyPenny—"

"*Stop! Shut up! Stop! Stop! Stop!*" Adam senior bellowed like an enraged bull.

Instant silence and cessation of movement.

The street vendors froze.

Doors opened and people crept onto porches.

Adam moved to the wall and set his half-empty drink on it. "Who are you people? What are you doing here?"

Their heads turned toward the wall slowly, in unison, with an odd cocked mannerism, an attitude of locating by ear rather than eye, as if dependent on some strange radar or sonar, not sight. "Ice cream . . . knives . . . cat's meat . . ." they muttered.

Justin Firbanks, Ninth Viscount Saltmare, a short, sullen boy, squeaked, "Hokey-Pokeys sell ice cream! Can we have some ice cream, Mr. Allen?"

†

Adam didn't even look at him. "No."

Justin pouted. "I want ice cream! I have my own money." Before Adam or Jocylen could move, he scrambled over the wall. "Come on everyone—my treat!"

Nightmare chaos. Children climbing and leaping, Adam and Jocylen tackling and tugging, trying to pull back first one, then another child; the street-vendors in motion, children scrambling among them, shrieking and laughing; Adam and Jocylen over the wall; the brute traders banging into them, each other, the scurrying children, grappling at the air with clumsy arms; the chimney sweep tripping over Eve, falling, his heavy brushes knocking Jocylen down; Adam lurching into the side of the Hokey-Pokey, bruising a knee; the shrill cries, now excited by some resonance of fear and hostility stimulated in the vendors, rising in volume and pitch toward the shrill peak of human voice that scrapes nerve endings like chalk squeaking on slate: *"Flowers! Fresh Flowers!" "Cat's meat man!" "Sam Hall—Chimney sweep!" "Ice cream!" "Rabbit!" "Muffins!" "Cheap Fish!" "Ripper strikes again!" "Sharp knives!" "Hokey-Pokey, Penny a lump; That's the stuff To make you jump!"*

Justin shoved a pound note at the Hokey-Pokey man.

The old man reached as if experimentally, unsure; he caught Justin's left arm on either side of the elbow; grinned maniacally as if pleased and excited by solid contact.

He bent the boy's arm backward until it snapped.

Justin screamed and fainted.

The knife sharpener staggered toward Adam. *"Sharp knives!"*

He lurched and Adam dodged too late and the bright blade skimmed Adam's left forearm, opening a long thin red line and stinging him. Adam shoved the vendor's chest with his right arm and the vendor fell. The knife sharpener sat curiously smelling the knife blade. Licked the edge. Blood was on his tongue.

He smiled. For a fraction of a second, his bright, fixed eyes cleared, as if his blindness had been lifted.

"Get in the house!" Adam shrieked.

The vendors froze momentarily and children clambered over the wall, dropping into the dark as Adam scooped the

†

unconscious form of Justin Firbanks into his arms and ran for the wall.

Jocylen, already over, turned and screamed, *"Adam! Look out! Behind you!"*

The knife sharpener was at his back. *"Sharp knives!"*

Adam tossed Justin, and Jocylen caught him, staggered, nearly fell, then stood upright. Adam seized his gin-and-lime, whirled, threw the drink into the hazel-marble eyes, ducked and then hesitated in horror.

The liquid slid down the knife-sharpener's eyes like water on glass.

"Sharp knives!"

Adam tripped the man, sending him sprawling, and did a two-handed vault over the wall. He took Justin back from his wife as they ran after the children toward the safety of their home.

The vendors were lined along the wall, straining against it but unable to breach it, as if solid things were unfathomable. They leered and cried into the dark yard: *"Cat's meat!" "Fish!" "Rabbit!"*

Adam and Jocylen burst through the back door just behind the children, and Adam laid the pale, wounded boy on the kitchen table, slammed the door closed and locked it.

"Joss—count the children and get them upstairs! Then phone the police. I'll lock all the doors and windows and bring Justin up to a bedroom. After you get the police, call Dr. Hastings. I think his arm must be broken and he's in shock."

Outside, the vendors calmed, stood stupidly for a moment, then regrouped.

They began to move in line down the streat again, like a shabby circus or carnival parade, marched in slow rhythm in and out of the pools of light, the lakes of dark, moving shadows once more. They resumed their mournful cries of minor commerce: "Fresh flowers! Flowers!" "Ice cream!" "Hot muffins! Ginger cakes!" "Sam Hall—chimney sweep!" "Rabbit for sale!" "Cheap fish!" "Whitechapel murder! Ripper strikes again!" "Sharp knives!"

They turned a corner. Only a high, shrill singsong trailed in their wake, like an echo dying down a barren mountain slope:

†

"Hokey-Pokey, Penny a lump; That's the stuff To make you jump!

Jocylen had watched the procession from a corner upstairs bedroom porch. The last sight she had of them was the chartreuse-and-raspberry-striped awning of the Hokey-Pokey, the possessed skipping and dancing of the small girl. Her nerves screamed at the sound of the obsessive chanting, the quatrain jingle, until she clapped her hands over her ears to shut it out.
When she removed them, there was silence.
Nothing audible on the pregnant night air.

Later, the Kennington police were politely reserved, attempting to mask their ordinary skepticism. Patrols could not locate the vendors. The only things that remained were the boy's broken elbow and the cut on Adam Allen's forearm, a few dead and rotten fish in the street and, in the grass, some flowers knocked from a vendor's basket. The flowers were dried beyond old, barely held their form under observation and dissolved into dust when touched. They had a sickly sweet smell that cloyed and gagged.
The report, written the next day with skepticism unmasked, was not passed on to the Metropolitan Police for several weeks.

Lees touched documents through the slot, but got nothing.
Topp read them silently and Lees recited them into a tape recorder, 91 percent verbatim, even as they progressed from reproductions of simple instructional signs:

NO RIGHT TURN ON RED

to children's stories:

That day when Pooh and Piglet tried to catch the Heffalump . . .

to newspaper stories and magazine articles:

As the Reagan era nears an end, Mrs. Thatcher remains the symbol of European neo-conservatism . . .

†

to a dictionary:

Coefficient of Performance, Thermodynamics. A constant that denotes the efficiency of a refrigerator, expressed as the amount of heat removed from a substance being refrigerated divided by the amount of work necessary to remove the heat.

to technical journals:

Notwithstanding the pioneer work done by Helgstrom and Bernier in Synchrogenetics, or Fraser's signal studies on termination dysfunctions in polydiffuse ortho-sychretic-genesis, it seems abundantly clear that the helix-labastrade . . .

As a sender, Lees was, again, nonproductive.

At the end of the day, Topp slumped in his chair and shook his head. "I'm bushed, certain. I tell you, George, it's like he's got a wire in my head and drains me dry. I can *feel* him pulling my thoughts out like a bloody vacuum."

Father Eric Mueller had left for his rescheduled luncheon with his publisher three times; each time he had forgotten something—a page of notes, his money, a clipping he wanted to share; three times he had returned to the rectory, retrieved the item and left, again, with the feeling of something missing.

The fourth time he stood in the courtyard, hesitant to leave. Again the sun was high, hard, and the fall air was tangy with the river.

It was as before: the arched door; the fork in the walk; the chapel and the rosebush.

"Lord. . . ?"

He listened.

"Lord. . . ?"

He walked, self-consciously, to the chapel door and opened it. The plank of light revealed no one; the chapel appeared empty. He closed the door, stared at the pewter handle.

He knew.

He was waiting for a call from Ann Lees, expecting it and not wanting to miss it and anticipating it. That was alright—

wasn't it? He was concerned for her. And for her husband. He was in this at the Lord's bidding, and only fools ran from such a call. That was all—wasn't it?

He knew.

Sometimes when they talked, he looked at the set of her head, just so, and light came streaming through her hair, and her radiance, even in her pain, shocked him. Or, talking on the telephone, he would strain to hear all the tones of her voice, try to see her in his head, imagine the fullness of her lips as her mouth parted to speak, and he would be struck by . . . recognition. Recognition of her, her womanhood; of himself, his manhood; recognition of . . . It was so hard to say, even in the privacy of his mind.

He threw back his head and laughed aloud. What privacy? He shrugged to God.

Recognition of the stirrings of romantic love, stirrings invoked by a mature, complete woman of subtlety, intelligence and warmth. And faith. The same faith as his own. And that was really it.

His subconscious was toying with a notion that was, per se, a natural, healthy inclination made impossible by the reality of the situation. Non-acceptance of such clear reality was rebellion and fantasy.

Father Mueller laughed again. You don't like this package? Fine. We'll take the same temptation and repackage it in a more sophisticated form.

He sighed. He knew he would have to dredge up his feelings and motives and look at them; kill the inappropriate desires—with compassion.

He reopened the chapel door and went in; his publisher could wait; some things were more important than others.

Lees and Hobart met in the library for a pre-dinner drink.

The room was vast and cool with modest light, a sanctuary of book-filled walls and soft furniture, muted colors and silent carpet, permeated by the smell of leather and a sense of serenity. Lees and Hobart nursed whiskies at opposite ends of a large couch.

Hobart stretched his neck, crossed his legs and tapped his teeth with the rim of his crystal tumbler. "I, er, wanted to

†

talk to you, eh, General"—wink—"because I begin to feel, heh-heh, rather a fifth wheel." Nod. "If you won't"—watch check, cuff shoot, drink sniff—"use me"—grin, wink, nod—"how can I be of service to you?"

The final phrase combined with the cool of the room to jar Lees with its echo.

"How can I be of service to you?" asks the bony bald man with kind brown eyes.

The cool office inside the blue door is dimly lit, a vast relief from the pitiless Texas sun. Young Lees stands tongue-tied, still sweating in his olive uniform. His blue eyes flick about the room restlessly, barely registering the plain hard furniture and tan walls and chipped linoleum floor, seeking to hide from the calm, even gaze of the gentle man.

"My name," he forces out, "is Jim Lees," and then rests, exhausted by the effort of conjuring the five words. He waits, hoping he isn't trembling.

The man waits. Finally, he says with a smile, "That's a good beginning, but it's not quite enough. Is there . . . someone you know here?"

Lees nods.

"A patient?"

Lees nods.

"A friend?"

Lees shakes his head—no.

"A relative?"

Lees nods.

"My father," he croaks, "Jack Lees."

"And you wish to see him, visit with him?"

Lees nods—yes, but his mind screams *no*! I don't want to see him! I don't want to be here! I don't want anything to do with him, but . . .

The man rises from behind his desk. "I think we can arrange that without too much difficulty."

"General—are you feeling ill?"

The bare fireplace came into focus and then, as he turned his head, Hobart's worried face. He really does look like a chipmunk, thought Lees irrelevantly.

†

He smiled. "I had a memory flash. I'm alright now."

Hobart leaned forward, intent, nervous mannerisms discarded. "Perhaps the memory flash was jogged by my query. If so, that might be something useful to talk about."

Lees shook his head. "Not just now, Dr. Hobart. Perhaps later."

After dinner Wednesday evening, Lees sat in an easy chair in another bedroom of the guest wing.

It was dark and on the wall were projected a series of slides. The slides progressed, over several hours, in complexity from colors to shapes to colored shapes to objects to scenery to people to scenery with people. Each slide was projected for a minute. Lees sat silently and concentrated on the images. Topp lay on a couch in the next bedroom, in darkened silence, trying to read Lees' thoughts. He spoke whatever he received into a tape recorder.

This test marked a significant change, for Billy Topp began to "read" Lees significantly. He scored 61 percent on colors and shapes, 59 percent on objects, and was able to give some accurate detail of scenery and people on 53 percent of those slides.

Topp nodded as Frounle read the figures. "For the first time, I felt the connection clear when the general was sending."

Lees agreed. "I felt a kind of tug in my head," he said.

Frounle was ecstatic. "It's obvious we're making enormous progress. Your power is growing."

Just what frightens me, thought Lees. And duty condemns me to cultivate my worst fear.

What Clive would later refer to as "the chases" and Hughes the "puzzle" began simply enough that Thursday morning, September 22, 1988, around eleven A.M.

Constable Felix Blatchford, having relieved himself in the men's WC, was strolling along the subway platform of the Whitechapel underground station when he froze. Straight ahead was a standing train. The door of the car directly in front of his was open. Framed in the doorway was a medium-

†

sized man in a tan whipcord suit, brown shirt and tan tie. His face was blunt-featured, bearded.
His eyes appeared to be as silver as polished coins.
He smiled directly at Constable Blatchford.
The door closed with a soft derisory hiss. The train rolled out of the station.
Lucian Nicholas! thought Blatchford. It's him! He ran for a telephone.
Nicholas changed from the Metropolitan Line to the Central at Liverpool Street and appeared a few minutes later at Holburn Station, changing from the Central Line to the Piccadilly Line.
Desk-Sergeant John T. Furbey, off duty, was making a train change the reverse of the silver-eyed cabbie and passed him on the platform. It took twenty rapid paces and half a minute for the glimpsed face to register on the sergeant. He stopped, turned, paused to be certain and then began to shoulder his way back through the crowd. He made it to the platform edge as the train pulled out and saw the face of the suspect through a disappearing window. The cabbie seemed to look at him, seemed to smile.
John T. Furbey ran for a telephone.
Both phone communications were received at the Yard by a switchboard trainee, Probationer-Constable Glen Godec, who took the initiative to call an all-car-alert as well as notifying Sergeant Clive.
Within minutes, patrol cars converged upon stations all along the Piccadilly Line. Patrol-Sergeant Dave Dahlby and Probationer-Constable Donna Hastings left their car just in time to see the suspect emerging from the Hyde Park Corner station. They gave chase, but he disappeared into the massive noontime crowd, and a scouring of the area for several hours by nearly fifty detectives and plainclothsmen could not locate a further trace of him.

At Hedgemore, a new phase of the tests began.
The bedroom light was muted. Lees lay on the bed, shoeless and in casual dress.
Frounle spoke soothingly. "So what we're going to do, try

†
167

first, General, is simple hypnosis. We're going to see if that can dredge up your dreams clearly enough to provide some useful detail. Later today, we may try hypnosis combined with some of the sodium amytol family of drugs. That process is a bit more rigorous because you don't so much remember the dreams as reexperience them. Clear, so far?"

"Yes."

"Are you relaxed?"

Lees laughed. "No, Dr. Frounle, I am not relaxed. I'm beginning to wonder if I will ever be relaxed again. Let's just get on with it, shall we?"

Frounle nodded. "Can you approximate the date when you began having the vision dreams?"

"I can do better than that. I can pinpoint it. I had the first dream on the night of October 9, 1985. I don't suppose I'll ever forget that date or the date of the second, when I knew this was going to be an ongoing process. The morning of October 18, 1985."

Frounle blinked. It made him look froggier. "I see. Quite precise. Then, we'll try for those two."

"Whatever . . ."

He used a gold pocket watch on a gold chain—time rocking gently back and forth beneath his somber, kind, froggy face.

"Watch the watch, General . . . see how it sways . . . the gold is attractive . . . you like the watch . . . you like the motion . . . you like the sway . . . you feel good watching the watch. . . ."

Lees lost the face, the room; he saw only the gold watch, the chain, the sway . . .

"You feel so good you are relaxing . . . relaxing . . . even getting tired . . . how surprising—your eyelids are heavy . . . they want to close . . . so just let them close . . ."

Lees lost the watch, closed his eyes.

". . . You're going to go into a peaceful sleep . . . you'll remember what is asked . . . you will recall the dreams vividly . . . you will sleep and tell us the dreams of October ninth first, then the dream of October eighteenth . . . you will remember the dreams and tell them to us as you remember— what you see and hear . . . I will tell you when to wake . . . I will say, 'General, the nap is over—wake,' and I will clap my

†

hands . . . when I do, you will wake and remember everything, but you will be rested . . . do you understand, General?"

Lees' voice was slurred, heavy, distant. ". . . Yes."

Billy Topp lay on a bed in semi-darkness in the next room. He was receiving already; he saw something round and shiny moving rhythmically; he heard snatches of Frounle's words. He felt as if he should take a nap.

Lees was in a hansom cab in Whitechapel.

The night air was grimy and heavy in the hot, narrow street. The driver whipped the horse, driving rapidly despite the close openings and angles of the fences and buildings. People jumped aside and pressed themselves flat against the fences and walls and shouted. The quirky gaslight revealed some faces, concealed others as they spun by. The seen faces were frightened. Lees was frightened. The people were pale and pinched and looked . . . lost. His clothes were tight, uncomfortable and the top hat felt heavy on his head. The noise of the horses' hooves and the iron wheels deafened him, kept him from thinking.

He felt strange and afraid.

The carriage rolled, slowing, into a broad street. The building and its legend loomed ahead:

The Great General Hospital
for East London

The cab stopped near a lamppost. There was a peephole from the driver's seat down into the carriage. Blind, silver eyes appeared in the dark.

" 'Ere's where you get out, guv. End o' the line."

Lees fumbled out of the cab, started walking as if pulled. There were crowds of people and he shrank from them as if diseased. Them or him? He didn't know. He walked. He walked rapidly, turned down a side street, was alone, hurried into angles. He heard a cry, ran, opened a door in a board fence, crossed a courtyard, exited through another fence into another street.

†

A house, steps, a fence, a man astride a woman's fallen body. A man with a knife.
Ripping her.
Cracking bones, tearing flesh, spraying blood.
Ripping her.
He turned, saw Lees.
They stared.
He was small, sallow-skinned, with lank brown hair and luminous eyes. He smiled.
"Too late."
Lees saw the blood-drained body. Shuddered.
The man rose and turned. His hands and wrists and forearms were covered with blood; the knife winked silver patches among the red ooze.
He began walking toward Lees.

"Leave that dream, General. Leave it. That dream is gone... do you understand me?"
Lees was sweaty and had been writhing on the bed as a patient might fight a straitjacket or restraints; he slumped back and his breathing slowed.
"Are you all right, General?"
"Yes."
"Shall we go on?"
"Yes."
"Then, I want you to remember the dream of October 18, 1985."

The cab, the streets, the people, the great street, Silver-Eyes, the clothes, the walking.
He passed a gas lamp with a crumpled newspaper caught at its base. He saw only the date: August 31, 1888.
The walking, the twisting side streets, the fence doors, the man, the woman, the knife.
Ripping her.
Recognition.
The Ripper coming for Lees.

"General, the nap is finished."
The sound of two hands clapping.

Lees sat upright, shivering and sweaty. In a few moments a drawn-looking Topp came in; he shook his head.

"Ugly dreams, General. Ugly."

Lees snapped, "I didn't ask you to invade them."

Topp opened his mouth, closed it and sat silently.

They listened to the tape recording.

Afterward, Lees shook his head. "Nothing new there."

Frounle said, "Fascinating."

"I'm glad you find my discomfort so intriguing," Lees snapped. "Would you like me to do it again?"

Frounle sighed. "Yes, General. This afternoon. With the drug."

Clive sat at his desk while a standing Hughes and Peters flanked him, resting their fists on the surface. The trio stared at a map of the London tube system spread out on the desktop.

Clive finished marking it with a black grease pencil. Hughes shook his head with distaste while Peters snorted, "Jumps right out at you, doesn't it?"

Clive nodded. "Whitechapel Station, Metropolitan Line; change at Liverpool Street to Central Line to Holburn; change to Piccadilly Line for Hyde Park Corner—the station nearest the first murder."

Hughes said, "Thumbing his nose at us. Going from the area of the original crimes to the area of the first re-creation."

Clive smiled. "Yes, but is he saucy enough to do it again? If he does, we can have him."

Peters frowned. "You're making it too simple. When will he ride and what line and where'll he start."

Clive pulled at an ear. "I'd think he'd ride peak hours again—if he's going to do it. Makes it easier to give the slip in a crowd."

"Yes," said Hughes. "And it doesn't matter where he starts. The second murder was here—on the Thames—so he has to ride either the Northern Line, Victoria Line, Circle Line or the District Line." He jabbed the map with an index finger. "And there are only five stations in the immediate area of the river-murder site. Pimlico, Vauxhall, Waterloo,

Westminster and Embankment. We cover those lines and those stations at morning, noon and evening rush hours."

Peters scratched his chin. "A man to a train on the lines and a trio for each station?"

Hughes nodded. "Yes. Emergency priority. Pull anybody from anything. I'll brief Sir Malcolm and buck any complaints straight to him."

Peters frowned. "Be a bloody big detail. Several hundred men at least."

Hughes said grimly, "However many it takes."

Clive smiled for what seemed the first time in weeks, smiled broadly and chuckled as he touched the map as if it were a talisman. "Come on, laddie—be too big for your britches just once more."

In the afternoon, the IV was in Lees' eyes.

The light shone through the vaguely amber fluid.

Frounle's voice was already distant. ". . . trying a number of members in the sodium amytol family to facilitate the memory-reexperiencing process . . . small doses act as sedatives, slightly larger doses as hypnotics . . . experiment to find the best facilitator for you . . ."

The watch was in front of Lees' eyes—the watch, the chain, the motion, the rhythm, the voice.

". . . relaxed . . . heavy lids . . . sleepy . . . remember . . ."

Dreams ran together and were jumbled.

Always the carriage and Silver-Eyes; sometimes the taxi as well; always the hospital; sometimes the walk was faster, slower, different details; always the newspaper—sometimes the year was 1888, sometimes 1988.

Always the woman.

Always the Ripper.

Always the *ripping*.

Always the recognition, the horror.

Always the fear.

In the evening, they tried another combination, another related drug. The results were slightly better, the dreams a little more differentiated, a little more sequential—but not fully.

†

Percy observed the evening session and was worried about Lees obvious discomfort and alarming blood pressure.

Lees was haggard and withdrawn afterward, and Ann watched over him as he slept. She sat in a chair near his bed with a soft light on. She tried to read a Graham Greene novel but kept setting it aside and staring at her husband, noticing the changes. His skin was pale and slack. Tension, worry and age lines looked like gouges in his face, like gullies and crevices. His eyes were hollowed and the sinking flesh beneath them was darkening. And he slept fitfully, curled tight, head buried and shoulders hunched, as if in defense against invasion.

She alternated between sorrow and sympathy for his ordeal and anger at his willfulness. She prayed for him, for the children, for others.

At 1:10 Friday morning, Bryan Fox, an unemployed actor, boarded the Victoria Line at the Oxford Circus Station. He was irritable after an evening spent at a producer's flat, where it had become all too clear that the producer was gay and more interested in Bryan's body than his career.

He settled into a seat and let the rocking motion of the train, the monotony of the barely seen tunnel walls, lull him into mindlessness.

In a few minutes the train stopped at Green Park Station. The doors hissed open and, at an angle, he saw a man walking toward his car—a man of medium height and stocky build, wearing a three-piece gray whipcord suit, a gunmetal shirt and navy tie. His face was blunt-featured, and he had sandy hair and a full beard. But it was his eyes Fox noticed most.

His eyes were dead silver.

He stepped into the car. The door hissed shut.

They were the only occupants of the car, but, as the train started, the man moved to a seat directly across from Fox, sat, raised his face and stared directly into Bryan Fox's eyes.

The silver eyes were awful. Bright as polished mirrors, but blank as stone walls, with no reflection inward or outward. And yet ... there were *things* in those eyes—shapes, movement, visions ...

Fox saw his mother lying in a pool of blood, stabbed by a

jealous drunken boyfriend. Bryan remembered being three years old and finding his mother thus, remembered the fear and anger and hatred and his tears of impotence. Bryan had the urge to kill the man sitting across from him.

The train roared through the subterranean cavern.

Things in the silver eyes, crawly things, neither human nor beast, creepy things without names.

Victoria Station stop; doors hissing open; five people leaving other cars; seven people entering other cars; doors hissing closed and the train picking up speed.

Silver eyes sucking his brain.

Fox saw himself shoving a radio, wristwatches, costume jewelry, a woman's gold compact inlaid with mother-of-pearl and inscribed *With Love* from her husband, a man's gold cigar case inscribed *With Love* from his wife—things he had stolen from a Knightsbridge flat—saw himself shove them across the counter of a grubby shop off Portobello Road; saw the pinched face of the man counting a mean stack of one-pound notes; saw himself grab the man's collar and shake him until he added ten notes to the small pile; remembered the grubby, soiled feel of the money, as if it had been packed away in grease for years; saw himself read the newspaper advertisement pleading for the return of the compact and cigar case—"items valued for personal sentiment"—with an offer of reward and a guarantee of "no questions asked."

Saw blood and fire in the silver eyes.

Felt murder and terror in his heart.

The man smiled at him and it was like an icy hand clamped on his intestines, squeezing until his bowels screamed in pain.

Stockwell Station.

The train was moving again and Fox was unwilling to lift his eyes from the bouncing floor, but saw something in the floor not really there: a face on a television program, a face in a newspaper reproduction of a photograph, the face of a man wanted in connection with the Hyde Park and river murders and the murder of a policeman, a blunt-featured face with sandy hair and full beard.

And dead silver eyes.

†

The face floated on the floor.

Fox's fear choked him, filled him, but, as if without consent of his will, his head raised up slowly, bringing the floating newspaper face up from the floor with it until it was superimposed on the man seated across from him.

They matched.

The man laughed.

Only the two of them in the car and no word spoken, no smile offered, no joke or jibe or quip or jest made, but he laughed and the laugh was completely absent of humor, with no comedy or satire or proportion in it, merely the vacant meaningless laugh of lunacy, a horrible laugh bringing with it the icy hand clamped to Fox's guts again.

It's him! Lucian Nicholas! The man the coppers want.

Brixton Station.

End of the line.

The doors hissed open. The man rose and walked out, his hard-soled shoes making the concrete of the platform ring.

Follow him! That's mad, he'll kill me.

Fox rose as if in a dream and stepped off the train.

They were alone on the platform, the man already distant, moving into shadow. The doors hissed shut. The train moved. Fox stood rooted and the man turned his head, looked over his shoulder, eyes gleaming. "Don't follow me, boy. Call the bloody police."

He kept on walking. Laughed. Disappeared.

Fox stared around. Brixton! he thought. What the fuck am I doing in bleeding Brixton? He had meant to get off at Victoria Station, his usual stop, and didn't know why he hadn't. Christ Almighty! What a balls-up!

He went to look for a telephone.

Lees awoke in pre-dawn with a suggestion of gray at the windows not illuminating the heavy darkness of the bedroom but graining the dimness just enough to imply shapes, intimate the existence of form in the negation of the lightless atmosphere.

Had he been dreaming of trains and tunnels?

Ann slept beside him, yet he felt alone.

†

* * *

Lees feels alone despite the kind, bony, balding man walking beside him under the oppressive Texas sun. It is a hundred yards across cracked clay and surface sand to the ward building where his father is a patient.

Lees says nothing, needing all his courage to keep from running, and the kind man recognizes his fear, keeps a considerate silence. Their feet make crisp, rhythmic sounds on the barren ground.

The ward looms ahead, a one-story concrete-block structure the color of faded whitewash with a flat roof. Set in one side is a green metal door with a small square of safety glass at eye level protected by metal bars. Above the door is a sign, freshly painted black letters on a brilliant white background. It seems to glow in the glare of the sun, to swim out away from the wall, the building, to drift in the air insolently, like a challenge, a seduction, an insult.

Lees sweats and walks doggedly and cannot take his eyes from the sign that grows as they near, until it finally seems to dominate the harsh landscape, the day, his mind, his life, the world:

VIOLENT WARD—MAXIMUM SECURITY
NO ADMITTANCE UNLESS ACCOMPANIED
BY HOSPITAL PERSONNEL

They stop at the door. The bony man fits a key in the lock, turns it, twists the knob. The door opens on a gray-painted corridor, a tunnel to despair. They step in and a guard peers out an open window square, nods at the gentle man.

"How yew, Dr. Ba-yuh-less?"

"Just fine, Fred."

The door closes behind them.

Lees jerked his mind away from Texas and back to Hedgemore with a wrench that felt almost physical. He slipped quietly out of bed and padded out to the balcony in his pajamas to smoke a cigarette and shiver in the chill dark

†

and fight another battle in the war raging across the weary landscape of his soul.

The report was on Clive's desk when he arrived in the morning and he digested it almost before he finished reading it.

He stared at the subway map: Green Park to Brixton. The nearest interchange station to Hyde Park Corner straight to the scene of the second murder. Damn! We forgot about Colson. Thought of the river murder as number two!

Clive experienced a moment of shame at such a cavalier dismissal of the murder of a brother officer and swore aloud. He didn't ride in peak hours! We'll have to cover clock-round!

He muttered aloud, "And I bet he'll not ride again until tomorrow . . . but, we'll have to cover today anyhow. Bastard!"

Detective-Sergeant Peters stared across their adjoining desks and shook his head. This case is sending old Clive round the bend. He's going potty.

Lees lay on the bed again.

He looked like a shackled animal. Percy had insisted on heart, pulse and blood-pressure monitoring. His left arm was cuffed; his chest was salved and electrodes attached; an IV stabbed into his right arm and the tubes and wires spread out from him in various directions, the visible ganglia of his ordeal.

He lost the people in the room, one by one—Dr. Percy; Nurse Logan; Hobart. Then, Frounle, leaving only the watch, the chain, the motion, the soft, slow voice.

He dreamt again.

This time the combination of drugs worked.

His dreams separated, individuated, accepted chronology. He dreamt seven of them in the two-hour morning session, and eight of them in the two-hour afternoon session.

The carriage, then the carriage that began as a cab. Silver-Eyes the Victorian driver, then Silver-Eyes the Victorian driver who first appeared as a contemporary hackie. The narrow streets, the Victorian refuse people, the broad street with the hospital, the walk. The passersby and the whore calling

†

his name and the newspaper snarled about the lamppost. The date alternating: August 31, 1888; August 31, 1988. The side street. The woman. The Ripper. The blood and recognition. The Ripper coming for him; then not.

Alone, in the next room, Topp, by now highly sensitized to Lees, rolled and writhed in agony and dread, receiving nearly all that Lees dreamt.

Frounle and Hobart listened to Lees' slurred recital of nightmare and watched his sweaty, muscle-tearing torture with fascinated repulsion. Percy and Logan stared at Lees, and at digital readouts, blips on monitor screens, with professional disapproval as his blood pressure peaked at 202 over 128 and his heart echo appeared, disappeared, reappeared.

Percy, backed by Cynthia Logan, argued for termination of the experiment; his patient was in danger. Frounle and Hobart left it to Lees, who refused to consider it. Topp sat, drained and listless, in a corner, kept silent, but secretly hoped Percy would prevail.

The Prince's Lily was a gentlemen's club not far from Belgrave Square. Founded in 1913 not long after the death of Edward VII and named in honor of the pudgy king's most famous mistress, Lily Langtry, the members still subscribed to the Edwardian sensibility—elegance, excess, social prestige and privilege, public propriety and priapic privacy, governance by an elite based upon bloodlines and wealth.

It was, predictably, the home secretary's club.

Lord Desmonde welcomed Stuart to a private luncheon room decorated with expensive classical erotica. Purple damask wall hangings depicted golden satyrs and nymphs. Figurines of Egyptian copper, Greek marble and pre-Columbian gold adorned small tables and wall niches, bearing their burden of disproportionately huge penises with a weary indifference.

Why does this place always make me feel, wondered Stuart, like a small boy seeking the privacy to masturbate?

Dezzi smiled. "I took the liberty of ordering, Malcolm. The steward said today's prime rib was exceptional, and the claret is not to be missed." He poured whisky for both of them, and they sat at a table covered with lemon linen. "Now, what happy news of progress can you give me?"

Stuart sipped his whisky and eyed the HS. "None, really."

Dezzi frowned. "That is too bad. The Cabinet are becoming restive. The government is taking a rather rude chafing from the press, the Chancellor of the Exchequer is shirty about the new estimates for detective squad overtime, and Sir Edwards William is no longer making himself a nuisance to me—he is now a nuisance to the PM."

Stuart sighed. "Dezzi, I wish I had good news, but I simply don't. Rather the reverse. I am preparing a report on the investigation to date. It is for your eyes and the prime minister's only. Would you like a verbal précis now?"

"Please."

Over rare roast beef and new potatoes, a brilliant Chateau Palmer '73, chocolate mousse and Stilton, cashews and brandy, Stuart took the home secretary through the discoveries of the investigation, step by step.

"So you see, Dezzi," he concluded, "we are in the awkward position of having each step of apparent progress turn out to be a regression. We are faced with facts that we cannot, presently, explain in terms of natural law."

"I *see*, Malcolm, why that report is for myself and the PM only. If that sort of poppycock ever got into general circulation, this government would be the laughingstock, not only of England, but of the entire world."

He doesn't get it, thought Stuart. Something different is going on here and he doesn't get it. Aloud, he said, "And I'm afraid the overtime estimates will be revised upward further, and dramatically. Hughes, Clive and Peters think that eighty underground stations must be occupied, clock-round, by a minimum of two officers per station. Along with the men needed to actually ride the trains, the detail will require a total of more than seven hundred men, per day, for an unforseen number of days."

The HS gawked at him. "My dear, Malcolm, that is twenty percent of CID's entire *force*!"

Stuart nodded grimly. "I know. And it only offers a *chance* of catching this Nicholas fellow. But if we don't take it, we'd

†

be exposed later as something far worse than humorous. We'd be irresponsible to the point of legal malfeasance and moral degeneracy."

Lord Desmonde stared at Stuart unblinkingly for a few long moments, then sighed.

"I suppose you had better go forward."

Stuart provoked another shocked stare from the HS with his simple reply: "I already have. I gave the orders at nine this morning."

"That borders on insubordination, Malcolm."

Stuart nodded. "Quite right, and you may fire me anytime you like, but *I* won't play politics with this case. I can't explain it, I can only describe it, but the issues here are far more important than my career." Or yours, he thought, but tactfully refrained from adding another repugnant item to the unpalatable menu he had already served to the HS.

In the afternoon Lees' drugged voice spoke haltingly.

". . . side street . . . walking . . . my legs are gone at the thighs . . . fog floating . . . a closed court ahead . . . stopping . . . blank building on my right . . . warehouse or something . . ."

His body went rigid.

Silver-Eyes was in his brain, muttering, shrieking, chanting. *"Won't work, guv. You'll never get it right. Through me! Come to me! Never get it right, guv—save through me. Never get it right, never get it right . . ."*

Lees screamed. "It hurts! Silver-Eyes in my head . . . not the dream . . . *Oh, God, it hurts!"*

Percy, Logan, Frounle and Hobart were rigid, staring at him, while in the next room Billy Topp howled in pain.

Silver-Eyes was in his head, looming like a mountain, caped and top-hatted and blank-dark where a face belonged but for the huge ball-bearing eyes. His cloak was fire and his hat was formed of squirming eels and his death-stench breath was in Lees' nose, choking him, and the voice would not stop.

"Doomed to fail. I can stop the pain! *Come to me, come to me, come to me, be mine and* I will stop the pain!"

In his hand was a wineglass. Fire reflected off crystal and

†

red liquid, shining like color, light, texture never imagined.

"Drink! Come to me! Drink and stop the pain!"

The wine was blood. Creatures slithered in it.

Lees screamed. *"No! No! No! Stop! Go away! Oh, God, the pain!"*

The heart monitor went beserk: 120 and climbing, for pulse; 217 over 117 and climbing for blood-pressure.

Percy scrambled to the IV and shut off the flow. *"Bring him out, Frounle! Now!"*

"When I clap my hands, General, the nap is finished. You will wake instantly. Do you hear me?"

"Yes! Yes! Oh, God, the pain!"

Frounle clapped his hands.

Lees' eyes opened, and he grabbed his head in his hands. He coughed and gagged and rolled over on the bed and vomited onto the carpet, vomited repeatedly, convulsively, vomited until he had dry heaves.

He sobbed, tears streaming down his face, his nose running freely.

Suddenly, his muscles spasmed, clenched, unclenched, trembled, knotted and bent his body backward until his back was a bow and he froze as if rigor mortis. He froze in that locked posture a minute, then collapsed face down on the bed, his body more fluid than matter, not so much limp as pooled.

He sobbed.

The team leaders sat in the library.

Dusk was coming on and the glow of the large fireplace was cheery. They sat in semi-circle close to the hearth, drawing sustenance from the crackling coal, the dancing flames.

Percy surveyed his colleagues' faces—Hobart; Frounle; Topp; Cynthia Logan. They were all wan, somber, as they sipped tea or munched listlessly on sandwiches and cakes, staring into the fire, hoping to find some answer, some solace from that primitive talisman. Even Hobart's restless body was quiet, still.

They're beaten, thought Percy. They're beaten and they don't know what to do.

†

The old man cleared his throat and spoke gently. "People, it's time to call a halt to this. That man is not going to be able to stand more without serious, lasting, physical damage to his heart. Possibly a fatal coronary."

They turned lifeless eyes toward him, listened and looked away, back into the fire.

Topp's eyes were circled so darkly he looked as if he had been beaten. He closed them, spoke in a hoarse whisper. "Fine by me. I'm all in meself. I'm not just gettin' pictures from the general, I'm gettin' his bloody pain. That cabbie lad is the devil." He shuddered. "Those silver eyes are enough to send you 'round the bend, just by themself."

Silence.

Hobart rubbed the bridge of his nose apathetically. "Don't we have to leave that decision to General Lees?"

Silence.

Frounle nodded. "It's not a decision for us, Dr. Percy. There are other lives, other issues involved."

Cynthia Logan shook her head, angrily fanning her short, dark hair. "No! We cannot, in conscience, continue—even if General Lees wants to do so. Dr. Percy is right. Our obligation to our patient is full stop! Now."

Silence.

Hobart clasped his hands in his lap and looked at them. "I'll admit that what is going on here is beyond my experience. I'm not a religious man—I've always rather prided myself on not needing that sort of thing." He sighed. "But what is happening here, to General Lees and Mr. Topp is obviously . . . real. I'm trying to see what it is . . . trying to understand it, but . . ."—his face squeezed—"this is painful for me to accept, even as a mere possibility, but I think Mr. Topp may have hit the thing precisely."

Silence.

Tears trickled down the face of the small man. "I . . . forgive me, I'm—" Cynthia Logan stretched out a hand and Hobart took it gratefully, then mastered his tears. "Who else can this silver-eyed figure be, but Satan . . . or one of his minions? And, if there is Satan—there is God. And, if there is God—he must be asking us to do something here."

†

Silence.
Frounle asked, "What?"
Hobart shook his head. "I don't know."
Topp sighed. "I'm not an intellectual or a professional man. Just a Liverpool dockie what got hit on his head and became sensitive to some of this stuff. But that silver-eyed gent is the devil. I'd just as soon quit, but I don't see how I can. If the general wants to keep at it, I mean."
Percy asked, "How much more?"
Frounle thought a moment in silence. "Probably one or two more sessions. We've gotten up to the last few dreams."
Percy closed his eyes. I'm the one who's beaten, he thought. May God forgive me.
He said, "If General Lees wants to . . . *one* more session."
Silence.
The fire flowed.

Lees' voice was low, slow.
". . . the woman is cleaved . . . half of her is . . . a Victorian drab . . . the other is a whore right off today's streets . . . yellow eyes . . . lifeless . . . he crosses the square toward her . . ."
The heart monitor was excited but not raging—pulse, 94; blood pressure, 168 over 93 but holding. Percy sat at one end of a wheeled metal cart with heart needles, electro-shock paddles and other emergency cardiac equipment; Cynthia Logan sat at the other end. They swiveled their heads back and forth between Lees and the monitoring machines.
". . . he hands her the pouch of gold . . . sets down the black bag . . ."
There was a momentary dimming in the power of the vision, the feeling of a shadow in the room. Lees stiffened and the machines began racing. Silver-Eyes was in his head and Silver-Eye's voice came from Lees' mouth so all could hear.
"That's all, guv. Ain't no more. You still 'aven't got it right, 'ave you?"
The spectators froze, staring at Lees, awed by the power of the deep, resonant voice. The machines raced on unnoticed— heart monitor more beserk than even the previous day; pulse,

†
183

139 and rising; blood pressure, 222 over 127 and rising.

"*Can't get it, eh, Guv! Come to me! Drink! Stop the pain!*"

Lees saw him and he was all fire and the crystal chalice was suspended in front of him, the red blood illuminated by the red flame.

"*Drink!*"

Lees screamed.

Percy came to, shot a horrified glance at the machines and shouted, "*Bring him out!*"

Lees grabbed his chest screaming and gagging.

Percy was on his feet. "*Bring him out! He's going into arrest!*"

Cynthia jerked the IV from Lees' arm as Frounle performed the instruction-clapping maneuver and Percy wheeled the tray to the bedside, shooting a glance over his shoulder toward the EKG monitor. "*Damn! He's in failure!*"

He grabbed the electro-shock paddles.

Lees left his body and ascended slowly toward the ceiling, looking down upon the scene. He felt almost perfectly peaceful save for a mild irritation at Percy and Logan.

Leave my body alone. It's over. I'm not there anymore.

He left them.

The mansion.

Hedgemore was visible below, despite the dark.

England.

Europe.

The world.

Dark blue sky.

He passed the moon, picking up speed.

Left the cosmos.

White light ahead.

A voice, gentle as a feather, firm as tested leather, musical and resonant and tangy-sweet, like a flute with no treacly undertone; clear.

"No. You must return. It is not yet time."

Was it Jesus speaking?

Lees felt enormous sorrow. He wanted to cry out but could not.

* * *

†

He was back in his body and his body was pain and Percy withdrew the huge needle dripping adrenaline and said, "He's back."

A wall of blackness, thick and textured and tangible. Lees was in the wall and the wall was physical pain and pain blocked out everything else, pain was an existence unto itself and it was Lees' existence.

Lees was pain.

Driving down to Hedgemore, late that night, Stuart tried to explain it to Vanessa.

"Considered more cold-bloodedly than I am prepared to do, it's only three murders of the hundreds a year in England. But there's an . . . atmosphere is the closest I can come, an atmosphere about this business that reeks of something more than . . . mere murder."

Vanessa shivered. "Mere murder is quite enough evil for me, thank you very much."

Stuart moved the Jaguar into the right lane to pass a slow-moving lorry. "Yes, but murder is, in some sense, understandable, explicable." He accelerated smoothly past the truck and crossed back into the left lane. "This is not."

"Malcolm, if you are trying to make me understand why you might have to sacrifice your career to principle, don't worry. It is your career and I have faith in your decisions." She leaned across the seat and kissed his ear. "And you can't imagine I fell in love with you over something as irrelevant as your being head of CID."

Stuart smiled. "And if your career as an actress continues to blossom, I can retire anyway and be your kept man."

Cynthia Logan unstrapped the blood-pressure cuff from Lees' arm on Saturday morning. Her pretty face framed by dark hair was smiling.

"One-fifteen over eighty, General. Miraculous." Her tone of voice was as if to a well-behaved child and Lees couldn't think of a reply. "Dr. Percy will be in momentarily, General."

She twitched out of the room, leaving Lees to stare out the window at a patch of rainy sky. Wet gray sky made a gloomy day and gray gloom was upon him, in him, like . . .

†

* * *

Lees feels himself shaking as Dr. Bayless unlocks a gray metal door set in a gray wall of the interior of the violent ward building.

Lees watches the door swing open.

The interior of the room is padded with what looks like thick yellow cotton quilting. There are no windows or furniture and the only light is from a bulb in the ceiling protected by a wire cage that segments the light into strange geometric shapes and shadows.

Huddled in a corner is Lees' father. His face is sweaty and his dark hair lank and graying. His strange lemony eyes are wilder than even Lees remembers. His upper body is encased in tan leather, a straitjacket that binds his arms.

Lees' eyes meet his father's.

A flicker of recognition crosses the possessed pupils, and he whispers, "Jim, boy—is that you?"

For less than a second the film of disease is washed away from the yellow orbs and something like sanity, hope, vision, shines out from them and it breaks Lees; he is flooded with anguish, sorrow, loss, pity and love. He is choked with emotion and dizzied by feeling. His voice cracks. "Dad . . ."

The yellow eyes film over again and are mad, shining like fire, and they freeze Lees' soul. *"Jim, boy!"*

His father struggles to his feet, working his way up the padded wall with his back.

"Jim, boy! You got to get me out of here! I have to warn the president!"

He writhes against the constraints of the straitjacket, pulling his arms as hard as he can until the muscles of his neck stand out like ropes and veins throb in his head.

"Get this off me!" he screams.

Then he stands still, panting, looking at Lees. He whispers. "Jim, boy, you came just in time." He licks his lips and darts a crafty glance at Dr. Bayless. "They say I'm crazy, but it's a trick. A plot. They want to keep me from the president, but I have to warn him." His eyes leave them and focus on the distance, as if seeing through or beyond walls. He whispers a soliloquy as if alone and playing to a larger audience. "He doesn't know. The president doesn't know, but I had a dream

†

... a vision ... I saw ... *them.*" His voice changes, becomes harsh, metallic, brittle and cruel. "They're coming—the niggers, the Jews, the papists, the spics—and they're going to take over and only the president can stop them, but he doesn't know." He swells with evident pride, seems to stand inches taller, beams. "*I have been chosen. I* am to warn the president."

His eyes come back to them. He glances at Bayless, then at his son.

"Jim, boy—he's one of them." He cackles. "Doesn't look it—oh, he could fool you, but not me. *Lees sees! Lees knows! I see inside him and he's a nigger inside!*"

Like a cat, unexpectedly swift, he jackknifes his body and roars, *"Bust me out, Jim!"* then runs forward, butting Bayless in the stomach, knocking him aside, staggers into his stunned son.

Lees instinctively lowers his shoulder, wraps his arms around his father's waist, drives him back into the room like the football defensive back he used to be, tackles his father and slams him to the padded floor. "Doctor—do something! Make him stop! *Please!*" The last word is a primal scream.

Bayless is beside him with a needle. "Hold him."

There is a hole in an arm of the straitjacket, an intended hole, circular and seamed. Bayless jams the needle into the exposed pink flesh, injects ... some drug.

Lees' father goes slack. Stares at his son in shock. Wonder. Horror. Fear.

"Jim ... boy ... you're ... you're one of them, too. . . ?"

The yellow eyes dull, glaze, close.

He sleeps.

Kneeling in the padded room, his drugged father prone before him, the doctor's face filled with compassion for the revelation of Lees' shame, he breaks again. His tough-young-soldier facade crumbles completely, leaving the boy that he still is revealed, naked, vulnerable.

Lee cries.

Dr. Percy's pink face invaded the rectangle of rainy gray sky in Lees' vision. Lees forced a smile.

"A very good blood-pressure reading, General."

†

"Yes."

Percy began to fit the cuff about Lees' left arm again. "I think I'll try it once more."

Lees said nothing, stared at the gray sky.

Lees is a very small boy.

His mother's plain round face hovers above him. Her expression is kindly but serious. She speaks to him, but he cannot hear her.

Percy unstrapped the cuff again, discarded it and sat. "One-oh-five over seventy-eight. Even better."

"Cynthia said it was miraculous."

Percy nodded, scratched his chin. "She has the experience to recognize a miracle. For that matter, so do I. Do you, General?"

Lees smiled. "I'm beginning to."

"Good. Sleep some more, now."

A stocky man of average height wearing a gray business suit and bowler and carrying a brolly, walked across the platform of the Stockwell Station. He had sandy hair, pale blue eyes and was clean-shaven.

Constable Richard Lund stared after him. No beard; eyes are wrong, but . . . something . . .

The man boarded a Northern Line train, moved to a window and turned to face Lund. As the doors closed, and before the train moved, he made a swift ducking motion with his head and Lund saw contact lenses drop into the man's thick hands. Then he straightened and smiled at Lund.

His eyes were dead silver.

The train moved, left the station.

Using his hand unit, Lund radioed Constable Menke on board the train. "Menke—Lund! He's in the fifth car, gray business suit, bowler; he's shaved his beard. Be careful!"

"I read you, Richard."

Lund then ran to a telephone to warn officers stationed in the next four stops—The Oval, Kennington, Waterloo and the Embankment.

Menke moved to the door between cars and tried it. It was

jammed and would not yield to handle-twisting, pulling or kicking. At the next stop, I'll pop out, run down to car five and jump aboard, Menke thought.

The Oval was coming up. The engineer began to ease the throttle down. The train picked up speed. The engineer jerked the throttle back and forth frantically, but the train continued to accelerate, not responding to the lever. He had lost control.

Constable Eugene Pankau stared in confusion and horror as the train rocketed through the station, the pale frightened faces of passengers staring back through the windows.

The lights went out in the train and people began to scream as it rocked madly on the tracks, its speed increasing to eighty kilometers an hour, then ninety.

Lights went out in stations along the Northern Line, and the sound of the train in the tunnel was seemingly amplified by the absence of light, until it was deafening, blood-freezing. It roared past Kennington and Waterloo on its journey beneath the Thames at one hundred kilometers per hour.

The terror was in speeding through the tunnel in utter darkness with no reference points visible, but the sound and the pressure and the rocking of the cars reinforced the knowledge of furious movement with no semblance of control left. A passage in enclosed lightlessness with all purpose and sanity removed like an existentialist's reverie of the movement through life toward death.

The screaming inside the train was claustrophobic and continual, uncountable decibels of outrage and fear.

The train finally slowed and came to a whispering stop one hundred meters from Embankment Station.

The darkness was complete.

The doors opened and a shadow leaped to the ground, the doors hissing closed behind him. The man who called himself Lucian Nicholas scampered along the tunnel to an emergency door for repairmen. He opened it and slipped through, closed the door behind him and climbed the stairs toward the street above.

It all took less than twelve seconds.

The train started up slowly and coasted into Embankment Station.

The lights came on. The doors slid open.

†

* * *

Stuart visited Lees' bedside after dinner and told him about the day's fiasco on the subway.

"So that's the report I got from Hughes on the phone. No one injured, thank God, but he slipped away again. And we've no explanation for why the train behaved as it did."

Lees nodded. "Fits in with the other things—the bonnet, the boat and all that."

"Yes." Stuart sipped his brandy. "That's why I'm beginning to wonder if . . . you're not the key to all this. Our best hope."

The words set up an echo in Lees' head.

"*I* don't know what the key is, or where our best hope lies," Dr. Bayless says gently.

Back in the cool building with the blue door, Lees regains some tenuous hold on himself. Venetian blinds striate the barren earth, as the cruel Texas sun waits outside like a growing malignancy.

"We've done all the physical testing possible. No tumor, no physical cause that we can determine."

Young Lees shrugs. "He's mad. A fruitcake."

Bayless smiles. "An accurate, if non-clinically phrased, diagnosis, but we'd like to find out why so there may be hope for a recovery."

Young Lees shrugs again. The psychic crap, is all he thinks. He wants desperately to be away, somewhere else.

"You can't help us?"

Lees shakes his head. "I'm no doctor. He was always dippy. Now he's just . . . worse."

Bayless nods. "I'm going to be candid with you. Though we can find no concrete cause for his mental condition, he is deteriorating—physically as well as intellectually. He's losing weight, he rests only when sedated, his heart and blood pressure are bad, his kidney function is poor and bowel function erratic."

Lees stares at him. "Are you saying he's going to die?"

"He might linger for years, but . . . he could go tomorrow from half a dozen causes—heart, stroke, kidney failure, something."

Be better for everyone, thinks Lees, and then is seared with guilt for the thought.

Lees sighed.

"I'm doing the best I can, Malcolm."

Stuart uncrossed his legs. "Yes. Frounle gave me an idea what the report will say. More or less, that if you're not psychic, no one ever was or ever will be. He's tremendously impressed."

Lees smiled. "It's not news."

Sunday afternoon, after mass, Ann and Father Mueller walked in the courtyard of St. Martin's. They stopped by a rosebush, and he caressed a red petal with his fingertips.

He looked up from the rose. "You can't leave him, Ann. It goes against everything we believe in, and he needs you more than ever . . . now."

She restrained herself from touching his silvery blond hair. Kiss me, Eric, she felt and thought. "And what of my needs?"

He stared at her sensitive eyes, mouth near. I want to take her in my arms. "I won't make light of your alienation, Ann, but . . . I believe sincerely that it's a temporary condition. That's one of the main ways we get into trouble, into sin. By thinking the emotion of the moment is permanent and irresistible."

Lees dreamt his own history.

Lees is a tiny tot.

His mother's plain round face hovers above him. Her expression is kindly but serious.

"Jimmy, your father tries to see things. Things that aren't there. He tries to get you to see things."

"Yes, Momma."

"Jimmy, that is madness. That is crazy. That is bad. You must not let your father get you to see things. You mustn't let anyone know about seeing things."

"Yes, Momma."

* * *

†

Police watched the eighty designated subway stations all day, but there was no sign of the man who called himself Lucian Nicholas.

Monday, Lees was taken off intensive care status.

He lay in bed, no longer wired to the EKG monitor, no longer connected to the oxygen tanks, no longer semi-comatose from sedatives. He was still groggy and drifted in and out of sleep, spending a moderate eight to ten hours a day in full consciousness.

Silver-Eyes had not returned nor had the visions, and he felt more peaceful than in the previous three years.

He thought about dying. *About having died.*

It was apparent that you didn't get away from this stuff just because you died. A central tenet of his lifelong belief had been that if you held on through life the problems would be over when they put you six feet under.

The end. Finito.

But no. Something else happened. Your spirit really was separable from your body. So there was no escape there.

Trapped.

Now what?

Lees had no clear answer, but he knew he could not fight anything any longer. He had not the strength and knew it; he had not the will and knew it. He had surrendered, and his only remaining problem was figuring out what it was he had surrendered to and what was required of him.

But he lacked energy and his thoughts were scattered.

The window next to his bed was at eye-level. The sun was low in the afternoon sky, but bright. He could see trees and a patch of field browning in solemn celebration of autumn. It was the sort of day on which he had loved to take his sons to football games or hunting in the Rockies. He had no wistfulness to be home and doing. The feeling was of pleasant memory and wonder that those things should have happened for him at all.

Dr. Percy entered the room.

Lees looked at the old man and saw that the pink of his skin was down, his eyes were sad and his shoulders drooped from fatigue. He walked carefully, as if he was afraid of falling, and, for the first time, he looked close to his age.

Lees thought, Somebody should help him.

Seeing Lees awake, he tried to brighten. "Coming around, are we, General?"

"Ready to run a marathon any day now."

Percy's eyes widened. "A chipper mood, too."

"I feel . . . better . . ."

Percy sat on the edge of the bed, looked at Lees thoughtfully.

Lees reached out his hand and touched Percy's elbow. "You have a pain here."

Percy nodded. "Shrapnel damaged the cartilage in 'seventeen. Acts up at times of . . . stress."

Lees cupped the elbow with his left hand and massaged it with his fingertips for thirty seconds, then let his hand drop.

Percy touched the elbow. "Pain is gone . . . feels a bit tingly, but . . . the pain is gone."

Lees smiled. "You're welcome."

Percy chuckled. "Yes, of course. Thank you."

The men eyed one another in silence. Finally, Percy said, "That was a psychic phenomenon . . . of some sort."

Lees nodded. "Yes, it was, wasn't it?"

"Bother you?"

Lees thought, then shook his head. "No." He shrugged. "It just . . . came. It was just . . . there."

"Real?"

"Yes."

"Something happened."

Lees nodded. "I'm told I died . . . briefly."

Silence.

Percy broke it. "I've had three previous patients die and revive. That's not many—four now in sixty years of practice. They all spoke of . . . out-of-body experiences."

Again Lees nodded. "Yes, but I'm not going to talk about mine. Not now."

"Bother you?"

"No, not really . . . except . . ."

"You didn't want to come back?"

"Something like that. Anyway, I don't understand it, but I'm not going to talk about it now. I'm comfortable with it."

†

"You've changed."

Lees hesitated. "I've given up something."

"Resistance?"

Lees smiled. "Yes, I suppose that's about as close to it as I could come now."

The police watched the underground again all day on Monday, but the silver-eyed cabbie made no appearance. The press was still writing and inquiring about the bizarre incident on the Northern Line, Saturday, but none of them had enough information or intuition to connect it to the neo-Ripper murders.

The one reporter in London who was closing in on the reality of the situation was the Vampire. And he was succeeding, not because of his virtues as a journalist, but because of his central flaw as a person: he was a drunk, and his source was a drunk. Traffic-Sergeant Jim Oliver was a thirty-five-year-old alcoholic, and like all alcoholics, he had a grossly inflated sense of his own importance, a grudge against the world for failing to recognize that importance and a compulsion to talk about the universal conspiracy to deny him his due recognition. The Vampire was a congenial companion in drunkenness because the physical addition of the disease had him in its death-grip, and he no longer cared to talk much, since talking interupted drinking.

"*I* should have had the detail. *I* put in for it and got passed over like always. And who did they choose—Eustace Dilling! A bloody acting-sergeant with his promotion not confirmed for three more months. That's who!"

"Rum go," said the Vampire. "What's so hot about the detail anyway?"

Oliver's round, characterless baby face assumed a look of craftiness. He glanced out of their booth and around the small smoky pub. "What's so hot about it is getting under the eye of the deputy commissioner CID, Sir Malcolm bloody Stuart himself."

The Vampire tossed back the last of his raw gin and snapped his fingers at a fat, apathetic barmaid for another round. "How'd it do that?"

Oliver tossed his head, flopping back a shock of his thick

†

brown hair, which was only beginning to recede at the temples. "Head of security detail at Hedgemore, Stuart's estate in Kent. Eighteen men on indefinite assignment."
The Vampire frowned. "What the hell for?"
"Some hush-hush project. Something to do with psychic experiments." Oliver laughed harshly. "Trying to solve the murders with a medium, I hear. Couldn't do any worse than the bugger-up on Saturday on the tube."
The barmaid slapped down a double gin and a pint of bitter. The Vampire paid for their drinks.
"What'd the runaway train have to do with it."
Oliver laughed again, drank, said, "Lucian Nicholas was on that train. Had been playing hide-and-seek with us for three days. Why'd you think there's so many coppers hanging around the tube lines these days?"
The Vampire shrugged. "I don't ride the underground. Didn't know there were."
Sergeant Oliver drained off half a pint at one go and wiped his lips, "Six or seven hundred men when you add up all the shifts."
The Vampire whistled.
Oliver nodded. "You'd think I could get one of those details, but no—I'll be stuck in traffic division forever. Hotshot CID boys don't want new talent to threaten their cushy slots."
"Rotten buggers," said the Vampire without feeling, and drained half his drink. "You say Nicholas was actually on the train?"
"Had him like that." Oliver grinned over a clenched fist. "Silly sods let him get away. Fits in with the funny business with the bonnet and the boat."
The Vampire kept buying drinks and Oliver kept talking and the Vampire listened, fighting the excitement rising through his alcoholic haze, trying not to let his drive show as one thought kept pounding in his brain.
This could be it! This might be my break! he wanted to shriek. *At last! Me!*

Tuesday, while the police watched the subway in vain once more for the man who called himself Lucian Nicholas, the

†
195

Vampire was busy following up Oliver's leads. He tricked one unwary constable, trapped a foolish detective-sergeant into giving him more information and used an outright bribe of one hundred pounds on Johnson, the smart-aleck lab technician.

Jim and Ann Lees held hands.
　It was his first walk outside since the heart attack and they strolled comfortably along the rim of the unnamed headland. It was near dusk of another beautiful autumn day, with a light wind and the failing sun at their backs. They stopped to watch the shattering waves and a gull gliding gracefully a few feet above the Channel's surface.
　He said, "I don't know. I don't understand what to make of the experience, but I'm not uncomfortable with it."
　"Do you need to talk to someone about it?"
　He hesitated.
　They resumed walking.
　"Probably, but—not just yet."
　They walked.
　"It changed you."
　"Yes."
　"For the better. You seem . . . peaceful."

Wednesday, at lunchtime, the antique globe lights of the Gay Hussar in Greek Street yellowed the aura of the small informal room and lent it an air of time past, empires risen and fallen, court balls and poetic soldiers. The authentic Hungarian cuisine had made it a Soho favorite of leftish Labor politicians and trendy show-business types years before. Lately, it was less in vogue and the slight decline in business had had an effect on the autocratic demeanor of the owner and his staff. Previously, a pair of customers like Felicia Bowen and Lisle Young would never have been seated, let alone served.
　Felicia Bowen was a lanky ash blonde with gorgeous legs, a thirty-three-year-old "model" (and part-time three hundred-pounds-a-night call girl) with a short list of bit parts on stage and in film. She was also a confirmed lesbian, a "speedball" freak who liked the heroin as much as the cocaine and was

†

suffering, unknown to herself, from terminal cancer of the pelvic region.

Lisle Young was twenty-eight years old, a *zoftig* brunette whose acting career had consisted of being the bosomy girl in a succession of period horror and adventure flicks that never quite attained B-picture competence. (She and Felicia had formed their friendship nine years earlier on the set of *The Undead of Swansea*—Lisle's first film and Felicia's last.) Lisle was also a chronic alcoholic who liked a spoon or needle now and then, a bisexual and well acquainted with casting couches as the most reliable means of keeping a hold on her tenuous career.

They had come directly to the Gay Hussar from an early morning party lubricated by copious amounts of drugs and alcohol and laced with pornography and varietal sex, and where the two had been cornered by a mysterious agent who had offered them one thousand pounds each for a long weekend "audition" at the country estate of an incognito producer. Both had accepted (it was the first time Lisle had taken a direct cash payment for her widely shared favors) despite being put off by the agent's sickening silver eyes. The "audition" was scheduled to begin Thursday, September 30.

They might (or might not) have made a connection between the surprisingly generous offer and the recent murders if they had been fully familiar with each other's acting credits. Lisle did not know that sixteen years earlier, Felicia had played Elizabeth Stride in an unmemorable chiller called *Blood of the Ripper*. (Shooting for Felicia consisted of two days at scale and three lines plus a scream in her single scene, so she did not remember it herself.) Felicia did not know that Lisle had played Catherine Eddowes six years before in *The Latin Ripper*, one of a dozen horror flicks she had appeared in during two years spent shuffling between West Germany, Spain and Italy. (Lisle would have had to consult her credit list herself to remember the part, since that period of her life was a boozy twenty-two-month sequence of no-budget horror-film sets where it was not worth the effort to differentiate one film or part from another.)

After partying all night, their grooming was slatternly, they smelled pussy-raunchy and alternated between the obnoxious and inane giggling of a drug high and semi-comatose stupor. Eventually, business downturn or no, the captain decided they were too disgusting to be tolerated, and ushered them out after tearing up their bill in his best Franz Josef-imperious style.

Felicia and Lisle giggled all the way to the cab, which they directed back to the former's flat for more pipe, spoon, needle and vibrator games.

At Hedgemore, Lees led Ann on an afternoon walk along the headland toward the lighthouse. A uniformed constable kept watch over them.

The lighthouse was only four stories high, a narrow column of pale stone with a curious wood-and-glass cupola atop it, now heavily shuttered in its abandonment.

Lees began to tell Ann, haltingly, of the family secrets he had hidden from her for so long. She was silent, expressionless, internally tense and torn by a tempestuous mix of emotions. Eventually, he grew tired, and they sat in the lee of the lighthouse with their backs warmed by the sun-heated stone.

It took him an hour and a half to narrate the main details of that hidden history. When he finished he rested his head on his hunched knees.

She sat staring out at the green foaming waves, as the shrill swooping gulls searched for sustenance in the cold deep waters.

"You could have told me."

"I was afraid."

"Of what?"

"Everything..."

Trapped by God, she told herself, and knew it wasn't true; consciousness and conscience had cornered her. Choice was still hers, but love made some options academic, theoretical. Wanton cruelty was too high a price for anything, and dreams pursued with disregard to love always turned to nightmares. To living hell. She could not nurse her anger, could not deny her love and life with this man, could not turn her back on him in his need.

She took him in her arms.

†

"Forgive me?" he whispered. "Can you ever forgive me?"
"Yes." She kissed him. "Hush, of course I can." She loved him.

That night, as they made gentle love, she held him in her arms, between her legs, with tears in her eyes, and refused to acknowledge the cause of her silent weeping.

Lees dreamed pillars of mist and overarching spider legs and cracking, crunching sounds and blood-stained silver eyes.

The London Daily   September 29, 1988

RIPPERGATE!

Scotland Yard COVERUP?
Psychic Police?

Special to the LD
From Carl Collins

This reporter has learned, from several highly placed sources at New Scotland Yard, that the Metropolitan Police are engaged in a conscious campaign to conceal important and mysterious details of the neo-Ripper murders from the public.
In the Hyde Park murder of the prostitute-porno-queen Polly Nichols, a black velvet bonnet was found by the body. Obviously new, it bore a maker's label, Hanby & Son, which was discovered to be the name of a Whitechapel milliner who went out of business shortly after the original series of Whitechapel killings. Most mysterious is the authoritative report that, in the month since the killing, the bonnet has disintegrated at a rate approximating three or four years per day. It is attested that the bonnet is now a shapeless pile of barely cohesive fabric just as if it were, indeed, 100 years old.
The one activity known conclusively of Mary Ann ''Polly'' Nichols, the original 1888 victim, on the day of her murder was that she bought a black velvet bonnet.
Similarly, in the Thames murder of ''Dark Annie''

†

Mackey, the prostitute-ecdysiast, the murder boat was a seemingly new steam launch of a type that passed out of common use around 1890. Again, in the three weeks since the second murder, the launch has ''aged'' at a premature rate. It is now reported to be unseaworthy, as might well be expected of an uncared-for century-old vessel.

Astonishing as these facts are, this reporter's most startling discovery is that New Scotland Yard are dabbling in the occult in their attempt to solve this baffling case. It is reliably asserted that a detail of eighteen police officers are serving as security at Hedgemore, the country residence of Sir Malcolm Stuart, deputy commissioner for Criminal Investigations Division. The security and secrecy is to guard a project of experimentation in psychic prediction. At the center of the project is an unnamed and mysterious medium who, it is hoped, may be capable of identifying the Ripper and preventing future murders.

The last item presently being concealed from the British public is the truth of the runaway train on the Northern Line underground so widely reported after last Saturday. Lucian Nicholas, the taxi driver wanted for questioning in the murder of Constable Colin Colson as well as in the neo-Ripper affair, was aboard the runaway train. He had been spotted riding the underground several times previously and a force of not less than 700 men had been detailed to guard the underground system and apprehend him. Despite these expensive, extensive and intense efforts, the suspect made good his escape.

We believe the public have a right to know. A right to know what is going on. A right to know if New Scotland Yard are behaving competently and correctly. If Sir Edwards William, the commissioner, or Sir Malcolm Stuart are not forthcoming, we believe Lord Desmonde, the home secretary, who bears direct responsibility for the Yard, should be held publicly accountable.

As the next murder evening in the original killings, the anniversary of the double event, is

†

upon us, we would suggest that time and public patience has nearly run out.

The Prime Minister of England sat in a high-backed leather chair at a small, round, leather-topped table in the anteroom just outside the Cabinet Room of Number 10 Downing Street.

Directly across from her, against the wall, stood a tall grandfather clock, its dark wood richly polished, its ornate gold-leafed hands indicating, correctly, the time as precisely 1:14 A.M., Greenwich Mean Time. The PM did not remember exactly whether that particular clock had stood in that particular place for a century or so or only for mere decades. No matter. For it was the idea of that clock that the PM adored; the clock, prosaically, told time; poetically, that clock embodied the meaning of time. For her, the meaning of time was the beauty of rediscovering tradition. Time, she thought; one can have no useful vision of the world without an understanding of time.

Directly to the right of the clock was a row of pegs. Each had a tag stating Lord Chancellor or Lord President of the Council or Foreign Secretary. The pegs were for the hats and coats of the Cabinet members, and Sir Winston had hung his on the peg for the First Lord of the Admiralty in this century, as his father, Lord Randolph, had hung his on the peg for the Chancellor of the Exchequer in the preceding century.

It was, of course, only a small example of tradition, but she believed that observance of minor custom was the sinew of discipline, as observance of major custom was its bone.

Just now, the pegs were full save only the home secretary's. The Cabinet awaited her inside and she was waiting for the home secretary, who was nearly fifteen minutes late—a breach of custom she cared for not at all.

As if the thought of her displeasure summoned him, at that moment the home secretary hurried into the anteroom like a small, slick cutter, trailing the deputy commissioner, CID, as a battleship in his wake. The PM remained seated and said sourly, "You're late, Lord Desmonde."

The two men pulled up stiff before her, immediately reduced to the demeanor of schoolboys likely to be caned by an angry headmaster.

"My apologies, Madam Prime Minister, but the traffic was brutal." The PM frowned, and Lord Desmonde hurried on. "I believe you have met Sir Malcolm before."

"I have, and on more pleasant occasions. Sir Malcolm, I have read your report. I do not know what sort of mental defectives you have working in the Yard laboratories, but I will hear of no more supernatural speculation. This is to be treated as an ordinary police matter. If these lunatics are dressing up in Victorian costume and riding about in hansom cabs and old boats and the underground, I should think that would make them all the simpler to capture. Do I make myself clear?"

"Quite."

"As for this General Lees—it is all very well to have a report from a parapsychologist stating that he is exceptionally psychic, but what has he done? He has advanced the investigation not an inch, but he may well make this government an absurdity. And for that, you and Lord Desmonde shall be held accountable. The Hedgemore project shall cease as of today. Is that clear?"

Stuart felt himself blushing furiously under her gaze and barely avoided stammering, "Perfectly, Prime Minister."

"Good. As for your requests, I reject them all and they will not"—she gave a hard glance to the home secretary—"even be presented to the Cabinet for discussion or consideration."

She paused and Lord Desmonde nodded. "Yes, Prime Minister."

She returned her gaze to Stuart and continued. "Do I need to enumerate them, Sir Malcolm? The extra staffing beyond what has already been granted you and the mobilizing of regular troops and reserves are expenditures vastly disproportionate to the gravity of the affair. Curfew on the future 'anniversary' evenings is an insult to London citizens. Personal D-Notice power for you is an absurdity—although you will manage to keep all the 'fantastic and confusing' details of this crime from the press. I will not read of occult rubbish in my morning *Times*."

"Yes, Prime Minister."

†

"I desire that this criminal shall be swiftly caught by ordinary police procedure and the entire business be reduced to the mundane, no matter how gory the actual murders may have been. If that is understood, you may go."

Stuart, still scarlet-cheeked and enraged, could not bring himself to speak again. He merely turned and left.

The Prime Minister eyed Lord Desmonde coldly.

He raised a brow and asked, "Something further, Prime Minister?"

"Yes, Dezzi. I want to warn you—do not dispose of Sir Edwards William at this moment. Do not raise this affair to crisis proportion in order to do so."

"No such intention has ever been mine, Madam Prime Minister."

"Good. You have in hand, I assume, a synopsis of the basic details of the crimes and the regular methods the police will be employing in their investigation?"

"I do."

"See that you confine your report to that. You may go in; I shall be along in a minute."

After the home secretary hung his bowler on his appointed peg, entered the Cabinet room and closed the doors behind him, calm returned to the anteroom. The prime minister surveyed the completed row of pegs with satisfaction. Had Walpole or Wellington administered rockets to their ministers on this same spot? Had an agenda for Peale or Palmerston included, as today's did, crisis in the Middle East, the horn of Africa, as well as in Poland and the Naval Reports? Had Disraeli paced this room, angered by the machinations of Gladstone, as she had earlier, fuming over the morning's statement by the nincompoop presently heading the Labor Party?

She was certain it was so; it was her comfort. Others had walked in her footsteps before her, had persevered and succeeded as she would. She was fond of Chesterton's defense of tradition and fond of quoting it: "We shall have the dead at our councils."

The irony was lost on her. One anonymous man, long dead, was infuriating her by intruding, unwanted, in her councils.

* * *

†

Dr. Percy set the blood-pressure cuff aside. "One-twenty-eight over seventy-nine." He smiled. "A most miraculous improvement. You look ten years younger besides. Good color, obvious energy, you even smile."

Lees laughed.

"To what should we attribute this turnaround, General? The diuretic"—the old doctor's eyes twinkled—"or a change of heart?"

Telling Ann, Lees told himself. Confessing, he almost admitted, but he scrubbed the word from his mind. Giving up my worst secret, that's what lifted the hypertension.

He smiled and said, "You tell me—you're the doctor."

Percy chuckled.

Once Stuart mastered his fury at the PM's dressing down, he debated internally for only twenty minutes before summoning Clive and Hughes to his office.

They had barely seated themselves before he said, "I'm going to disobey the prime minister." Clive's face was placid, Hughes' startled. "I'm going to bring Lees up here this evening as we had planned. See if he can't 'get' something to help us. If it doesn't succeed . . . it will probably mean the end of my career."

He rose from behind his desk and crossed to the wall of glass, as much to give room to his subordinates and avoid embarrassing them, as from any desire for a view of the autumn rain dousing Wellington Barracks. He thrust his hands in his trouser pockets. "That's all very well for me—what about you? I can't impose that sort of risk on you. If either of you would like to be taken off this case now, say the word. I would understand, and it would probably be the wisest course for both of you."

Clive shrugged. "In for a penny—in for a pound."

Hughes smiled at Stuart's back. "Not a chance. I have the feeling that this thing is . . . well, building. I sense tonight will be even more extraordinary. I wouldn't miss it."

Immensely moved, Stuart could only say, "Thank you."

The plastic insect came on through the thickening dusk with a metallic clacking, like a ratchet loosely geared. Its entire

†

head was one clear eye, colorless, translucent, curved and hard, unblinking and pitiless.

Schmetterlink, thought Lees.

The awkward German for *butterfly* was inextricably linked in his mind with helicopters, had been since his hundreds of rides in gunships over the rice paddies and jungles, and he wondered for the umpteenth time whether he would ever be able to see or hear a helicopter again without thinking of it as an iron butterfly, without having the word—*schmetterlink*—pop into his consciousness.

Probably not, he decided.

There was no pad at Hedgemore, so an area of the headland had been squared with several strings of Christmas lights. The RAF helicopter approached from the Channel, bobbing in the gusty wind. It found the area, hovered and lowered slowly to a landing so smooth the craft barely rocked as it touched down.

Good, thought Lees. I have a pilot who's not a cowboy.

He turned to look at Ann. Their eyes met; his were calm, as were hers, and love was suddenly back in them completely. They hugged fiercely, parted quickly. He turned and stooped, trotted to the helicopter and climbed inside.

It rose cleanly and beat back out over the Channel waters that were becoming indistinct in the swift fall of night.

The pilot was uncommunicative, and Lees was just as glad. The whirlybird found the Thames and followed it up to London. From the air, the city was a festival of lights that seemed ironically cheerful to Lees, as if it were preparing for a celebratory evening rather than an anniversary of savagery.

His mind suddenly clouded.

Fog; moving serial shapes; a blonde, a brunette; cracking sounds; shrieks; spider legs; rolling fog.

Lees hardly noticed the helicopter's descent or the quiet touchdown on the pad atop the recent additions to the Yard towers. He thanked the pilot for the comfortable flight and clambered out.

Stuart, Hughes and Clive were waiting for him.

At 8:50 P.M., three men entered the Haymarket Theatre.

Sir Anton Newbury, the playwright and director, led John

Bates and Terry Stanton, youngish leading men, inside and turned on the lobby lights.

"I know we've been over it and over it, but that second-act curtain just doesn't quite . . . click. I've two pages of new dialogue and I just want you to walk through them. I need to *hear* the lines aloud. From the stage."

Bates rolled his eyes, but Stanton merely shrugged amiably. Being cast, as unknowns, for Newbury's next play, *The Trial of Oscar Wilde,* due to open in ten days, was the break of their young careers. They were prepared to accept unusual demands, especially an eccentricity so mild as an unscheduled reading of new material for a scene that *was* unsatisfactory.

Sir Anton handed each of them a pair of typescript pages. "Go on down to the stage while I get the work lights up."

They sat on the stage in the dark until Anton, from the light booth, brought up the working spots.

The set, an Old Bailey replica, was brightened in the foreground, but remained shadowy upstage—gloomy, but somehow substantial-feeling, heavy with darkness.

Anton called down from the booth. "I forgot to lock the door. Look over the lines and I'll be right down."

Bates took his place standing in the dock, while Stanton crossed to the defense table. They began to read the pages silently.

Newbury, retracing his steps, was absorbed in ideas for possible further changes and did not notice the low sounds from the lobby. He strode, head down, toward the entrance by the ticket-taker's stand, but motion and noise brought him out of reverie and he froze a few feet from the stall.

A crowd clogged the lobby.

Hundreds of people were filing into the Haymarket, Victorian people in 1880s evening dress for theatre, and as they passed, moving slowly, with a curious expression on their pale faces and in their bright eyes, they held out shiny yellow tickets in the direction of the stall and dropped them. The tickets fluttered to the floor in twos and threes, making a pasteboard mound.

Newbury swiveled his head to take it in as people passed within inches of him without a flicker of recognition.

Silk hats, flowered bonnets, wing collars and cravats, floral-print dresses and velveteen gowns with daring bodices, tails and studded shirts, polished boots, beards and mustaches, piled, rolled hairdos. Pale papery-thin flesh and shiny marble eyes and blank fixed stares of stimuli-deprived creatures.

He bent and retrieved a fallen yellow ticket, straightened up and read the pasteboard:

> The Haymarket Theatre Management Presents:
> *Golden Girl*
>
> A comedy in 3 acts   September 29, 1988
> by   9:00 P.M.
> Randolph Friar
>   Admit One
>   Orchestra B5

He swallowed hard. He had an intuition—remain silent and wait until the Victorians finished filing into the theater.

Bates and Stanton heard the inner doors opening, heard a light conversational hum and the sound of many feet. They turned and peered out into the dark. The house lights came up.

Victorians were filing into the seats, quickly filling the ground floor and the staggered tiers of the three balconies.

The actors stared at one another and back at the eerie audience.

The house lights dimmed. The curtain came down. Rose again. The stage lights came up and the audience began to applaud.

Dead silence for ten seconds. Then light, polite applause as when a star makes an initial entrance.

Bates muttered, "What the hell. . . ?"

Stanton shrugged, and they saw the heads of the audience begin to move back and forth in some slow strange motion for some reason they could not discern.

Silence.

The actors stared at the audience. An explosion of laughter

startled them, causing them to flinch and cower as if struck.

Bates asked, "What do we do?" The laughter died away, exposing the last two words. They saw the head motion begin again and felt a sudden restlessness in the audience, which was cut short by an explosion of laughter that had barely begun to run down when another cascade of merriment rolled upward at them.

Silence.

Laughter.

Silence.

Laughter and applause.

They saw Newbury in the wings, the forefinger of his right hand to his lips indicating silence, his left hand making a cautious gesture of beckoning.

Laughter.

The actors began to edge toward the wings.

Silence.

Floorboards creaked. "Shit!" said Bates, and they froze.

Silence.

The head motion began again. The front-row patrons edged forward in their seats, preparing to rise, their heads turned toward the two actors stopped in their attempted exit.

An explosion of laughter so loud it seemed to shake the very walls crescendoed and rose again and again and again.

Bates and Stanton ran tiptoe offstage, and, under the cover of roaring, chuckling, guffawing and wheezing, the three men bolted out a side stage exit, slamming the door behind them. They stood shaking in the chill air.

Sir Anton Newbury said with emotion, "You young men have great acting careers ahead of you. You know when to shut up!"

Stanton said, "*I* also know when to exit—let's get the hell out of here!"

It took them half an hour to locate a policeman and another fifteen minutes to persuade him to investigate.

They waited outside while he entered to take a look.

He found nothing but an empty theater and a mound of bright yellow tickets from another century.

†

* * *

Stuart's office was tense despite the small table of food, sandwiches, cakes, tea, bouillon, despite the quiet tones of conversation, despite the hour—11:22 P.M. (nearly two hours before the precise anniversary of the third and fourth killings). Lees felt an almost eerie inner peace. He looked at his three companions.

Clive was haggard from the frustration of the hardest, best, sustained work of his career, with no tangible results to show for it. Hughes was keyed-up, electric. Stuart was outwardly cool, detached, in control, but Lees sensed his inner strain and did not have to be psychic to do so. He had described in all the detail he possessed the fog, shapes, women, images that were coming to him several times, and all of them had tried out ideas seeking clarification.

Now Lees said, "There's a unity in it. It feels all of a piece, as if I ought to be able to see the whole, and the details would come clear spontaneously."

Hughes nodded. "Me, too. Something sticks in my head about what you've described as if I know what it is, but it doesn't completely come to me."

"I'm at sea." Clive shrugged. "Can't make fish nor fowl of it."

Stuart nodded. "I don't get any sense of it."

Hughes said, "Perhaps, it's like one of those times you're trying to remember the name of an actor in an old film and you can't conjure it up no matter how hard you try. Later, you wake up in the middle of the night and say, 'Dennis Price.'"

Stuart was short. "Unfortunately, we don't have the luxury of sleeping on it."

"No," replied Hughes, "but perhaps if we draw our conscious attention elsewhere the thing might surface. Jim, why don't you tell us something about youself—maybe talk about your Vietnam experiences. As an Englishman, I've always wondered what that was truly about for Americans."

The Ripper worshipped alone.

His dressing was ritualized, almost devotional in mood—first the broadcloth trousers, linen shirt and waistcoat, the grainy textures no longer grating but now familiar to the skin, somehow sensual as physical symbols of the power, the release to come. From them to socks and half boots; slow, careful adjustment of the gray, silk cravat; easing into the suit coat; the final adornment of cape and top hat.

Again, thought the Ripper. It shall come again.

The door-mirror image of the late Victorian gentleman ready for an evening out was the same. The low light shadowed, softened the room.

Again, thought the Ripper. Stronger this time, more splendid, more powerful, more profound, more . . .

The electric shock at the base of the skull, and the building shook as if being pulled apart by time, then steadied. The gas lamps hissed hungrily.

The Victorian furnishings had replaced the contemporary. The wallpaper in a rose-and-gray rococo floral pattern was somber near to gloomy.

More! thought the Ripper, his face luminous with mounting need. More powers!

A shaft of black light coming in through the pentagonal stained-glass window passed, undisturbed, through the awning over the four-poster bed and made a solid black pentagon on the cream coverlet.

The Ripper turned from the mirror.

Yes!

He stared into the black light; flaming faces flickered and faded; shrieks only the Ripper could hear sounded cacophony.

"Yes! More!" the Ripper bellowed aloud.

The edge of the pentagon began to trace itself in thick, red liquid, moist and tacky, bordering itself in blood.

"Oh, yes!" shrieked the Ripper, limbs liquid with ecstasy.

The small black bag was on the floor beside the bed.

It opened itself.

The knife blade gleamed hypnotically from inside.

The Ripper knelt, removed the knife reverently, lifted it and placed it in the center of the pentagon.

Lees saw all this in his head.

He sat on the couch in Stuart's office, eyes wide and staring fixedly at the ceiling, sweating, entranced. He saw inside his head the scene inside the Ripper's room and tried to relate the horror while seeing it. The schock made him mutter, skip details, made his narrative disjointed, quirky.

"Mirror . . . image . . . low light . . . man . . . curly hair, dark hair, muttonchops, mustache . . . What?! . . . *Gas lamps!* Room different . . . older . . . darker . . . *What is that?"*

He was silent some seconds.

Stuart, Hughes and Clive exchanged swift, furtive glances.

"Black light . . . it's black light . . . on the bed . . . a pentagon." He shuddered and covered his ears; his face was contorted in pain.

The Ripper stared into the black light.
The knife blade glowed.
Red-hot.
White-hot.
Its aura was fire.
A face was in the fire, glowing, a Victorian face, like the new Ripper, but not a twin—sallower skin, darker eyes, clean-shaven save for long sideburns; hatless, with lank, lighter hair. But the eyes. The eyes were burning like the new Ripper's eyes. Mad, wanton, ravenous.
The old Ripper spoke.
"Your night has come round again."
The new Ripper whispered, "Yes, master."
"The powers grow."
"Yes, master."
"Use them and they shall increase for yet a fourth night."
The old Ripper glowed, grew, expanded as if to burst the blade and materialize.
"And the fourth night shall not be yours alone!"
"Yes, master."
"The fourth shall be—
"*Ours!*"
The old Ripper diminished, faded, fled. The blade became white hot.
Red-hot.
Gray.

†

Cooled until it was as cold as ice and hard as stone.

The black light withdrew, but the new Ripper remained kneeling, head bowed, eyes closed.

Praying.

Lees choked out the last words: "... praying ... the Ripper's praying and ..." His eyeballs rolled up as if disappearing into his head as he blacked out.

Clive fetched salts while Stuart brought brandy.

Felicia Bowen and Lisle Young were coked to the gills and had finished three bottles of champagne between them. They had dressed in party pretties for the journey to the country and had their overnight bags packed.

They stood in the foyer of Lisle's Knightsbridge flat.

The taxi glided to a stop in front.

It was 11:41 P.M.

Revived, Lees shuddered.

"The pain in my head ... seeing that was the worst I've ever felt." He froze. "Two women ... the ones I dreamt ... they're in a taxi ... the driver has silver eyes ..."

"Where are they, Jim?" Stuart asked softly.

"Don't know ... streets, houses, trees ... look vaguely familiar, but ..." He tightened his lips, shook his head.

"Shouldn't we go to the patrol car now? We'll be mobile as Jim sees more," Hughes suggested.

Stuart nodded.

They moved.

It was 11:53 P.M.

Lees' eyes were closed.

Fog, serial shapes, the women, cracking sounds, spider legs, shrieks.

"It's coming," he muttered.

Clive slowed in the desultory traffic of Birdcage Walk while the others turned in their seats.

"The fog curls ... but it isn't fog—it's steam and ... the shapes ... the women ... the cracking sounds and ... spidery legs ... but they're not ... they're metal overhead, like

†

girders . . . almost decorative . . . under glass, arched sooty glass, and the cracking sounds . . . no, crunching sounds, like gravel, no—cinders underfoot and the shrieks are whistles and the shapes are—*Trains! They're in an old train station full of steam locomotives!* with an arched dome of glass laced by black-iron girders.

Lees opened his eyes.

"Which one?" wondered Stuart aloud.

Lees closed his eyes and the picture was clearer.

"I've . . . I think I've been there . . . before—yes, I met Ann there when I came back from a NATO conference at Brighton."

He opened his eyes and smiled.

"Victoria Station."

Even stoned to the max, Felicia and Lisle were overwhelmed by external stimuli as they descended to the platform level of Victoria Station with Silver-Eyes at their elbows, guiding them.

The platform was moderately busy with late travelers in Victorian dress moving about slowly to and from trains. Steam poured from engines and porters humped freight and luggage and the whistle shrieks echoed to the sooted glass overhead and, barely visible through the network of girders, the clouds of gray smoke.

The women looked at each other.

They were Victorian. In dress and manner and look; worn, used, sick, with no visible defenses, no sophisticated makeup or clever couture or artfully focused lens to conceal as much as reveal. Their natures, their lives, their consciousnesses, were naked, as clear and repugnant as leprosy's open sores. Only the chemically elongated lag between thought and action prevented them from screaming.

They hated one another as one despises the all-too-lucid mirror.

In a dream-state of chemicals, time-warp, shock and manifested self-loathing, they glided under light pressure from Silver-Eyes, moved across the platform and onto a train.

The Ripper was waiting to show them to their separate and private compartments, their richly furnished anterooms to hell.

†

213

Silver-Eyes left them and walked forward, the cinders exploding and imploding underfoot, to the engine.

He mounted the empty cab; blew the shrill whistle.

It was 12:01 A.M., September 30, 1888.

Again.

Stuart and Lees, followed rapidly by Hughes and Clive, ran into the station and pulled up halfway down the stairs to the platforms, halted by a physical resistance, like a field with a waterlike quality of restraint—not insurmountable or impenetrable, but another medium, having a different set of internal laws and requiring another set of physical responses and actions.

The scene shocked them in its broad outline, overwhelmed and awed them in its scope, in its fine detail, filigree and brushwork.

Hughes was entranced. The familiar setting, transformed, pulled his eyes in every direction.

Steam engines. Stroudly D-class tank engines, nearly a dozen venting heavens of steam that insinuated around, over and through the lower tiers of black-iron girders, like cumulus among the triangles; blunt-nosed, squat, heavy-metal vehicles designed by William Stroudly for function *sans* grace. A potpourri of carriages: wooden and slope-roofed, of unequal heights and uniform, stubbed length; center-aisle walk-throughs interspersed with outside-door compartment-entrance-only cars; some gay in fresh coats of black, red, white and green paint, some dulled by use to an indistinct dinge.

Competing placards advertised Pears and Hudsons Soaps (the former favored by the Prince of Wales), Bovril and Nestlés Milk, Mellins Foods and One-All Manures and Seeds.

Figures flirted with the harsh artificial light of gas lamps, the refuge of shadows and steam. A long-weekend crowd of gentry moved back and forth across the scarred wood; women with flowing multi-layered skirts, tight bodices and strapped waists, or men—wing-collared, top-hatted, Prince Albert-coated, with gold watch chains dancing, bearded and mustached richly; they were all well-fed-looking, but oddly pale

†

despite the brisk evening, undoubted avid consumption of amusing clarets, distinguished ports and fine cognacs.

Lees and Stuart stared at each other dumbfounded. They had entered the station dressed in contemporary casual clothes suitable for action. Now, Stuart was clothed in a camel-color suit and a caped gray houndstooth overcoat with matching deerstalker hat, while Lees was top-hatted and Prince-Albert–coated with a snowy silk scarf. He might have mingled with the station crowd at that moment—12:12 A.M., September 30, 1888, unnoticed—especially since he was no longer clean-shaven, but now sported a neatly manicured beard.

Whistles shrieked. Steam vented in loud angry blasts and expanding mushrooms. Cinders crunched, cracked, exploded under the feet of hustling stewards and porters. People shouted excited holiday greetings.

"Where are they?" asked Stuart, coming out of his daze.

Lees pointed.

Several tracks away, a train was just beginning to move. The silver-eyed engineer laughed at them, blew the whistle. They ran down the steps and around the end-of-track platform, past the DINING AND REFRESHMENT ROOM, and jumped onto the cinder roadbed.

Clive and Hughes trailed after them. Clive jostled an arrogant-looking swell, nearly fell, and Hughes caught him, restoring his balance as Clive shouted, *"Watch where you're bloody well going, you ignorant sod!"*

The whistles stopped; steam hissed low and hostile. The Victorian passengers, porters, workmen, engineers slowed. Stopped. Began an odd turning back and forth of their heads.

Hughes and Clive stared around at them, truly noticed them for the first time, how deathly pale the skin was, almost thin enough to see through; button-bright eyes and fixed, blank faces; the queer cocked heads turning, as if listening intently.

"Christ! Look at these mad buggers, will you, Inspector?"

The man Clive had jostled turned his eyes, unseeing, toward the sergeant. Other Victorians angled their bodies toward them, began to shuffle slowly, tentatively, in their

†

direction. The man grappled the air, almost grabbing Clive, and the sergeant lost his already frayed temper, hit the man in the mouth with his beefy fist.

The man staggered backward and Clive's fist stung and there was blood on the Victorian's teeth, tongue. He licked it and his eyes cleared momentarily.

Lees and Stuart dodged between cars and crossed to the center track. The train was beginning to build up momentum and was ten yards away and gaining on them.

They lowered their heads and sprinted. Their hearts pounded, breath shortened.

Silver-Eyes shrieked the whistle and Lees could feel him laughing at them.

They closed to a yard, but couldn't seem to shorten the gap.

Lees was a tall slim man, Stuart a bull—stamina versus strength and both waning.

They increased their pace, muscles rubbering.

The train quickened.

Half a yard, but barely holding ground.

Stuart grasped Lees' armpits and shoved him forward; Lees grabbed the railing, got a foot on a step, pulled. Stuart dove and swung his body using the railing for leverage, hooking his feet on the train platform and clambering over the railing, grunting and sweating. They collapsed in a tangle, breath roaring in their throats like wind through a bent tunnel, rasping their inner tissues like a wire brush.

The train was leaving the station. Leaving Hughes and Clive behind. With the Victorians.

The train rolled out of Victoria Station and into the crisp fall nineteenth-century air.

Stuart gasped, "Jim . . . you okay? How's your heart?"

Lees wheezed, "Can't tell. My lungs've already collapsed, so I guess it doesn't matter."

They pulled themselves upright as the train rocked and rolled onto the railroad bridge across the Thames.

They stood stock-still and stared.

To the west, coming under Chelsea Bridge, ghostly in the

†

moonlight, was a three-masted clipper ship with all plain sail set.

She gleamed, hull up in calm water, creamy white with discreet red piping and her sails a pale India blue. She came on, swift and silent, sailing like a dream of spices and tobacco and exotic fruit, dusky women and tropical birds, warm trade winds.

Her crew was active in the rigging, on the decks, swarming in bare feet, white duck trousers and blue jerseys, looking like uniformed insects in a frenzy of obscure purpose.

Her name—*Calico Dancer*—was brassy bold along the bow.

She had just unloaded a cargo of rum and sugar from Jamaica and hemp from Haiti, was outward bound for cocoa and coffee from Venezuela. She went down with all hands in a hurricane off Barbados in August 1890.

The train was across the river, fleeing into Wandsworth.

Stuart and Lees shook themselves away from the lure of the vision, looked around.

Stuart said, "This bloody train is a *moving* time warp."

The Ripper entered Felicia Bowen's compartment.

She was seated, face turned to the window, stupefied in her fading cocaine haze at the Victorian garments she wore and the Victorian train and the Victorian suburbs through which it rolled, dazed by the bony, ugly, diseased face in the glass, a face from another era, a face that was not her and had always been her.

She saw the Ripper's reflection.

A man not much larger than herself with the dress, the look, of a Victorian dandy, glowing brown eyes projecting the consuming fire within.

"I am Elizabeth Stride," she said, and knew not where the words came from.

"I know," said the Ripper in a voice thick with another kind of disease, a mixture of hatred, bent love, sexual role jealousy and perversion, compulsive violence.

She turned her head, looked the Ripper in the eyes. "You must free me."

†

"I know."

"You must kill me."

"I know. I will."

He set the black bag on the seat.

It opened of its own accord.

She smiled; saw the gleaming knife within; smiled. She felt a warmth flood her, a release, a peace she had never known before and, commingled with serenity, a desire, a heat, a sexual passion hotter and stronger than all the lusts she had satiated throughout a life of multiple fantasy hedonism.

She stood.

The Ripper smiled tenderly.

"Hurry," she whispered, "hurry—I'm ready."

The Ripper grasped the knife, lifted it free.

She tore her tattered dress open from throat to waist, ripped again and it was open to her thighs.

"Hurry."

The Ripper presented the blade and she kissed it, touched it, licked it with a hungry tongue.

"Hurry."

She shrieked joy-terror-release as the blade leapt into her throat and slashed across, deep. Blood sprayed as her eyes rolled back into her head in the final inward turning, the last escape attempt—dying willfully. Her legs gave out and she crashed against the seat, slid to the floor with limpness already in her lifeless limbs, and the Ripper was on her.

Whimpering noises came from the Ripper's throat—glee, ecstasy, desire, release, the heat of momentary gratification of an unfillable need.

He ripped her.

Blood squirted, bones and cartilage cracked and popped with electric sound and flesh parted before the honed edge and his power.

He ripped her!

The initial squads of reinforcements that Clive had radioed for from the car came bursting into the station and immediately stopped, standing transfixed by the sight of time warp.

A sergeant pointed. A crowd of Victorians had hold of Clive

†

and Hughes and were wrestling them to the platform. Several had their mouths open wide as if to bite.

The train had just left the station.

Before the policemen could move to rescue Hughes and Clive the transformation began, like watching a wipe-transition in an old motion picture.

It began at the far end of the platform and proceeded to pick up speed at the train exit; as it moved, all the Victorians in its path, all the century-old advertising signs and physical objects disappeared; traveling behind the dissolve came the ordinary and routine inhabitants and objects that made up Victoria Station in September 1988.

All returned to the natural, leaving only echoed images on the retinas of the stunned policemen.

Hughes and Clive, suddenly freed, fell to the platform.

A contemporary porter and passengers, passing, gave the fallen officers odd stares of curiosity and, in some cases, contempt.

Lees said with wooden calm, "He's killed her. Elizabeth Stride is dead . . . he's ripping her."

They plunged down the center aisle of the carriage, flinging open doors on either side, glancing in and moving on, startling perfectly proper Victorian ladies and gentlemen with their frantic pace and movement, wild eyes and sweaty disheveled appearance.

One car, two cars.

The rickety, bouncing coupling platforms.

They stopped.

The blank back wall of a carriage faced them, immobile, unyielding.

"Shit," said Lees.

"Bloody hell," muttered Stuart.

They looked at one another.

"Up seems to be the only way."

"Can you do it, Jim?"

Lees grinned. "My heart won't get better standing here. Impotence has never had a calming effect on me."

Stuart laughed, locked and cupped his hands, made a step

for Lees. Lees placed his foot and Stuart lifted with all the power of his sixteen stone, heaved his friend up. Lees grabbed the closest metal ventilation tube and pulled himself up, spread-eagled on the roof.

The wind and the slipstream of the hurtling train were strong and tugged at him as he slewed his body around to face rearward, extending an arm toward Stuart.

The huge man stood on the coupling platform railing, grasped Lees' arm, forearm-to-forearm, and jump-pulled, grabbing the ventilation shaft with his other hand and levering himself up.

They lay prone, faces near.

The cold air was like a knife.

The whistle shrieked Silver-Eyes' taunt.

The train, accelerating to the point where speed almost negated friction, seemed on the verge of leaving the track altogether, had no margin between motion and destruction.

"My God, I had no idea these old trains could do this speed!" shouted Lees.

Stuart nodded. "Must be going sixty-five miles an hour!"

It was 12:39 A.M., September 30, 1888.

They had passed out of County London into County Kent and roared through the quaint station at Wrothham, passing startled, angry passengers waiting to board and welcoming parties for passengers expecting to disembark, hurtling on toward West Malling.

The moon was full, bright, revelatory. The countryside was dark-green, almost navy in the reflected light, tree-studded and intermittently forested; spiky lines of stone walls jigsawed the land; country church spires and warmly lit farmhouses and rural pubs softened the night.

They closed on a stately home of England ablaze in a glory of artificial light, forty visible windows incandescent from total inner illumination and terraces, gardens, grounds glowing with hundreds of strung lanterns ribboning several hundred yards in every direction from the mansion.

Music, gay music, party music, ball music filled the air with graceful presence, a sublime ease mingled with excitement, laughter, joy. Celebration of life was tangible as wood smoke, crisp as the moon and as alluring as the rustle of silk

†

or heady as the subtlety of a great and complex champagne.

A series of great doors to a ballroom revealed at a distance formal men and gowned women dancing, sharing conversation, wine, laughter, gaiety. There must have been more than a hundred people inside and the grounds were crawling with solitary strollers, couples, trios, quartets. Cigar ends flared and dimmed like out-of-season fireflies.

They were almost upon the estate.

A tall, golden-haired, Nordic-faced woman in a superb white gown and shoulder wrap stood on an upper terrace, elbow-length-white-gloved hands resting lightly on the wall. She turned her head slowly from side-to-side, scanning the gardens below her as if searching for a particular form and face.

"Alexandra . . ." whispered Stuart.

Lees looked at him.

"Alexandra," repeated Stuart. "Princess of Wales . . . she looks exactly like the photographs, only more . . ."

The track described an arc around the estate boundary, turning their perspective of the scene, rounding and softening the angles of sight as if they were stationary and the party scene revealed was an intricately arranged moment on a vast and slowly rotating stage prepared perfectly for their small brief audience.

Nearby, in a small alcove of the garden's ornately patterned hedges, a man and a woman embraced. The light from a single lantern above and barely beyond one hedge wall was indirect and the interior of the alcove could only be seen from their vantage point.

The woman was tall, wasp-waisted and large-breasted, with auburn hair towered and tiered; gowned stunningly in bold red, with diamonds gleaming from gloved wrists and arms, her hair, her ears and her pale throat. She had a fur wrap across her shoulders and one of the man's meaty hands was slipped inside, squeezing her left breast while her hands rested lightly on his shoulders and their bodies pressed together at waist and thigh. Their faces melted together and mouths were busy.

He was shortish, stout, bulky, excellently tailored for a formal evening and, pulling back from her, revealed a plump, beautifully bearded face. In his left hand he deftly held both a champagne glass and a priapic cigar.

"Bertie," said Stuart, and Lees nodded.

"I recognize him."

Stuart said drily, "The Prince of Wales was notorious for his marital indiscretions."

The train fully rounded the curve and their last glimpse of royal infidelity was the figure of Alexandra, still solitary, still slowly turning her face, still scanning, still searching—an image frozen in their heads for life in the tension of irresolution.

The train rocked dangerously. The whistle shrieked.

"Damn!" swore Lees.

"Got to move!" shouted Stuart.

Lees looked around and asked, "How will we see?!"

"Have to dangle over the edge. Look in the compartments upside down."

Lees nodded.

Stuart shrugged. "You take that side; I'll cover this one."

They edged along the roof, peering into and dismissing the curiously pale and blank occupants or empty interiors of the half-dozen compartments on each side that comprised the contents of the carriage.

Stood, braced, leapt dangerously to the next roof and repeated the process. Came to a center-aisle carriage, jumped down and raced through, whipping open doors like mad machines, finding nothing. Climbed laboriously up to the roof of another side-access car and repeated the process.

At 1:11 A.M., September 30, 1888, they jumped down to enter another center-aisle car, the sixth in a nine-car train, and halted midway in their routine.

The tiny room had been redecorated in blood.

Red, crimson, dark wine and near-black shades at various degrees of dryness splotched walls, windows, seats, floor.

And the pale body: cracked open, sliced and mutilated.

They froze, staring, chilled bone-deep by the insufferable sight of inexplicable brutality.

Stuart slapped his forehead, grabbed Lees and shook him. "We're doing this all wrong! Use your power—*see him! Where is he?*"

†

Lees shut his eyes and groaned, "He's with her. Her compartment is . . . in the carriage . . . just behind the engine."

They turned and ran.

The next carriage was close-ended. They repeated their climbing routine, stood upright, tentatively found footing on the roof—and halted.

A figure emerged from the dark, climbing the car's other end, rising slowly into view, filling the air with a huge caped and top-hatted and powerful form.

Lucian Nicholas stood facing them, laughing horribly.

The Ripper entered Lisle Young's compartment.

Lisle was a hag in the window and she knew her doom when she saw the Ripper's image and she wept bitterly.

The Ripper tried to soothe her, said softly, "It's time."

"No!"

Whispered, "It really is for the best."

"No!"

"You once portrayed Catherine Eddowes . . ."

She stared; the vague memory of a horror film surfaced.

"It has always been your destiny."

"No!"

She stood and backed against the door, implored with hands, face. "No! I can change! I can be better! I can . . ." Her mind fumbled for something, anything convincing and dramatic to show how complete her conversion from self-absorbed uselessness would be. "I . . . I"—her eyes widened and she smiled triumphantly through tears—"*I can become a nun!*"

The Ripper laughed hysterically.

Lees and Stuart fought for balance against wind and fear and unstable train motion as they edged toward the giant barring their way.

Nicholas laughed and extended his arms, his hands palms up, making a come-hither motion with his fingers. "Come on, lads," he cooed, "try me!"

They advanced slowly.

He turned, more swooping than leaping to the roof of the next carriage. He turned again and laughed and motioned them on again. "Come closer, lads. Try *me!*" He backed confidently toward the middle of the car.

Instinctively, Lees and Stuart moved together toward Silver-Eyes.

His hands were invisible in motion, seizing their throats and lifting them bodily at arms' length. He spread his arms outward and dangled them like marionettes out to his side, their bodies suspended above the ground rocketing past, dangling above fatal, body-breaking falls and supported by only Silver-Eyes' strength and will.

He laughed madly, and his rancid breath choked them.

"Think you're a match for me, lads? Think again!"

He laughed with glee, reveling in his power over them. He began to loosen his grip, eyeing one, then the other with sadistic glee to measure their terror as he did so.

The bag opened.

The Ripper withdrew the still bloody knife.

"Accept it, cow."

"No."

"Prepare to die!"

"No!"

"Yes!"

She fell to her knees. *"No! Please!"* Words tumbled from her mouth. "Anything—*please!* I'll do anything you want!"

The Ripper laughed.

"Anything!"

"That's more ridiculous than you know," the Ripper muttered and laughed again.

Stuart felt the grip loosening about his throat and knew he was about to die. The words of the Lord's Prayer came to him and he prayed aloud. "Our Father, Who art in heaven . . ."

Lees knew they were going to die, was unafraid, felt only the urge to say something, fumbled for good words. He heard Stuart and joined in. ". . . Thy kingdom come—"

The prayer was chopped short by the crashing together of their skulls as Silver-Eyes smashed their bodies together and dropped them as if burnt to the roof of the carriage. They fell in a tangle, ears ringing, dazed.

†

"*None of that* HIM *shit!*" screamed Silver-Eyes, and in one motion, he turned, soared past the car's end and dropped down out of sight.

They shook themselves apart and crawled.

To car's end.

Saw Silver-Eyes rip the last coupling bolt free with his hands.

"*No!*" screamed Stuart.

Nicholas laughed.

The cars began to separate, and they could feel their carriage begin to slow almost immediately.

"No," croaked Lees.

Silver-Eyes laughed.

"Then kiss me, Catherine Cow!"

Her lips were on the Ripper's and desperately hungry and she reached out with her hands to feel, touch, squeeze, and pressed hard with her body, smashing her tits flat and opening her eyes wide, startled by the sensation.

The Ripper slit her throat.

Blood everywhere.

Hot blood spurting.

The Ripper drank.

And let her fall.

Was on her.

Ripped her.

Silver-Eyes had climbed back to the engine, and the train sections were now separated by a quarter-mile. The whistle shrieked one last nasty cry as engine and single carriage disappeared around a curve of track.

"No," said Stuart listlessly.

Lees dropped his head. "Doesn't matter. She's dead. That's over."

"Again."

"Yes."

The carriages rolled on with draining momentum, and they noticed they were slowly approaching the station in Little-Storping-on-Whitby, would come to rest almost perfectly aligned with the passenger platform. But it was now 1:43

†

A.M., September 30, 1988, and they were the eunuch train's only live passengers. It was empty otherwise save, for the ripped body in the bloody compartment.

Stuart stood, his bulk emphasized by the odd outfit of caped houndstooth overcoat and deerstalker hat, a look of ineffable sorrow on his face as he stared into the distance at the lonely track where the Silver-Eyes express had disappeared.

Lees, suddenly exhausted beyond bearing, sat down abruptly with his legs dangling over the side of the halted carriage. He folded his hands between his legs, his shoulders slumping, head down with his silk top-hat, Prince Albert coat and silk neck scarf giving him a look of disheveled elegance.

Night birds and insects made noise; otherwise the village was quiet.

They remained motionless.

At 2:22 A.M. a heavy fog hung over the southern and southeastern suburbs of London.

In Sydenham, the grounds of the Crystal Palace (converted to a national sports center) were blanketed thickly. Despite the moderate temperatures, the pond was frozen solid. No snow had fallen, but the pond, banks and surrounding ridges were carpeted with a cold fluffy powder.

Several dozen warmly bundled Victorians—men, women and children—ice-skated on the pond in repetitive patterns. A cape-coated man bumped a small girl. She fell to the ice, wailed. He stopped and helped her up and he and her mother comforted her. Then he skated off, making a circuit of the pond.

He bumped the same small girl. She fell to the ice, wailed. He stopped and helped her up and he and her mother comforted her. Then he skated off.

Above the pond, on a natural terrace of protruding boulders, stood a leafless tree, its spiky limbs spidering the fog with crooked-claw branches. Grasping the tree trunk some five meters up were the blunt stone forelegs of a statue—a giant prehistoric monster looking vaguely like a dinosaur. It was reared up on hind legs, stretching eight or nine meters skyward, looming darkly above the tableau: a ponderous idea—half real, half artist's black imagination. In the night fog its damp surface seemed to breathe, and it poised itself as if momentarily energized with savage life to uproot its companion tree and fling it down upon the placid scene of the skating Victorians.

The wailing girl was comforted again.

The man skated off.

Priscilla Fortescue, fourteen, had decided to surrender her virtue to Rollin Sykes, fifteen.

They had been coming, late at night, to the Crystal Palace grounds for more than a month. They generally snuck out of their respectable middle-class homes around 1:30 A.M., proceeded to the woodsy area of the park, necked (and lately) petted and worked themselves to the brink of intercourse by 2:30 or so. Priscilla had always halted them there and, after frustrating decompression, they were ordinarily home, safe in bed, by 3:15 or 3:30.

Pris had finally agonized her way through to the decision to give her body as well as her heart and longing. Not that she hadn't felt a little out of step making "such a big deal about it," in the phrase of a thirteen-year-old friend and confidante. Still, some true inner instinct had guided her not to make light of final physical intimacy, and Rollin, also a virgin, had pledged his love without demanding sexual capitulation.

They walked comfortably and quietly together.

They were both tall, he six feet even and she five-eight, blond and slender. Pris was self-absorbed, once the decision was made, alternating between tingling anticipation and narcissistic fears of bodily inadequacy. Rollin didn't mind her distractedness. Somehow he sensed this might be the fateful night and was so excited he already had an erection. He was grateful for the thick blanket draped over his left forearm, carried so as to conceal the bulge in his tight jean pants.

They came out of a stand of trees and stopped.

They stared at the snow on the ground.

"There hasn't been any snowfall . . ." Rollin said wonderingly.

Pris frowned. "It's not cold enough."

They listened and heard scraping sounds and a muffled child's cry floating on the night air, drifting through the fog.

†

They stared at one another in the dark.

They walked softly over a small rise and down to the edge of the pond, and stared in disbelief at the skating Victorians. A man and a woman in the center of the pond comforted a small girl. The man skated off. The girl stopped sniffling.

Silence save the sound of skate blades cutting ice.

The Victorians skated in long swooping arcs, gliding, circling, swinging and swaying about the ice. They often skated close or at each other, seeming destined for collision but sliding away and apart just before contact, as if choreographed for some graceful pantomime of avoided disaster.

Pris and Rollin watched silently, mesmerized for several minutes.

At center ice, a cape-coated man bumped a small girl. She fell to the ice, wailed. He stopped and helped her up and he and a woman comforted her.

Rollin shook his head. "Didn't they do that same thing when we were walking up?"

"Yes, and how can the pond be frozen over? It's nowhere near cold enough."

Their voices carried strongly on the still air. Two skaters collided and fell to the ice, sliding into a third, who tumbled over them. A small boy lurched and fell onto the bank beneath the towering tree and looming stone monster.

The Victorians slowed, stopped.

Rotated their heads from side to side.

Listening.

Puzzled, Pris and Rollin stared silently.

The skaters resumed slowly.

A woman in fur hat and fur-trimmed waist-jacket over a long heavy wool dress circled toward them. She looked about twenty-five and was darkly pretty, with a plump, pert, preposterously pale face. The sound of skate blades was grating and the woman's runners dug deep, kicking up small puffs of ice in her wake.

Pris asked, "What is this?"

The woman did a reverse stop a meter away and turned her head back and forth.

"Why are you all in those costumes?"

Skaters tumbled, slid, fell; others stopped.

†

Listened.

"Are you deaf? Blind? Dumb?"

The woman brought her button-blue eyes to bear on Pris.

"Answer me!"

The woman skated to the edge of the pond, her arms and hands groping the air searchingly, seized Priscilla's arm.

Pris screamed.

Rollin reached out. "Let go of her!" He took the woman's arm and tried to free Pris.

The Victorians gathered themselves for motion.

The woman tugged Priscilla, dragging her toward the ice, and Pris screamed.

The skaters were moving, coming at them.

Rollin bent back one of the woman's fingers with both hands using all the strength he could muster. He had never felt someone so strong.

The woman's finger snapped, hung limp, broken. She registered no reaction, no pain, no feeling, kept dragging Priscilla onto the edge of the ice. The Victorian skaters closed on them, looming with pale irritated faces, groping hands, dead marble eyes.

Pris was crying and Rollin cursed.

The eyes were on them, at them.

He kicked the woman's feet and she slipped, fell, and two men tumbled over her into a heap as she lost her grip, flailing the air for balance and becoming the center of a whirlwind of falling bodies.

Rollin grabbed Priscilla's arm, but she fell and a small boy grabbed her ankle in a grip of iron, and she screamed as Rollin tugged, but the boy was too strong for him.

A man grabbed Rollin's throat, choking him toward blackness, and he felt his consciousness going, sight fading, the nightmare scene blurring. He dropped and kicked the man's legs, and they both fell, and Rollin pushed as they collided and the man tumbled aside down the bank.

The boy bit Priscilla's ankle and she shrieked in horror and pain as his teeth tore through cloth socks and ripped flesh and came away dripping blood, flecked with tissue. His eyes cleared and he smiled straight at Rollin, a hideous, beastly grin of wolfish blood-pleasure.

†

The others hesitated.

Sniffing.

Rollin seized the boy's coat collar and bottom, lifted him in fury and pitched him point-blank into the knot of skaters, sending them tumbling and knocking one another down like bowling pins. Bodies slid in all directions on the ice. He grabbed the fallen blanket and threw it in the face of the nearest man still standing, shoved the man's chest and he fell, slid, setting up another ripple of tumbling and collapsing skaters.

Rollin seized Priscilla's hand, pulled her to her feet.

They ran.

As they crested the small rise, they looked back.

Skaters were clambering to their feet. Half a dozen were trying to walk on the bank but stuck their blades in soft ground or fell clumsily. The small boy was on all fours, sniffing and licking the snow where blood stained it, trying to crawl along the trail of blood left by Priscilla's ankle.

They ran into the woods, panting, crashing over dead fallen limbs, crushing leaves underfoot. They stopped to catch their breath. Turned to go. Pris shrieked.

They had turned directly into another of the giant monster statues that dotted the grounds, a Victorian menagerie of grotesque mythic beasts. It seemed to totter on its stone base, reach for them with huge legs.

They ran and came to a clear space and stopped again to catch their breath, but immediately stiffened, stared, shook.

The fog was drifting up and away from them like a theater curtain being raised at a torturously slow pace, revealing a rising meadow terraced and hedged and gardened; vast pools dotted with fountains spraying columns of water higher than any man; stone urns and statuary and Victorian strollers crossing marble squares, climbing broad stone steps bounded by fluted heavy railings lined with more statuary and urns, a giant building rising two hundred fifty feet into the parting fog; centered and topped by a huge arch that sat upon rectangular descending tiers, each wing stretching away in geometric regularity, each section a repeating series of iron supports and grillwork clearly visible through the seemingly endless walls of solid glass.

†

Two thousand feet wide. More than four hundred feet deep. Thirty miles of guttering and two hundred miles of wooden sash bars visible. Nine hundred thousand square feet of glass housing nineteen thousand exhibits being viewed by a thousand or more of the pale, blank, unswerving Victorians.

Built in 1851 in Hyde Park.

Moved to Sydenham in 1854.

Burned to the ground in 1936.

The Crystal Palace risen from the past like a mammoth, glittering, jeweled Phoenix.

Rollin croaked hysterically, "Jesus Christ! It's the Crystal Palace!"

Pris began to cry again.

It gleamed and glowed from the gas lights within, beautiful and monstrous in its scope and reexistence.

"Oh, God," said Rollin.

His voice, Priscilla's sobs, carried on the night air.

The mob of Victorian strollers in the gardens and on the terraces slowed.

Stopped.

Began to turn their heads in a cocked, listening posture.

Pris and Rollin saw them.

Ran away into the night and fog.

Reflections From the Ripper's Journal

The ruthless, sleepless, unsmiling concentration upon self which is the mark of Hell.
—*C. S. Lewis*

MARCH 1987

I have struggled all the long month with the question.
  Be this madness or no madness?
  No one knows, no one can imagine the tortures of the damned I have suffered these long days. I fear for my sanity, but...
  I examine other paths.
  Forgiveness. Oh, revolting! To become, in fact as well as appearance, one of those dull sheep who note not slights and injuries—or worse—who, noting, readily excuse and forget. To live without pride or sense of place, to fawn and grovel and be ordinary as the common run of men. Impossible! I will not have it so.
  Truce? Then I—not she—should pay the unbearable pain of my unrepentant hatred, my fury. I will not have it so.
  But be these ideas mad? Let me settle this issue.
  If this be madness, let me examine the causes of these feelings, these desires, these facts, events and ... these plans? (Have I progressed to plans?)
  Causes of hatred:

1. She pretended to love me, but never did.
2. She has stolen, from me, all that I hold dear; love, hope, self-esteem, birthright—all!
3. She has always been loved; unjustly, I have not.

Are these just causes for hatred?
Yes.
What penalty, what revenge shall satisfy hatred?
  My justified hatred is an inferno that warms and sears and lights my soul. My justified hatred is a sword that cleaves me

from others, from wee, blind creatures who cannot, will not see the truth about her.

Shall such heroic hatred be satisfied with puny penalties or tepid revenge?

Never!

Death is the only possible penalty; the only just revenge. And no mere death, no quick and painless poison or barbiturate, no brief merciful fall, no easy ignorant death—she must know she is to die and know terror; she must know why she is to die and suffer anguish; she must see her death coming; she must feel her death happening; she must cry out in pain with no possible help, see her own mutilation, see her body cut open, torn, Ripped—yes, ripped!

If my hatred is just, and it is; if my hatred is all-powerful, and it is; if such supreme rage demands she be ripped to pieces in foreknowledge of her death, its just causes and in indescribable agony, and this is demanded; if these things be true—there must be a reason, a cause, a purpose for the convening of events.

The events:

1. My just hatred and its demands.
2. Her name.
3. Her age.
4. The Ripper centennial.

What cause can there be?

There must be purpose and purpose supposes logic and logic supposes a mind and a mind supposes a being, an entity.

What purpose can there be—for the purpose discerned will indicate the nature of the being, indicate the identity of the being.

The purpose must be the recreation of the murders.

Why recreate?

Because the initial creation was not fully satisfactory.

Who would have been left unsatisfied?

The Ripper?

Satan?

Both?

†

Both.

So all these things must be convening because I *am* to be his new instrument and shall, in some way, join with the old Ripper. I *am* to commit the fresh slaughter and bring the new terror.

I am chosen!
He must be seeking me; I shall seek him!
I accept!
I am chosen!
I will be his new Ripper!

MAY 1987

I have found the other cows!
If she is to die for her name, they will die for theirs; their names would have to be the same as his victims. It was laughably easy. All I had to do was open the book and there they were (perhaps the book is another reason I was chosen). There they were, just waiting to be slaughtered.
But there is more.
It will require more.
I will require help.
I must go to the source.
I must contact him!
Now that I have found my path, the release, the ecstasy is beyond imagining—transcendent, nearly beyond feeling. As when, the other day, I saw a picture in a book of the Ripper's final victim. I nearly fainted with pleasure when I saw the mutilated, putrescent thing. I came as I realized that is what I shall do to her, that grotesquerie shall be her. Tears of joy welled in me and I felt my wet hate trickle down my legs, smear my thighs, and I have never felt so fulfilled before.
And this was only thought, realization!
Ah, but the deed!
I have scoured the ancient books and writings for the ceremonies and rituals that are necessary. I shall begin. I shall pray to him!
My existence, my real existence, has narrowed to this single, overwhelming flame. I live my ordinary life, in fact am better at it for being freed, but it is nothing save motions, gestures, the vacant posturing of the unsuspecting, to the unsuspecting. It is a mask, a refuge, and I am safe, well and truly hidden. No one knows my fierce, true existence, but my destiny is clear before me and I am exultant.
I shall pray to him!

†

III
Mary Kelly

The devil is no fool. He can get people feeling
about heaven the way they ought to feel about
hell. He can make them fear the means of grace
the way they do not fear sin. And he does so,
not by light but by obscurity, not by realities
but by shadows; not by clarity and substance,
but by dreams and the creatures of psychosis.
And men are so poor in intellect that a few cold
chills down their spine will be enough to keep
them from ever finding out the truth about anything.
—*Thomas Merton*

III

Mary Kelly

OCTOBER 1, 1988

Rumors were rampant in London.

Many of the rumors were grounded in fact, garbled fragments of reality, but such odd fact and curious reality that they lent themselves to more than ordinary embellishment, misunderstanding and skepticism.

The squad of police who arrived at Victoria Station just as the time warp was pulled out by the leaving locomotive were talking—talking to journalists, other coppers, family, friends and acquaintances with no thought to the Official Secrets Act.

The account of the incident at the Haymarket Theatre was given great play because of the fame of Sir Anton Newbury. This prominence, in turn, lent support or credibility to the strange story of the reappearance of the Crystal Palace as told by Priscilla Fortescue and Rollin Sykes.

Phoned reports to the police and press from eyewitnesses along the route of the murder train numbered more than five hundred. Many cited momentary bizarre effects as the train passed—changes in physical surroundings, sudden appearances of hansom cabs and carriages and numbers of pale, sullen strangers with the look and garb of Victorians.

Still, it was Saturday, the weekend, and Scotland Yard could hold press and public at bay temporarily. So the detritus of the murders, two mutilated bodies on two sections of elderly train separated by twenty-some miles, was attended to in the customary manner. Hughes and Clive were left to oversee the pulling together of the routine investigation, while Stuart and Lees retired to Hedgemore to consider the latest failure. It was agreed that Hughes and Clive would drive down to Kent for a Sunday-afternoon conference to discuss

†

the massive shakeout sure to be coming as a result of the latest Ripper anniversary.

11:09 P.M.

Constable Parker James was one of the fruits of Stuart's most innovative yet traditional programs during his tenure as head of CID. It was a return to emphasis on and expansion of localized foot patrols.

Scotland Yard, despite the advent of the squad car, had always maintained a force on foot, but Stuart decided to allocate substantially more men to it and to strengthen the old neighborhood concept.

Teams were assigned to city areas and patroled them for eighteen-month tours, with optional reassignment for an additional year-and-a-half tour. This enabled officers to become intimate with an area of the city, its residents, businesses, lifestyle and law-enforcement needs.

Parker James had been rotating nightly within the adjoining areas of Bayswater, Maida Vale, Marylebone and St. John's Wood for nearly two years. He was so familiar with the life of the area that he functioned easily and quickly as an anticipator of trouble, protector of persons and property, mediator of disputes and security-blanket figure for the inhabitants. He was ideally suited to the job by his youthful (twenty-eight years) vigor; fair-haired good-looks; large, athletic and reassuring build; easy, outgoing personality and active intelligence, which was mirrored in his friendly gray eyes. Most of all, he loved the assignment, and his clear enthusiasm endeared him to the people he served.

A case in point was Chumly Wells, a fiftyish, widowed, childless, pensioner drunk who could be counted on to show up on Constable James' beat Fridays and Saturdays, fully intoxicated. He was a lonely old man, and James would greet him warmly, have a short chat (always mentioning the possibility of help for Wells' drinking problem) and make sure he got a cab or bus or train to his Hampstead home.

On this night, they were walking along Lord's Cricket Ground when they saw the Thomas Tilling Horse Bus parked beneath a streetlamp. The island of yellow light seemed

†

grainy, like an old crude photograph inserted in the frame of clear night and smooth dark.

The bus was bright red and gay; the team of black horses were richly groomed, docile and handsome. Double-decked, with an open-air upper and enclosed lower, it had three lace-curtained windows to a side and sported bold advertising signs:

Job Horses	T. TILLING	Private
Weddings	JOB-MASTERS	Omnibus
	Chief Office-Peckham	
NESTLÉS MILK		HUDSON'S
Richest in Cream		SOAP

A rear platform provided entry to the six-passenger inner compartment or access to curved wood-enclosed brass-railed stairs to the nine-seat upper. A huge pale man bundled in a heavy broadcloth overcoat half-sat, half-stood on a braced platform above the horses, but below the railing of the upper seating. A long snaky whip and silk top hat completed the driver's uniform.

He turned his head and Parker James, stunned by the sight, slowed, stopped. Cast-Iron Billy, he thought. Chumly Wells, so drunk he saw nothing out of the way in the apparition of a Victorian horse bus, broke into a trotting shuffle and sang out cheerfully over his shoulder, "See you next week, Constable! Thanks again!"

He leaped to the rear platform as the driver cracked the long whip, the bus lurched into motion and James came out of his daze.

"Chumly! Wait!"

He ran.

The bus picked up speed and turned northwest onto Wellington Road, disappeared. A hissing sound caught James' attention in mid-stride and he turned his head, slowed again, stopped, stared. Up. The streetlamp was nearly twice his

†

height, a bulbous clear-glass iron-framed globe that tapered outward as it rose and gave off a grainy yellow light from the flame of its sulfureous gas-jet.

Mad, he thought.

He ran for the corner.

The horse bus was out of sight.

He cursed under his breath as he ran for the nearest call box.

Cast-Iron Billy? he wondered.

The wind of motion through cool night air was bracing, head clearing, and Chumly Wells walked, holding the rail, toward the front of the omnibus. He leaned close to the driver, asked, "What's the fare, old son?"

Cast-Iron Billy cocked his head oddly and a furrow of irritation knitted his brow; his voice was loud, sharp and hostile. "Abbey Road to Golders Green via St. John's Wood, Marylebone and Hampstead Heath!"

He swung the whip sharply in a back and forth arc, the tail grazing Chumly's cheek and drawing a thin line of blood.

"*Sod you!*" yelped Wells, jumping back and grabbing his face. He brought his hand away and it was smeared with blood.

Cast-Iron Billy yelled, "*Abbey Road to Golders Green via St. John's Wood, Marylebone and Hampstead Heath!*"

Wells pulled away, staggered to the rear and the stairs. The bus was clattering along too fast to get off. He fumbled down to the door, opened it and stepped into the interior, closed the door behind him.

A lurch of the bus sat him in an empty seat with an unceremonious thump. The compartment was close, stuffy, and he gazed about in whisky haze trying to orient himself. The next seat was occupied by a silent, sullen ape of a workman in a shabby suit, dead-pale stubble-covered face beneath a coal-dusty derby. He held an empty tin lunch pail in his lap; turned his head slowly, awkwardly.

Sniffing.

In front of Chumly sat a couple. He, a bulky blond youth with pale arrogant face above wing-collared Victorian evening

†

clothes; she, a pale delicate young woman of thin dark-haired beauty in fur wrap and satin gown.

They had the air of interrupted chatter and turned their heads slowly, sniffing. Murmuring.

"Marvelous ball..."

"Freddie Thistlewaite was ever so dashing."

"The new dances are exciting."

"Miranda was radiant..."

Chumly shook his head; tried to clear the whisky trance enough to understand what was wrong with ... all this. He looked. The glass windows were shined squeaky clean and the hourglass-shaped lace curtains with floral pattern were laundered, starched and homey.

For 1888.

The thought, Horse bus, penetrated his drunken brain.

"What's going on here...?"

The trio of heads began to move slowly back and forth with a cocked-ear attitude.

"Bloody driver whipped me for no reason. Cut my face."

The faces angled toward him in a searching attitude, bodies swiveling in seats. They sniffed. The woman licked her lips.

"Are you people deaf? I asked—what's going on here?!"

The couple's voices were low, but thrilled, excited, as the trio edged toward Chumly Wells.

"Marvelous ball..."

"Freddie Thistlewaite was ever so dashing."

"The new dances are exciting."

"Miranda was radiant..."

The woman reached out, groped, touched his split cheek. Her hand came away blood-smeared. She sniffed it. They all sniffed.

"What?!..."

She licked her fingers like a cat.

Her eyes cleared briefly, and he saw naked desire in them, obsession unrestrained, primitive lust in waves as powerful as an ocean, hot as the sun. His whisper was horror: "Oh ... no!"

The men groped, grabbed, seized him by his arms.

"*Let me go!*"

She put her arms around his neck and opened her mouth wide; red tongue and white teeth, rancid breath.

He struggled and screamed, but they were too strong, too eager, too ferocious. Bore him down.

"Marvelous ball! . . ."
"Freddie Thistlewaite was ever so dashing!"
"The new dances are exciting!"
"Miranda was radiant!"

The driver cracked the whip.

The horses charged and the gay red bus clattered and rumbled through the night, rocking and swaying, the thundering hooves and roaring wood wheels drowning the screams of pain and fear, the shrieks of ecstasy from within.

Parker James climbed into the patrol car and the driver asked in a sarcastic tone, "All right then, Constable. Where did your bloody runaway horse bus go?"

James conjured up the image of the omnibus in his mind, remembered the band of black-and-white tile about the body that proclaimed the route: ABBEY ROAD ST. JOHN'S WOOD MARYLEBONE HAMPSTEAD HEATH GOLDERS GREEN

"Head up Wellington Road toward Hampstead."

The sergeant, sitting next to the driver, snorted. "Right. Hampstead it is. Good a place as any to trail the wild goose."

Twice, enroute, nervous pedestrians flagged them down to enquire if the Thomas Tilling Horse Bus they'd seen had anything to do with the Ripper murders.

Constable Parker James took no satisfaction from the altered looks the driver and sergeant began to give him.

They found Chumly Wells on a deserted grassy knoll at the edge of Hampstead Heath. He lay on his back with his legs spread-eagled, his arms flung wide. His skin was pale from exsanguination and already cooling. His clothes were torn apart.

His throat was ripped out.

His chest was ravaged.

The thin light of the sergeant's torch showed different sets

†

of tooth-marks in the tissue around the wounds, as if someone or something had savaged huge chunks from his throat, shoulders, chest and stomach.

The driver was shaking silently and the sergeant passed a hand across his eyes wearily. He moved his torch to Chumly Wells' face.

The eyes were wide open, dilated, smooth, slick like mirrors and reflected a fixed image—the face of a pale-pretty, dark-haired and delicate young woman, her red lips parted, white teeth gleaming, an expression of unbearable desire on her face.

Parker James turned away. The nightmare connected in his mind with a conversation of several weeks before. Two residents of the area, Hugh and Meg Brandon, had become good friends and they had shared with him their spooky experience with the boy match-seller. He couldn't see how to relate the two incidents in the stifling limits of an official report, decided he would have to talk to someone in authority.

After the night and day he'd had, Clive didn't appreciate being roused from his sleep by an enterprising constable who'd gone to the Yard and secured his home telephone number. But after he'd heard the first few details of Parker James' story, he agreed to meet him at an all-night tea-and-sandwich shop on Oxford Street.

By 4:44 A.M., they'd finished two pots of tea, a roast-beef sandwich each and several slices of pie. James had also finished his recital of the incidents.

"The tyke didn't do anything else? Just screamed at them?"

"No, that's all. They kept repeating that he moved his head . . . well . . . almost as if he were blind, as if placing them by sound."

Clive nodded. "That fits in with what I saw at Victoria, and with the early reports about the Haymarket and the incident at Sydenham. That's not for publication, mind."

James nodded.

Clive asked, "Sunday your off-shift?"

"Yes. Think I'll have a proper sleep-out."

Clive smiled; there was some rough justice in duty commanding him to turn tables on the younger man. "Afraid not, Constable. First, you and I'll have a look at the late Chumly Wells; then, we'll pop back to the Yard to collect notes and meet Chief Inspector Hughes for a drive down to Kent."

A cold afternoon rain pelted the French doors of the library at Hedgemore, obscuring the view of the trees that masked The Shoots.

Inside, six men sat in a semi-circle of stuffed chairs facing a brisk coal fire and nursing drinks. For half an hour, Stuart, Lees, Hughes, Clive and Cochran had listened to Parker James. The young man had handled his narrative well despite a certain nervousness at reciting for the deputy commissioner, a chief inspector, the senior sergeant in CID and two retired American general officers.

"There's just one last thing," he said. "The driver of the omnibus. I don't exactly know how to put it, but I think I *recognized* him."

Clive frowned. "Why didn't you tell me before. We'll want to get men right on it! Time's awasting!"

"Well," drawled James, "it's not quite like that. It's . . . an oddity."

Lees grimaced. "Everything about this business is odd."

"Yes, sir. The thing is, my father was something of a buff on Victorian transport. Steam engines, hansom cabs, and . . . horse buses. He collected books and articles and photographs, and he shared his hobby with me. Thomas Tilling had a famous employee, a driver of his omnibuses in the seventies and eighties. I still have some of my father's collection and there are any number of photographs of the man. Cast-Iron Billy was his name."

Clive made a face of disgust. "And you're going to tell us Cast-Iron Billy was driving this Thomas Tilling Omnibus down Abbey Road last night."

James shrugged. "It certainly looked like him, Sergeant. His name popped into my head as soon as I saw the driver."

Stuart and Lees exchanged glances. Stuart smiled gently. "Don't feel bad, Constable. Friday night, on our harumscarum train trip, General Lees and I passed a country home where a Victorian dress ball was in progress. We believe we saw Albert Edward, Prince of Wales, and Princess Alexandra in the gardens."

"Oh." James digested that idea. Smiled. "Thank you, sir."

Stuart turned to Clive. "Sergeant, you said that Constable James' story had combined with some other reports to give you a theory."

Clive finished his tea and set the cup aside. "Yes, sir. I'm not happy with what I'm about to say, but . . ." He produced a box from his pocket. It was wood, a matchbox with a colored label: BRYANT & MAY'S ALPINE VESUVIANS. "We stopped, on our way down, at the home of Mr. and Mrs. Brandon. He was kind enough to lend us this box, the matches he bought from the strange boy. As you'll note, it is a nineteenth-century box of matches, and looks it. Paper label faded, discolored, peeling at the corners; wood soft and rotting. Just as you'd expect. But Mr. Brandon says the box was new, fresh, looked of recent manufacture when he bought it. Said he chucked it on a shelf and hadn't looked at it again until today." He frowned. "This box clearly links the match-seller incident with all the other barminess. It happened after the first murder and, as far as we know, it was the first 'out-of-time' incident that occurred separate from a murder evening. And it was small. Nothing much happened except a nice young couple got spooked. Last week I received a report that had apparently slipped through some crack or other.

"Just after the second murder, there seems to have been another incident. A young art student was taking a late-night walk and, on Heneage Street, was attracted by what he described as a glowing wall. A wall plastered with nineteenth-century advertisements. He even recognized two of the theater posters because they were examples of Victorian poster art used in a textbook he'd studied. Anyway, he says, as he looked at the advertisements he seemed to experience the products. Music hall crowds and noises, the sailing motion of a cross-Channel packet. He got physically ill and ran away.

"That's a second incident where nothing too terrible happened except for a good fright.

"Then we have the incident of the street traders down by

The Oval. We've all read the report—does anyone want to challenge its linkage to the rest of this?"

There were head shakes and murmured nos.

"In that incident, things got out of hand. Young Viscount Saltmare had his elbow broken and the barrister, Allen, received a cut on his arm. And if they hadn't fled into the house"—Clive shrugged—"who knows?"

"That gives us an incident with physical harm inflicted between anniversary evenings two and three. And, on Friday, we have the Haymarket Theatre thing, involving several hundred of these throwbacks or whatever they are, just before the train murders. Right afterwards, the event at Sydenham where a young boy and girl were attacked and—they say—the bloody Crystal Palace reappeared. And last night we have a man, well—eaten to death on an omnibus.

"What I'm getting at is: each Ripper re-creation seems to be more *elaborate* than the previous one, and the intervening 'incidents' are growing in a sort of parallel."

Stuart rose and crossed to the fire. "Sergeant, you have set the situation admirably." He warmed his hands, then thrust them into his pockets and turned to face the other men. "We have to anticipate, and one event that requires thought is the near certainty that within the week, I will either be given the chop or have to resign."

The other men stared at him, then exchanged glances of consternation.

"Sir Edwards William?" Hughes asked.

Stuart nodded. "He can no longer be pacified with sanitized reports and précis, and given the situation, one can hardly blame him." He stared at the French doors, the streaky wash of rainwater against the glass panels. "He has informed me that he will make his complaints public tomorrow. Whoever is brought in as head of CID will be unfamiliar with the case and, in the ordinary sense, resistant to notions of the supernatural. Assuming that, I suspect General Lees or the product of his gift will not be welcome. Yet I believe that if there is to be a solution, it will come from Lees. The team is disbanded as of yesterday, but I will continue to offer the hospitality of Hedgemore and whatever help my private resources can muster. Jim?"

†

Lees smiled. "Of course. I will stay on, and—push for a breakthrough."

"Good. I am also assuming that the case officers"—he smiled at Hughes and Clive—"will wish to be kept informed of any progress."

Clive nodded and Hughes said, "Certainly."

"Then discreet communication will be necessary. I should like to suggest that Constable James, so conveniently to hand, be temporarily reassigned as administrative assistant to Sergeant Clive. And that General Cochran, if he is willing, be liaison to Constable James. That would keep meetings and communications one step removed from the chief case officers and from Hedgemore."

Pat Cochran grinned. "Suits me."

Parker James nodded. "Done."

"Good. Now we will have to await the events."

They all looked at Lees.

The world press had been treating the neo-Ripper murders as a gore-oddity feature with a sidebar of historical resonance, but the weekend reports out of London were sufficiently provocative to cause a news-value reassessment.

An invasion of foreign journalists began on Monday and continued throughout the week. The attention of the globe turned slowly toward London, the city that had been—in late Victorian and Edwardian times—the hub of the world.

This emphasis was, once more, a soft halftone, like an echo at the margin of hearing.

Monday morning, Sir Edwards William called a press conference at the Yard's new press-reception center.

Sir Edwards, a florid, beefy John Bull-type Englishman, sat behind a bank of microphones, uncomfortable in the harsh glare of television lights.

He read a prepared statement:

"For more than a month the priority of New Scotland Yard has been the investigation of the neo-Ripper murders. As the recent article in the *London Daily* by Mr. Carl Collins has charged, many vital details of the inquiry have been denied the press and public.

"The conspiracy is internal as well as external. During this investigation, the prime minister, the home secretary and Deputy Commissioner Stuart have contrived to keep the pertinent workings of the investigation from me.

"My protestations and implorings have been to no avail. I have been prevented from carrying out the duties and responsibilities with which I am charged.

"Under the present circumstances, I am left with no honorable alternative. I have, today, tendered my resignation as Commissioner of New Scotland Yard to the prime minister."

By Tuesday, Sir Edwards' resignation had the government in full crisis. In Parliament, the opposition called for a vote of no confidence, and the government survived by only one vote.

The PM called a full Cabinet meeting to address the crisis at five P.M.

The Prime Minister settled herself in her leather armchair midway down the table in the Cabinet room. Van Loo's portrait of Walpole stared dourly down on her as the clock on the mantelpiece registered 5:11. The modest coal fire at her back glowed benignly, unlike the furnace of fury inside her.

The Cabinet sat in silence.

The prime minister moved her cold stare across the face of each minister until it came to rest on the poker-faced countenance of Lord Desmonde. Her voice was acid. *"Perhaps* the home secretary should like to advise the government about the departmental squabble and the domestic crises that have conspired to bring this government within a single vote of falling."

Desmonde's manner was diffident; his voice bland. "In what respect would the government care to be enlightened?"

"You may conform, Lord Desmonde, to the five Ws of journalism—who, what, when, where and, most importantly, why."

Lord Desmonde crossed his legs. The silence was deafening. He realized his political career was in the balance. He might never again sit at the long table, each position indicated by the dark, leather-bound note folders above a ministerial title below. He saw, with satisfaction, that none of the folders were open, no one had taken up a pen. He marshaled his thoughts.

†

"No notes," were his first words.

There were several affirmative nods and the prime minister said, "Agreed."

"I believe the government is acquainted with the fact that Sir Edwards William is an ass."

There were numerous smiles and a few chuckles; the PM was unmoved.

"He was appointed Commissioner of New Scotland Yard by my predecessor, who has since departed this mortal life, so I shall not speculate upon his motives for the appointment.

"Nonetheless, the man is an ass. Worse, he is ambitious. Worse still, despite his nominal registration as a Conservative, his chief friends and supporters in the house are Liberals and Labour and Social Democrats."

He stared up at the portrait of Walpole. Walpole remained dour.

Desmonde brought his gaze to meet the PM. "Madam Prime Minister, for reasons known only to yourself, I have been instructed, since I took this post, that it would be politically inexpedient to sack Sir Edwards. Obedient to your wishes, I have, for some time, maneuvered him into a position where he holds his office in name only. I have done so in order to protect this government from his traitorous ambition and in hopes of inducing him to resign. He has not done so and I have not been allowed to fire him and he has been a thorn in this government's side, unpulled and festering, for years.

Lord Desmonde uncrossed his legs, sat up and leaned across the table in the direction of the prime minister. "He has resigned. Leave him. He will fade away. But, reinstated, he would become a deadly infection in this government!"

There were numerous nods and several "hear-hears" around the table; the PM remained unmoved. She leaned toward the Lord Desmonde. "You speak well to Sir Edwards; you say nothing of the current crisis."

"I have asked Deputy Commissioner Stuart here, as he can give a clearer account than I; I left him waiting in the anteroom."

Silence fell on the room again. It was if the home secretary had slapped the prime minister.

†

The PM did not explode. She mastered herself, nodded and spoke with tongue of honey that does not cover the vinegar. "Then you may fetch him, Mr. Home Secretary."

Lord Desmonde glanced at the buttons in front of the PM's chair used to summon those waiting in the anteroom and, briefly, toyed with the notion of reaching out and stabbing the appropriate one.

The Cabinet tensed.

Desmonde submitted.

He rose and strolled to the doors, opened one and motioned Stuart inside. Stuart sat in a vacant chair at the foot of the table and Lord Desmonde resumed his normal seat.

The PM's tone remained icy. "Sir Malcolm, be so kind as to summarize the current state of the Ripper crisis and investigation."

We are the straw men, thought Stuart, staring down the long table at the cautious rows of faces turned to him. "That, Madam Prime Minister, is somewhat difficult. The normal side, the ordinary side of the investigation, proceeds along conventional lines: examination of the physical evidence; circulation of the perpetrator's description; inquiry into the background and associates of the victims. All very routine, all proven method, all briskly undertaken by an enormous number of CID staff, and *all*, in my opinion, utterly useless."

Silence descended on the room again.

Salisbury never had this problem, thought the prime minister. What do I do now? She said, "You're going to talk to us about the supernatural, aren't you?"

Stuart nodded. "If you wish me to speak intelligently on this matter, I shall have to do so."

"By all means, speak intelligently."

Stuart recited the supernatural side of the case. He discussed the implications of the physical facts and phenomena. He finished with a summary of the Victoria Station train ride, which elicited ministerial stares ranging in expression from fascinated incredulity to irritable dismissal and outright contempt.

No one spoke for some time after his recital. Finally, the PM broke the silence. "Thank you, Sir Malcolm. That will suffice." After he left, she shook her head. "This case has ob-

†

viously unhinged Sir Malcolm. We shall all hope it is temporary." She turned to Lord Desmonde. "He has to go."

The HS nodded. "Obviously."

"And, clearly, if it was impractical to give Sir Edwards the chop previously, it is *impossible* to allow him to resign now."

Cabinet ministers nodded and murmured assent.

The prime minister closed the meeting with the same icy formality that she had used to open it. "Lord Desmonde, it shall be your task to carry the olive branch to Sir Edwards and see that he accepts it. *Publicly.*"

Thursday, Sir Edwards William withdrew his resignation at another press conference where he also, gleefully, announced the firing of Sir Malcolm Stuart. Chief Inspector Hughes was appointed Acting Deputy Commissioner for CID until a permanent appointee could be named.

By Thursday afternoon, Stuart had cleaned out his desk at the Yard and the security force at Hedgemore had been recalled to London.

Stuart sat in his Duke Street study placing the personal items and files he had taken from the Yard in his private desk. Steady October rain tattooed the casement windows, darkened the day and hid Grosvenor Square from view.

Vanessa Cilone opened the door quietly, stopped and looked at her lover. His posture was still upright and straight, but his movements were slow and distractedly deliberate, his face tired and sad to dreaminess.

"Malcolm," she said softly.

He swiveled his chair to face her fully.

"I heard the news on the set. I came straightaway."

He restrained tears, held his arms wide and she flew into them. "Oh, Malcolm, darling, I'm so sorry. They're such awful fools to abandon the best man they'll ever have."

He hugged hard, stroked her hair. "Poor girl—you've put your money on a flat-footed horse who's been scratched from the race."

She leaned back in his arms and looked at him. "Malcolm Stuart, it's not you that's been scratched. It's *their* silly race that's been called."

†

He laughed and squeezed her. "Oh, you are a grand girl, my Vanessa."

They looked at one another. "Marry me," he blurted.

Her eyes widened in shock.

He took her expression of surprised disbelief for distaste. "I'm sorry. I shouldn't have asked that. I suppose the moment provoked—"

"Malcolm!" she snapped, cutting off his disclaimer. "Don't you dare retract those two words. I have been waiting and hoping for more than two years that you would speak them to me. You may not have them back and I accept and just you try to get out of that!"

He stared at her—stunned. "You do? You will? You want to . . . marry me?"

"Why, you great fool—you mean you didn't know?"

He shook his head.

Her face softened; she whispered, "More than anything else in life I wish to be Mrs. Malcolm Stuart."

"Lady Stuart," he corrected drily. "They haven't stripped me of my knighthood."

She laughed.

And they made love and talked for hours excitedly, making plans, sharing emotions—even their mutual fears, which had kept them from discovering their mutual desire for public and official commitment.

She called friends and arranged a spur-of-the-moment weekend at Hedgemore, a party to "cheer Malcolm up." Stuart relaxed listening to her chatter and grinned like an inane boy—for that moment, the happiest man in London. Healing grace turned a day of disaster into a day of joy, and Stuart's sense of failure and humiliation was lifted by love.

During the week 567 journalists of all qualities and descriptions descended on London.

A candidate for the very best might have been Jake Morgan. Semi-retired at sixty-six, he was an intense, stocky man, with salt-and-pepper hair, and gentle yet penetrating eyes. A three-time Pulitzer Prize winner, he had, in the fifties and sixties, been the finest political writer in America. In 1969 he had abandoned his syndicated column, and he now only covered stories or subjects worthy of book-length treatment. He had come to London to investigate whether or not there was a book in the Ripper crisis.

He checked into a suite at Brown's, unpacked, lit one of his fine, ubiquitous Manila cigars and began calling people. A World War II fighter-pilot, he had married Janice Duncan, daughter of a Scots lord, so that he not only knew everybody in or out of power in North America, he also knew everybody in England. He simply began calling friends and finding out things.

A certain candidate for the very worst among them would have to have been Bridget Genaro Garcia, twenty-seven, roving anchorperson for the Eagle Broadcast Network. A lush-bodied, dark-haired, olive-skinned sexpot with startling blue eyes, her education, training and experience prior to her EBN elevation were a high-school degree from Yuba City, California, four years as a child-bride/housewife to a nomadic and drunken oil-worker, two years as a divorcee-waitress in Texarkana, Texas, two and a half years as a semi-successful model in Indianapolis, Indiana, and Denver, Colorado, and three and a half weeks as a weather-girl for the local television station in Aspen, Colorado.

She was entirely the creation of a media poll. EBN, six months into its network infancy, had commissioned the largest media poll ever undertaken in search of the "perfect" news-star. More than five hundred thousand viewers of network news had been questioned and the resulting profile was young, sexy, female, ethnic-but-not-black. The top executives of EBN, vacationing in Aspen and mulling the results of the poll, were presented with an on-screen live image of the poll's conclusion—a young sexy female of Irish-Italian-Hispanic descent.

They signed her to a two-year contract at $250,000 a year, trained her for three months in voice, diction, poise and remedial reading and foisted her on the public. In her six months on the tube, EBN's ratings and market share for their nightly news had rocketed them into second place, only fractions of a point away from first. EBN had, the week before,

†

negotiated a new six-year contract with her that started with an annual salary of $2,000,000 and escalated to $4,000,000 per annum by 1993.

She arrived in London on the afternoon of the seventh with her permanent entourage of cameramen, light and sound technicians, researchers, producers, directors, assistants to everybody, gofers to everybody, manicurists, hair-stylists, cosmetic advisors, wardrobe supervisors and three round-the-clock escorts for her four toy poodles (three males named Sam, Arnie and George after her EBN bosses and a bitch named Bridget; "I let them do to her what I don't let the big boys do to me"). Her demands upon arrival were an entire new wardrobe ("Something sort of like a sexy version of whatever they wore when Jack-the-Ripper was doing his thing"), new hairstyle, makeup and an exclusive interview with the Prime Minister ("or the police chief, somebody like that").

Only the latter request was unfillable.

She made her first broadcast from London on Friday evening, the eighth, in an emerald velvet dress with rose-colored lace and ruffles highlighting a low-cut, sculpted bodice that accented her cleavage and with her silky, black hair waved and trailing long down her left shoulder and peek-a-booing over her left eye like Veronica Lake playing a nymphomaniacal milkmaid. Having failed to secure the PM, BGG, as her press releases referred to her, fell back on a practice widely honored in television "journalism"—she interviewed another journalist.

And, because the Rippergate scoop had made him the "hot" reporter in town, she chose the Vampire.

For his debut on international television, he got a good haircut, bought a new suit and groomed himself with a concentration he rarely gave that civilized task. He also used restraint on his alcohol intake (sipped only a pint throughout the day). He spoke in a relatively lucid manner and made an acceptable appearance.

He also made a reasonable impression upon BGG. She invited him to dinner and, afterward, back to her hotel suite, where she encouraged him to do to her "what she didn't let the big boys do." And he did it well enough that she asked

†

him to stay the night (and do it several more times). By morning, they were making plans for their "relationship," both personal and professional.

Thus the Vampire entered what he had always supposed was heaven.

On Saturday, twenty-two additional house guests arrived at Hedgemore.

They descended on the estate in a leisurely stream—many of them the familiars from Duke Street parties—and soon cluttered the grounds with their strolling, riding, hunting, swimming or merely conversation or reading and eating what seemed an endless tea.

Dinner was black-tie and, at the pre-dinner cocktail hour, Malcolm announced his engagement to Vanessa. The response was hearty applause, cheers and a procession of individual congratulations and toasts.

At dinner, Jillian announced, "I have wonderful news."

A quiet fell over the guests. The rows of wineglasses glowed in the muted light from the cut-crystal chandelier. The fresh orchids floating in silver bowls, the multi-colored gowns of the ladies and the evening dress of the men glistened with the sleek aura of occasion.

"As many of you know, Vanessa has just finished filming, taping and still photography for the new Scent of Love Perfume advertising campaign, which is the largest project of its sort ever undertaken by a British firm. It will make Vanessa's face instantly recognizable around the world. Malcolm and she will be wed the first week of December and will honeymoon until early January in France."

There was a round of applause and "hear-hears."

Lees heard General Sir Arthur whisper to Mary Cilone, "I believe the Riviera is wheelchair-equipped now. It will be a great convenience for our Vanessa to be able to provide care for her bridegroom."

Mary whispered fiercely, "Hush your wicked tongue, Arthur."

Jillian resumed. "My announcement is not so beautiful as theirs was, but is still something of a smasher. Ambassador

Pictures has set script, director and casting of their newest production—*Penny Dreadful*. Shooting will begin the last week of January in Geneva. The film will star"—she paused for dramatic effect amid some oohs and ahs—"Vanessa Cilone!"

Underneath the loud burst of applause, Sir Arthur said, "She'd better leave Malcolm at home. They say the thin air and winter cold is difficult for the elderly heart."

"Arthur, you are hopeless!"

"Of course I am, Mary. It's part of my charm."

The Leeses danced a few slow numbers in the grand ballroom, but, for the most part, they sat and drank the fine champagne and enjoyed the music. Occasionally, other men came and took Ann to dance.

Lees felt slightly tipsy, very relaxed without a thought in his head for murder or magic or madness. He left to relieve himself once and, returning, met Jillian. "General Lees, you haven't danced with me yet," she said brightly.

"I'm afraid it would be a debacle for you and a chore for me."

She laughed, and he noticed how tall and pretty she was in her dark-haired, angular way. Taking his good arm, she said, "Then shall we have some air?"

They strolled out the front door and began circling the mansion on the gravel drive. The night was moderate with an emotionally neutral moon and the starred dome a clear deep blue.

"Your news was rather spectacular, wasn't it?"

"Oh, yes. This is the picture that will make Vanessa an international star. The script is one of the best spy thrillers I've read. Very sophisticated, very glamorous, believable action, good pace and wit with a cutting edge."

"You should do the reviews."

Her laughter tinkled in the upper range contrasting with the soft grinding of pebbles underfoot. "I'll suggest it to the Sunday supplements."

"Good money, or is it impolite to ask?"

They stepped onto a country-stone walk as she smiled. "Agents think it's impolite only when they've sold their clients cheaply. I managed to price her rather dear—two hundred thousand and a profit participation. If the script films as well as it reads, we'll be able to pick and choose scripts and name our price after this movie. But what a bore I am being. Talking nothing but shop when *you're* the one having genuine adventures."

Wind riffled lawn grass.

Lees shook his head. "My adventures are just what I want to forget. And films are a world I know nothing about. I am fascinated, not bored."

"You are a charming man."

They stopped beneath a heavy oak.

The naked limbs moved sinuously in small wind and Jillian's hair ruffled lightly. The silver light muted their features highlighted their glamorous clothes, made them appear to one another as beautiful people in an aura of celluloid romance, irresistibly attractive. Without consciously knowing how, Lees found her pressed close. Her lips were warm, her perfume light and pungent, her body supple.

He wanted her and it shocked him.

She stepped back slightly, aware of his sudden tension.

"Don't worry, Jim. That was just a dream-wish of what could only be in another place, another time, another life."

"Yes," was all he could say and his voice was thick, unnatural.

They turned of like accord and resumed walking. Their footsteps made nearly no sound on the stones. They rounded the far corner of the mansion and caught sight of the poolhouse.

"Feel guilty?"

"Yes. And . . . well, stunned. I've never been unfaithful to Ann. Even mentally or emotionally."

They turned onto the cement walk toward the poolhouse.

"That's rather wonderful," said Jillian wistfully.

They stopped suddenly.

In the shadow of the poolhouse another couple embraced, kissed, pressed close and made small, soft groanings to the rapid touches of swiftly moving hands. An angle of moonlight revealed Sir Arthur and Mary Cilone, and Lees glanced quickly at Jillian. Her lips pressed tight, but her shoulders had the sag of resignation. Lees led her back around the mansion, quietly and rapidly. She didn't speak until they were back on the gravel.

"Would that my father were as committed to fidelity as you are, Jim."

They paused.

"Are you alright?" he asked.

She nodded. "Yes." She shrugged, "I should be used to it. It's been going on for more years than I know. Not just Aunt Mary. Daddy has always been a ladies' man."

"Your mother?"

"Oh, she and father have led separate lives for eons. They'd divorce but for his bloody career."

They walked slowly.

"Aunt Mary's been a widow for a dozen years, so she's okay, but father . . . he's been known to romance married women and other . . . types . . . and he has no conscience about that."

"Don't be too hard on him, Jillian."

She eyed him speculatively as they paused at the front doors. "You're naive, aren't you, Jim? You kiss a girl under the influence of champagne and moonlight and feel guilty, while the world around you is full of truly wicked wounds."

He shrugged. "Champagne, moonlight, whatever influences—I'm married. That means I'm not supposed to kiss other women. Especially not with lust in my heart."

She laughed. "Was there lust in your heart?"

He smiled. "I'm afraid so."

She shivered. "Let's go inside. I feel the chill."

The party continued for hours, but Lees felt his energy fade, and it wasn't long before he and Ann excused themselves. Still, he had a hard time getting to sleep. He didn't like his feelings of guilt, and he was actively repulsed by the sordid scene near the poolhouse.

The sanctuary at St. Martin's was gloomy Gothic, heavy stone and dark, with vaulted ceilings that left Lees feeling far too small for the room. The congregation was also thin for the surroundings—perhaps a hundred in a sanctuary intended to hold five hundred.

The ritual and the liturgy in the missalette were confusing and made him feel alien and uncomfortable. But there were three moments he rather liked.

Father Mueller was the celebrant, and in his homily he said, "The blessing and the curse of the twentieth century is Dynamic Man.

"It has been a century in which God has helped us to accomplish much in science, technology, the arts, medicine, economics, psychiatry, self-knowledge and self-expression. But we have often given ourselves *sole* credit for these accomplishments. We have thought of ourselves as Dynamic Man—that Godlike creature capable of anything, without limitations and completely in control of our destiny. This has made our century one of raised expectations and great hope.

"But this is also a century in which we have failed at much.

"There have been world wars with slaughter in the millions, and the horrors of the Holocaust; hundreds of 'lesser' wars; the persistence of poverty and hunger, hatred and disease and violence; totalitarian conspiracy and the cowardly appeasement of the comfortable; the threat of nuclear Armageddon and the surrender to evil and self-enslavement; the oft-times meaningless search for purpose through pleasure-without-love in the forms of alcohol, drugs, uncommitted sexual conduct, material wealth and possessions, mad music and expensive thrills.

"If Dynamic Man be true, the failures as well as the triumphs are solely ours. And failures of such monstrous dimension have bred a century also of despair.

"But a Christian must be an optimist, for Christ's message was *salvation*—not damnation.

"The outcome is not in our hands.

"We must work with love, charity, goodwill and determination *as if* the outcome of events depended upon our efforts while always remembering that all our labor is in vain without the saving Grace of our Lord and Redeemer Jesus Christ.

"Dynamic Man is an ego trip that rockets straight to hell on earth. True awareness of our mortal frailties and limits is the humility that saves and leads us joyfully to heaven in this life."

Lees wasn't quite sure he could trust the message yet, but he liked it. He liked being let off the hook for once. Not for effort, but for *result;* the idea that some force, some power larger than himself had responsibility for the ultimate turn of events, was a peaceful and heartening concept.

He also liked the blessing of the bread and wine. The symbolism was comfortable—a communal meal of celebration. Holiday dinners had always been important and uplifting occasions for himself, Ann, and the children, grandchildren. He could accept that part of the service, and saw the sense of focusing around it.

"What did you think?" Ann asked outside on the sun-washed steps.

Wind from the river pushed at them and Lees raised his voice against it. "I enjoyed it. It relaxed me, but I doubt if you'll make a Catholic of me."

Passing parishoners turned to stare, startled by his words. Lees and Ann noted their shocked glances, laughed. She said, "Father Mueller said he would meet us at the restaurant in half an hour."

The Slender Gourmet was in a bow-fronted Victorian house situated on the Embankment near Cheyne Row. Father Mueller had secured the best table in the front dining room, a padded booth set in the canted-glass bow-front that was dappled by warm sun and the shadow fragments from overarching tree limbs. The surface of the Thames was molten gold.

The priest had changed to caramel-color slacks and a royal-blue polo shirt under a tan crew-neck sweater. With his tanned face and silvery-blond hair he might have been an aristocrat or an actor, but the captain and the waiter greeted him simply as "Father Mueller."

Lees ordered a neat whisky, Ann asked for a vodka martini, while Mueller had mineral water; he suggested the chef's salad accompanied by a plate of cheeses and crusty brown bread.

"How did you like mass?"

Lees smiled. "It was a little . . . strange."

Mueller chuckled. "You should have tried it in pre-Vatican-Two days. In Latin, with the altar distanced and the priest's back to the congregation, it was really disconcerting to visitors."

The priest and Ann shared a fleeting smile, acknowledging the shared experience and the initiated's right of amusement at the past foibles of a mutually loved institution.

Lees felt the exclusion and an image flickered in his brain—Mueller and Ann holding hands—then was gone, leaving him with an insinuation of vertigo.

"Ann said you wanted to talk to me."

"Yes." Lees stared at the mint-color flocked wallpaper.

Mueller prompted, "How can I help you?"

Lees met his eyes. "This is hard."

Mueller's face was sympathetic and he nodded, but kept silent.

"I . . . I have come to believe that I need spiritual advice. I think I need to ask for God's help, and I don't know how to go about it." He sighed and slumped back in his chair, finished his whisky and sat silent, exhausted by the effort of admission.

Ann bit her lip to keep tears of relief inside.

"And you would like me to see if I can suggest a possible path?"

Lees nodded.

The waiter brought their meal, began serving.

Lees clamped his jaw. Silver-Eyes was in his head and his voice was low, ugly: *"Don't trust 'im, guv. 'E wants yer wife!"*

The waiter withdrew.

"Jim, you're pale—are you ill?" Ann asked.

"Silver-Eyes," muttered Lees, "in my head."

Tree-limb shadow wavered on the cranberry-colored linen tablecloth, made a point of sunlight wink off the rim of Mueller's water goblet. The priest's face was concentrated, intent. "Did he speak? What did he say?"

†

Silver-Eyes shrieked, "Don't trust 'im! 'E wants to fuck yer woman!" and Lees flinched at the stabbing pain in his brain.

Ann's voice was hesitant. "Jim. . . ?"

He looked out the window, but the river surface was too bright and he closed his eyes against the pain. "He said not to trust you. He said . . . you want Ann."

Silver-Eyes was gone.

Lees opened his eyes and Mueller met them. "Are *you* asking?"

Lees nodded.

"Want is too active a verb. I was a man before I was a priest and I remain a man. Your wife is, in all ways, an uncommonly attractive woman. That is all there is or could be to that."

Ann stared at her lap. "And Father Eric is an attractive man. I felt that especially when you were struggling so hard. You were so alienated."

An image in Lees' head—moonlight; Hedgemore grounds; Jillian's soft lips. Foolish impulses, thought Lees. Foolish, but not unforgiveable.

He took Ann's hand, squeezed it, smiled. "Silver-Eyes must be desperate."

They began to eat.

"You'll be staying on at Hedgemore?" Father Mueller asked.

"Yes. Malcolm invites you to come down as well. If you can arrange the time away."

Mueller smiled. "I can come down Tuesday and stay for the necessary length of time. I believe I'm being called as you are."

A tour boat plied the center of the Thames, sparkling white and crowded with passengers, passed between a brace of framing autumn-bare trees, momentarily composing a picture of setting, motion, light, force and distance that Turner would have been proud to paint.

Most of the guests had returned to London, so dinner at Hedgemore was a limited affair—Malcolm and Vanessa, Jim and Ann, Jillian and her current actor beau, Franklin Thorn. During the dessert, Lees mentioned, "Some of the dreams

†

I've had the last week seemed to suggest that Jillian might be in some danger. I don't—"

He stopped talking because Jillian had dropped her spoon and turned white.

Everyone stared at her.

"Jillian...?" asked Thorn.

She shut her eyes and shook, trying to master her fear. Finally, she set her hands flat on the table and exhaled. "I knew it."

Vanessa's brow wrinkled. "Knew what, Jilly?"

"I've been so scared and felt *silly*, so I was . . . afraid to tell anyone about my fear."

"What fear?" Malcolm asked.

"My name. The Ripper's last victim was named Mary Kelly—wasn't she? I never use it, but my middle name is Mary. Jillian Mary Kelly."

"My God," said Vanessa, "I'd completely forgotten that. You were named after our Aunt Jill and my mother. And you're twenty-four—just as the Ripper's Mary Kelly was."

Stuart leaned back in his chair, frowned. "What makes you think you'd be *the* Mary Kelly?"

Jillian picked at the tablecloth using long fingers like nibbling tweezers, stared at her plate. "Just . . . bad feelings. Nothing I could make any sense of or talk about. That's why I haven't said anything about it to anyone."

Stuart looked at Lees. "Jim, do your dreams show Jillian being attacked by the Ripper?"

Lees shook his head. "No. I wouldn't have kept them to myself if they had. One showed her being blown through a plate of glass, another had her drowning in the Thames, a third seemed to be a horse-riding scene. She had some sort of accident, hurt her head and fell."

Stuart said, "Well, it'll certainly be easy enough to take precautions to protect you, Jillian."

Lees apologized. "I'm sorry for blurting it out so baldly, Jillian."

She forced a brave smile but remained pale, shaken. "No, that's all right, Jim. I'll feel better now that I can talk about it openly."

* * *

†

Lees dreamed the Tower raven.

He dreamed his father talking to a woman with her back turned and a pale face sinking in the golden waters of the Thames and couldn't tell if it was Jillian's.

He dreamed mean streets and pale sullen faces, crowds of hostile Victorians with blank, fixed expressions and shiny dead eyes.

Monday, October 11, Sir Edwards William informed Hughes that he would be Acting Deputy Commissioner for CID for the duration of the Ripper crisis only. He also said he wished to be thoroughly involved on a daily basis and would be ruthless with dismissals at the slightest sign of information withheld or any further dabbling in "that parapsychological hogwash."

The Yard's main discovery of the day was the résumés of the latest victims, which revealed that Felicia Bowen had played Elizabeth Stride in *Blood of the Ripper* in 1972 and Lisle Young had played Catherine Eddowes in *The Latin Ripper* in 1982.

Clive said, "Seems as if the link between old victim and new gets more oblique with each murder."

Hughes nodded and stifled a yawn. "Buck the report on up to Sir Edwards. Maybe *he* can tell us why."

North of Leicester Square begins the Seven Dials area of central London. Once a teeming slum, a thirty-two-year project had driven Shaftesbury Avenue (named after the social-reformer ninth Earl) and Charing Cross Road through the heart of the district. The slum clearance was not fully successful until the 1950s—a century after it was begun.

Gilt Street was a lately fashionable cul-de-sac northeast of Piccadilly Circus. Only a block long, it was lined with modernized rowhouses and ended in a tiny traffic circle surrounding a dot of grass that passed for a minaturized park. Arching across the sealed end of the street stood a handsome contemporary two-story apartment block, the Bunburry Arms. Discreet (if expensive) management had attracted an exclusive and wealthy client list to the Bunburry, composed entirely of married gentlemen who sought privacy for affairs—if not of the heart, at least of the body.

The best flat in the building, 2C—second floor front, left end—was rented for secluded improprieties by General Sir Arthur Kelly.

That evening he was—so he thought—entertaining a young actress client of his daughter. Sir Arthur made love to Monica Day three times between dinner and eleven P.M. He made love to Monica Day because he made love to all the women he brought to his various beds. Sex was, for Sir Arthur, a highly sophisticated, orchestrated and choreographed performing art, an exercise in strength, stamina, control and virtuosity. Necessarily, the object was not emotional bonding or pleasure, but applause.

Monica Day did not know this or, had she known, would she have spared it much thought. She did know that his lovemaking was emotionally detached and self-conscious, physically competent and unsatisfying despite the trimmings of roses, dinner, champagne, elegant surroundings, romantic music, soft lighting and artful mirrors.

In short, she'd had better.

Had, in fact, had better the night before, so her protestations of rapture were as perfunctory and unenthusiastic as Sir Arthur's mechanical rhapsodies to her youth (twenty) and beauty (considerable).

For his part, Sir Arthur was too arrogantly dense to examine any lack in himself, but recognized, with irritation, the insincerity of her assurances that the evening's couplings had "transported her." In short, he thought her a dull girl. Like all of them.

Wrapped in a scarlet-and-black silk robe, he padded across the thick carpet of the darkened lounge to the wet bar for another bottle of champagne. He opened the door of the small refrigerator and, by the interior light, selected a bottle from half a dozen lying on their sides.

Mums, he thought. No use wasting a choice vintage on a tedious child like her. She'd never appreciate it; is incapable of appreciating the best.

He closed the door and straightened in the dark.

None of them truly appreciate . . .

†

He glanced out the near window, took a step forward and stood by the curtain, stared out into the night.

Gilt Street was transformed.

The street was narrower and dim, from the only remaining street lamp's (centering the dot of grass) inability to penetrate the narrow passage between the decrepit Victorian tenements that had replaced the modernized row houses.

The tenements had lower-floor stone facades and brick uppers primly divided by a thin line of masonry, an architectural straight-rule, like a mouth pressed tight in disapproval. The gloom was broken only by occasional light from some of the arched doorways and the few recessed windows not covered by stout wooden shutters and fell heavily like grained yellow boards dropped thoughtlessly into the confined unwelcoming street that was hardly wider than an alley.

It's happening again.

Pale sullen people stood or squatted before the houses, some fully in shadow, some partially betrayed by the slabs of light. They were quiet or talked desultorily—fat women in dark dresses or long skirts; stooped, round-shouldered men in tatty black coats and wool caps; pinch-face children who all seemed to have weak chins hovered near their parents in clumps or played circumscribed listless games.

They are dead, but they live! he thought, and a strange excitement thrilled him.

He looked down. The awning of the Bunburry Arms was visible, its green and red stripes just as they always were. He looked toward the end of the street. The time reversion seemed to have gone from Gilt Street's opening right up to the tiny traffic circle and then to have . . . run into some invisible obstacle? Or . . . run to the limit of its energy? Something.

Sir Arthur stroked his chin.

One-A and 1C were between tenants, being refinished. One-B was at his country estate for the month, while 2B was on the Continent. He hadn't seen 2A for several days so . . . it was possible that he and Monica were the only people in the building. The only living contemporary humans presently at the scene. . . .

†

Yes, this will be amusing.

He closed the curtains.

She lay naked amid the rumpled sheets, her supple beauty carelessly displayed as if a thing of no value or consequence. She yawned.

"Took long enough to find a bottle of champagne." Her brow knitted. "Where is it?"

Sir Arthur lounged in the doorway, hands in the pockets of his robe. "I changed my mind."

"What?"

"I changed my mind. I don't want to drink more champagne with you. I don't want to fuck you anymore. I don't want you at all. You're a dull girl and the finer things are wasted on you. Get dressed and get out."

She goggled at him. When she regained her voice she said, "You must be joking."

"*Au contraire*—I am completely serious. Get dressed and get out."

"Jesus!"

He returned to the dark lounge, sat and smoked.

She came out of the bedroom, sloppily dressed, in three minutes. Her body moved with the electric quavering rigidity that rage brings.

"You ought to have your wang stuffed and mounted. It'd be more bloody use that way. And you know where you can have it stuffed!"

Sir Arthur was silent.

She slammed out the door.

He ground his cigarette in an ashtray, opened the bottle and poured a glass of champagne, a choice vintage. Then he crossed to a window and opened the curtain enough to see out.

Monica cursed him under her breath in the elevator. Don't give a damn if she is my booking agent, I'll give Jilly a blast about her asshole father!

The elevator stopped. The door opened with a sigh that echoed her own.

She stepped out into the deserted lobby, her head down, ignoring the pale light and modern Swedish furnishings, and strode to the heavy wooden door wondering if that might be too emotional, too rash.

A girl can't jeopardize her career, and there's other ways of getting back. Spread the word a bit about what a lousy lay he is and get the girls giggling at him—make sure he knows why they're laughing at him. That'll fix him proper.

She pushed through the front door and let it slam loudly behind her, walked rapidly across the pavement with her spiked heels beating out a tattoo of violence in the still night air.

She looked up, gasped, "God!" and stopped.

The pale people with bright eyes and fixed faces stopped. The Victorian wretched angled their heads toward her. Listened.

She looked up the block and it seemed too long and too narrow and she couldn't see into the street beyond. She looked at the people—dirty, unkempt, frozen in their shabby clothes and their bodies tense with the stillness. They looked so grubby, so pale, so poor, so hostile.

So hungry.

She edged backward and her heels made a scraping sound on the pavement.

Bodies turned fractionally. Ears cocked like sonar homing in on her.

She ran to the apartment building door and shook the handle of the locked barrier and faces turned at the sound of her vigorous tugging on the heavy door and, over her shoulder, she saw the nearest man, short and swarthy under his wool cap, with strange, dark skin around his lids like eyeshadow, begin to move toward the Bunburry Arms.

Others followed.

She jabbed the button beside the discreet gold plate that said only 2C and the muffled sound was audible in the still street.

The Victorians were coming.

She pressed the button again and held it down, sobbed, "Open up, you bastard!"

The Victorians were closing.

She used both hands to hold down all six buttons and the

†

272

buzzer sound heightened. Whirling her head in terror, she looked upward and saw the parted curtain at a window of 2C.

Sir Arthur looked down upon her, his face an emotionless mask. He sipped champagne.

The Victorians were shuffling up the walk, stumbling onto the grass, surrounding her, and she pounded on the door, shrieking, "*Open up! Open the door for pity's sake!*"

A small girl touched her dress and Monica screamed and whirled and ran. The girl held tight and the dress tore and Monica knocked down a fat woman and ran, pushing, shoving and dodging the grappling hands and arms and broke through.

She ran directly across the street to the dot of grass in the center of the tiny traffic circle, but she was sobbing and screaming and wobbling on her high heels and the small swarthy man caught her, seized her around the waist and pulled her down, fell on top of her. He leaned close as the other Victorians clotted around her and his breath was foul, leaned toward her neck with his mouth wide and jagged yellow-and-black stump-teeth wet, saliva-slick, gleaming.

She screamed.

And disappeared from sight beneath the ravenous Victorians.

That is even better than sullying one's own hands, thought Sir Arthur. That is like remote control. Forces are loosed and one learns . . . rather too late . . . not to be a dull girl.

He had a rigid erection.

Closed the curtain.

The parcel arrived in the early post Tuesday. It was addressed: Chief Inspector Richard Hughes, Acting Deputy Commissioner, CID, New Scotland Yard, and wrapped in plain brown paper. Inside was a shoe box. Lifting the lid revealed a gelatinous mass of tissue, a welter of caked blood and a bloodstained plio-film container in which could be seen a long rectangular envelope of Yellow-Moon Notepaper hand-inked in Phoenician Blue.

Clive blanched. "Christ!"

Hughes swallowed his nausea. "Part of the Eddowes surro-

†

gate's kidney if our new Ripper is still following the old script."

He secured the letter:

October 10, 1988
From Hell

Chief Inspector Hughes
Acting Deputy Commissioner, CID
New Scotland Yard

New New Boss:

My bloody appetite bid me,
So I ate half of Eddowes' kidney;
I enjoyed a rare treat,
Human blood and human meat.

You can have all the rest
And if it will digest—
I'll send you more
From the next little whore.

So far—we've played the old score,
But new notes are in store;
Time for some surprise
Says the man with silver eyes.

Yours truly,
Jack-the-Ripper

The smell of the decaying tissue was gagging, and Clive breathed through his mouth, "To the lab?"

Hughes replaced the lid, shaking his head. "No. First send it over to Sir Edwards William's office. He wants to be thoroughly involved, so he says."

Monica Day's body, or what was left of it, lay on the dot of grass at the end of Gilt Street. The cul-de-sac had reverted to its 1988 form during the night, and one of the tenants of the fashionable rowhouses found the girl's savaged corpse at 8:11 A.M.

Clive and Hughes were on the scene by noon and interviewed Sir Arthur, the only tenant on the Bunburry Arms premises, over a light lunch that he provided. He had identified the girl and admitted the assignation—"a perfectly charming evening"—but denied seeing or hearing anything after she left the apartment sometime between eleven and eleven-thirty.

Afterward, Hughes asked Clive, "Why do I feel that insufferably smug fop knows something? Something more than he's telling?"

"We," said Clive, "the question is why do *we* feel that arrogant bastard knows more than he's telling?"

Father Eric Mueller was dropped off at Hedgemore by a brother priest shortly after eleven a.m., Tuesday morning. He brought with him a scuffed tan leather suitcase, a blue cloth book bag almost bursting its seams with paperbacks, and a cardboard cylinder almost as high as his shoulder. He immediately rejected the quarters provided for him in the guest wing, asking for something more isolated instead.

Stuart consulted Granby, who suggested the small abandoned lighthouse that had been used as a study by Stuart's father. Mueller agreed and by mid-afternoon it had been thoroughly cleaned and provisioned by the servants and Mueller installed. He had asked Lees to join him for a late afternoon tea.

It was nearly a half-mile walk along the cliffs to the lighthouse, but pleasing on the warm fall day. The lighthouse was a bleached-stone column four stories high and topped by a wood-and-glass room that looked not unlike a penthouse apartment. It wavered in the sun as Lees approached, appearing to tremble and waffle as if it were insubstantial, liquid and pliant.

He pushed open a heavy wooden door at the base of the column and stepped into a gloomy cylinder, narrow and obscure compared with the sunlit outer world.

He climbed.

The circular iron stairs were faded black and tight, steep. The exertion was dizzying and breath-robbing. Lees felt claustrophobic in the tube, wondered if his heart would give out and he would fall, die alone on the barren metal stairs.

He climbed.

The stairs ended at a landing.

He stepped onto the floor and leaned on the stair railing, breathing hard and momentarily stunned, his eyes blinded by the vast suffusion of light after the dim cylinder.

The room was circular and carpeted in a bleached butter shade. It had a built-in bed, built-in desk and bookshelves, built-in wall-benches stretching around the entire perimeter, a built-in kitchenette and one door (presumably to a WC). From the room's waist to its twelve-foot ceiling, however, it was entirely glass, save only the stair landing and door next to it. The glass was angled outward top to bottom, the ceiling area a circle not more than twelve feet in diameter while the floor area was more than twenty feet in diameter.

The sensation was immediate and overwhelming.

Sun.

Light.

Everywhere.

More as an environment than an illumination of an environment and a sense of seeing everything serially and completely at the same time—the rolling Kent countryside, woods, Hedgemore, the meadows and cliffs, the sea and sky. It was more than a sense of being enabled to see. It was a powerful revelation of being unable *not to see* any longer.

Father Mueller sat at a small table in the kitchenette area sipping beef tea and watching Lees with a speculative expression on his face. "General, come sit down. Rest. Have some tea," he said gently.

Lees crossed and sat in a chair next to Mueller, caught his breath and said, "Thank you. That's quite a climb."

Mueller nodded. "Yes, but what an unexpected reward for having made the effort."

Lees nodded. "A total surprise."

"The best rewards are often unexpected."

They sipped tea in silence.

Cutting the Channel's green-gray waves was a British missile-cruiser, steaming in solitude down from summer port at Scapa Flow, bound on some obscure exercise of post-imperial chest thumping. The men watched the sleek gray vessel loom directly opposite them, swift and powerful and self-contained, self-sustained, filling a disproportionate share of the glass

†

wall with ominous metal muscle. Crewmen were dwarfs at distance and only intermittently visible. The warship might have been a ghostship with a life and spirit of its own, inhuman.

"The apex of worldly power," said the priest, "capable of destroying cities, murdering millions."

"Yes," muttered Lees absently.

"And all it would take to sink her would be an immoderate gale in mid-ocean, a few unmanageable waves. She could capsize or steam straight into a mountain of water and disappear without a trace in the twinkling of an eye without another soul ever being aware of the tempest."

Lees pried his gaze from the passing cruiser and eyed the slender man next to him.

"A lesson?"

Mueller smiled. "A reminder. Those who seek or exercise power need to be constantly aware of its true source. God has loaned so much power to humans that we often forget, think it comes from us or belongs to us."

Lees mulled that over in silence. "And I am seeking power?"

The priest answered, "Deciding what we want is a good way to begin. Why don't you tell me what the experiences are that led you to ask my help. In detail."

Lees let his eyes wander as he recalled the circumstances of the previous six weeks. As he spoke, he gazed absentmindedly at the stern of the warship until it faded from view; at the water that no longer marked its passing; the rough meadow grass along the cliffs that bent with the wind.

It took more than three hours. The light died away with the afternoon. By the time Lees narrated the time-warp experience, it was so dark their faces swam in lamp light, and all else was dim or shadowed or dark.

Mueller set out a plate of rough bread and wedges of cheese, poured more strong beef tea.

"Your experience with the British Railway system was ... impressive. What do you make of that?"

Lees smiled. "I don't know. Magic?"

"And who motivated the magic?"

"The man with the silver eyes, I suppose."

"And who is he?"

Lees smiled again. "You want me to say the devil."

The priest shook his head. "I only want you to say what you know or believe. No more, no less."

"The devil is what makes sense even if it doesn't make sense—if you know what I mean."

Mueller chuckled. "Yes, I do. And what you want is to stop the Ripper murders, thwart the silver-eyed man?"

"Yes."

"Then you are, indeed, seeking power. Great power."

That night, Lees dreamed.

He was high up, in a cold room, as if frigid air was blowing through it.

He stood still, seemed unable to move.

He felt the wind on his back, had to brace his legs to stand upright.

A body flew past him from behind.

It was Jillian Kelly, and her face was a mask of terror and fear. She screamed for help and stretched her arms out to him as she flew across the room, then hit a large window.

It shattered in slow motion and shards and slivers of glass tore Jillian's face and body, sent blood spurting from countless wounds.

She screamed as she blew through the window.

Fell.

Lees woke shaking.

Wednesday morning was rainless gray in Kent, the sort of threatening sky that promises showers, but never delivers.

Father Mueller looked up from his steaming mug of cocoa. "Do you know what Saint Thomas Aquinas said?"

Lees looked out the glass wall of the lighthouse at the choppy channel and laughed. "No, I haven't the foggiest."

Mueller smiled. "Aquinas held that it was possible to reason logically and irrefutably to the existence of God. He also held that to do so, to argue fully and honestly every queer question or hair-splitting argument—to argue completely

†

would require all of a man's time for all of his life. And that is what he devoted his life to—a painstaking process of writing out the logical debate over the existence of God."

Lees raised his eyebrows. "You want me to read all of Aquinas?"

Mueller laughed and shook his head. "No. There isn't time."

"Oh, good," said Lees with feeling.

The priest chuckled, "But Aquinas also proposed—that since most humans aren't called to a lifetime inquiry of his sort—that God, in his infinite mercy and wisdom, gave us revealed religion. That is what we shall try to do. Get you some revelation."

"How?"

"We might try for some conscious contact with God through prayer and see what happens."

Lees stared at him. Swallowed hard. "Right now?"

Mueller smiled. "What are you uncomfortable with in the idea of praying?"

"I don't know . . . I guess that's it—I don't know how or what to pray for—or who I'm praying to."

"We'll make it up as we go along."

"I beg your pardon?"

"We'll use words that are comfortable and just ask for help, strength and guidance. You can choose your own conception of God."

"My *own* conception?"

"Sure. The idea is to get closer to God, not farther away, and all of us are merely making guesses about his nature. Why don't you spend today thinking about what kind of God you *could* love and respect. Make a list of qualities if that will help. Tomorrow, we can talk about that and—if you want—pray to that God. We'll see if he answers."

Bundled warmly, Ann and Vanessa cantered their horses through The Rides, then slowed them to a walk as they approached the country stone wall that bounded the estate. The two-lane blacktop beyond was a careless gunmetal ribbon in the aqueous light.

Vanessa shook her head and her hair flowed about her

shoulders. "No, I never had a father to know. He died when I was two years old. The closest I've had is Uncle Arthur, but"—she smiled bitterly—"he's not much of a father-type. You don't want your father to seduce you—at least I don't."

Ann's eyes widened. "Oh, no."

They reached the stone wall and their horses stopped.

"Oh, yes. He tried when I was seventeen, tried for six months or so, like I was one of his military campaigns. If it wasn't for Jilly, I wouldn't ever see him, even if . . ." She sighed.

Their horses bent their heads and began to nibble tentatively at the rough grass.

"Mother's mad about him. Been sleeping with him for ages. Keeps hoping he'll get a divorce and marry her. I can't imagine why—he'd just cheat on her."

Ann shook her head. "A man like Sir Arthur is very sad. He's sick and lost, and has no idea what it's all about."

They heard a rumbling sound from up the road, but, glancing, saw nothing, paid no attention.

Vanessa smiled thinly. "Jilly says I fell in love with Malcolm because I wanted a father figure for a husband, but that kind of psychologizing is cheap and too easy by half."

Ann shrugged. "A good marriage is made up of all kinds of relational elements—lovers, friends, companions, brother-sister, father-daughter, mother-son. The trick is to strike the right balance of elements."

Vanessa opened her mouth to speak but stopped. The rumbling grew louder, and they turned their heads to look up the road again.

A two-horse wagon came clattering around the bend at the crest of the near ridge and picked up speed on the approaching descent.

They stared.

The horses were dapple gray, the wagon dark wood with iron-rimmed wheels, the rear set half again larger than the front pair, and covered by a high tan canvas stretched over iron ribs. An advertising message had been stenciled on either side of the canvas in large black letters:

IND. Coope   EAST INDIA
        Co's   P A L E
IMPERIAL STOUT   & Burton
                               A L E S

The driver was a skinny little man in black trousers and boots, white shirt and unbuttoned vest, with a soft-billed railroad cap pulled low and a straight twig-stemmed pipe jammed in his mouth. He was old, his hair thin and fluffy, his flowing guardsman mustache white like the bristles of his poorly shaved chin. His anthracite-colored eyes were bright buttons and his skin paler than a white winter sky.

Their horses became nervy, pawed and sidestepped at the approach and, as the wagon came parallel, Vanessa's reared and whinnied while Ann's backed and snorted.

The driver turned his head back and forth slowly with an odd-angled and listening attitude. His eyes passed across theirs and they saw no flicker of recognition of their existence. The wagon rolled past rapidly, curved up and away and disappeared over the top of the next hill.

The rumbling grew fainter.

Died away.

They exchanged frightened, wordless stares, turned their still-nervy horses and galloped back toward the mansion.

Stuart, Lees, Cochran and Mueller listened to the women's description of the wagon incident. Stuart turned to Cochran. "Pat, I'd like you to go up to London tomorrow. See Griffin and Yardley's, a security firm on Oxford Street. Arrange for a detail of a dozen men for Hedgemore. They can bill my bank directly."

Cochran nodded.

"Fortress Hedgemore," muttered Lees.

Mueller met Lees' eyes and nodded.

Lees walked alone after dinner, thinking about what sort of God he could love and respect.

†

Later, he dreamed.

Piccadilly Circus filled with Thomas Tilling horse buses and carriages and hansoms. Circling over and over and over again. The sidewalks and streets filling with pale people, Victorians with fixed faces and bright eyes and a hostile air.

Thursday, the rain came, heavy pale rain that striped the air and painted all exterior surfaces with a wet gleam, like high-gloss lacquer or slick film-stock.

The lighthouse was dimmed, swam with blue-green hues like sitting in an aquarium while Lees and Mueller shared the priest's ubiquitous hot chocolate and scones.

"I would like my God to be loving, forgiving, generous, understanding and—present."

"By present you mean. . . ?"

"I want to know He's there. And cares." Lees shrugged. "Otherwise, what good is He?"

Mueller smiled. "Sounds not unlike the father you always wished you had."

"Yes."

"Good. Let's call Him up and see if He answers."

Lees looked apprehensive. "Should we kneel?"

"What would be most comfortable for you?"

"I'm not . . . sure."

"Perhaps if we just continue sitting and merely bowed our heads?"

Lees nodded. "And could you . . . say it this time?"

Mueller nodded and they bowed their heads.

Silence except for the sound of rain on the windows. The priest's voice was soft, steady. "Heavenly Father, we have been brought to this task—discovering Your will for Jim Lees—by Your divine intervention and guidance. We cannot, of our own devices, complete your appointed work. We humbly ask You to clear our minds and spirits and hearts of distractions that we may become more aware, more receptive of Your direction."

Silence.

"Would you like to add anything, Jim?"

"I . . . I ask this also."

†

Silence.

"Amen."

Walking back to the mansion, Lees was thoughtful, but he noticed he was not troubled by his thoughts; they turned in his mind easily, frictionless.

That night, after Ann went to sleep, he got out of bed, knelt and prayed silently.

Heavenly Father, I have turned my face from You in arrogance and fear and pain, but I am sorry, and I ask your help. Help me to . . . to be better . . . to love better . . . Please.

He felt a warmth at his neck and shoulders, as if large gentle hands rested there, then a sensation of lightness, relief, as if something had been lifted.

He slept deep and dreamless, thick and full rest.

Friday, it rained again, all over England.

The dozen Griffin & Yardley's security guards got wet moving into their quarters in the servant's wing of Hedgemore and patrolling the grounds in billowing yellow rain-slickers and hard-billed navy blue military-style hats.

Lees got wet walking to and from the lighthouse.

Everyone else stayed inside the mansion.

Hughes stood at the window overlooking Wellington Barracks. The parade ground was deserted and wind whipped sheets of rain across it as if some divine scouring process were bent on eradicating all soot from sight in preparation for the Final Inspection.

He turned from the glum morning view to . . . it was still hard for him to think of it as *his* office. He hadn't moved any of his personal things into it and still half-expected to wake from a bad dream and see Stuart standing ready to pass marching orders for the division. Stuart's division. But it wasn't Stuart's division anymore—it was Hughes'.

He turned back to the wet world outside. An idea, an impish idea, floated to the surface of his mind. Despite all the press uproar and sensational accounts of the events in recent weeks, the government was still taking a business-as-usual, nothing-out-of-the-ordinary-is-going-on attitude for public consumption. But Sir Edwards William, had, in his reacceptance of the commissioner's post, made the public pronouncement that "there will be no cover-up ever again so long as I head the Yard." A subordinate could hardly be blamed for taking a superior at his word.

Hughes chuckled.

Then the Vampire came to mind, and he grinned and laughed out loud. It would be a gamble, but . . . he was already risking his career many times over. One more roll of the dice wouldn't be that much extra strain.

And it certainly would be fun.

He laughed again.

Saturday broke sunny and warm. Mueller and Lees walked in the woods of The Shoots, while birds sang and squirrels scampered.

"I don't know how else to describe it. I feel better, easier . . . freed in some manner."

"I don't know how it could be described much better. So the God of your conception seems to be at home and taking calls."

Flickering between trees at a distance they saw flashes of dark blue in motion; a security guard on patrol.

"Yes. Can I ask you—what is your God like?"

"Much like yours."

"I thought . . . I had the impression that the Christian God was—well, angry and punishing."

The priest smiled. "Many people have that concept. God's not responsible for the misapprehensions people allow themselves. Most of the prophecy and evidence is to the contrary. What's punishing about a God who forgives sin as soon as it's asked for?"

They walked in silence.

Lees asked, "Is it really that simple? That easy?"

Mueller stopped and Lees faced him.

"Yes, Jim. It's not God who can't or won't forgive people. It's *people* who can't or won't forgive people. Or themselves."

* * *

†

Sunday morning, Lees went with Ann and Mueller to mass in Folkstone. The sanctuary was sparsely populated, and the elderly priest's frail voice did not carry well. His homily was brief and drifted away from Jim, who knelt and prayed while the others approached the altar to receive communion. He peered closely at the faces of the faithful as they returned to their pews, tried to see if anything had happened to them that was visible. One attractive woman's eyes were glistening with tears, but her mouth was smiling and her clear skin seemed to radiate light energy.

What does that mean? Lees wondered.

Sunday night was overcast, moonless.

Four security guards patrolled the grounds of Hedgemore.

The outside world continued to froth and churn, but the supernatural appeared to have taken a break, apparently resting, as if gathering strength.

Waiting.

At Hedgemore, all was focused on Lees and Mueller, but at a distance. They were separate, working and, perhaps, oblivious, as if time and space would stop while they completed their necessary task.

There was no rain in Kent, and the lighthouse was light, and light was the lighthouse. Lees and Mueller sipped hot chocolate while Lees reread the three-by-five file card Mueller had given him with, as he said, "Three ideas."

1. I am powerless over circumstances and my life has become unmanageable by me.
2. I have come to believe that God can restore my life to sanity.
3. I have made a decision and a commitment to turn my life and my will over to His care and His protection.

"I'm okay with one and three, but 'restore to sanity' in two—what does that mean?"

"One definition of insanity, useful for this context, is trying a failed solution repetitively in recurring situations—trying to solve the same problem over and over again with the

†

same failed attitudes and behaviors while always hoping for or expecting a different result."

Lees puffed on his cigarette; Mueller blew cigar smoke rings. Lees said, "Ummm."

"Problem?"

"I see what you're saying, but you'll have to connect it for me."

"All right, let me illustrate. You have a car that won't start; dead battery. But you decide, for whatever reason, the battery is fine, you just need more air in the tires. You put air in them. Won't start. You inflate them more. Still the car won't start. You overinflate the tires until they explode but still won't check the battery. You go out, buy new tires and begin the process all over again. Insanity?"

Lees chuckled. "Yes."

Mueller refilled their cups, replaced the pot on the stove, recrossed to the table and sat down. "How much different is that from what we see all around us in the ordinary routines of life? People feel unhappy, alienated, sometimes even despairing and what do they do?"

Mueller sipped cocoa.

Lees stared at him, nodded. "We try any solution but God."

"Exactly. The loudest voices of the twentieth-century shout stridently that the spiritual dimension is an illusion and far too many of us are afraid to contradict that clamorous chorus. We'll try Freud's solutions, or Einstein's or Darwin's, or Marx's or John Paul Getty's or Madison Avenue's or Hollywood's—we'll try any solution but the one that has worked for billions of people throughout the four thousand years of recorded history."

"God's solution."

"Precisely."

Lees sipped hot chocolate and stubbed out his cigarette. "Sort of like the quote you threw at me when we met at the Dorchester—'contempt prior to investigation.'"

Mueller smiled. "Yes. Glad you remembered our atheist friend, Mr. Spencer."

"It's a powerful statement. And this insanity applies to me as well?"

"Let's see, shall we?"

†

"How?"

"Inventory your life. Divide it up into three sections. One—how much time have you spent, approximately, in a state of joy or happiness or excitement or contentment, with a sense of purpose and of doing well, loving or being loved, the sense of being in the right place at the right time doing the right thing."

"In the flow of life."

"Exactly. Two—how much time in the doldrums. Nothing too bad but nothing exactly good or right either. A vague sense of discontent, occasional irritableness, restlessness, a feeling of being out of tune, like a note not precisely struck."

"Uh-huh. And section three is the pits."

"Yes. How much time in a state of active disquiet. Anger, frustration, palpable boredom, alienation, sorrow, depression, pain, loneliness—any kind of overt negativity."

"I see."

Lees stared out at the light through the light. He found his eyes fascinated by an oak tree at the edge of small forest, drank in its asymmetry, its gnarled trunk and knobby limbs, the orange-red of its last few dying leaves.

Mueller watched Lees.

Lees sighed. "Sounds depressing."

"Why?"

Lees smiled. "I believe I've spent a lot more time in states two and three than in the first state."

Lees and Mueller walked in the woods of The Shoots. The air was clean, crisp and clear. Dead things—leaves, twigs—cracked and crunched underfoot.

Mueller asked, "What did you find in your inventory?"

"As best I can reconstruct, I've spent about six years in state number one—joy or contentment; say twenty-five or so years in number two—the doldrums, out of tune and twenty-seven or so years in number three—pain, anger, all kinds of frustration."

Mueller stopped and searched Lees' face. "Truly?"

Lees stopped, stared back. "Yes, why?"

"That's a very long time to spend feeling so badly."

"Father, I don't think I spent more than a full month of

days in any state other than negativity for almost the first eighteen years of my life. Until I met Ann."

Mueller nodded and they resumed walking.

"So out of fifty-eight years, you've spent more than half a century being unhappy, out of tune, feeling bad to a greater or lesser extent?"

"Yes."

"What conclusion do you draw from that?"

They walked in silence. A jay chattered at them from a nearby naked tree limb. Through the trees were visible fields and meadows and sun and wildflowers, weeds, sky—so much ordinary beauty that the eye often forgot.

"My way—and I don't just mean my unusual 'power'—my way has never *worked.*"

The priest heard the catch in the general's voice, glanced at him and saw tears trickling from the corners of his eyes, said softly, "Yes. And it hurts . . . doesn't it?"

"Yes. It makes me feel . . . such a fool. Such a madman." He stopped and bent over at the waist, breathing rapidly, hyperventilating yet almost choking, almost gasping for breath.

Mueller put a hand on his shoulder and spoke softly, almost whispering. "Why mad?"

"All . . ." Lees squeezed words out like stones, "all those years . . . all those years of hurting . . . of feeling terrible, and always trying so hard . . ."

"Trying what?"

"Work!" he shouted angrily. "I'd feel bad—I'd work; I'd fear the power—I'd work; I'd be unsure of Ann—I'd work; I'd worry about the kids—I'd work, I'd worry about money—I'd work; I'd . . . I'd hate my father—I'd work. . . ." Lees panted, exhausted.

Mueller nodded. "Your battery was dead and you kept putting air in the tires."

"Yes."

Mueller stood up and Lees straightened.

"Does that answer your question about sanity?"

Lees laughed, brushed tears from his face. "Yes. Now I *know* what you meant."

"Good. Do you have to keep on doing that?"

"I can't."

†

* * *

Another day, Lees and Mueller sat in the lighthouse again.

"Jim, what do you think about the ideas on those cards now?"

"I'm comfortable with them. I even"—he grinned boyishly—"rather like them."

"Good. Then shall we internalize them?"

"How do we do that?"

"Say them aloud. Pray them. We can do it together and add any other thoughts to God that come to mind."

Lees thought about it, nodded. "All right. And I think I'd like to kneel this time."

They knelt in the center of the room.

Light was all around them.

They bowed their heads.

They were bathed in light, felt the heat on their bodies.

Mueller started slowly and Lees joined in hesitantly; but their voices gained strength quickly.

"We are powerless over circumstance, and our lives have become unmanageable by us...."

Pause.

"We have come to believe that a power greater than ourselves—You, Lord—can restore our lives to sanity...."

Pause.

"We have made a decision and a commitment to turn our will and our lives over to Your care and protection...."

Pause.

Mueller continued. "We do so freely—"

Lees echoed him, "We do so freely..."

"Dear Lord, please take all of us—"

"Dear Lord, please take all of us..."

"To mold as You will—"

"To mold as You will...."

Pause.

"Amen."

They rose and sat together in silence on one of the wall benches. Lees lit a cigarette, smoked it, then stubbed it out, leaned back and closed his eyes. The light warmed the small of his back and he smiled.

Mueller asked, "How does it feel?"

†

"Peaceful."
"Prayer often does that."
Silence.

The light was so in the room that the light was the room and the room was the light and lighthouse was building's proper name.

"Yes," said Lees finally, "I think I'll have to pray more often."

"You might try praying those ideas in the evening before you go to bed and in the morning when you wake."

"Yes."

"And now you have made a decision and a commitment, so you might also ask God to reveal his will for you—to you—on a daily basis. One day at a time."

Lees nodded. "And the power to carry it out?"

"Yes."

Lees lay in bed, in the dark. Ann slept quietly beside him. He said his prayers in his head and ended them with a whisper. "Oh Lord, please help me to see Thy will and grant me the power to carry it out as You would have me. Amen."

He waited. Was not inspired.

He waited. Prayed again.

Waited. Was not inspired.

He felt puzzled and a little disappointed, then wondered what he was waiting for and felt a little silly. A burning bush in the bedroom would be a pain in the ass as well as a miracle, he thought, and giggled quietly. Presently, he drifted off to sleep.

The woman's back was toward him.

She was slender and had long hair.

Something about the shape of her . . . was . . . familiar?

She began turning slowly, turning slower than slow-motion film, turning with barely a hint of motion, turning until his eyes ached to see her and he reached out a hand to grasp her shoulder, speed her turning. . . .

Silver-Eyes.

Shrieking.

†

"You'll never get it, Guv!"
The fire and the chalice.
"Come to me!"
The monstrous hated black-blank face and the dead silver orbs.
"Drink!"
The spotlights, the audience, the sweat and smoke, his father's pale leering face.
His fear.

The light came on and he was thrashing in the bed. Ann sat upright next to him, her hand still on the lamp switch, staring at him, sleepy-eyed, pale, concerned.
"Jim?"
He sighed and rubbed his eyes and reached for his cigarettes, smiled at her as he shook one loose from the pack and said, "That part of me seems to have come alive again."

In the lighthouse again, Lees described the dream. Mueller listened thoughtfully as they ate pancakes and rashers and sipped tea.
"You seem to have had an answer."
Lees swallowed bacon, nodded. "Yes. Now if we can just figure out what it means. Is God always so cryptic?"
Mueller chuckled. "Usually. Who was the woman?"
"I don't know."
"Certainly you do."
Lees laid his knife and fork aside, stared. "I do?"
"Certainly."
Lees thought in silence. "The . . . next victim."
"That would be my guess."
"So that the message is: see her?"
"Which would. . . ?"
"Save her."
Mueller nodded. "I think that's it."
"Which is right where we started."
"Not quite. Now you are accepting God's will, not running on self-will. In this instance, they seem to coincide—save the woman, stop the Ripper, so it may appear to be a hair-split-

ting distinction. It's not. You had to submit before you could use the gift. Acknowledge the gift, but also acknowledge the giver."

Drizzle drummed soothingly on the window. Lees watched drops slide down the glass, spreading, dissolving.

"Silver-Eyes," he said softly, "came because . . . the power is . . . coming toward me?"

"That's a good enough speculation. What about the nightclub scene?"

Lees lips tightened.

"Jim?"

Lees sighed, looked away. "My father . . . used to . . . when I was very young, he forced . . ." He squeezed his eyes tight, shook his head, could not continue.

Mueller put a hand on his shoulder.

"It's all right. Stay with it, and let it out."

Silence.

"Talk to me, Jim . . ."

Lees bent over at the waist, sighed.

"Talk to me, Jim."

"He forced me to perform . . . in his nightclub act. I hated it. I was frightened of the people, the noise, the faces. I hated it all, and I—hated him!"

Lees laid his forearms on the table, rested his forehead on them and mumbled something.

"I'm sorry, Jim, I couldn't hear you."

Lees lifted his face. "I haven't talked to anyone—not even Ann—about that for nearly fifty years . . . not since I stopped complaining about it to my mother."

Mueller smiled gently. "This may come as a surprise to you, but in my job I'm used to hearing secrets."

Lees managed a small laugh. "First confession, Father?"

"Something like that."

Lees dropped his face back onto his arms.

Mueller rose, crossed to his book bag, rummaged through it and extracted an extremely thin paperback. He brought it to the table, sat and laid it by Lees' arms.

Silence. Five minutes passed.

Lees finally straightened, looked at the book: *Healing of Memories*, by Dennis and Matthew Linn.

†

The priest said, "I think the last part of the dream's message is that your anger at your father is the memory that needs healing. Read this book today. Don't bother with the written excercises until we talk about it."

Lees looked at the book with an expression that conveyed fear, loathing and dread.

Lees had had a bad night filled with grim dreams—Silver-Eyes, his father, bloody women and dark streets, black taxis and the frustrating woman with her back to him who turned too slowly, never came far enough around for him to see her.

He was grumpy and monosyllabic, uncommunicative as he ate dry toast and marmalade and drank scalding tea. Mueller looked at him, at his head down hunch-shouldered posture. Resistance, he thought. And resistance must mean we've struck a nerve. *The* nerve.

Aloud he asked, "Did you read the book?"

Lees muttered, "Yes."

"What did you think?"

"Not much."

Mueller stood and stretched, took his tea and walked to the far glass wall, stared out at the choppy Channel below.

"What didn't you like?"

Lees was silent.

Mueller considered a gull on the wing, skimming the surface. He remembered a small girl's pronouncement from years before—"There are two kinds of birds. Sea gulls and plain birds"—and smiled to himself. He stretched again and yawned. The day was gray and overcast and made him feel sleepy, though he had had a good night's rest.

"What didn't you like?"

He heard the sound of a cup banged down, but did not turn to face Lees.

"I told you—I'm not Jesus, and I never will be!"

"And I told *you*—nobody expects you to be Jesus, not even God."

"*That* book does!" roared Lees.

Mueller smiled. He let the reverberations of Lees' anger settle before he replied. "The book *suggests* we try to imitate Jesus in the arts of forgiveness and healing within the limits

†

of our abilities. That we recognize the Christ in us and in others." He turned and looked at Lees' angry face. "What's the matter, Jim? Is it just unthinkable to forgive your father?"

"Yes!"

Lees dropped his head and Mueller stifled a laugh at how little-boy-afraid-of-a-spanking he looked. "I thought we made a commitment the other day."

"I knew you'd throw that at me."

"Well, did we or did we not?"

"I didn't agree to forgive my father."

Just like a sulky little boy, thought Mueller. "When I make a commitment, I consider it binding. I can't take it back just because I begin to dislike some of the hard work, the difficulty, the pain that it entails. That's not commitment—that's what the politicians call keeping your options open."

Lees was silent. Mueller sat and crossed his legs and sipped tea.

The silence stretched. Finally, Lees buried his face in his hands, mumbled.

"I didn't hear you, Jim."

"How can I forgive that bastard?"

"Then you agree that God is calling you to forgive your father?"

"Maybe."

Silence.

"You know, Father—a lot of this seems pretty . . . well, *abstract*. I mean, it's a curious way to go about trying to stop a murder. Makes the murders seem . . . almost irrelevant."

"Think of it as a paradox. The murders are dead-center at the heart of the evil—*are* the evil. But they are also a diversion, a smoke screen for evil."

"You've lost me."

"Would you agree that these murders are pretty unusual events?"

"I'll say," Lees snorted.

"Would you agree that they are evil writ large, evil in broad bold strokes, evil easy to grasp as evil?"

"Yes."

"As such, are they justly symbolic of the smaller, the ordi-

†

nary, the commonplace and often unnoticed evil that we are all prey to—the snub of a friend or acquaintance, the back turned to a lover, the rude remark to a waiter, the hidden anger or resentment or envy, the self-destructive egocentricity of an alcoholic or the smug, cruel indifference to starving children, the infidelity of spouses or the neglect of parents—all those times when we good, decent, ordinary people injure ourselves and others and God's love and then say to ourselves, 'Well, I'm only human, everybody does it, I'm doing the best I can, I couldn't help it?'"

Lees nodded. "I see. Larger evil is clearer, easier to focus on."

"Yes. And dwelling obsessively on extraordinary evil permits us to let ordinary wrongs in ourselves to go unnoticed and unhealed or, if recognized, then justified—'I'm not as bad as that, I haven't murdered anyone.' But, of course, I have. I have murdered you and me with ten thousand tiny cuts."

"Then the murders are irrelevant?"

"In *that* sense. But in another sense, they are the heart of evil, for they are where small evil, unhealed, leads. Sin breeds in the dark places of the heart like a mutant virus—furiously active, wildly contagious, toxic and terribly terminal."

Lees stared out into gray light. "Stalin was the product of an unhappy childhood—is that it? Sounds like Social Psychology 101."

"Nothing wrong with that diagnosis. It's the remedy that's demented. You can't fix a society from the top down. You can't even fix another human being. You can only heal yourself with God's help. And become an instrument in the healing of those around you."

Lees smiled wanly. "Which is all another way of saying I'm supposed to . . . forgive my father."

"I think we'd reached tentative agreement that the dream had three parts—the turning woman, the next victim that you should attempt to focus your power on saving."

"Yes."

"Silver-Eyes' reappearance, indicating he will fight us."

"Yes."

"The nightclub memory, indicating a healing necessary to

free your gift. That seems to strike to the core of your resistance. You have hated the gift all these years because your father tried to use it and you in ways that were terrifying to you."

"Yes." Lees lit a cigarette. Exhaled. Sighed. "It's so . . . hard!"

Mueller nodded. "Perhaps it's time for some further motivation." He rose and crossed to the desk, lifted a long cardboard cylinder and began removing the plastic cap. "Most of us, as we discussed, spend our lives being called to fight rather ordinary, almost banal or tedious evil." He began pulling a large rolled paper poster from the tube. "But, occasionally, some of us are called to confront extraordinary evil. You and I seem to be in that position, and I anticipated we might need a visual reminder of the enemy to keep us focused. I had this poster made up to special order. I fear the printing shop people thought I was bizarre and I can't say I blame them. . . ."

He unfurled the poster.

It was three feet by five feet, black-and-white—a grainy enlarged reproduction of a century-old photograph.

A wooden bed center foreground shoved against a wooden door center background. A wooden table right foreground pushed up against the bed. Bed linens twisted up, exposing a substantial portion of the mattress and the crude wood slatting of the bed. The door and visible wall planking, as well as headboard, mattress, bed and table obviously stark, cheap, unadorned and of careless manufacture, hard unsympathetic use. The look of bleak, despairing poverty of matter and mind and soul.

The crumpled linens atop the bed were covered with dark patches that the eye slowly recognized; they were soaked in blood. The body on the bed was only identifiable as a woman because it was partially clothed in a dress; a dress whose front was completely slashed away, leaving visible only a puffed sleeve to attest that the rent garment was indeed a dress. The face was bloody and featureless, crisscrossed with slashes and cuts and with much of the skin stripped off to reveal the skull beneath. The ribs were bared and bloody, with most of the

†

chest flayed away. Her breasts were in a bloody pile on the bedside table.

Her left hand was shoved into the open bloody hole where her stomach had been split open. Her legs were spread, the nearer invisible beneath the twisted cloth of dress and sheets, the far one bent at the knee, thigh peeled down to stark bone and bloody wads of tissue. Between her legs was a bloody heap of extracted organs, inseparable and unidentifiable to the eye.

The image of the whole was overpowering, radiated repulsion as physical waves that pushed against Lees and he lifted, crossed his arms to ward them off, turned his head instinctively.

Lees and Mueller were pale.

The silence shrieked.

Mueller whispered, "Mary Kelly . . . the Ripper's final victim." He rerolled the poster, laid it back on the desk and sat in a chair across the table from Lees.

Lees' hands shook as he raised the cup to his lips.

The tea was cold.

The day was grayer still outside, and the room dimmed and the world was visibly scarred before their wounded eyes, was diminished.

They sat without speaking, exhaling audibly, letting slow color return to their faces. Lees lit a cigarette, his hand still trembling, and the priest lit a cigar.

"That is evil crystallized, clear, unmistakable."

Mueller nodded. "And, Jim, I believe in my heart of hearts, I believe with every fiber of my being, I believe that Jesus forgave the Ripper . . . forgave even that."

Lees stared at the priest as if viewing a lunatic. His face turned red and his neck swelled, muscles contorting against years of tension and rigidity.

Mueller whispered, "If Jesus could forgive even that . . . can you not forgive your father?"

Lees dropped his face into his hands.

Mueller whispered again, "Can you not forgive your father?"

Lees sobbed.

†

* * *

Later, Lees read from *Healing of Memories:*

> I have seen people shuffle into the psychiatric clinic with long lists of physical symptoms which evaporate one by one as they begin to forgive their parents.

Lees closed the book, keeping his place with his finger, bowed his head and exhaled. You're saying, he thought, You're saying, Lord, that I will feel better if I . . . forgive? Lees sighed. "That's hard," he said aloud.

Mueller agreed. "Of course it is—the principle is that of total surrender, total acceptance."

Another day, Lees read: "Can a person who doesn't love himself love God?"

Mueller grinned. "How can you love a God that made an unworthy you?"

"Ummph," said Lees. "I hadn't even thought about *loving* God. I just thought I had to obey him."

"We learn to love God because he loves us, but we really can't love God or others if we don't love ourselves. Let's work on that. The heart of your hurt is the feeling of powerlessness and terror of your traumatic childhood experiences. You were powerless, and the experiences were frightening. The inaccuracy is in blaming yourself. You *felt* you ought to be able to change things; since you couldn't, you assumed there was something wrong with you. Your hatred of your father is really self-hatred."

Lees grunted. "That makes sense, but it sounds too simple."

Again Mueller grinned. "All true principles are simple. The rule is that if you can't explain it easily to a child, it isn't a true principle."

"Ummph," said Lees.

Lees found mass peaceful and warming. He realized he was beginning to look forward to Sundays because Sundays meant mass.

What was the comfort? The rituals of the liturgy? The

†

calm, expectant air of the church? Just the sight of other people who, by their presence, announced they were also seekers of this mystery called God?

What is this all about? he wondered. What now? Am I wanting to be a Catholic, too?

The next day, Mueller read aloud: "Do I really desire healing?"

Lees looked at him. "Are you asking me?"

"Yes."

Lees stared at the drizzle speckling the surface of the sea and searched his mind, his heart, his soul. Finding no resistance in any hidden corner, he smiled and nodded. "Yes," was all he said.

The rain returned to fall on Hedgemore, and the first week of November had become chill unto cheerlessness. The lighthouse room was gray in the afternoon.

Lees read: "Be angry and sin not . . ."

He looked at Mueller with a question in his eyes.

"You need to admit anger, pain, sorrow, fear—any wounding emotion before it can be healed. Acknowledge it, feel it, see it, experience it, but don't act it out. If a man insults you, anger will precede healing and forgiveness, but it is not necessary to hit him. Or even return the insult."

"So we need to talk more about my anger at my father?" Lees rubbed the edge of the table with his palm. "I don't know, Eric. We seem to get farther and farther afield and . . . nothing's happening in my head. I've even stopped dreaming the turning woman. That part of me has shut down again."

Mueller turned up his palms. "We are either going to have both faith and trust or we are not."

"I suppose so."

"Good. Shall we talk about your father?"

Jim and Ann walked along the cliffs in late afternoon. They were bundled warmly against the sunless cold, their cheeks red from the wind and temperature. They held gloved hands.

"I never knew," he said, "until I started talking with Eric. I never knew *how much* hurt and anger I had stored up."

†

They paused naturally, of synchronized impulse, and stared out at the channel. They could not see far in the gray light. A large ship moved in the distance, obscured, half-hidden in twilight.

"Once I started, I flowed. The venom and sorrow all came boiling out. And I started hearing myself. It shocked me."

Tears were in the corners of her eyes.

He bowed his head. "I realize now how much all that has distanced me from you, from the children."

Tears were in his eyes, too, and he struggled with them. "I'm so sorry, Ann. Can you forgive me?"

She squeezed his hand. "I do. I will."

Something good *can* come, he thought, from anything . . .

Lees woke, startled. What? he thought.

The moon laid a silver river through the French doors that ran across the carpet and piled up at the dam of the far wall.

He was still half-asleep, disoriented. He sat on the edge of the bed and gazed absently into the pale stream. The cold, reflected light riveted his eyes. Pale . . . shimmering . . . thin, but hard . . . a banked fire from an alien world . . . silver . . . silver bright . . . silver like . . .

He sat entranced for minutes.

Thoughtless, he rose and dressed and stole out of the room, through the darkened mansion, outside into cold, clean air, past the poolhouse, across the meadow grass, which whispered against his shoes, brushed his pant cuffs, walking mindless and straight, unswervingly, in the stream of silver light that encompassed him, illuminated him as if he were a shade, straight on to the cliff, as if to walk the river of moonlight upward into the heavens to its source.

He stopped at cliff's edge with an inch or so of shoe tip beyond the rim.

He stared up.

Straight into the bright full orb of silver.

Stared.

Wind caressed his cheeks gently.

Sea sounds lapped at his ears.

He stared into the pitiless heart of the moon.

Stared vacantly, without thought.

†

Expectant, seeking revelation.

The moon separated, becoming twin eyes, dead eyes, all surface and reflection with no vitality, no inner life, no heart or soul or song.

A figure without a face.

Silver-Eyes in the night sky larger than a mortal mind could encompass. He laughed, and the world shook. Lees flinched, but did not notice the crumbling of bits and pieces of earth along the cliff's edge.

The northern Maine nightclub is small, cramped, hot. The crowd of fifty-three patrons is standing room only and drunk, noisy, sweaty. The air is blue with tobacco smoke, unbreathable. They are there for LEES SEES.

The curtain goes up.

Lees is five-and-a-half years old and center stage with his father under hot lights. He sees the faces—paunchy and weathered, scrawny and weathered, pale from generations of malnourishment or red from decades of drinking. And the eyes—glittering, excited, alight, expectant, ravenous. Hungry.

Lees is terrified. He looks up at his father. His father has no face, only cruel dead silver eyes.

His father's no-mouth whispers, "Stop shivering, you whelp. Be a man. Be a man—hate me!" Shrieks, *"Be a man! Hate me! Hate me, son! Be a man!"*

Tears form in little-boy-Lees' eyes and he shakes his small head, croaks, "No! No—I will not hate you, Father. And you are not my father. I will not hate my father. I will not hate you."

The figure seizes his tiny shoulders, shakes him violently, shrieks, *"Hate me!"*

Little-boy-Lees shuts his eyes. "I won't, won't, won't won't won't . . ."

Lees stood alone on the cliff edge, staring into the milky glare of the twin moons.

"You don't hate me?" Silver-Eyes roared. *"You will hate me!"* and he laughed and the earth rocked and bits, wedges fell away from the cliff's edge.

†

Lees stared into the silver light.

The top hat and cloak disappeared.

The moons merged, became one again.

Lees stared into the moon and there was a woman in the moon, a long-haired woman with her back to him, afire like the burning ice of diamond glow and turning, turning, turning, so slowly slowly slowly . . .

A cloud crossed the moon and blotted out the sky.

Pitch dark. Wind rising.

Lees was blinded by the sudden black, could not move. Silver-Eyes laughed somewhere and the earth shook; rain came in torrents, wind-whipped.

Thunder.

Lightning.

Lees ran, back to Hedgemore, back to the mansion, streaming wet with one thought pounding over and over in his brain, his heart . . .

I forgive my father, I forgive my father, I forgive my father . . .

Lees and Ann and Father Eric and Pat Cochran went to mass in the village on Sundays and Lees learned to look forward to it.

And Lees prayed and talked with Mueller.

And Lees dreamed.

And there was the eerie quiet, the stillness from the other side—a waiting . . .

On Saturday, Malcolm, Vanessa, Pat Cochran and Ann drove up to the Duke Street house, and Hedgemore was left to Lees and Father Mueller and the servants.

Lees stayed with Mueller in the lighthouse.

They talked late into the night.

"I just don't know, Eric. I have acknowledged *him* and asked forgiveness and direction, yet the dreams are still unclear to me. Is there some further surrender?"

Mueller shook his head. "I don't know. Keep asking."

Lees grinned ruefully. "At least, in the army, you *knew* what the orders *were*."

Mueller chuckled. "And then complained about them, no doubt."

Lees laughed and nodded. "All the time. Constantly."

Lees knelt in the humble stone church of the village. The light was dim and the sounds soft. Eric stepped out into the aisle, joined the procession moving toward the altar to receive the host, healing Grace.

The words echoed in Lees' head: "Lord, I am not worthy to receive You, but only say the word and I shall be healed."

The light played tricks with his eyes.

The slim stream of villagers in rough or casual contemporary clothing seemed to swell. He rubbed his eyes. He seemed to see a procession of ancients in robes and sandals, knights in armor and princes in royal regalia and serfs in rude jerkins, Occidental and Oriental faces, many skin tones and shades, clothing and bearing from all ages and places, the last two thousand years. The procession shimmered in his mind, moving backward out the door of the village church and stretched through time as well as distance. The throng was enormous and patient and stretched farther than mortal eye could see, filled with the mighty and the humble of the human family, with sad faces and faces saved by joy and faces corrupted by the world and faces sculpted to peace by pain. It was the long, unending procession of all the saints and sinners who had, for two millennia, declared themselves followers of Christ Jesus, had turned to the best of their poor abilities toward His Truth, His Light and His Way. The people who broke bread and blessed wine in His Honor, the Living Church, warts and all.

Lees' eyes misted and his heart softened; warmth and peace and serenity moved in him.

When his eyes cleared the church was simple stone, the congregation a modest assortment of Kent villagers; all was as before. And nothing was as before.

The lighthouse room was light and light was the room and they swam into the light, Lees across to a curved bench, where he sat on a cushion and sighed relief from the climb,

†

Mueller to the kitchenette, where he began putting together a pot of chocolate. "Fried eggs, grilled tomatoes, a few rashers suit for breakfast?"

"Sounds perfect."

"Then that's what we'll have. I try to never trifle with perfection."

Everything was brilliant—benches, chairs, table, windows, woods, ground and grass and cliffs and beaches, sun, sand, sky, sea. Everything was brilliant and everything glowed, shone, sparkled, radiated, emanated, grew, glistened, shimmered. Everything was alive with light.

The smells of chocolate and bacon filled their nostrils. Mueller concentrated on the preparation of the meal. Lees lit a cigarette, exhaled and leaned back at peace, closed his eyes.

"Father?"

"When did we switch back from 'Eric' to 'Father'?"

"Just now. Just for now. Just for this moment, because I want to say something that makes me feel uplifted and humbled at once and together."

Mueller swiveled his upper body to look at Lees. The priest's expression shifted from whimsy to sober curiosity. "Then by all means call me 'father.'"

Lees nodded. He spoke softly, but the words set up a resonance not unlike faint and distant music. "Father, I want to become a Christian. I want to become a Catholic."

Nothing is lost, thought Eric. Nothing is ever wasted.

†

304

NOVEMBER 8, 1988

Stuart came down from London to drive Lees and Mueller back to the city. The day was overcast, gray, not as wet or bleak as the day Stuart first drove the Leeses down to Hedgemore, but colder, more hard-edged.

Stuart drove competently, easily. The atmosphere was informal, but with an undertone of pressure, the pressure of deadline, of unbending time.

"What are the arrangements for tonight?" asked Mueller.

"We should be at the studio around nine. Collins and the Garcia woman will interview the three of us for half an hour. Then Jim gets a few minutes to make his pitch."

Lees looked out the window, smiled bleakly. "All the years I denied my . . . gift. Now I'm going on international television to proclaim it."

The priest said, "You can't say God doesn't have a sense of humor."

Lees could not quite laugh, but did nod agreement.

Stuart continued. "After the television broadcast, an unmarked car will be waiting for us, and we'll be smuggled into the Yard. Hughes and Clive are risking everything. . . ."

The men grew silent.

They passed through a village of Tudor inns and bungalows lining a sharply angled street, designed as if to encourage the traveler to stop.

"What about Jillian?" asked Lees. "I still have these dreams that seem to point to her danger. And most of her name is accurate—Mary Kelly."

Stuart nodded. "Jillian, Sir Arthur, Vanessa and Ann will stay at Jilly's apartment tonight. Hughes has designated a patrol force for the building."

†

The rest of the drive to London was mostly silent, each man wrapped in his own thoughts, fears and apprehensions.

The Vampire was tranquilized by six double Scotches and the generally lowered level of energy that several weeks of near-continual sex with Bridget Genaro Garcia had caused. He sat a few feet from her in the studio, and the high-voltage aura of sensuality that she still radiated caused a throb in his being like a low level toothache. He wondered at her undiminished appetite and increased energy with not so much awe as hopelessness bordering on despair. They were the current "in" couple, the chic twosome being touted by the celebrity-gossip panderers. They were the objects of intense EBN buildup not unlike the old movie studios' publicity campaigns, and their linked names regularly popped up in gossip columns, "news" items and Sunday supplement feature stories. But the Vampire was not fooled by all these trappings. He had found himself in this situation overnight because of a hot story and could disappear overnight when the story grew cold. He had some illusions about himself, but not many that ran bone-deep. He was not a good jounalist; he was not attractive; and he was not a great lover (was in fact certain that his present overextended efforts were for BGG substandard and barely passable and, anyway, he knew his pecker couldn't keep up the pace much longer). In short, he now had everything he ever thought he wanted and it all weighed him down, made him nervous and apprehensive.

Still, he covered it well. That night he looked as good as he ever would. His scarred face was made up cleverly to hide the worst blemishes and give him a rugged appearance, his hair was styled expensively and well, his body clean and deodorized, powdered and cologned. His elegant gray six-hundred-dollar EBN blazer and slacks matched BGG's gray blazer and skirt. His deep blue shirt, oxblood tie and shoes radiated a muted, wealthy glow.

He glanced at the wall clock, which showed 9:29 P.M., London time. He looked at Lees and Mueller and Stuart seated on the far side of BGG and they seemed calm enough. He shot BGG a reassuring smile and turned his attention to the main camera. Seconds later the red light went on and the producer pointed at him, signaling that he was live on EBN as well as on, via satellite feed, almost every broadcast network, syndicate and local outlet on the planet, save only those behind the Iron Curtain.

He introduced BGG, Lees, Mueller and Stuart, and then they spent twenty-five minutes "chatting" (from a hastily written script) about Lees—his gifts, his struggle, his visions—and Father Mueller's work in spiritual guidance, as well as Stuart's view of the crisis.

The last minutes of the broadcast were the *quid pro quo*, the payoff for the incredible scoop of an anniversary-evening interview with the "Ripper psychic," as Lees would come to be called. Lees was allowed to make an appeal—on his own and uncensored.

The cameras closed in on him.

He was tired-looking but not haggard, handsome but not flashy and well groomed in a tan sports jacket, navy turtleneck and slacks. He was awkward, but not nervous, hesitant but not evasive, and what he *was* spoke louder than words: a sincere and honorable man groping to find the right in a terrifying and baffling situation.

"I'm not used to this sort of thing and wouldn't undertake it if the situation weren't extraordinary, and if circumstance had not thrust this role on me."

His blue eyes were brilliant and thoughtful in closeup.

"I don't pretend to completely understand my gift, or what this whole crisis means."

The lines of his attractive face were deeply etched by stress and fatigue. It gave depth of character to his handsomeness—suffering visible.

"But I have come to believe that neither I nor anyone else can do anything useful without the help of God. I don't pretend to understand God, either, but I believe He *is* and He loves us all. And I believe He will help us . . . if we ask."

Lees leaned forward in his studio chair, as if to physically reach out to the watching billions.

"I'm going to ask you to do something. Anyone who can see and hear me, anyone who believes in God, from whatever faith or perspective—Christian, Jew, Buddhist, Muslim, Hindu—whatever—or anyone who even *thinks* there *might*

†

be God—I ask you to pray tonight. Go to your churches or synagogues or mosques or temples or your homes or wherever you happen to be, and take just a few minutes to pray . . . I wouldn't presume to tell anyone what to pray, but I believe prayers are the last, best hope we have. Thank you and God bless."

In Pakistan and Nepal, in Saudi Arabia and Israel, Sri Lanka and Chile, Kenya and Canada and Connecticut, all around the globe, people watched the program, listened to Lees and looked at one another—or looked inward, or outward, or upward—and recognized the simple sincerity of the appeal, the honest humility of the motives.

People prayed.

Kneeling in churches or living rooms, lying in bed, staring at the ceiling in the dark, outside in brilliant sun or under the canopy of a starlit night, in between classes or instead of a coffee break, while driving or walking or cycling or jogging, in alleys and apartments, along avenues and amidst the barren desert, high atop mountains or dwarfed by vast plains and endless sky, beside lakes and streams and rivers and upon the high seas, people prayed.

People prayed rosaries and chanted mantras and fumbled for words of grace in quiet informality, repeated ancient Hebrew forms, Hindu forms, Buddhist forms or said millions of paternosters. People prayed in the name of Allah and Moses and Buddha and Jesus and Mary and all the Communion of Saints. Within minutes after the broadcast, millions of people prayed, then tens of millions, and as the hours passed, hundreds of millions in a growing tidal wave of the faithful, the repentant, the good-hearted, the humble and the unsure, until the early morning of November 9, 1988, called, loudly or softly, clearly or obliquely, swiftly or slowly, but irresistibly, called nearly four billion human souls to seek the aid and comfort and solace of their maker. People prayed for the Ripper's capture, the Ripper's destruction; the defeat of the devil; the clairvoyance of Lees; Lees' comfort, safety, sanity and redemption; for the prevention of murder and no harm to befall anyone; for swift or terrible justice; for lost souls; for mercy; for universal peace and brotherhood; prayed the words of their hearts and spilled out to God the endless sea of their

†

hopes, fears, frustrations and anxieties, their woundedness and healing, their pain, their joy, their love.

People prayed.

Jillian's building, in the northeastern end of lower Thames Street, was an enormous postwar office block that had, the previous year, been renovated to a height of eighteen stories. Jillian had been one of the first tenants of the new addition, and had picked a suite of rooms—a three-room office and two-bedroom flat—on the top floor.

Eustace Dilling, who had managed the Hedgemore security detail so admirably he had been promoted to sergeant, headed an on-site security force of twenty-four constables, all armed with service revolvers. By 12:48 P.M., he was satisfied with the arrangements and the positioning of the offices, and had called the Yard to pass a report on to Clive.

At 1:09, Sergeant Dilling knocked on the door of the flat, was admitted by Jillian and took up a post in an Eames chair that he moved to the railed balcony overlooking her sunken lounge.

"Sure you won't join us for a bite of late supper, Sergeant?"

Dilling grinned at Jillian. "No, ma'am. Thank you, but I'll just sit up here quiet as nevermind and you won't know I'm here."

Sir Arthur muttered from the bar. "*That*, at least, is a relief."

Vanessa and Ann, sitting at table, stared down at their sandwiches and tea while Mary Cilone shot Kelly a disgusted glance.

At 2:59 A.M., Hughes hung up the phone after a last-minute conversation with Sir Edwards William. More than fifty thousand men—police, army and reserves—patrolled the city by foot and automobile, jeep and personnel carrier. Roadblocks and patrols were especially heavy around the previous murder sites, in parks, railway and tube stations, public places and all locations where previous "incidents" had been reported.

The PM had not agreed to enforced curfew, but had publicly requested a voluntary curfew and closing of restaurants and pubs at midnight. Early reports were that cooperation was

†

good. Public traffic in the city was less than forty percent of normal and many establishments had closed by eleven P.M.

The entire city was poised and waiting. The world was watching and held its collective breath.

"Bloody fool," muttered Hughes, staring at the now silent telephone.

"That's insubordination," suggested Stuart.

Hughes smiled. "What's one more count after all I've piled up?"

Lees stood at the window wall. The greenery of St. James Park and the Palace Gardens were deep velvet intimations in textured night. The lights of the city glittered like hope in the dark.

Images in Lees' head.

Sunlight, hot and liquid and blinding. London streets in rapid succession—Portobello Road, Kensington High Street, Chelsea Embankment, Edgeware Road, Outer Circle, Warwick Way, Park Lane, Old Bond Street, Holburn Viaduct and Ludgate Hill, Bishopsgate, Threadneedle Street and . . . Whitechapel Road.

Mueller noticed the rigidity of Lees' posture. "Jim?"

"I'm seeing things."

Stuart, Hughes, Clive, Cochran and James turned their eyes to him.

"The city . . . streets from all over the city . . ."

The streets were impassable. Autos and lorries and buses were jammed side-by-side and nose-to-nose with horses and carriages and wagons and horse buses. The streets and sidewalks, parks and buildings and alleys were choked to bursting with people, contemporary people in modern clothes, and pale button-eyed Victorians. The translucent Victorian faces were fixed confusion and hostility, and their heads moved back and forth slowly, or remained cocked in a listening posture.

Something snapped.

Victorians seized moderns, struggled and wrestled and beat them to the ground, strangled and choked and bludgeoned them. Bit them. Tore their throats out and fell on the bleeding bodies and savaged the carcasses, ate them like wolves.

†

Ripped them!

The streets were riots, civilians and police and the army in hand-to-hand mortal combat, and the Victorians—with blood-cleared eyes and supernatural strength—winning. Their eyes were mad and their ferocity unquenchable and they felled dozens each and increased the attack. Soon, the streets were littered with bodies and the gutters ran with blood.

Lees leaned against the window, whispered, "What was the population of London in 1888?"

Hughes frowned, shrugged. "Four, maybe four and a half million."

Lees whispered, "If this murder isn't stopped . . . most of them are coming back."

Sergeant Dilling accepted a second cup of tea and yawned. "Pardon me, ma'am. Bit short on sleep."

Jilly smiled. "Not to worry, Sergeant. I won't tell that you were yawning on duty."

Dilling chuckled. "Bless you, ma'am. If they sacked every copper who got dozy on shift there wouldn't be a policeman left in uniform."

Jillian descended the white-carpeted stairs and crossed to the conversation area filled with clean-lined padded sofa and chairs, a slate coffee table and chromium lamps. She sat next to Vanessa and picked up her glass of white wine and sipped it, held it in both hands like a talisman.

"I don't believe it."

"Believe. . . ?"

"I cannot, I will not, believe I am . . . the intended . . ."

Vanessa put a hand on Jillian's arm reassuringly. "I know. I don't either. I can't believe this horrid affair has really anything to do with . . . us. Our family. But it was wise to take precautions."

They glanced at Sir Arthur and Mary Cilone sitting at the table, playing gin rummy. Ann was in the spare bedroom, napping.

Jillian glanced at her watch.

3:11.

They sipped wine.

Dilling yawned.

†

Jillian smiled at Vanessa. "The sergeant and Ann have given me a yearning. I'm bushed. I think I might stretch out for a short nap. It's not so long before it will be past the . . . time."

Vanessa patted her arm. "Good idea."

Jillian went into her bedroom. Vanessa crossed to the windows.

The electric lights of districts in view were comforting. She could see the implication of some few autos by their headlight beams and a figure on foot here and there, on near streets, dwindled by height and distance to miniature stature.

Below, to the east, just outside the city boundary, loomed the dark shape of the Tower of London.

Vanessa placed a slim hand at her throat, remembering that the White Tower housed the exquisite Norman chapel of St. John the Evangelist side-by-side with displays of the instruments of torture and execution that were the commonplace of past royal politics and power.

The barracks housing the infantry regiment, the Yeoman Warders and Yeoman of the Guard was an elongated rectangle by the north wall. Next to it an insubstantial appearing darkness was the church of St. Peter-in-Chains.

She shivered, but could not keep her eyes from wandering morbidly across the black bulk of the famous prison. They drifted to the south, to the river and Traitor's Gate, where many a nobleman and noblewoman, fallen from favor, had entered their last quarters under the sentence of death that was the fullest flare of royal displeasure. Beyond were the twin cylinders of Wakefield Tower, which housed the crown jewels, and the Bloody Tower, where the Little Princes, Edward V and, his brother, the Duke of York, had been murdered and buried by Henry VII and the deed pinned on his tragically maligned predecessor, Richard III.

She could not, in the dark, pick out the spot where Anne Boleyn was beheaded and shut her eyes as dread came home to her, broke through the walls of her defenses.

"Horrid place," she muttered, and a tremor ran through her. She realized she had never seen the Tower for what it was. Colorful history, she had thought, or jewels and royalty and pageantry. Yet the fat ugly ravens kept there as bizarre

†

pets *were* the proper Tower birds—black, sleek, sordidly symbolic of a monument to institutionalized cruelty, legitimized betrayal and torture, legalized venom and murder coated with the "fool's gold" patina of royal privilege and will, political necessity and the "divine right of kings."

Her fantasy world of safety and security was somehow shattered, and she felt the long-dead arms of the ancient murdered stretch out to her, supplicating and entreating, seducing her to join their ghastly parade of savagely shortened lives. Finally, she was afraid to the marrow.

The sudden sound scalded her nerves and she jumped. She turned, her heart racing. Sergeant Dilling was snoring slack-jawed and open-mouthed. Tears stung her eyes. She gulped wine and exhaled loudly.

They will give him such a rocket for sleeping, she thought. She touched her face with a trembling hand, gulped wine again and turned back to the north windows, tried to let the bright electric lights of the mazelike streets soothe her.

Jillian got up from the bed where she had sat moodily. She crossed to her wardrobe, unbuttoning her blouse as she walked. The single bedside lamp provided little light and the room was dim, gloomy.

She turned the handle.
The door swung free.
Slowly opened.
Let sparse light illuminate the shadowed interior.
The Ripper was in the closet!

On Porchester Place, a small dark-haired boy with bright marble eyes and deathly white skin stood with a tray of matchboxes strapped to his chest. He waved a box of Bryant & May's Alpine Vesuvians and hawked his wares.

"Matches! Best brimstones! Ha' penny the box! Matches!"

Not far away, on Abbey Road, Cast-Iron Billy cracked the whip, held the reins of the team pulling the Thomas Tilling Horse Bus and cried out the route: "Abbey Road to Golders Green via St. John's Wood, Marylebone and Hampstead Heath!"

On Heneage Street, a warehouse wall glowed in the dark.

†

Century-old advertising posters in black-and-white and primary colors radiated color, sight, smell, texture. A music-hall piano tinkled an eerie tinny tune.

In her house near The Oval, Jocylen Allen awakened and sat up in the dark.

She strained her ears, heard nothing, slipped silently out of bed and crossed to a window. Her heart beat insistently and her hand shook as she fingered back a curtain, stared out at the streetlamps, the damp night.

A hokey-pokey popped around a corner and began rumbling up her street, its chartreuse-and-raspberry striped awning flopping with motion. A ragamuffin little girl danced alongside and her high piping voice carried on the still air: "Hokey-Pokey, Penny a lump; That's the stuff To make you jump!"

At 3:15 A.M., Stuart asked Lees, "Still nothing?"

Lees shook his head sadly.

Stuart shrugged. "I can't sit here any longer. Let's go to the car. We'll drive over toward Jillian's flat." The others stared at him and he said defensively, "We've no better idea."

Lees nodded. "You're right, Malcolm. And the safety of loved ones is the primal duty. We'd be less than human if that wasn't more important than . . ."

The others nodded.

Outside, wet was falling; not rain, not even drizzle; just wet. Surfaces glistened, were damp and footing was slick treacherous. The auto pulled out on to Victoria Street with Clive driving, Mueller beside him, Lees and Stuart in back. The second auto carried James, Hughes and Cochran.

Lees felt pressure in his head as Clive turned onto the Victoria Embankment after traversing Parliament Square and jogging briefly on Bridge Street. The pressure built, but nothing came.

They approached Cleopatra's Needle. Suddenly, Lees bent nearly double from sudden pain in his head. "Aahh, aahh, aaahhh!"

"Jim—what is it?!"

Images.

Vanessa Cilone, windows and lights, a bedroom, a closet

door opening in dim light, a featureless face with thick curly dark hair beneath a top hat.

Pain.

Silver-Eyes in his head.

"He's . . . he's . . . he's with them. *The Ripper is with Vanessa!*"

Clive jammed the accelerator pedal to the floor and tires squealed, the rear end shimmied and the police car jumped and streaked away.

Jillian smiled to herself, reached into the wardrobe and lifted the top hat and wig from the featureless wooden head. She took the costume and the bag and laid each item on her bed. Her eyes caught the silver-burlap wallpaper and the small Klee.

Not long, she thought. Not long and you will be something else. Again.

She trembled with anticipation, and her loins were wet.

Lees pressed his hands to his temples and choked on the pain. "Oh, God, oh, God . . . oh, God—the Ripper's dressing and the Ripper is . . . oh, God—*It's Jillian!*"

"*No!*" screamed Stuart like a man mortally wounded.

Lees' head was filled with Silver-Eyes and Silver-Eyes conjured a vision.

Jillian in the moonlight.

Her perfume.

Her soft lips.

Lees was nauseous and tears flooded his eyes, as he rolled down the window, leaned his head out into the swift stream of air and vomited exhaustively.

Jill-the-Ripper, fully garbed, opened her bedroom door a crack and called, "Father, could you come here a second?"

She stood behind the door as she opened it for Sir Arthur. She closed the door.

He saw her; the knife in her hand. His eyes widened in surprise and he opened his mouth, but no words came.

The Ripper chuckled. "Finally left you speechless, Father?

Finally secured your full attention? Good," she whispered, "time to die," and plunged the knife directly into her father's throat before he could move or make a sound.

A young army lieutenant crossed into Hyde Park from his detachment's post at Hyde Park Corner and stopped at the edge of Rotten Row.

Victorians in finery paraded the sidewalks and horses and carriages circled the mile of turf.

A constable assigned to the Haymarket Theatre turned to stare at the glass doors. Could have sworn I heard something, he told himself.

Inside, the stage lights had come up and the Victorian audience was laughing.

The stone dinosaur stared blindly down on the Crystal Palace pond where Victorians skated in a silence broken only by the sounds of sharp runners slicing ice and the crying of a small girl who had been bumped and knocked down.

Not far away, a squad of soldiers stared dumbstruck as mist parted, revealing the gardens and walks and statuary and stairs and the monstrous building of pale-blue ironwork and masses of sheet glass rising and glittering in the night like a fantasy jewel.

The Crystal Palace risen again.

Jill-the-Ripper knelt over the bloody body of her fallen father and bowed her head. The bloody knife lay on his chest and the blade glowed. There was fire in the blade and his face was in the blade and his eyes were luminous, volcanic, and the Ripper whispered . . .

Lees said softly, "She's killed Sir Arthur. She's . . . 'praying' . . ."

Vanessa frowned at the distant lights of the far reaches of Spitalfields and Barbican. They puzzled her. They were not purely white and strong now, had shifted to a dimmer intensity and gave off an odd yellow tinge.

She watched and shifted her eyes. The lights were still white, strong. She shifted her eyes back.

†

She couldn't be sure, but it seemed as if another outer row of lights were now dimmer and yellowish as well.

She watched without shifting her eyes.

Another row changed.

What? she wondered. Less light? Yellow?

She noticed that there were fewer headlight beams moving in the closer, white-lit areas, but none in the yellowed rows.

She did not know where the words came from, but she thought, Gaslights are yellow.

Gaslights?

Time warp, she thought.

Her knees buckled and she put a hand to the window to keep from falling. The realization overwhelmed her with adrenaline-fed terror. The entire area encircling her was a moving time-warp.

Headed straight for her.

Jillian rose and grasped the knife, crossed to the door, opened it a crack and said in a husky voice, "Vanessa . . ."

Vanessa turned and stared at the door with her limbs trembling and blood pounding aching heart and throbbing head.

"Vanessa . . ."

She backed against the window wall shaking so hard she vibrated the glass.

"Vanessa . . ."

She stared at her mother, Mary, who was frozen in fear, seated at the table. Her mouth and throat were dry to cracking and her tongue seemed a giant gland choking her.

The door swung open.

She saw Jill-the-Ripper, recognized her, shrieked, "*Sergeant Dilling!*"

The Ripper shook her head. "Chloral hydrate in the second cup of tea. He'll be out for hours. You could pour scalding water on his head and he wouldn't wake."

Vanessa slid down the glass to her knees, tears tumbling out of her, shoulders shaking in despair, grief and fear.

The Ripper stepped into the room.

"Why?" sobbed Mary.

The only answer was the stabbing electric shock of the time-warp. The office block was no more. The policemen in

†

the building were caught in a change where no space existed for them, disappeared from time, their beings suspended. The patrolmen about the building found themselves amongst unfamiliar buildings, wearing unfamiliar uniforms, disoriented and not quite able to remember who they were or what they were supposed to be doing at the moment. Where the office building had stood, a row of semi-detached Victorian homes, numbering eleven altogether, now stood.

It was 3:24 A.M., November 9, 1888.

Again.

Clive brought the car up from the Blackfriars' Bridge underpass curve in a rear-end sliding sixty-kilometers-per-hour charge as he accelerated the short stretch to Queen Victoria Street.

Too late, Stuart shouted "Look out!" as they clipped the rear corner of a red horse-drawn omnibus filled with working-class Victorians headed to the inner city for early morning shifts. Both vehicles spun in opposite directions, the omnibus turning over and breaking one horse's leg and the other horse's neck while the sedan slid into a gaslight post, bending it over to near horizontal with the impact shattering the fixture's flow regulator, so that the flame shot out at a slight upward angle like a tilted six-foot Bunsen-burner.

Westward along the street was a series of auto–carriage collisions and a milling confusion of Victorians and moderns, the latter staring at the anachronistic mixture of details, the indigestible juncture of times. Eastward, the people, vehicles and buildings were completely Victorian.

"Time-warp," muttered Clive and Stuart.

"Time-warp," groaned Lees.

As they watched, two Victorians attacked moderns; fights broke out. The screaming began.

Clive said, "Sir, we're at last a kilometer-and-a-half from the office block. This time-warp must have a three-kilometer radius."

Stuart snapped, "Yes, and no time to lose. Let's get on."

Clive shook his head sadly. "She won't start up, sir. Impact's done something to the engine."

†

Lees said, "Did you say three-kilometer radius, Sergeant?"

"Yes, sir."

"My London layout's not perfect, but wouldn't that take in Whitechapel?"

"Lord, yes," exclaimed Clive.

Stuart frowned at them, snapped, "What are you two nattering about?"

Lees seized his arm. "Time-warp, Malcolm. Everything occurring exactly as it did a hundred years ago. Whitechapel!"

"Oh, *God!*"

"Vanessa and Jillian . . . *and* now, the original Ripper stalking the original Mary Kelly—*again!*"

Stuart leaped out and the others tumbled after him. "Clive, Hughes, Pat, Constable James, head for Whitechapel—you know how to find Miller's Court, don't you?"

They nodded.

"Jim, Eric, come with me!"

They all ran.

A light rain fell on Whitechapel.

The gentle sluicing cleaned the sky of coal dust and rinsed the grime from the slum buildings and streets, filling the rain gutters with a steady stream of fresh water carrying away the outer stains of the refuse district.

Mary Kelly, a passably attractive street whore, strolled along Goulston Street not far from her Miller's Court room. She desperately needed "work," although she'd already had two customers earlier that evening. She owed thirty-five shillings back rent on her room to McCarthy (the whores who lodged in his tenements and rooms were known as McCarthy's Rents—the cash from their street sex transactions provided him with most of his income and them with little more than lodging and booze) and he was pressing her hard for payment. Even the light rain and moderate chill made her cough and shiver. Her morning sickness had not left her and she was afraid she might not keep her last tot of gin down.

The night was discouraging enough and the hour uncomfortable enough that custom was hard to find. Indeed, if she were not so desperate for funds, Mary Kelly would have spent

†

the night indoors. As it was, she had to desert the side streets and small lanes where she often plied her trade and seek the larger thoroughfares. Even they were mostly deserted.
She stood still.
A hansom carriage came clattering down the street.
She turned toward it and mustered a saucy grin as it passed. She could not see into the dim interior, but she noticed the hackie's queer silver eyes beneath his top hat. She saw, thought, moved and felt as she had a hundred years before, but she had had her free will restored.
She and the Ripper.
Silver-Eyes needed the choices repeated.
The choice for prostitution and banal tedious evil.
The choice for murder and slaughter.
The choice for terror and pain and death.
The carriage rolled on by.
She turned away, shivering again in her thin dress and shawl. Too fancy, she thought. Too fancy for the likes o' me.
She resumed walking south, thinking she might just pop into the Black Garter Pub two doors on—not that she'd have a drink, mind—she'd not earned enough to satisfy McCarthy's black soul, let alone treat herself. Just pop in out of the wet for ten minutes. To let the cold from her bones. 'Course they did have illegal after-hours prices for regulars. A big mug of buttered rum punch'd cost no more than an ordinary-time tot. Be almost a *crime* to pass it up.
She turned into the doorway, sensing something.
The clatter of horses' hooves and grind of iron wheels had not disappeared, merely stopped. She looked back north along Goulston Street and saw the cab halted at the corner of Wentworth. The passenger was alighting. She watched as he turned south and began walking back toward her. The carriage turned west onto Wentworth and disappeared.
She stepped back onto the sidewalk.
The man came walking, walking, walking. He was well-dressed—she could tell even at distance—and as he approached, she noted a small black bag in his left hand. There was something familiar about the slender figure and the set of his narrow shoulders. She strained to see his features, and as

†

he approached closer, began to enter the soft light thrown by the pub windows, her eyes widened.

He stopped two paces away and smiled at her.

"You!" she blurted, then curtseyed in embarrassed confusion. "Sorry, sir—I mean M'Lord—I mean . . . is that right?"

"Close enough," he said in a mellow baritone.

"What'd you be doing in these mean streets, er, M'Lord?"

"Why, looking for you, dear girl." He smiled. "Looking specially just for you."

Half a block on the seven men saw a deserted hansom cab parked on the street. Hughes shouted, "We've the farthest to go?"

Stuart nodded. "Take it!"

Clive leapt to the driver's seat, and Hughes jumped on the running board, hooking an arm through the window after James and Cochran clambered in. Clive cracked the whip. They flew up Queen Victoria Street toward Cornhill, Leadenhall and Aldegate High Street beyond.

"We'll just make it!" shouted Clive.

Hughes nodded.

"And then we'll have the answer to the century-old question!"

Hughes stared at Clive.

"We'll know!" shouted the sergeant. "We'll know who Jack-the-Ripper was!"

Yes, I suppose we will, thought Hughes.

An open-air carriage came leisurely toward the trio. It was empty and driven by a man in emerald-and-gold livery.

Stuart hissed, "We'll jump on this side and push him off."

Lees and Mueller nodded, and as the carriage pulled even with them, they grabbed the sides and scrambled up, over and into the passenger compartment. The rocking and small sounds caused the driver's brow to furrow and his head to cock, listening. Stuart stood on the forward passenger seat and raised himself to his full height, grabbed the driver's shoulders and flung him bodily out and away, while Lees

†

clambered up to the seat, seized the reins, whipped them up and down as the driver landed in the street and rolled several times. The horses responded and the carriage leaped ahead down Queen Victoria Street toward Cannon and King William Streets and Lower Thames beyond.

It was 3:33 A.M.

The bedroom was broad and dimly lit by a four-candle chandelier. The heavy oak furniture shone dully; the blue-gold-silver Persian carpet was soft underfoot. Jillian, having forced Mary and Vanessa into the room at knifepoint, now closed the door swiftly and leaned heavily against it. The body of Sir Arthur lay crumpled and unmoving in one corner.

Vanessa and Mary and Jillian stared at one another in a triangular tableau. Vanessa shook her head, dazed.

"Jillian—you're my cousin, my friend, my agent, the woman closest to me in all the world. I've always loved you. Why?"

"Because I've always hated you."

"Why?" whispered Vanessa.

"Because you have stolen everything from me!"

"Stolen what?"

"Everything I've always wanted or dreamed about or desired. I'm a good-enough-looking woman, but cousin Vanessa was always *beautiful!* You made me appear plain by contrast! I'm bright, but cousin Vanessa was always charming. All the men I wanted always fell for Vanessa! Always the star! Always the attention, the affection—yes, even the money! While Jillian takes the leavings, the handouts, the crumbs!"

"But, Jilly, I never knew—"

"*Of course you didn't!* You think I'd *ask you* for what belonged to me *by right?!*" The Ripper breathed heavily, panted with the exhaustion of release, pent-up emotion acknowledged after years' frustration. "Even that," she said thickly, "even that—all that—I *might* be able to let go, but you stole my birthright, and that I could never forgive—you *cow!*"

Vanessa's voice quavered with terror and confusion. "Birthright? I don't—"

"*Understand?!* Don't understand. Of course you don't, but ask your mother. Why do you think your dear Uncle Arthur doted on you so much? Paid you more attention than his own daughter? Sometimes forgot my birthday, but never yours?

†

Gave you parties and presents and holiday trips he never gave me, not unless I was tagging along with the two of you? Why? Why does he resent Malcolm so openly? Why has he given you all the love I ever wanted and was always denied?"

There were tears in the Ripper's eyes.

Vanessa shook her head, dumbfounded.

The Ripper whispered, "I'll tell you why. Because you're not my cousin, cunt! You're my sister!"

"*No!*"

"*Yes!* Yes, you are!" the Ripper hissed. "Your slut mother was fucking daddy blind before either of us was born. After your father's death, I overheard them talking once. We were just twelve then. They talked about you—what they owed *you* as parents. *You!* Always you, always Vanessa, and never Jillian. You are my *hated* sister and your true name—not mine—is *Mary Kelly!*"

The Ripper threw back her head and laughed sickeningly.

Miller's Court was a short cobblestone cul-de-sac, and Mary Kelly led her famous customer up it in the rain, holding his arm gently.

"Fancy," she said "a girl loike me and a gent loike you." She stopped at the squalid one-room bungalow, reached through a broken corner of the doorglass, unlocked and opened it.

They stepped into darkness.

She struck a match and their faces were illusions in the air. She touched it to the wick of a candle on her bedside table. The tiny aura floated in the room.

"Shall we have a fire? There's some coal in the grate."

"That would be splendid."

"Can I take your bag?"

"No, just . . . get ready while I start the fire."

"What's in it?"

He smiled. "A special treat I like to take around with me on nights like this."

The lieutenant had made the mistake of summoning his men by orders barked in a loud voice.

†

The Victorians found him, seized him, bore him to the ground and ripped him open with their teeth.

When the thirty men of his command arrived, the Victorians attacked.

Rotten Row was a battleground, with a hundred Victorians in close combat with the soldiers, who only had crowd-control rubber bullets. The Victorians were picking them off one by one, a private here, a corporal there, seized and carried under flailing and kicking and screaming, beaten and bitten and ripped and savaged and eaten.

The Victorians whose eyes had cleared were now moving out of the park.

Looking.

Hunting.

The carriage sped down Lower Thames Street, the vast, imposing shadows of the Tower of London looming ahead, casting a symbolic judgement across the evening, indifferent time sitting in judgment of puny men and their frail efforts to combat terror, sin, murder and evil.

The carriage rolled to a stop in front of the row of eleven semi-detached homes. The trio stood in the carriage and stared at them.

Stuart swore, turned to Lees. "There's no time for a search! Where are they?!"

Jill-the-Ripper's eyes were filmy, distant. Her voice was thick, as if drunken or drugged.

"It becomes its own reward, you know . . . the thrill, the anticipation . . . the killing, the cutting, the blood. I thought I just hated *you*, but I hated them all . . . all the cows . . ." Her voice dropped to a sick, dreamy whisper. "I loathe all women—all of us—we depend on men, we give them power over us, we think ourselves incomplete without them . . ."

Vanessa was afraid to speak, but her mind raced with agonized argument.

The Ripper muttered, "I *loved* killing them . . ." Her eyes burned.

Her whisper was intense. "Not so much as I am going to

†

enjoy you—my pet! I'm going to cut you and slit your throat . . . and *rip you!*

The door to the adjoining bedroom opened.

Ann Lees stood in the doorway, staring uncomprehendingly.

Jillian's eyes moved to her.

Mary Cilone ran at the Ripper, but she was too quick, whirled and stabbed in one motion, burying the blade in Mary's stomach and tearing upward with the strength of hatred.

Mary screamed, "Run, Vanessa! *Run!*" and shrieked with the pain of her disemboweling as the Ripper stabbed, twisted, tore and ripped her. She sagged to the floor, bleeding, dying, whispering, "I'm sorry, so sorry . . . Run, Vanessa . . . run . . ."

Mary Kelly sat on the bed in the shabby room. The candlelight was weak and her shift was thin. She shivered.

The Ripper crouched by the fire and, satisfied it was lit, swiveled his head to look at her. Cow, he thought.

He smiled.

She smiled, patted the bed. "Coming, M'Lord?"

He nodded. "Just let me get my bag."

Adam and Jocylen Allen stood at their bedroom window holding their terrified twins, Adam and Eve.

The street was lined now.

The street vendors were back.

"Fresh flowers!"
"Hot muffins!"
"Rabbit for sale!"
"Sam Hall—chimney sweep!"
"Cat's meat man!"
"Ice cream!"
"Ripper murders another in Whitechapel!"
"Sharp knives!"
"Hokey-Pokey, Penny a lump; That's the stuff To make you jump!"

* * *

†

Soldiers in Sydenham were advancing on the Crystal Palace, which was lit from within by gas lamps, giving off a yellow shimmering glow of thousand-pane refraction in the night. Hundreds of Victorians were visible within the towering structure—pale blank faces, walking slowly and rhythmically.
The point soldier climbed the steps.

Clive raced the short block on Whitechapel Road, nearly standing the hansom cab on end making the accelerated turn onto Goulston Street. He began reining in parallel to The Black Garter and applied the hand brake until the iron wheels screamed against the damp pavement and the friction shot sparks a whiff of smoke the scent of heat.
The men clambered to the pavement. Their way to the warren leading to Miller's Court was blocked by a small crowd of Victorians—workers, idlers, the poor, hard pale men with sullen faces already turning their heads at the alien, unremembered sound of this carriage, these men. One thickset man near them was making tentative searching motions in the air with his arms and the others were separating very slowly in a line across their intended path.
Cocking their heads.
Moving them slowly from side-to-side.
Listening.
Groping.
Clive, Hughes, James and Cochran edged toward the end of the line as quietly as possible, preparing to flank them. Suddenly, Parker James stubbed his toe, swore softly, reflexively.
The Victorians froze.
Clive darted around the end of the line, was past them, running, fumbling his pistol free as he ran.
The Victorians made a complete line across the passageway, blocked Hughes, James and Cochran.

"Where are they?" repeated Stuart.
Lees scanned the row of homes. Nothing.
He bowed his head. "Our Father, Who art in—"
Mueller and Stuart bowed their heads, joined in. "Hallowed be Thy Name, Thy Kingdom come, Thy Will be done . . ."

†

The prayer completed, Lees and Mueller crossed themselves and raised their eyes. Lees swung his gaze from left to right along the row of houses, pausing a second at each facade—nothing—until his eyes rested on the last home in the row. Images swam in his head—Vanessa and Ann; Jill-the-Ripper, knife in hand.

"The last one. The far house. The one nearest the Tower."

They ran to it and up stone steps. The plain wood door was locked and too heavy to break down. Stuart pushed the others aside and produced his pistol, took aim on the lock and squeezed the trigger.

Nothing.

He stared at the revolver. Swore. Time-warp had changed the new double-action police positive model to a nineteenth-century Lee Enfield model, single-action, which required cocking before firing. Stuart pulled the hammer back, aimed, fired, and repeated the process. The primitive shells vented powerful cordite aroma and smoke and the explosions were deafening at close range.

The lock shattered, and Lees kicked the door inward, led the men inside.

Clive ran heavily, winded and shaken, the last few steps to the tiny hovel. He stopped, braced himself, raised his right foot waist high and kicked in the door.

He stepped inside to an eerie-light frozen tableau—Mary Kelly on the bed, the Ripper with his back to her having just removed the knife from the small bag. He took two steps toward the Ripper. The pistol felt extra heavy and awkward as he raised it, but he paid no attention to the sensation.

"Scotland Yard. You're under arrest."

The Ripper turned.

They were only a few feet apart and even in the diffuse light the Ripper's features were instantly recognizable to Clive from old photographs.

"*You!*" he blurted as he leveled the revolver at the man's chest an arm length away. "You're Jack-the-Ripper?!"

"Yes," the man hissed.

He hurled himself at Clive, and Clive squeezed the trigger three times before the knife sliced deep into his throat.

†

"*Oh, murder!*" yelled Mary Kelly, and she trembled, shook, cried on the bed.

Clive swayed on his feet, bleeding, dying, staring dumbly at the traitorous revolver that had failed him, at last recognizing it as a single-action Lee Enfield. He tried to cock the hammer, but his strength was fading fast. The Ripper knocked it from his hand and it clatter-bounce-slid away across the floor.

The Ripper's face was inches away, his breath hot and ugly, his features locked in the dying sergeant's brain, the image he would carry into eternity. "You," he whispered one last time and fell.

Clive was dead.

The Ripper turned toward Mary Kelly, who lay on the bed, paralyzed with fear.

"Now, my dear, having dispensed with the unexpected appetizer, shall we proceed to the *entrée*?"

The others all gave in, flashed through Vanessa Cilone's mind as the Ripper walked toward her. Anger welled in her. Not me, by God!

She reached for a pot of flowers at hand, seized and threw it in one motion. It caught the Ripper a glancing blow on the forehead, shattering the vase and staggering Jillian.

Everything wavered as the Ripper's eyes glazed for a second. Everything hesitated, wavered, as if environmental reality might transform once more.

The men in the house hall felt the existential tremor, glanced at each other.

Jillian's eyes cleared and everything settled, firmed. Blood dripped from her forehead.

"Bitch!"

She leapt and slashed out with the knife, catching the dodging Vanessa high upon her left cheek with a downward slice that ripped flesh open from cheekbone to jaw. Blood spouted and Vanessa shrieked. She jerked away, pushed over a chair and ran for the door as the Ripper turned chasing and sprawled to the floor, foot caught in a chair.

The door was locked.

* * *

†

Images—the Ripper falling, Vanessa at a locked door, Ann throwing things at Jillian—swam in Lees' head and he felt them as a directional beacon, ran for the stairs. He flung the words "Top floor" over his shoulder.
They raced up the stairs.

Jillian was up.
Vanessa raced for the bed, seized and flung a pillow backhanded. The Ripper parried it with her knife, slashing it away and loosing a cloud of goose feathers into the air as Vanessa dove onto the bed and rolled in one motion across it, back onto her feet and into a crouch. She braced her hands against the wooden frame and shoved the bed straight at the Ripper, knocking her from her feet once more.
"Bitch!"
Ann grabbed a chair.

Lees pointed, and they raced down the hall toward the end door, Stuart shouldering to the front, cocking the revolver and firing on the run. The roar was deafening and the lock shattered; pieces of metal and wood flew in splinters as the door swung inward from the impact and Stuart leapt into the room.
Vanessa was trapped against the far wall and the Ripper's arm raised with knife ready to plunge into her throat. Ann was advancing on Jillian with a chair.
Stuart cocked and fired in one motion.
Sound, smoke, smell, confusion.
The bullet hit Jillian's shoulder and spun her around and ripped the knife from her shocked fingers, sending it sliding under the bed. Her eyes glazed with pain, her mind lost focus.
Time trembled.
Her eyes refocused.
Lees saw Whitechapel in his mind, saw Miller's Court, the body, the whore, the Ripper with knife prepared. He shouted, "Clive's dead! Hughes . . . I don't know? The Ripper is going to kill Mary Kelly again!" He stared at Jillian.
She backed away, sulky-faced, whimpering softly in her

†

throat—the bully halted and revealed, as always, for the coward-victim-cretin beneath the cruelty.

"It's in her head, Malcolm. The time-warp is in her head. *Knock her out!*"

Stuart did not pause to think, knowing instinctively he had time for only one telling punch and it dare not be pulled. Necessity combined with his fear, outrage and months' of frustration as he stepped forward gathering his sixteen stone into whistling uppercut that landed at the precise spot for maximum effect, knocked the Ripper unconscious even as it lifted her body high into the air and sent it flying.

White light and electric shock.

A soldier opened the door to the Crystal Palace.

It exploded.

Thousands of tons of glass and tens of thousands of tons of metal hurtled outward and upward, and shattered and filled the sky with shards of pale blue iron, and pale translucent flesh and yellow light and crystal glass and flame and smoke in a shower of the energy of released hatred spewing.

Time righted itself.

It was 4:14 A.M., 1988.

The City of London was of a piece again.

They were in the office block, in Jillian's eighteenth-floor flat.

Jillian hit the glass window wall spread-eagled and with the full surface of her backside. The momentum of Stuart's heavyweight hit was fueled by the electricity of the time reversion, and she shattered a six-foot-square section of the tempered glass and continued through, pinwheeling and tumbling end-over-end to the hard, real, indifferent and unforgiving ground below.

The Ripper landed with an audible impact of breaking bones and pulping tissue, bounced, settled and was dead.

The deep cut on Vanessa's face was not life threatening, but it left a permanent puckered white scar across her left cheek. It did not diminish her true beauty to those who knew and loved her and she developed a Veronica Lake peekaboo hairstyle that drooped across the left side of her face. The scar did

†

bring an abrupt end to her modeling-acting career, but she was not greatly saddened. She and Malcolm were married on Christmas Day (Lees was best man), and within three years they had produced two healthy children, a son and a daughter.

The Lees remained in England for six months while he recuperated. Father Eric Mueller gave him a course of intensive instruction, and baptized him into the Catholic Church at Easter, 1989.

The government crowed over its "triumph" and designated Sir Malcolm Stuart man-of-the-hour. He was appointed, three months later, head of the British equivalent of the CIA.

Sergeant Clive was buried with all the honor the Metropolitan Police Force could muster. Stuart lobbied for and obtained Clive's posthumous promotion to deputy inspector, which increased his widow's pension substantially.

The press had a half-year feast on the neo-Ripper crisis, weeks of headline stories mining the details, followed by months of features, articles and books reexploring the well-trod ground. But, as he had throughout, the Vampire produced what, in a way, was the last word on the final chapter. He did it in his usual, brief, raunchy, irrevereant manner, with a concluding, extra-edition headline:

SPECIAL EDITION   SPECIAL EDITION   SPECIAL EDITION

The London Daily   November 9, 1988

JACK AND JILL!

†

Epilogue

And ever near us, though unseen,
The dear immortal spirits tread;
For all the boundless universe
is life—*there are no dead!*
  —*John Luckey McCreery*

February 29, 1996

Pikes Peak was snow packed and gleamed even in the gloom of a dimming dusky day. Cold wind whipped fat flakes of fresh falling snow in lateral gusts across the air. The light was gray and hard, made winter more palpable.

The casket lay in the open grave.

A squad of smartly uniformed soldiers fired crisp rifle salutes into the chill air, resonating echos of honor and sorrow across the cemetery. Several hundred mourners paraded by in the quiet reflection that authentic solemnity stimulates. They dropped roses into the grave or tumbled trowels of earth onto the coffin, making sharp sounds in the silence, cadences of ritual farewell. The protective awning beside the grave whipped and rustled, cracked when the wind gusted.

Sir Malcolm and Lady Stuart stood next to Ann Lees, his huge paw supporting her left elbow. Lady Stuart was stunning in black and only when the wind riffled her long blond hair across her left cheek could the scar be glimpsed like a frightsight in a mild game of children's scaredy-cat peekaboo. Stuart was still a handsome bull of a man with only now some white beginning to highlight his temples.

Father Eric Mueller supported Ann Lees' right arm. He looked relatively unchanged by the years. His blond hair was slightly more silver, the furrows of his face were etched fractionally deeper, his clear blue eyes displaying the extra maturity of pain-gained wisdom, but he still radiated serenity.

Ann Lees was older and looked it, but she was an attractive woman, despite her tear-and-wind-reddened face.

Stuart whispered to her, "Jim was a true friend, one of the bravest men I've ever known. A great man."

The wind whistled mournfully.

"He came far—very far," said Father Mueller.

†

Snow drifted by.

Ann nodded. "These last seven years were the best. He became . . . he used his gift to help people . . . freely. He never interfered, but . . . was always there when he could . . . be of service."

She looked out at the files of grief.

"Half these people never knew us until after he converted. See the boy over there?"

Her friends looked at a ruddy-cheeked teenager, dark-haired and handsome. The boy dropped a blood-red rose into the grave, crossed himself.

"We met his family at St. Paul's, our parish. Jim . . . how do you say it? Jim saw that the boy had cancer in his leg. The family were put off, but at last they had tests done. It was true, and so early it was . . . it was almost incipient rather than actualized. Just a tiny tumor, and they got it all. That was five years ago. He's had no recurrence. . . ."

The priest said, "Jim is with Jesus, Ann."

She nodded. "Yes. I believe that."

Wind cracked the awning loudly, and they started involuntarily and glanced upward.

A tiny tunnel of sun broke through the clouds, made a cone of gold light encapsuling the very top of Pikes Peak. Against the blue-silver slopes muted by the lonely sky, the pure white snowpack of the harshly angled ridge glowed.

White.

Light.

Gleaming promise.